Ne
The A...
Companion

By C.J. Carella

To Scott! Watch out for Ginsu!

Published by Fey Dreams Productions, LLC

Copyright @ 2014 Fey Dreams Productions, LLC. All rights reserved. All rights reserved. This material may not be reproduced, displayed, modified or distributed without the express prior written permission of the copyright holder. For permission, contact cjcarella@cjcarella.com

This is a work of fiction. All characters appearing in this work are fictitious. Any resemblance to real persons, living or dead, is purely coincidental.

Acknowledgements

My deepest thanks to the special reward Kickstarter backers, whose generous help made this project possible. Benjamin Barton, Ken Clover, Scott Coady, Erik Fischer, Jorel Levenson, Jack McCrary, Scott Palter, Michael Pierce, Paul Singleton, Terence Thyr, and Brad Whitcomb. Thank you all, and hope you enjoy your characters in the stories!

Introduction

Back in 2005, in the wild and primitive days before Twitter and the iPhone, I started working on a superhero setting for the roleplaying game book *Beyond Human* (a book that would remain unpublished as of March of 2014, alas). I wanted to create a setting a little different from the standard comic book fare where the world remains largely unchanged despite the presence of godlike beings in it. As a fan of alternate history, I had a lot of fun making costumed superheroes show up in the early 20th century and generally make a mess of things.

Fast forward to 2012. I started writing the story, set in that alternate world, of a faceless vigilante who stumbles into a sinister conspiracy. The story mutated into the tale of the young woman the vigilante encounters early in the story, and *Armageddon Girl* was born. After the novel was finished, I found myself writing short stories involving other characters in that setting, and figured a collection of those stories and other essays would make for a nice Kickstarter bonus reward when I used that crowd-funding program to finance the book's publication. This book is the result.

New Olympus is not a direct sequel to *Armageddon Girl*. The sequel, *Doomsday Duet*, is in the works and will be released soon. If you are only interested in following Christine Dark and Face-Off's adventures, this isn't the book you want, although fans of Ms. Dark do get to meet her mother and find out why Christine was named after a Stephen King novel in the story "Hungry Love."

The stories in New Olympus are presented in chronological order, beginning with "Deguello" (set in 1937) and ending with "Death At A Con" (2010). They offer glimpses of the world, set in different times and places, from World War Two to the Sixties to the early 21st century. They involve some people you will recognize from the novels, and introduce others who may play a role in the sequels. The stories also feature several characters named after and created by a number of generous Kickstarter backers who gave me a chance to immortalize them, so to speak, in three of the tales in this book. I hope they (and the rest of you) enjoy reading those portrayals as much as I did developing them with their help.

About a fifth of of the book consists of essays describing the setting's history and current status, as well as ideas on using the world of *Armageddon Girl* in roleplaying games. Thus this project comes full circle, from original RPG setting to novel back to RPGs. That section is not as detailed as I would have liked, but to truly flesh out a fifty-year history of the world (and provide rules, character stats, and other RPG elements) would take at least an entire book (or three). Perhaps one day, if there is enough interest, I will write a full roleplaying sourcebook for New Olympus. Until then, I hope the gamers among my readership get some use out of those chapters.

My humble thanks to all you readers. Thanks to you I'm doing what I love most.

C.J. Carella
March 9, 2014

Deguello

Barcelona Front, Outside Vacarisses, Spain July 8, 1937

There was a dead horse just a hundred yards from Martin Long's position. It stank. It stank badly enough to be noticeable among the thousand other stenches of war. Somebody should do something about the stinking beast. Its bloated body offended Martin's sensibilities in a way the hundreds of human corpses he had seen since joining the Abraham Lincoln Brigade no longer did.

"It's getting pretty ripe, isn't it?" Sam Decker – the man who claimed his name was Sam Decker – said after risking a quick peek over the edge of their trench. Decker knew what he was about. He never looked up from the same position twice. The *Nacionales* had a couple of good snipers on their side of the line. Martin's best friend in the Brigade, a skinny New York Jew called Lenny, had found out how good the snipers were a couple of days ago. Poor Lenny had poked his head up and one of the bastards had plugged him right in the kisser. Martin had seen the back of Lenny's head burst open, spraying blood and brains everywhere. They'd killed Lenny, those bastards.

Somebody should do something about the stinking horse.

"It's going to be a hot one," Decker went on, not bothered by Martin's silence. Decker wasn't bothered by much, certainly not by Martin's dislike of him. "In more ways than one."

He smiled at Martin's raised eyebrow. "Word is Franco's boys are going to hit our sector today or tomorrow."

"When did you hear that? Over breakfast with Colonel Modesto?" Martin asked.

Sarcasm made no impression on Decker, either. "That's Lieutenant Colonel Modesto, and no, I haven't had the pleasure. No, the writer told me."

"Ah." The writer and his woman often came by the Brigade's sector to chat up the American volunteers who had thrown their lot with Spain's doomed Republican government. Decker had spoken privately with the writer a couple of times. They knew each other; they did not like each other, but there was a measure of respect between the two.

Martin had finally figured out who Decker really was in the last few days. Well, him and Lenny, not too long before Lenny went and stopped a Nationalist bullet with his face. "So what did he have to say?"

"Not much, but I could read between the lines. Ernie isn't big on sharing. He let on that we might want to be careful in the next day or two."

"That's swell." If the *Nacionales* pushed hard on the Lincolns, he didn't think the Lincolns were going to hold them off. Martin's day had started out lousy, thanks to the damn dead horse. It wasn't going to get better.

"*No pasaran!*" Decker said, sarcasm seasoning the Spanish phrase. Martin chuckled bitterly. 'They shall not pass' had been one of the more popular refrains of the Republic back when it controlled Madrid. But the Nationalists had passed, and passed, and passed some more. Madrid had fallen earlier that year, and the woman who had originated the refrain had ended up in front of a firing squad. You'd think Isidora Gomez's death would make people think twice before using that 'They shall not pass' claptrap, but the Spanish loved their little romantic gestures just about as much as they loved martyrs.

The Republicans had raised a bumper crop of martyrs, and there were plenty more where they came from.

"What are you doing here?" The question surprised Martin even as it came out of his mouth.

"Who, me?" Decker responded. "Enjoying the pleasures of the beautiful Spanish countryside, of course."

"Bullshit."

"Fighting the spread of Fascism on behalf of the workers of the world, of course."

"Bullshit."

"Why don't you tell me, then?" Decker sounded genuinely curious.

"I know who you are," Martin said. Might as well get the truth out in the open. The air stank of dead horse and the day was going to be fucked anyway.

Decker didn't try to make any denials or feign ignorance. He started rolling up a cigarette while he spoke. "Lenny finally figured it out, didn't he? He always had more brains than he let on, the poor bastard. I'd thought the hair dye and the beard would be enough to keep me safe."

"You're Daedalus Smith," Martin hissed, keeping his voice low enough not to be overhead by the other men in the trench. The distant rumble of artillery helped mute his words. Nobody was paying much attention to either of them in any case. Neither man was very popular, and the other men of the platoon were having their own conversations or catching quick catnaps. "A filthy capitalist arms dealer. What the fuck are you doing here?"

That accusation, spoken in a slightly louder voice, would amount to a death sentence. There were plenty of men in the Brigade who'd shoot Daedalus Smith on sight. Decker – Smith – didn't look too worried. Martin made sure his Mosin-Nagant rifle was within easy reach, just in case the industrialist tried anything. Smith didn't make any moves, however, just looked at Martin with a cold, thoughtful stare.

"Two reasons," Smith finally said. "First, I wanted to see the elephant before the big war started."

"The big war?"

"This little shindig's just a dress rehearsal, pal. The real thing's coming, and coming soon. You'd think we'd have learned better after the Great War, but Hitler's bound and determined to have a war, and it only takes one guy to start a fight. I have no love for the Bolshies and useful idiots of the Republic, mind you. A bigger pack of imbeciles and charlatans the world has never seen. But we're going to be fighting the Nazis, and I wanted to see them in action."

"You said two reasons."

"I wanted to see Hitler's Teutonic Knights."

"The Knights?" Martin had to laugh at that. "Propaganda and smoke and mirrors," he said with a sneer.

"And who won Guadalajara for the Fascists?" Smith countered. "Mussolini's Praetorians were there. Three of them, at least. And one of the Knights. He's the one who won that fight."

Martin had heard the stories. The Lincolns had not fought at Guadalajara, but they had been among the forces hastily evacuated from Madrid before the city fell. Rumors about the supermen who had spearheaded the attack had spread like wildfire, helped along by triumphant Nationalist, Italian and German propaganda.

"Pull the other one," he said, a trifle less sure than he'd been seconds before. Martin had watched the newsreels about the '36 Olympics, only months before he'd left Pittsburgh just a few steps ahead of the law. He'd seen the footage of the flying man with arcs of electricity dancing from his hands – they called him Donnar or Donner or something like that. Martin had laughed about it. It had been a Nazi trick, stage wires and film editing. It had to be a trick. Smith's expression showed the capitalist believed every word of it, however, and seeing that shook up Martin's certainties. Smith might be an exploiter, but nobody though he was gullible or a fool.

A cold feeling spread through Martin's guts. He'd been under artillery fire and aerial bombardment, but the idea that men could fly and throw lightning bolts scared him on a different level. He could accept a world with bombs and murderous Fascists in it. But this…

Smith noticed the change in Martin's expression. "They're real, all right," he said, not gloating or triumphantly, but in a cool, almost sympathetic voice, sounding like a kind doctor delivering some very bad news to his patient. "I've seen them. Not the Italian or Kraut versions, not yet at least. We've got our very own Neolympians, what the Germans like to call Aesir, in the U.S. of A. There's a fellow in New York who can bounce bullets off his chest and bend steel with his bare hands. I've met him."

Martin shook his head but said nothing. He found himself groping for a cigarette. There were only a handful of smokes left in the battered pack in his pocket, but he needed something to steady himself.

"The Praetorian Guards aren't much," Daedalus continued as Martin lit up. "One uses this big anti-tank rifle as his personal weapon and he can shoot the wings off a fly with it, but that's not what broke the front at Guadalajara. The other two are no great shakes, either – one can fling balls of fire, if you can believe it, but from the reports I've read they hit only as hard as hand grenades. The last one is bullet-proof and strong enough to overturn armored cars. But the German, that's the one that got the boys of the Thälmann Battalion to run, and that's what broke the Republican line. They were Krauts, too, but our Krauts, good Reds like you." Martin bristled at that but took a long drag of his cigarette and kept silent. "Somewhat fitting, a super-Kraut routing other Krauts, I suppose."

"Who was it?"

"He goes by the name Shatterhands, or Shatterhand. Stupid name, isn't it? The way the story goes, Hitler gave the Knight that nickname. It comes from some books he used to read as a kid. And it's not a German word for Shatterhands, either; the name is in English. Funny fellow, that Hitler."

"What can he do? Fly? Spit flames out of his mouth?" Martin could not believe he was having this conversation.

Smith opened his mouth to answer but shut it abruptly when loud music started playing from the Nationalist lines. The melody was sad and mournful at first, but soon became harsh and martial, its loud notes resonating even from the distance between the battle lines. "Ernie was right," Smith hissed.

"That music..."

"That's Shatterhands' idea of a joke. He had it play at Guadalajara, too. It's *El Deguello.*"

Deguello? Martin searched through his rudimentary Spanish. If it didn't involve food or fucking or shooting, he didn't know much of the local lingo. "What's that mean?"

"Throat-cutting," Smith explained, drawing a finger over his own neck to emphasize the translation. "It means 'No Quarter.' It means Shatterhands is going to hit here."

The music stopped. A few seconds later an explosion went off close by. Much too close. The shelling started in earnest, the Nationalists' cannon pounding on the Republican lines.

Artillery was bad, the worst part of the fucking war. Bullets could kill you, but explosives tore you apart, and it didn't matter if you were a coward or a saint or a hero, shockwave and shrapnel reaped you just the same, and if a shell burst through the trench's overhead cover and went off in your hole, you were done, nothing you could do. Martin had gotten used to many things since arriving to Spain, but the monstrous impartiality of artillery still got to him. He screamed and raged and pissed his pants as the earth shook and near misses deafened and battered him. Around him, men dealt with the horror in their own ways. Some prayed silently or called for their mothers, others let loose with every word of profanity they knew; most merely screamed wordlessly just like him. Smith closed his eyes tightly and clutched something hanging from a chain around his neck. A crucifix, Martin guessed with contempt during a brief lull in the barrage that lasted long enough for him to regain some measure of composure. Martin caught a glimpse of the object when Smith shifted his grip on it: it wasn't a crucifix, but a slender metal rod with a few strange symbols carved on it. The artillery started up again and he had no more leisure to wonder about it. There was only time to scream and endure.

Before the last of the artillery died out, noncoms and officers were already screaming and cajoling the men to come up and fight. The Nationalists were coming. One of the Brigade's machineguns started up, its stuttering bursts joined by another one a few seconds later. Their death-song helped steady Martin's nerves as he scrambled for the edge of the trench, his Mosin-Nagant rifle at the ready. Smith was right there beside him, as were all of the other Lincolns hale enough to fight. Two weren't: someone he didn't recognize was lying face down on the dirt, not moving at all. The other was Lazlo 'the Lizard' Slizard, who'd taken some shrapnel and was howling and squeezing a gushing wound on the side of his neck. Even as Martin started to rush towards him, the Hungarian's eyes rolled in his head and he slumped down, silent at last. Martin shrugged and turned away from the corpse.

A kaleidoscope of images, sounds and smells followed, things he didn't remember clearly at the time, things he knew from experience would come visit him later, in dreams or awake or when eating or having sex with one of the local girls, sudden remembrances that would freeze him for a second or three, lust or hunger or sleep gone and forgotten while he relived them. All of that was distant and meaningless now. All that mattered was the feel of his rifle hitting his shoulder hard enough to leave bruises as he shot and shot again at the antlike figures rushing to and fro, crawling or running from cover to cover. He fired the gun dry and used a stripper clip to put another five rounds into the rifle, fired it dry again, reloaded and fired it dry again.

There were vehicles moving among the men, armored cars and tanks, their machineguns clattering as they sought out the men in the trenches. A burst of heavy bullets kicked dirt in Martin's face. A few yards away, someone's cursing was cut off suddenly and finally as one of the machinegun rounds hit someone. He didn't think he had enough piss left in him, but his bladder let go again at the near-miss. He ignored it just as he ignored the kick of the gun against his bruised shoulder, ignored the sight of the dead horse exploding into flying gobbets of flesh when a mortar round hit it.

The Nationalists stopped coming forward. Some took cover and shot back. Others tried to go back the way they'd come and were picked off by machinegun and rifle fire and the occasional mortar round. Planes droned overhead and Martin braced himself for the wail of Stukas diving on their position, but the aircraft moved on. Looking for better targets, maybe. Martin didn't care why, glad enough to be spared. He felt a moment of savage satisfaction while watching the backs of the retreating Nationalists – until he saw the figure running forward.

At first, his eyes refused to accept the sight. A man in a bright gold and scarlet uniform – no, not a uniform, a *costume* – just didn't belong in a modern battlefield. He made a perfect target, and two hundred riflemen and both machineguns opened up on him, drawn by the colors and motion. The man in gold and red was running incredibly fast – faster than that colored sprinter from the Olympics, Owens, possibly as fast as a speeding car – but he wasn't faster than a bullet. He was hit dozens of times, maybe more. Even as Martin shot at him, he saw spurts of dirt erupting all around the running man like raindrops of lead. But the man neither wavered nor fell. A mortar round went off a few yards in front of the costumed man, and he ran unscathed through the shrapnel that Martin knew had slashed the place where he'd been. Nothing human could have survived that.

Nothing human had. Martin had no piss or shit left to give, but he felt his bowels loosening nonetheless. He looked around the trench, seeing his fellow veterans exchange wide-eyed glances. A fear deeper and more primal than the terror the artillery had inflicted infected the men in the trench. Many, possibly most, disregarded it and kept on shooting; you learned quickly enough that turning your back on an enemy just got you dead quicker. But some, even some who Martin knew were no cowards, wavered and fell back. Some ran and kept running even after Sergeant Morelli turned his Thompson on them and mowed down two of them.

Smith didn't run. "That's him!" he yelled, and Martin heard a disturbing note of eagerness in the capitalist's voice. "That's Shatterhands!"

Martin ignored him and shot at Shatterhands yet again. The gun didn't kick, producing only a mild click. Empty. He reached for another stripper clip and had just loaded it when he saw Shatterhands leap in the air, an impossible leap, at least fifty or sixty feet high and well over a hundred yards in length, an impossible leap that put him within twenty yards of the trench line and maybe thirty yards to the left of Martin's position. He turned to follow the leap, dimly noticing the Nationalists were moving forward again.

Smith grabbed him and threw him face-first onto the ground just as Shatterhands landed.

The world exploded.

He opened his eyes some time later. It couldn't have been very long; echoes of the explosion were still making his ears ring dully. There was wet dirt in his mouth and dust in his nose. Martin coughed, spat and raised his head. The trench had partially collapsed around him. Dirt, unmoving men and pieces of men lay all around him. The dirt floor was muddy with blood. An explosive shockwave had traveled the length of the narrow enclosure, tearing everybody apart.

He was unharmed and had no idea why.

Dimly through the dust and smoke, he saw a figure turn around one of the trench's corners. Smith. Martin picked up his rifle and numbly followed the capitalist, driven by some instinct he could not explain any more than he could understand why he still lived while everyone he'd known for the past year had been turned into unfeeling, uncaring gobbets of meat. He turned the corner, and saw an entire section of trench had been obliterated by the explosion. An open crater had replaced the fortification. Of the men manning that section, nothing remained but some gore and scraps of cloth and flesh.

In the center of the crater, Daedalus Smith faced Shatterhands.

Close-up, the German was not as impressive, despite the shiny and still perfectly clean costume. He was a man of middle stature, athletic but not handsome, his blunt features coarse and dull, with beady blue eyes staring balefully under a mop of dark brown hair. His hands were large, abnormally sized for his body, and they were trembling: not shaking in fear, but vibrating as if they contained some powerful engine that was revving up. The Teutonic Knight and Smith were exchanging words, and as Martin joined their stretch of trench, Smith said something else in German. Martin understood not a word of it, but whatever it was infuriated the Knight. He rushed Smith, his oversized fists ready to pummel the industrialist. He moved impossibly fast, as fast a cat, too fast for Martin to shoot, not that he had a clear shot anyway with Smith between him and the German.

Smith was faster.

Martin had seen Smith fight. His sometimes-cultured speech had gotten under the skin of some of the more class-conscious Lincolns, and he'd been in more than one brawl. The industrialist had won every one of them. He might sound like a prissy college boy, but he fought with economic ruthlessness and knew how to box like a pro. But he'd never moved as quickly in any of those fights as he did now, sidestepping the German's hammer blows with such grace the whole thing seemed like steps in a prearranged dance. The Knight's fist hit one of the crater's walls, and the impact was literally explosive, sending a shower of dirt in every direction and generating a wave of overpressure that knocked Martin off his feet. The man's nickname made sense to Martin now.

As the German tried to recover his balance, Smith struck him three times, two powerful jabs to the body and a right hook that connected solidly with the Knight's neck. The punches sounded as loud as gunshots, and Martin was sure they would have broken a normal man's bones. Against this opponent, however, they had as much effect as the bullets the Lincolns had fruitlessly poured on him. Smith backpedaled; the German followed him, a grin enlivening his doughy face. Martin shot him in the head. He either missed or the bullet struck and bounced off unnoticed.

The capitalist's retreat had meant to buy him enough time to reach under his uniform and rip the metal rod from the chain around his neck. He held the object like a weapon, not unlike the roll of quarters Martin had carried around in Philly for special occasions. As he dully worked the useless rifle's bolt to chamber another useless round, Martin saw Smith reverse direction and charge Shatterhands, ducking under a wild swing to get in close. The metal rod in his hand was beginning to glow. It produced an unearthly combination of golden and purplish-black hues the likes of which Martin had never seen before. Smith grappled with the German for a second and made a stabbing motion with the rod, striking the Knight on the side of the neck.

Shatterhands screamed in pain. He fell back, Smith holding on to him, as the multi-colored light flowed liquidly from the rod and curled around both combatants in sinuous tendrils of light and smoke. The German convulsed helplessly as the tendrils played over him. "Fuck you, Fritz!" Smith shouted, a maniacal smile on his face. Martin briefly considered shooting Smith. He now understood why the capitalist had known so much about Neolympians; he was one of them. Only fear that the bullet would be as useless against Smith as against the German stayed his hand.

A blinding flash of light filled the crater, blinding him.

Martin blinked furiously, trying to clear his vision. When he could see again, Smith was staggering towards him. The industrialist dropped the metal rod: the object was twisted and misshapen, as if it had been melted in a furnace. Shatterhands was lying where he had fallen, moving feebly. "We have to go," Smith said.

"What..?"

"We have to go!" Smith repeated, rushing past Martin. "It didn't work! Damn me, but it didn't work!" He started scrambling out of the trench. As before, Martin followed the man's lead, even if it meant running out in the open in a world ridden with shrapnel and machinegun bullets.

The two men joined the rout of the Lincoln Brigade. The Nationalists had rallied, and Shatterhands' destruction of the trench line had been too much for too many men. Martin ran, short mad dashes for cover, pausing once in a while to turn and shoot at the approaching enemy. He knew what to do; he'd been in several similar retreats before. A few Lincolns didn't run; they manned the one machinegun that had survived Shatterhands' attack and bought their comrades some time with their lives. As he fled, Martin heard a thunderous explosion once again and the machinegun fell silent. The German demigod was back in action.

After that there was only terror and thirst and a taste like ashes and metallic dust in his mouth.

* * *

"Merriman's dead!" Fred Keller yelled. The Lincoln Brigade's commissar had been yelling the same phrase every few seconds, answering a question nobody was asking. The man walked aimlessly back and forth, just another obstacle to the fleeing men. "Merriman's dead!"

The news of the Brigade commander's death meant nothing to Martin. He had made it to the rear along with other survivors of the battalion and all that mattered to him was escaping before the Nationalists and their creature reached them. At some point he had lost track of Smith, but as he greedily drank water off a canteen he'd pilfered off a dead soldier, he spotted the industrialist. Smith was having a word with a wagon driver. Martin reached them just as Smith handed the driver a wad of bills. The driver licked his lips, visibly considered the offer, and nodded curtly.

"Glad to see you made it," Smith told Martin as casually as if they had run into each other at a baseball game. "I've secured a ride. Care to come along?"

"They'll shoot us," Martin said. The Republicans for deserting; the Nationalists for being Republicans. Even ditching their uniforms would not help; either side would check their shoulders for the unmistakable bruises firing a rifle made, bruises that meant death for a man out of uniform.

"The Republic's done," Smith replied curtly. "While Shatterhands was breaking the front, the Red Baron himself led a sortie and hit the rear with some new attack airplanes armed with incendiary bombs. Barcelona's burning. The Republic is dead. All we can do is get out of here."

Martin reeled at the news. He'd known the cause was doomed, known it after Madrid fell, known it after each shameful retreat, let alone the rout he'd just experienced. He realized now he'd still held onto a shred of hope, however. Hope that the Western Powers would intervene and bring the Fascists to heel, perhaps. Hope that eventually the people would rise against the Nationalist propaganda that had so successfully mystified them. All his hopes died when he heard Smith's words. The capitalist was right: there was nothing left but survival.

The wagon attracted a motley crew of followers on the long march towards

Barcelona, or whatever was left of the city. A handful of Lincolns from the rout at Vacarisses. Members of other International Brigades. Republican deserters. Civilians fleeing from the vengeful Nationalists. They joined a throng of refugees filling the roads, occasionally strafed by German aircraft but largely left alone. There was little point in attacking the fleeing remnants of the Republican armies. Word was a new government had been formed in Barcelona, and it was suing for peace. Only Franco's insistence on an unconditional surrender was slowing down the process, but soon enough the Republicans would throw in the towel and give the Fascist bastard and his German and Italian masters whatever they wanted.

On the first day of the march they found the writer. The self-assured man Martin had seen was gone, gone like his black beret and glasses. Only Smith recognized the dazed man walking alongside the road in torn and bloody clothes. Smith took him in, got him on the wagon and heard his story. The writer didn't say much at first but Smith got it out of him. He had been in a military convoy fleeing the disaster, a convoy that had gotten hit by the Red Baron's personal attack aeroplane, the Dragon Craft that did not use propellers and traveled at impossible speeds. The writer's woman had died in his arms. "They killed Martha." That was mostly what he said during the two days he spent with them on the road to Barcelona. "They killed Martha." On the third day he bought or stole someone's service revolver and put it to his head. The gunshot in the night went unnoticed by the exhausted refugees among the other noises of disaster. Martin found the body that morning.

"Dammit, Ernie," Smith said as they buried him. It was all the epitaph he got. They buried the body and kept moving. They could see Barcelona now, or the pillars of smoke rising from the smoldering ruins of the city. Sometimes they encountered people clogging the roads while trying to flee the city. Nobody knew anything.

It was chaos and hell.

Barcelona, Spain August 13, 1937

Martin Long found Daedalus Smith at a bar in Barcelona. The bar's windows were boarded up – glass couldn't be found for love or money in the city – but the place was still open, and although the hooch served there was vile, it did the job to drown one's sorrows just fine.

Smith was in a rumpled suit; it had seen better days but was still a damn sight better than Martin's own civilian clothes. The industrialist had a woman on his lap and a half-empty bottle in his hand. As Martin walked to his table, Smith gulped down the last of the hooch and threw the bottle against a wall. The locals started at the sound of breaking glass but otherwise ignored him. They'd likely been paid well for their patience, Martin thought sourly.

"What are you still doing here, Long? I thought you'd been repatriated already."

"I missed the boat," Martin replied as he sat down. A new bottle of booze was placed on the table along with some glasses. Martin poured himself a drink. "I wanted to talk to you one last time."

"Sure, why not? Got nothing better to do. Off you go, Manuelita," Smith told the woman, sending her on her way with a swift slap on her ample rump. "What's on your mind, Long? You missed your chance to denounce me to the Commissars. There's no Commissars left, although I'm sure Franco's equivalents are just as nasty." Smith filled the other glass and emptied it in one gulp.

"What happened back there?" Martin asked. He looked intently at the capitalist. Smith was drunk, but his eyes were not as dull and unfocused as they should be after a long night of imbibing.

Smith refilled his glass. "I like you, Long," he said before gulping down the drink. "You're an honest man, for a lousy Commie. Commies and Nazis. They'll be the death of us unless we do something about them."

Martin said nothing and waited.

"What do you want to know, Long? Were you wondering how we survived Shatterhands' little trick at the trenches? It was my talisman. It had several uses, you know. Created a protective... there are no good terms for it, call it an aura or an invisible shield if you will. It blunted the explosion's shockwave. Without it we'd both be dead. Well, you'd be dead most certainly. I might have made it. Glad I didn't get the chance to find out one way or the other, though."

"What else did it do?" Martin asked.

Smith had another drink. "It was a lure. For their kind. That's why old

Shatterhands picked that particular stretch of trench to hit. Aesir are creatures of instinct and intuition, you see. Something, some form of foretelling for all I know, something draws them towards spots where trouble is likely. The talisman was designed to replicate that effect. It acted like a beacon."

The realization Smith's metal rod had gotten all his friends killed should have filled Martin with rage. He felt nothing but the need to have another drink. He did.

"There was more to it, of course," Smith went on. "The device's primary purpose was to steal power from a Neolympian, or Aesir if you'd prefer, and transfer it to me." He refilled his glass and looked at it with eyes that had gone cold and hard. He set the full glass down, untouched. "And it failed. Failed completely. Almost killed me in the process."

"You're one of them. One of those things," Martin said softly. He already knew, but wanted Smith to admit it openly.

Smith nodded. "Yes, Long. It took me a while to realize it. I'm not like Shatterhands, or Donner. I'm much weaker. Pathetic. Barely better than a mere mortal."

Slow excitement spread warmly through Martin's guts as his free hand gently touched the grenade concealed under his jacket. His final errand might be more than a fruitless gesture after all. This close up, with the grenade going off under the table, the blast would tear both men apart below the waist. Nothing human would survive it. Maybe something barely better than a mere human would not survive it, either.

"Don't do it, Long."

Martin stared at Smith, who didn't look drunk anymore. "I know you have a little care package for me under your jacket. I noticed it the second you came in. Not a pistol, no. Something bigger. By now you've figured out a pistol would do you no good, haven't you?"

"I will see you in hell, Smith."

"Why, for God's sake? I saved your life. Several times, as I recall."

"You should not be."

"No room in the dialectic for the likes of me, is that it? How can one hold the proposition that all men must be equal, when beings like Shatterhands make it so obviously untrue? The Fascists have it so much easier than you Reds, sport. They don't mind worshiping their new gods."

"You should not be."

"And yet here we stand. Killing me will not change that. I aim to do good in this world – and yes, to do well too. I think my gifts will be very useful when the Nazis make their move. You are doing everyone a disservice, Long. Come on, keep your present in your pocket, and I'll buy you enough drinks to make you forget all about Neolympians. What do you say?"

Martin's grim expression didn't change. "If I can rid the world of one of you, that is enough for me. There can't be that many of you."

"You should see if anybody around here knows how to play *El Deguello*, Long. It would suit the occasion. To answer your question - no, there aren't very many of us. Less than a hundred by my estimates, but those are little more than wild guesses. But there is no telling how many more will show up in the future, since I have no earthly idea how it is that we exist in the first place. Maybe one day everyone will be just like us." He finished his drink and stared Martin in the eye. "So if you're willing to personally see me to hell, Long, you might as well get to it."

There was nothing left to say. Martin pulled the grenade's pin.

Smith ripped open his shirt, revealing a new metal rod hanging over his chest. Martin's eyes widened with shock, and he had just enough time to realize his gesture had been futile after all.

From the outside of the bar, the explosion was dull and unspectacular, especially for a city still reeling from the massive bombings of the previous month. There were no glass windows to blow out. The wooden boards withstood the explosion fairly well, except for a few holes punched through by stray pieces of shrapnel. The grenade blast was followed by a second or two of silence before the screaming began. The front door opened and patrons stumbled outside, some clutching at bleeding wounds, others staggering around in shock.

Daedalus Smith, unharmed and unmarked, shouldered past them and walked away into the darkness.

Visionary

New York City, New York, September 19, 1938

"I am sorry, Dr. Horowitz," the man from Edison Electric said. He did not sound the least bit sorry.

Hiram Horowitz sat up straight and held on to his temper. He was a large man, six feet five, with a broad-shouldered physique that most people found intimidating. In most ways he looked almost exactly like his father, a butcher by trade, a kosher butcher by vocation, a man respected by those in his community but largely despised by the greater world outside. Hiram's dreams had led him beyond the confines of Crown Heights, braving the hostility of the *goyim* in pursuit of a greater destiny.

The officious little man from Edison Electric had just slammed the door shut on that destiny.

"Mr. Davis," Hiram said, speaking slowly and enunciating every word carefully. He had spent most of his teenage years working hard at not sounding like a Jew, carefully excising all Yiddish from his vocabulary, altering the rhythms of his speech, and turning his back on the way his family had raised him. He'd done all this, despite feeling all but certain that, no matter what he did, he'd always be viewed as nothing but a filthy kike. "Mr. Davis, you were there when I demonstrated the device. It works. A panel of experts from Columbia University examined it with the utmost care and pronounced its effects were real. The Jupiter Device can capture the energy produced by lightning bolts and store it for future use. Its value to this country – to all of mankind – is undeniable."

"I was there, Dr. Horowitz," Davis said, agreeably enough. He was a slight man with a pinched face and prematurely receding hair, and he looked very uncomfortable in what promised to become a confrontation of sorts. "I was unequivocally impressed by the device, and I enthusiastically supported its development by the Edison Electric Company."

"What is the problem, then? Why did you just tell me my contract is being canceled?"

"The device cannot be reproduced, doctor. Please, let me explain," Davis added hastily, forestalling another eruption from Hiram. "The prototype you gave us to study does work, it works perfectly well. So well, in fact, that the research facility in Menlo Park is using it to power its main laboratory even as we speak. The problem is, we cannot duplicate it."

"What do you mean? The blueprints I gave you – "

"We have followed all the design specifications you provided when we purchased the patent," Davis interrupted. "Every version of the device we've built does not work, however. When struck by lightning bolts, the prototypes are simply destroyed, storing no power whatsoever. Furthermore, they do not seem to attract lighting strikes with any degree of reliability, unlike the original device."

"That's impossible!" Hiram said. His cheeks felt warm, and he knew they were flushed with the anger that always bubbled below his normally placid countenance, the anger he labored so hard to suppress. Three years' work, and this pathetic little man was telling him it was for nothing?

"Nonetheless, we find ourselves unable to reproduce the effect of the Jupiter Device. Again, I am sorry, and Edison Electric is in no way accusing you of fraud or malfeasance of any kind. We did confirm the efficacy of the original prototype, after all. But we cannot honor our contract if we cannot build copies of your device, Dr. Horowitz. We are prepared to allow you to retain the funds we advanced, and to return to you full ownership of your patents. Please do keep in mind we would be well within our rights to attempt to recover those funds, given that the designs we purchased are simply impossible to manufacture."

Hiram drew in a deep breath, but held it in and did not explode into an angry tirade. He would not give this simpering fool the satisfaction of making a scene. "What you are saying, then, is that your facilities are unable to duplicate work I performed in my personal laboratory, using common tools and materials."

"That appears to be the case, yes," Mr. Davis agreed. "You are of course welcome to try other companies."

"I should have been directly involved," Hiram protested. "If you'd allowed me to supervise the development process personally..."

"We did try, Doctor, as you well know."

Hiram looked down. It was his temper, of course, and his abrasive personality. He did not suffer any kind of fool, and he did not work well with others. He'd learned as much during his years at Columbia and then Harvard. Some of it had been anti-Semitism, of course, but some of it was his own fault. His two-month tenure at Edison Electric had been a miserable time for everyone concerned, and he'd agreed to hand over the work to others with undisguised relief. Except now it appeared the damn fools couldn't do anything right without him!

"If this is an attempt to defraud me, you can rest assured my lawyers will take action," he said in a deep, rumbling voice that made Mr. Davis flinch as if the threat had been physical rather than legal.

"If we could do anything with your designs, Dr. Horowitz, we wouldn't be having this discussion in the first place. You are welcome to seek legal counsel. We have, and are satisfied our response is legal and appropriate."

Ruined. He was ruined. Nobody would touch his patents once Edison Electric's failure became public knowledge. Mr. Davis might be careful not to accuse him of fraud, but many others wouldn't. His reputation would be destroyed in a matter of days. The money those bastards had so magnanimously allowed him to keep was gone already, spent on other projects – projects he wouldn't be able to complete now, or to sell even if he did. A part of him briefly considered reaching across the desk and snapping the little man's neck. He could do it, and easily. Hiram was freakishly strong even for a man of his size, something several people had discovered when they'd tried to bully him.

No. Violence here and now would not do him any good. He would act later, when he had a plan. They had taken everything from him.

He would have to figure out a way to take it back.

New York City, New York, October 6, 1938

"What's a cute tomato like you doing in a place like this?"

Linda Lamar ignored Detective Gonzaga's idea of witty repartee and stuck to the business at hand. "Can you tell me what happened here, Detective, or do I need to go above your head?"

"Crime scenes are no place for a dame," Gonzaga grumbled, but went on to answer her question. "We're not sure yet. The victim's body is badly burned. Some sort of industrial accident, mebbe."

"In this part of the Bowery? The only industries here are bootlegging, gambling and racketeering," Linda said.

"It's possible the body was dumped here," was the detective's curt reply. "We're working on it, Miss Lamar. Give us a little break, will you?"

"Can I see the body?" Linda knew she was pushing her luck. Gonzaga liked her somewhat, and was willing to cut her some slack as long as she didn't mind some fairly weak attempts at flirting along the way, but asking to stick her nose in the middle of an investigation? Her chances weren't all that great. Still, nothing ventured, nothing gained.

"No can do, Miss Lamar."

"You can call me Linda, you know," she said. She almost batted her eyelashes at him, but the very idea made her sick to her stomach. "And you know I won't blab."

Gonzaga looked around. He was the only detective around; the uniformed cops were concentrating on keeping a small crowd of rubberneckers from trampling all over the crime scene. He thought about it, and shrugged. "All right, you can have a quick peek, but you owe me one, sister. Linda." He smiled at her and led the reporter to the scene.

As such things went, it wasn't much of a crime scene. An alley in a bad area of the Bowery, not that there were many good areas in the Bowery. A sheet-covered body lay near a wall.

"He hasn't been there for long," Gonzaga commented, leaning over the covered corpse. "Some concerned citizen called it in – and then somebody in the department went and called *you*," he added in an annoyed tone. "And if I find the louse who did..."

"Reporters cannot reveal their sources, Detective."

"Call me Bob, Linda."

"Of course, Bob." The stiff under the sheet better be worth the trouble of getting on a first-name basis with Gonzaga. That was just the kind of thing that might give a fellow ideas, very wrong ideas when it came to Linda Lamar.

The detective started lifting the sheet. "Brace yourself. It's not a pretty sight."

It wasn't.

Linda had seen lots of stiffs before, starting with her uncle Grant, who'd keeled over during one memorable Thanksgiving dinner when she was seven. There had been plenty more since then; it came with the territory when you worked the crime beat for the *World's Journal*. There'd been gunshot victims, stabbings, one bludgeoning and a particularly gruesome dismemberment with an ax, Lizzie Borden style.

This one still took the cake.

"What on Earth happened to him?" Linda asked as she crouched over the man's corpse.

"Damfino. Never seen nothing like that."

From the waist down, the corpse was relatively unscathed, enough to see he had been wearing grey flannel pants, Argyle socks and black shoes. From the waist up...

"Those are the worst burns I've ever seen," she said, trying to stay focused on the facts. Some of the man's skin and flesh had been burned black as tar. Linda could smell something horribly similar to the scent of pork chops wafting from the corpse. The burns were worst around the collarbone area, which had been charred to the bone. The man's face had melted off his skull. Linda's stomach was doing flip-flops, but she acted cool as a cucumber. Too many people already believed dames had no place in this kind of business, and if she got sick in front of the cops, she would be proving them right.

Where the skin hadn't been burned to a crisp, she saw weird red marks, scar-like red patterns running under the man's skin in a pattern. The marks reminded her of something, but at first she couldn't put her finger on it.

"There's another big burn on the fellow's back," Gonzaga said. "A through-and-through burn. The medical examiner's going to have a field day."

Something clicked in her head. "Lightning."

"Beg pardon?"

"Those red marks, they're called Lichtenberg scars, or Lichtenberg burns, something like that." Linda pointed at the pattern on the unburned portions of the man's skin. "They happen when you get struck by lightning."

"I'll be God-damned, pardon my French," Gonzaga said. "Lightning? The poor schmuck died in a genuine act of God? Don't that beat all?"

"Victims of an act of God usually don't end up dumped in an alley in the Bowery," Linda pointed out. "And I don't remember any thunderstorms in the city in the last month."

"First you tell me it's lightning, and now you're telling me it ain't? Just like a broad, changing her mind from one sentence to the next."

Linda glared at the detective. "What I'm telling you, *Bob*," she said, turning the name into an insult with her tone of voice, "is that whatever killed this man worked a lot like lightning. It just couldn't be natural lightning. At least I don't think it could."

"Oh, that's just fuc... swell," the detective replied. "One of those."

"That'd be my guess." Under the horror and disgust, Linda felt a brief burst of excitement. This had to be 'one of those,' a Special Case. They were becoming more common every year, as real life was becoming more like a tale straight out of a pulp magazine, or even a four-color funnybook. "One of those, or some newfangled gizmo." Those were also popping all over the place, wonderful and impossible weapons, tools and vehicles. Linda strongly suspected the two phenomena were related.

"You can't be writing nothing like that, you hear?" Gonzaga said. "Not until the medical examiner says what's what."

"Don't worry, Bob. I'll keep the story under my hat for now." *Until I find out what's what,* she thought but kept to herself. *Then I'll have my own little exclusive.*

* * *

Jimmy 'the Weasel' O'Malley hurried towards his new hiding place. Tonight was no time to be caught alone on the streets, not after Lazy Eye had been found in a back alley looking like a badly-cooked hamburger patty. Someone was gunning for Freddy Razor's mob, and Jimmy, being a member of said mob, felt like he had a target painted on his back. Time to make himself scarce until things quieted down. The Weasel figured he'd hole up in some fleabag motel and try to get in touch with

Freddy in the morning. He picked up the pace, wishing the news about Lazy Eye hadn't reached him when he was drunk like a skunk. He was still a bit unsteady on his feet, and it was a good five blocks to the fleabag hotel.

An ominous laugh erupted somewhere behind him.

The Weasel froze for a second. It couldn't be, could it? He was afraid to look behind him, but even more afraid not to know who was there. He turned around, and his fears were confirmed. A figure stood a few feet away, wrapped in a cloak, wearing a gas mask that obscured his features.

"Oh, shit."

The Lurker laughed again. Jimmy took off running.

Fear was a great motivator. The Weasel ran like he'd never run before, ran until his heart was pounding on his chest like a sledgehammer and he could barely breathe. He vaulted a fence as if he was in the Olympics, ran some more, and made a right turn into another alley.

The Lurker stood at the end of the alley, waiting for him. Jimmy tripped on some trash and ended up on his hands and knees in front of the cloaked figure.

"Jimmy the Weasel," the Lurker said; his voice was a harsh whisper that sent chills down Jimmy's back. "I have some questions for you."

"Jeeze, mister! I didn't do nothin'!" Jimmy protested. The Lurker's mirthless laughter shut off his denials. "All right, all right! Whaddya want to know?"

"Who is after Freddy Razor's mob? Who killed Billy Lazy Eye?"

"I dunno, mister! We got no beef with nobody!" Jimmy knew that answer wasn't going to satisfy the Lurker. Stories of what happened to people who crossed the mystery man deepened his panic. "Wait, wait, I think it was Levine's mob! Freddy got into a tussle with Red Levine's gang a few weeks back, but everyone thought that was over with. It's got to be his people who're gunning after us. I hadn't heard his mob could fry a man like a side of bacon, but that's what they did to poor Lazy Eye."

The man in the gas mask didn't say anything for a few seconds. If he thought Jimmy was lying, things were going to get mighty hairy mighty fast. Finally, the Lurker spoke. "You should get out of town, Jimmy. Things are going to get ugly around here." There was a blur of shadowy movement, and the Lurker was gone.

Jimmy had people in New Jersey. He figured this would be a great time to visit. Maybe for keeps. Freddy Razor might be mad about it, but Jimmy figured that, with the Lurker involved, Freddy's opinion wasn't going to matter for much longer.

* * *

"Doc, I think we're in trouble," Horace 'Chip' Nelson shouted before another burst of submachine gun fire drowned out all sound.

"You figured that out just now? You shoulda been a private dick," grumbled Robert 'Sims' Klondike after the shooting stopped. The massively built Sims crouched as low as he could behind some cargo crates, but the cover was woefully inadequate for someone his size. "Doc, we gotta do something or they're gonna fill us full of lead!"

"Quiet, you oversized orangutan!" admonished Chip. The former Navy Intelligence officer cursed when several bullets punched through one of the crates. "Doc will figure something out faster if you stop bothering him. Right, Doc?"

Kenneth 'Doc' Slaughter said nothing, ignoring his companion's byplay while he coolly assessed the situation. He and his two assistants had arrived to a warehouse on the waterfront a few minutes before, following a lead on some very rare and valuable stolen goods, and had stumbled into a gang of heavily armed men. The thieves had managed to pin down Doc and his friends with a barrage of automatic fire. Sims was right; if they didn't do something they would soon be surrounded and cut down.

Doc was armed with a weapon of his own invention, a .15 caliber machine pistol that fired a variety of ammunition. The gun was currently loaded with non-lethal anesthetic darts; he had managed to shoot down two of the thugs before being forced behind some crates by several well-aimed bursts of automatic fire. His three companions were even less well-armed. Sims only had his hand and feet; Chip carried an ornate cane that could telescope into a fighting staff, which did him little good while hiding behind several stacks of crates, surrounded by a dozen heavily armed men. Their enemies were firing from behind cover, and he couldn't shoot at them without becoming exposed to their counter-fire.

Unless... "Hand me your cane, Chip," Doc said. Chip did so without hesitation. As soon as the stick was in his hand, Doc rolled towards a tall stack of crates. The sudden motion triggered another burst of shots, but none of the bullets hit him. A quick glance had shown Doc the proper angles and distances involved in what he needed to do. He shoved the cane under the bottom crate and used it as a lever to topple the stack of wooden boxes. Under the lacquered wood finish, the cane was made of a light but amazingly strong alloy of Doc's invention, and, driven by his extraordinary strength, it easily caused the high stack of boxes to collapse towards the largest concentration of shooters. The falling boxes forced the men to scatter into the open, where Doc could pick them off with rapid but accurate shots from his pistol. Six gunmen went down in as many seconds.

The loss of over half their number unnerved the remaining thugs. They fled, followed by the taunts of Doc's companions. "You'd better run, you idiots! Doc made a monkey outta youse!" Sims shouted gleefully.

"That's funny, you calling anybody a monkey," Chip said to his friend. Sims' nickname referred to his simian features and enormous size, which could most kindly be referred to as 'gorilla-like.'

Doc paid no attention to the byplay. As soon as the remaining shooters ran, he launched himself after them. He caught one of the fleeing men by the nape of the neck and lifted him off the ground as if he weighted no more than a cat. He did not shoot his captive. The curare-based nerve toxin in his bullets would render their targets unconscious for several hours, and he needed answers now.

The man's struggles were fruitless; he could no more break Doc's grip than he could have bent a bar of solid steel. His flailing fists hit Doc a few times, doing more damage to his knuckles than to the blonde giant holding him. Doc flung the man against a wall, stunning him. "That's enough of that," he said.

The thug cowered against the wall as Doc's companions joined him and surrounded the captive. "Fuck me sideways, it's Doc Slaughter!"

"Not your lucky day, is it, bucko?" Sims said derisively. "You took a shot at Doc and the Fantastic Five. Not very smart."

"Two out of the Five, anyways," Chip corrected pedantically; Doc's other companions were away at the moment.

The cornered man watched the byplay with wide eyes, clearly too scared to say anything. "Who hired you?" Doc asked him in a stern tone. "Who's been stealing field effect transistors all over the city?" The electronic devices had been stolen from two universities' laboratories and an Edison Electric facility over the last few days. The solid-state transistors were mostly experimental creations with no practical uses, but Doc knew only too well that seemingly harmless tools could be used for very harmful purposes. The thieves had shown themselves to be willing to use force to achieve their goals, which meant they were up to no good. "Who hired you?" he repeated.

"Awright! Awright, I'll tell ya! We was..."

There was a sudden change in the air around Doc Slaughter, combined with a sudden premonition of doom that sent him into action before his conscious mind could begin to process the information. He jumped, slamming Sims to the ground with his feet and using the falling giant as a launching platform to hurl himself towards Chip, knocking him down as well.

A blinding flash of light filled the warehouse. Doc felt unbearable heat scorching his back right through the tough fabric of his clothes, even as his body was wracked by electrical currents. A thunderous crash shook the entire building an instant later. Doc hit the ground rolling, ignoring the pain and shock as he looked for a target. The warehouse's lights had been shorted by the attack, and in the darkness he was only able to catch a brief flurry of motion as someone fled the warehouse. He pulled a mini-flashlight from a pouch on his belt and used it to illuminate the scene, although the burning stench filling his nostrils gave him a good idea of what he would see.

The shooter they had been interrogating was dead, struck directly by the lightning-like bolt that had barely missed Doc. The man's flesh had been charred to the bone, leaving behind nothing but an unrecognizable, blackened corpse.

"I'll be dipped in... What the hell was that?" Sims exclaimed.

Doc fought off a surge of frustration. The mysterious weapon's wielder was gone. "Whatever it was, it must use the transistors the thieves were procuring."

"We're in some real trouble then, Doc."

Doc could only nod at that.

New York City, New York, October 7, 1938

"Mr. Clarke?"

John Clarke turned towards the unfamiliar voice and found himself looking down on a tiny wisp of a woman, barely a few inches above four feet, slender and beautiful, at least from what he could see of her face. Her eyes were concealed behind dark glasses. Her skin was dark, her hair black and curled.

"Can I help you, Miss?" he said politely, suppressing an impatient urge to ignore the woman. He'd been on his way to *The World's Journal*, and he needed to hurry if he wasn't going to be late. Mr. Wilkins, the *Journal*'s editor, had no tolerance for malingerers, and he was wont to make his feelings on the matter profanely clear.

"I have a job for you," she said softly. "I have a job for Ultimate."

Cold dread gripped John. "I don't know what you mean," he replied, the denial sounding weak to his own ears.

"Your secret is safe with me, John Clarke," the strange woman asserted calmly. "But thousands will die if you don't act. Otherwise I would not be doing this."

John relaxed minutely. Worries about his secret and Mr. Wilkins' reaction to his lateness faded away. The woman's words were an irresistible lure. Why else had God or Providence gifted him with his abilities, if not to help people? Why else had he dressed in that silly costume that had recently been immortalized in the pages of a comic book?

"Let's go somewhere and talk, then," he said, all business now. He'd be late after all.

* * *

Gonzaga hadn't shared the dead fellow's name with Linda, but her contacts at the NYPD had coughed up the info quickly enough. Bill 'Lazy Eye' O'Grady had run with a tough mob before someone had deep-fried him and dumped his body in that alley. Lazy Eye had worked for Freddy 'Razor' Shaughnessy. Freddy Razor ran a few rackets around the Bowery, mostly protection and gambling. The connection might explain why someone could want O'Grady dead, if not how that someone had done the deed.

Even more interestingly, another charred corpse had been found later that very night. Details were still sketchy, but none other than the notorious Doc Slaughter had been involved in the incident. The story was getting bigger and bigger.

Linda hung up on the flunkie at the NYPD when the fellow started getting tiresome, and looked up from her desk just in time to see John Clarke come in. Clarke was the new golden boy at the *World's Journal,* a big palooka with a stupid-looking mustache and the shoulders of a Brooklyn Dodgers defensive lineman. He was late, but Mr. Wilkins was off playing golf with the mayor, so he was safe enough. His eyes met hers, and he greeted her with a shy smile. She scowled at him. Clarke had scooped her too many times already for her to feel chummy towards him.

Her scowl didn't deter him from walking up to her desk. "Good morning, Linda."

"What's so good about it? That was a rhetorical question, by the way." He started to stammer an apology, but she cut him off again. "What do you want, Clarke? I'm busy."

"I'm working on a story…"

"That's swell, Clarke. So am I." *And if you try and scoop me, I'll have your guts for garters.* She didn't say that out loud, but her glare expressed the sentiment quite clearly.

"It's about that inventor, Hiram Horowitz," Clarke went on. You wrote an article about him last year."

"Yes, I remember him. He's giving Doc Slaughter a run for his money when it comes to creating new gadgets and contraptions. What about him?"

"Did you find anything that might lead you to believe he would be involved in something illegal, or dangerous?"

Linda's brows furrowed in concentration. Nothing came to mind right offhand. Had she missed something? She remembered her brief interview with Mr. Horowitz fairly well, another big guy who did not appear at all like a scientist until he opened his mouth. The man had not been very friendly – which was unusual; in her experience, most fellows tried to be on their best behavior around her – but otherwise he'd been fairly ordinary, almost boring, in fact. All he wanted to talk about were all his new inventions. She'd done a little digging on the man's background, just in case. Sometimes the most boring people would have some very interesting skeletons in their closets.

"There wasn't much to the fellow," she admitted. "I'd have to look up my notes, but going off the top of my head, a couple of his cousins ran with Red Levine's mob. That's about it, though."

"Red Levine; he's an enforcer for Lucky Luciano, isn't he?"

"Allegedly, sure. Nothing we could print, of course. No evidence, and witnesses either change their stories or find themselves suffering all kinds of unfortunate accidents."

"Do you think I could have a look at your notes, Linda? It could be important."

"Why, Mistuh Clarke, Ah surely could," she said in an atrocious attempt at a Southern accent. Scarlett O'Hara she surely wasn't. "And I will, as soon as you tell me why you want to know about Mr. Horowitz and his wonderful gadgets."

"I got a tip claiming he's trying to do something that might endanger a lot of people."

"Now that's interesting. Is it a good source?"

"It was very persuasive, you might say."

Linda was tempted to tell Clarke she could only have her notes if he let her in on the story, but she had to keep chasing after the leads on the Lightning Bolt Murders. She decided to be a good sport and let the big lug have the info. The way she figured it, if he was busy chasing Horowitz he wouldn't get in her way. "I'll get them for you." She got up from her desk and ruffled through the battered file cabinet where she kept her notes, fairly sure Clarke was ogling her all the while. Men! "There wasn't much to tell, as far as I remember. Other than the cousins, and I don't think he's really in touch with them, the man was clean. Ivy League graduate, no criminal record, has made a nice pile of dough selling his patents. Here you go," she finished, handing him the folder. "That's all the dirt I could dig up. Nothing good enough to make it in the article. It was a puff piece anyways, a 'local boy makes it big' story. You actually think he's up to something?"

"I hope not," John said. "Thank you, Linda. You just saved me from a lot of legwork. I owe you one."

"And don't you forget it, Clarke."

He gave her another shy smile and walked to his own desk. He really wasn't such a bad fellow, she thought. If he were a bit more assertive, he might grow on her. Oh, well. She had more important things to do. Linda turned back to her story.

Someone had fried one of Freddy Razor's goons. She was pretty sure Freddy wasn't going to take that lying down. If the other dead body was also one of his, then a gang war might be in the offing. Things were going to get ugly, and when things got ugly they became newsworthy. If she played her cards right, she would have a front-row seat to some mayhem.

* * *

Twisting ribbons of actinic light lashed at the Empire States Building, shattering glass and cracking stone and concrete. Off in the distance, a skyscraper started leaning drunkenly to one side, the slow collapse accelerating until the structure struck another building in an explosive impact that created a cloud of pulverized masonry. Pillars of smoke marked places where the other strikes had sparked fires.

New York burned under a lightning storm of impossible power.

The apocalyptic vision that Cassandra had shared with him fluttered behind John Clark's eyes as he approached a seemingly abandoned facility in Queens. The idea that Hiram Horowitz could be responsible for such a disaster seemed ridiculous, risible even, but John couldn't dismiss the images the seer had shown him. Unfortunately, there was no evidence the man was involved in anything criminal or dangerous. John needed actual evidence before he could make any accusations or take action.

The only thing Linda had been able to find about Horowitz was the existence of a cousin, Yitzak Horowitz, who had been linked with Samuel 'Red' Levine's mob. Beyond that dubious link to organized crime (there were no indications Hiram and his cousin had socialized with each other after their respective Bar Mitzvahs) Horowitz was clean. He was a genius inventor with several patents to his name. Wealthy and successful inventors usually didn't resort to crime.

How successful had Horowitz been, though? John noted that the Linda's article mentioned the inventor's greatest achievement had been the sale of a new power generator to Edison Electric. A few phone calls later, John discovered that the deal with Edison Electric had fallen through a few weeks ago. That provided a motive, if nothing else.

After some more digging, John had tried to find Horowitz. He'd quickly discovered that the inventor no longer resided in his apartment and had left owing last month's rent, something his landlord had been quick to volunteer. His office in the city had also been abandoned. That left this building in the garment district, a former factory that had fallen into hard times; Horowitz had purchased the building and converted it into a workshop. John walked up to the front door. It was locked, and the lights were out, which was unsurprising since it was long past business hours.

John considered his options. He mostly preferred to work within the law, but Cassandra's visions had made it clear time was of the essence. If there was any information about Horowitz in the building, he needed to find it. With a rueful shrug, he walked into an alley behind the building and quickly took off his suit, revealing the tight costume beneath. He removed the folded cape and boots from a briefcase and hastily put them on, feeling self-conscious as he did it. It was a necessary evil, he told himself. If he was discovered breaking and entering, it would be best if the perpetrator was identified as the mystery man known as Ultimate, and not as John Clarke, law-abiding journalist.

The building was a four-story affair. John gathered himself and leaped up, propelling himself forty feet into the air with a single bound. All of which was wondrous, except he didn't clear the top of the building as he'd planned, and wasn't able to find a handhold before plummeting back towards the ground. John landed with bone-crushing force, bounced off, and rolled to his feet. "I need to work on that," he muttered to himself. If he jumped too high he'd miss the building altogether and land somewhere at random; a few months ago he had overshot his target and crashed through the roof of a fortunately unoccupied car. Before that, he had destroyed numerous awnings, a hot dog cart, and a storefront window. He had spent a good deal of his meager salary anonymously paying the owners for the ensuing property damage. None of the incidents had made it to the papers, or the comics. They still grated, though.

John gritted his teeth and tried again. This time he gauged the force of his jump correctly and landed on the top of the warehouse. There was an access door on the roof. It was locked but he effortlessly broke the lock, reminding himself to find out how much a new lock would cost for when it was time to make restitution.

The top floors of the building had clearly been used mostly for storage and were covered in dust. John quietly went down to the lower levels. It was dark, but he had brought a flashlight. It cast a circle of light, revealing a well-stocked workshop, with machine tools and assembly tables that had clearly seen some recent use. A few unfinished devices lay on the tables, but their purpose completely eluded him.

John spent a few minutes fruitlessly searching the place before his inhumanly keen hearing picked up two cars stopping near the building. A number of men got off and approached walked toward the workshop. John hid himself behind a large table and waited. He listened as the newcomers came in.

"… so I says to her, I says, 'Listen, baby, and listen good. I ain't takin' no guff from no broad!'"

"And then you woke up." Laughter. "Come on, Mel. Everyone knows Tammy left you for that Navy puke."

"Everyone, shut yer traps! I want to get all them boxes loaded up nice and quick. We've got lots to do tonight, to make up for yesterday's mess. Chop chop!"

"Sure, Yitz, anything you say."

John peered at the men from his hiding place. They looked like they'd be more at home shaking down small business owners than carrying boxes filled with the electronic components he had noticed earlier. He noticed most of them bore weapons: revolvers and pistols were tucked in their waistbands or in shoulder or belt holsters. One of them, the only one not busy lifting boxes, had a larger weapon in his hands, something roughly the size of a sawed-off shotgun. Either Horowitz was making use of his underworld contacts, of the underworld was making use of him. Either way, it was time to intervene.

John stepped out into the open. "I don't think those belong to you," he said loudly. The gangsters froze and stared unbelievingly at him for a second or two. "If you put the boxes down and explain yourselves, nobody needs to get hurt," he went on.

The gangsters sprang into action. Two of them dropped the boxes and ran for the exit. The rest reached for their guns. John rushed the closest one and drove a fist into his stomach, doubling him over, and followed up with a hammer blow to the back of his head that sent him sprawling to the ground. He had suppressed his inhuman strength before striking, but the blows were enough to put the thug down for the count.

Two of the remaining men fired away at him. They were no farther than ten yards away, but most of their shots missed. In the two years since he had started a career in crime-fighting, John had noticed that guns were surprisingly inaccurate, especially in the hands of untrained criminals. Only two bullets struck him from a barrage of over a dozen shots. An impact on his shoulder bounced off, barely noticeable. The other shot struck him on his left cheek. It stung him slightly, but that was all. Even a few months before, the shots would have hurt him more. Was he getting used to being shot, or was he growing tougher with time? He didn't know.

This wasn't the time to think about those things, of course. He rushed the closest shooter and brought him low with a right cross to the jaw. As John turned towards the last two men still on their feet, the fellow with the shotgun-like weapon brought it to bear and opened fire.

Blinding light flashed forth, and pain.

He was on his hands and knees, the smell of his own scorched flesh filling his nostrils. His head was ringing and he couldn't see. A painful burn on the left side of his collarbone throbbed with every heartbeat. Distantly, he heard voices.

"I got 'im! I killed Ultimate!"

"Look out, Yitz! He's still moving!"

"I'll blast 'im again."

Another shock struck John on his right arm. A surge of heat hotter than anything he had experienced before was followed by a wave of electrical shock that coursed through every nerve of his body, knocking him on his back. He lay twitching on the ground, unable to move.

"Zap him again, Yitz!"

"I can't, dammit! The fucking gizmo ain't working no more! Let's get outta here!"

Some time passed before he could get his muscles to work again. John struggled to his feet. The burn on his torso was almost gone, healed off by his inhuman recuperative abilities, but his wounded arm still pained him and he was unsteady on his feet. The thugs were gone; they had managed to drag off their fallen buddies and some of the boxes they had come for. He must have been in a daze for longer than he'd thought.

Nothing had hurt him to that degree before. For some reason, the realization brought him measure of comfort. *Remember, you are still mortal.* Triumphant Roman generals had a slave muttering those words to them during celebrations, to temper their arrogance. Realizing that there were things in this world that could injure or even kill him made John feel strangely better about himself and his place in the world. Not that the actual experience had been pleasant, of course.

The weapon matched Cassandra's vision far too closely. Hiram Horowitz had somehow built a device that could generate lightning bolts, and the weapon was in the hands of gangsters. Nothing good could come of that.

John had to do something about it.

***

Uh, oh, Linda Lamar thought as she looked down the barrel of the Colt .45 aimed directly at her face.

"Now what's a dame like you doin' in a place like this?" Freddy Razor said, echoing Detective Gonzaga's words from last night, except that Freddy sounded a lot meaner than the policeman had. "You'd better have somethin' to say, sister, and it'd better be somethin' good."

Linda should have known better than to try and sneak around one of Freddy Razor's known hangouts, a garage in the Bowery that doubled as a meeting place for his gang. One of her underworld contacts, a waitress with a penchant for dating the wrong kind of guy, had let her know that Freddy had called a meeting at the garage. Linda had traded her usual dress and heels for blue jeans and sensible shoes, and had tried to sneak around the back of the garage. Unfortunately, one of Freddy's goons had spotted her.

Her first inkling that something was wrong had happened when she felt a gun being pressed against her back. She'd had no choice but to walk into the garage, where Freddy Razor had started waving another gun in her face. Linda looked around. The garage was mostly empty except for a few stripped down cars and half a dozen rough-looking men. They all looked angry, scared or both, and none seemed happy to see her. Their leader was no exception: the big and burly Irishman glared at her with murder in his eyes. Freddy Razor's red hair and ruddy complexion were great at expressing anger. Linda, a redhead with a fiery temper herself, could sympathize, although she would have been more sympathetic if the anger wasn't aimed at her.

This would be a great time for Ultimate to show up. The man in the cape seemed to have a knack for appearing at just the right time to save her bacon. One could only hope this was one of those occasions. "I'm gonna ask you again," Freddy said. "What are you doin' here? I ain't gonna ask you three times."

"I know someone's gunning for your mob, Freddy," Linda said levelly. "I wanted to find out who it was."

Freddy's eyes narrowed. "I know who you are. That lady reporter at the *World's Journal*."

"Guilty as charged," she replied. "I'm not looking to give you any trouble, okay? I'm after whoever fried Lazy Eye. Maybe we can help each other," she continued hopefully.

"Oh, yeah? You hear that, boys? She wants to help us." Some of the men laughed at that. "We don't need no dame's help to handle Red Levine's gang. I don't care what they used to kill Lazy Eye. We'll get 'em. But before we go get 'em, maybe you could help us, in another way." Freddy Razor raised the gun and started reaching for her with his free hand; his angry scowl was replaced by a hungry leer. "Maybe we can have us a little party before we leave."

The lights went out.

Linda ducked away from Freddy Razor as the men around her started shouting in the darkness.

A sinister laugh echoed throughout the garage and silenced everyone.

That wasn't Ultimate.

Linda hit the ground just as one of the panicky thugs started yelling. "Oh shit! It's the Lurker!" A second later, people started shooting. Linda crawled on her hands and knees, catching glimpses of the action around her as muzzle flashes provided brief moments of illumination. She saw a man clutch at his chest and go down in the space of two gunshots. In the midst of the deafening reports, she heard other men scream in pain and terror. Off to her left, she caught a glimpse of a cloaked figure making an impossible leap across the room, twin Mauser pistols in his hands firing in quick succession. Someone fell across her legs, soaking her jeans with blood. She kicked the dying man off her and managed to reach one of the stripped-down cars, where she could get some cover from all the gunfire. It would be a shame if her first-hand look at the Lurker in action ended with her catching a stray bullet.

The battle didn't last long. Freddy was the last to fall. She saw him fire several shots at the elusive cloaked figure, none of which hit anything. Freddy's gun made a few clicks after it was emptied. There was a final muzzle flash, which revealed the cloaked man with the gas mask, and Freddy went down. Silence and darkness filled the space that moments before had held half a dozen men.

The Lurker laughed again.

Somehow, being in the dark with the mystery man was scarier than being surrounded by armed thugs. She didn't let her feelings show, however. The Lamar family didn't raise wimps or quivering daisies. "Lurker? Is it safe to come out now?"

The only answer was another burst of laughter. A few nerve-wracking seconds later, the lights came on again, revealing the sprawled bodies of Freddy Razor and his gang. The Lurker was nowhere to be seen. Just like in the stories, the man in the gas mask just wasn't much of a conversationalist.

Linda rose to her feet, forcing herself to ignore the corpses surrounding her. Out in the distance she heard police sirens. It might be a good idea to make herself scarce before Gonzaga or some other cop decided to hold her for questioning. As she left, Linda considered Freddy's comments before his untimely demise. He'd mentioned Red Levine; hadn't she just handed John Clarke a bunch of notes with

Levine's name in them? Notes related to that inventor, Hiram Horowitz. Horowitz, who had invented several gizmos involving electricity. Linda didn't believe in coincidences.

Clark had scooped her again, curse him.

Well, maybe not, she reassured herself as she got into her car, which she'd parked not too far from the ill-fated meeting place. For one, she might well get a front-page story just out of the massacre she'd just witnessed, which might make up somewhat for the terror and the nightmares she'd be having for God knew how long. For another, John's angle had involved Horowitz himself, not his gangland connections. Linda might still get ahead of the mild-mannered oaf.

Linda looked at herself on the car's rearview mirror. Her face was stained with a spatter of blood. She didn't remember getting splashed with gore, but there it was. Her hands started to shake; she had to wait until they had steadied before she could drive away. Luckily nobody spotted her while she got herself together. Meeting the Lurker had been a bit more exciting than she'd expected. Being nearly murdered or worse had also taken its toll on her.

She could only hope things wouldn't get any worse before they got better.

* * *

He'd never expected things would go so badly.

Hiram Horowitz tried to force himself to concentrate on his work rather than reflect on the circumstances where his poor choices had led him. He couldn't quite manage it. He'd gone from being a reputable and well-respected scientist and inventor to a failure and possible fraud, and from there he'd become an outright criminal. His downfall had been as rapid as it had been absolute.

"None of this was supposed to happen," he muttered to himself as he connected more of the precious solid-state transistors into the huge device he'd been working on for the last several days. There was still a chance at redemption, however. If he could get this latest version of the Jupiter Device to work, it wouldn't matter what anybody thought of him. He would be able to show the world a modern marvel that could provide all the power New York City would ever need. He would drive Edison Electric out of business in one fell swoop. He would show everyone he was no fraud.

Everything would be all right then, as long as he could hide the dark twists and turns his journey had taken.

He'd needed money, more money than he would be able to raise on his own. With no legitimate alternatives left to him, he'd turned to his cousin. Yitzak Horowitz's unsavory associations had long been a source of sorrow and scandal in his family, but Hiram had swallowed his pride and tried to secure a loan from his cousin's underworld friends. Yitz himself had been surprisingly sympathetic to his plight. "Whaddidya expect, Hir?" Yitz had said over a glass of beer after Hiram had related his troubles. "They robbed ya, that's what they did. They ain't gonna let no hebes like us get ahead in this world."

Yitz had been willing to help, but he'd needed some sort of collateral. When Hiram tried to explain his device in a way someone with a fourth-grade education could grasp, Yitz had – rather ingeniously, one might add – suggested some practical if unsavory applications for the Jupiter Device. Reluctantly, Hiram had built a weapon for his cousin. Hiram hoped his hoodlum relative wouldn't get into too much trouble with it. In return, Yitz had provided funds and a new workshop by the city docks, a building that not too long ago had been used to warehouse illegal liquor. When the materials Hiram needed had been beyond their resources, Yitz and his men had gone and stolen them. It had been regretful but necessary.

Hiram was almost finished with his most ambitious project to date: a massive version of the Jupiter Device, capable of generating enough power for the entire city, and possibly much of the tri-state area. He would demonstrate the device's capabilities in a most dramatic way: an impressive lightshow over the entire city, sending arcs of lightning soaring harmlessly over New York's skies for everyone to see. The demonstration would convince all the skeptics, and soon he would be building similar devices for Chicago, Detroit, and every other large city in the country, and eventually the world.

Nobody would look too closely at the financing of the original device – or the provenance of its components – once its power and efficacy became apparent, or so he hoped.

Hiram wiped his forehead and examined the connection he'd been working on. A part of him resented doing the menial installation work like some mechanic, but he'd come to accept the only way his creation would work was if he personally oversaw every step in its construction. Cousin Yitz had provided him with a number of workers who had helped with the basic construction, but everything else he had done with his own two hands. He had been working nonstop for several days, pausing only to eat or catch a couple of hours of sleep here or there. As the device neared completion he'd even foregone eating. Neither hunger not sleeplessness bothered him. His creation was almost finished.

"How's it goin' Hir?"

Hiram turned towards his cousin. Yitzak Horowitz was a good four inches shorter than him, and much less heavily built; he had a weasel-like cast to his face and demeanor, which together with the malevolent glint in his eyes made his criminal inclinations abundantly clear. The customary smirk on Yitz's face was missing, however. He looked angry and worried. Several of his thugs were there as well, some laden with boxes of equipment, things Hiram had requested before he realized he could finish the device without them.

"I'm just about done, Yitz. Is everything all right?"

"Nope. Nothin's awright, Hir. We ran into some trouble, and your gizmo ain't workin' no more. We coulda gotten arrested on account it stopped workin'. The first time I used it worked great. I did a whatdayacallit, an experiment out in the Bowery, and got one of Freddy Razor's boys. Worked like a charm. Even better, I just got word that Freddy got his mob together and the fuckin' Lurker wiped them out for us, so we don't gotta worry about them no more."

Hiram frowned at the news. His invention, used for murder? He supposed such a result should have been foreseeable, but the actuality of it bothered him.

"But when we were getting more of that stuff you need, we ran into Doc Slaughter and his gang. And the stupid contraption stopped workin' at the worst time."

"I told you the weapon could only hold a few charges. How many times did you use it?"

"Three, four times? I tested it a couple times first, then used it on Lazy Eyes.

Then I had to shut up Sammy before he could squeal to Doc Slaughter. That happened last night. I couldn't make the damn zap gun work until the last minute, but the one shot I got off took care of Sammy and almost did for Doc and his pals, too, but then the damn thing stopped working and I had to change that cappa-something bit in it."

"The capacitor," Hiram said.

"Yeah, the cappawhazit. Then tonight we ran into fuckin' Ultimate his own damn self, when we were emptying your old workshop to get the stuff we couldn't steal last night. I hurt 'im bad with your gizmo, Hir, I did, but the damn zapper died on me again before I could finish him off, and now the fuckin' Invincible Man is gonna come gunnin' for me. Gunnin' for us."

"Dear God," Hiram said. He'd worked with Doc Slaughter while still in college, and even considered at one point to try and join the ranks of his inner circle, before realizing he'd much rather be his own man. Slaughter was one of the few men who could figure out that the components Yitz and his men had stolen had ended up in the Jupiter Device. That was bad news. And what about Ultimate? "I thought the Invincible Man was just a tall tale," he told his cousin.

"He's real, all right. I knew that before I ever laid eyes on him," Yitz retorted. "And he's for real, too. Bullets done bounce off of him, just like in people was sayin'. But your zapper, it put him down. Down, but not out, see? Now he's gonna be lookin' for us."

Ludicrous. The idea that a man's skin could shed bullets was simply impossible. And yet Hiram could not simply discount Yitz's testimony. Too many seemingly impossible things were happening all over the world. Even his own creations were stretching the limits of the possible, if not actually breaking them. The words from the officious bastard at Edison Electric came back to haunt him. What if his inventions only worked because they were being driven by his will instead of physical, natural laws?

Hiram shook his head. He couldn't dwell on those things. "Can they find us here?" he asked his cousin.

"I dunno. None of the guys Doc Slaughter nabbed last night knew about this address, except for Sammy, and I made sure he couldn't blab. Tonight we got away clean from Ultimate. We're safe here, I think. But you need to fix the zap gun, Hir, just in case, and mebbe get us a couple more of them. Just in case."

"No," Hiram replied firmly. This had gone far enough. Two men had been killed by the weapon he had handed his cousin. He couldn't afford to be seen as an accessory to murder, not if he had any hopes to regaining his good name. "I told you, I'm finished. As soon as I demonstrate my invention, everything will be all right. City and state governments will line up to have me produce copies of the device. There will be more than enough money for everyone, Yitzak. You'll never have to commit another crime again."

"None of that matters if I get nabbed for the crimes I already done, Hir," Yitz replied. "And if that happens, you'll be heading to the big house too, you hear? So I'm gonna have to insist on getting them zap guns. If Ultimate comes after us, we gotta put him on ice. Same with Doc Slaughter, or anyone else getting' in our way."

Dammit. Dammit all to hell. Hiram barely stopped an angry outburst that would gain him nothing and tried to consider the situation. If Slaughter or that Ultimate fellow discovered Hiram's involvement with the underworld, he was doomed. He'd already faced the loss of everything he'd worked so hard for. It seemed as if every step he took to try to escape his fate only led him deeper into the abyss. He needed to wipe the slate clean somehow, but was he willing to pay the price to do so?

He was a man with a vision, with a purpose. The Jupiter Device was but a stepping stone towards his destiny. He could transform the world, lead humanity to a Golden Age. All he had to do was get through this hurdle.

"What's it gonna be, Hir?" Yitz asked. He and his henchmen were getting tense.

Hiram smiled at them. "I'll get you your 'zap guns,' and more, cousin. I have a plan, Yitz. A plan that will solve all our problems."

Yitz smiled back. "I always knew you had it in you, Hir," he said approvingly.

Hiram hadn't known he had it in him, not until that very moment. It was interesting, how easily he had made the decision to commit murder.

New York City, New York, October 8, 1938

"I really wish you'd stay in the car, Miss Lamar," Doc Slaughter said. He was an imposing man – at least an inch or two taller than Ultimate, Linda had gauged after meeting with him, and blessed with the looks of a Norse god – but if he thought he was going to push her around, he had another thing coming.

"You have two choices, Doc. Let me tag along with your merry men, or I'll go off on my own and get into who knows what kind of trouble."

"There is a third option: we could lock you up in the trunk."

"Just try it, buster. You'll live to regret it, I can guarantee that."

Doc Slaughter sighed heavily. Linda figured people didn't usually say no to the big blonde guy. "Very well. Just try to stay out of harm's way. The only reason we're going after our quarry on our own is because I fear the police is not equipped to handle their exotic weapons. I can only hope the precautions I've taken will be enough to deal with them."

"That, and we don't want some cop on the take to spill the beans about our little hunting expedition," Sims Klondike said from the front seat of the large bronze-colored sedan, a large car with ample room for Doc, Linda, and Doc's two companions. Sims leered at Linda from the rear view window. "Don't you worry, Miss Lamar. We'll take good care of ya."

"I doubt Miss Lamar would enjoy your idea of care, you big ape," Chip chided him.

Linda rolled her eyes but didn't say anything. Sims might look and act like an ape, but his attitude was the same as that of the other men in the car. Chip Nelson was unfailingly polite and had perfect manners, and Doc Slaughter himself was cool and aloof, but they all were treating her like a child, which was as infuriating as it was unsurprising.

When she heard about Doc's encounter with a lightning gun, she'd figured she would share her information with the adventurer and get a better story. As it turned out, Doc had learned of the location of the weapons' workshop from one of his own underworld contacts. Linda's information had added a few pieces of the puzzle, though, just enough that Doc had felt obligated to let her tag along, or perhaps he'd been worried might prematurely let the cat out of the bag. Linda could live with the man's attitude as long as she got her scoop.

Doc's car came to a stop near a block of warehouses by the docks. It was after business hours, and the place was mostly deserted, but Linda could see the lights were on at one of the buildings. "That's the place," Doc confirmed. "Our informant wasn't lying."

"What's the plan, Doc?" Sims asked.

"We go in quietly, and try to take them by surprise."

The group approached the warehouse, sticking to the shadows, and sneaked around the back of the building. A door there was invitingly open. That looked suspicious to Linda, but Doc Slaughter led the way and he made it inside without incident. The rest of the gang followed, with Linda bringing up the rear.

The interior of the warehouse was dark except for a spot near the center, where a large machine stood, surrounded by spotlights. The device was twice as tall as a man, a boxy contraption of metal and rubber with a control panel full of lights and levers; thick cables extended from it and disappeared into the shadowy areas in the warehouse. It was humming at a steady rate, and some of its components were glowing with a bluish hue. Linda smelled ozone in the air and felt the small hairs on her arms stand up.

Standing by the machine was a large man in a lab coat she immediately recognized as Hiram Horowitz. He appeared to be unaware of their presence as he adjusted some levers and buttons on the large device.

"Doctor Horowitz," Doc Slaughter called out. His companions spread out to both sides of him, their guns at the ready.

Horowitz turned around to face them. "Doctor Slaughter. I was expecting you. Is Ultimate with your group by any chance? No? That's all right. I believe he will be joining us shortly."

"I'm placing you under arrest on suspicion of grand theft and murder," Doc said.

"Slander. Baseless slander. I committed no crimes, not until now, and only because that's the only way I can protect my reputation. Only by silencing my would-be accusers will I be able to continue my work in peace. I am sorry it had to come to this."

"Don't try anything, Horowitz," Sims growled. "Make a move and I'll plug you."

"You really need a better class of henchmen, Slaughter," Horowitz said. "Mine, for instance, know how to stay quiet until needed." He made a small gesture with his head, and Linda heard movement all around them. She spotted men moving into position from behind boxes and shelves in the warehouse. Several of them were holding strange silver tubes. She didn't have to guess what those things were.

"Kill them all," Horowitz said. Sims shot him even as he said the words but the inventor ducked with amazing quickness and avoided the burst of gunfire.

Lightning and thunder filled the warehouse.

* * *

The biggest problem with wearing a costume was finding a good place to change.

John Clarke parked his car near the warehouse that – his informant claimed – held the workshop that had produced the lightning weapon. He'd found a dark alley, changed into his Ultimate outfit and dropped his civilian clothes and the fake mustache back into his car before heading towards his quarry. *There must be a better way to do this*, he mused.

He was sure he was walking into a trap. Someone had spread the word about the warehouse location, and done it much too conveniently. His foes would be waiting, no doubt armed with the lightning gun that had almost killed him the previous night. He would have to be careful.

He was almost to the warehouse when the lightning storm started.

There were flashes of light and loud explosions coming from inside the building, but that wasn't all. John looked up to the sky and saw storm clouds swirling in a pattern centered on the warehouse. Bolts of lightning erupted between the cloud formation and the warehouse below, dozens of strikes in a handful of seconds. The spectacle looked all too much like the vision Cassandra had shown him.

There was no time to be careful.

John didn't bother looking for a door. He covered the distance to the building in a single bound and crashed through a wall. The interior of the warehouse had become a battlefield of sorts, where half a dozen men unleashed twisting arcs of electricity on four figures in the center of the building. Three of them were twisting in agony under the lightning bolts; the lone survivor was somersaulting away and proving to be an elusive target. John didn't pause to see who the victims were. He moved in a blur of motion, striking three of the lightning wielders in a couple of seconds and leaving them unconscious on the ground.

John saw the fourth figure fall, struck by two blasts at the same time, and cursed himself for not being fast enough. Two gunners remained and they fired at him. He avoided one shot and sent the attacker sprawling to the ground with a punch, even as the last bolt of lightning struck him on the left shoulder, staggering him. He ignored the pain and subdued the last man with a bone-shattering blow.

Strange. The last time he'd been hit had been a lot more painful. It seemed that whatever didn't kill him only made him stronger.

Only one figure remained on his feet, a tall man in a lab coat. He wasn't holding a weapon.

"Horowitz."

"That's *Doctor* Horowitz," the man in the lab coat hissed. "So you are the amazing Ultimate."

"You are under arrest, Doctor," John said.

"We'll see about that." Horowitz turned towards his machine. John leaped towards him at inhuman speeds, but he wasn't fast enough.

Blinding light struck him down.

* * *

Hiram Horowitz was flung against the Jupiter Device by the sheer force of the lightning storm unfolding mere feet away. His face and every bit of exposed skin hurt; it felt as if he'd been badly sunburned. None of that mattered, however. The device had worked, and it had stopped the Invincible Man in his tracks. He'd channeled the power of an artificial lightning storm into a single point, transfixing Ultimate with multiple bolts. The lightshow he'd prepared to use to dazzle Manhattan had become a Biblical weapon with which to smite his enemies.

Half a dozen continuous arcs of electricity transfixed Ultimate. No human being – no living thing – should have survived, but the man in the silly grey and red costume was still moving, although those could just be mere galvanic reflexes. The humanoid figure should have been completely carbonized, however, and although the searing lightning bolts were burning Ultimate, they had yet to consume him. The impossibility of it all shocked Hiram to the core.

The world of scientific certainties in which he had grown up, to which he had spent his life trying to contribute, was crumbling before his eyes. He found himself overcome with loathing for the writhing figure that lived on while being struck by enough power to destroy a city. He had set up the ambush to get rid of any potential accusers, and incidentally to also eliminate his cousin and his fellow criminals, but now all he cared for was to destroy the abomination before him.

Hiram turned to his machine and drew more power from the skies above. A part of him was terrified of the risks involved in overusing the device, but he ignored it.

Ultimate had to die.

* * *

Linda Lamar painfully regained consciousness as thunder and lightning exploded nearby. Her hair was standing on end and she had painful burns over her shoulders and waist, but she was alive, thanks to Doc Slaughter and the protective gizmos he had cobbled earlier in the day.

The blonde genius had figured out how to build a harness that channeled and ground out electrical currents. He'd built enough of the harnesses to outfit himself and his companions, plus a certain nosey reporter who'd insisted in tagging along. The proof that devices worked was very simple: she had been hit by one of the lightning guns, and she was still alive. Not feeling great – the harness straps had partially melted off and burned her even through her clothes – but alive. Eight or nine goons had shot lightning bolts at them. Doc and his companions had taken down a few of the gangsters before being struck. The last thing Linda remembered was seeing a twisting arc of electricity reaching toward her. She had survived, however.

Linda looked up and saw Ultimate being wracked by repeated lightning strikes.

The bolts of energy striking Ultimate were painfully bright to look at. Even from dozens of feet away, Linda could feel their power. The costumed hero should be dead already; he certainly didn't look like he would survive for long. Linda looked around: Doc and his companions were stirring weakly, but none of them was going to be ready for action in time.

She had to do something.

Doc Slaughter had offered her one of his home-made machine pistols, but Linda had politely declined it in favor for her trusty .38 revolver, a gift from her father when he'd realized he wasn't going to deter his precious daughter from getting a dangerous job in the big city. After the incident with Freddy Razor and the Lurker, Linda had decided that bringing her gun along was a good idea. She retrieved the revolver and considered who or what to shoot.

Gunning Horowitz down was an option, but it wouldn't save Ultimate and she didn't have it in her to kill someone in cold blood. Instead, she took aim at Horowitz's machine and started shooting. She had spent plenty of time at the range, and her aim was good. She went for the control panel of the contraption, figuring a few bullet holes there wouldn't do it any good.

One shot, two, three. The gun reports went unheeded in the deafening lightning storm. On the fourth shot, though, the machine started sparkling and smoking, and Horowitz noticed that. He had time to scream "NO!" before her fifth shot hit his creation.

The demise of the Jupiter Device turned out to be fairly unspectacular. The bolts of lightning transfixing Ultimate vanished, and silence filled the warehouse. The blinding flashes were replaced by the weak warehouse lights. The huge machine sputtered for a few more seconds and went still.

"No," Horowitz said.

Ultimate struggled to his knees. Horowitz took a look at him, cast a venomous glance at Linda, and ran away. Linda thought she had one more bullet in her gun, but shooting a man in the back did not appeal to her. In the ensuing years, she would bitterly regret that decision.

The Invincible Man looked didn't look very invincible at the moment. Most of his costume had been torn off, and his skin and flesh were horribly burned. Yet, even in the few seconds since the artificial storm had stopped, she could see the wounds start to fade.

"Thank you very much, Miss Lamar," he said weakly, still on his hands and knees.

"Aren't you going to be chasing after Horowitz?"

"I would, but I can hear..."

The meaty sound of a well-connected punch came from behind the machine, and Horowitz staggered back into view, twirled clumsily like a drunken ballerina, and went down for the count.

"... laughter," Ultimate finished, and Linda caught the now familiar laugh of the Lurker. The sneaky mystery man had shown up late to the party, but had arrived in time to take care of Horowitz. She thought she saw a dark form moving in the shadows, heading for an exit. The man in the gas mask certainly had a flair for the dramatic, although Linda would have appreciated it if he'd shown up before she'd gotten half-fried by lightning.

The Lurker wasn't the only one adept at disappearing. When she turned back towards Ultimate, he was gone as well. She hadn't even gotten a good look at his face. Oh, well.

Doc and his companions were getting up. Sims and Chips looked much the worse for wear: the former looked like a bull gorilla that had been set on fire long enough to burn off all of his fur, and Chips' dapper suit had been ruined, along with his composure. The two companions did not trade any banter as they marveled at their survival.

"Are you all right, Miss Lamar?" Doc Slaughter asked her. He had been struck multiple times by the lightning bolts. His clothes had been shredded just as badly as Ultimate's, and his harness had been completely destroyed, but he looked ready for action, not that there was much left to do. The torn clothes just helped show off Doc's impressive physique. Linda idly wondered if the man was seeing anybody.

"I'll live," Linda said. She indicated the unconscious Horowitz. "You'd better keep an eye on him. The Lurker knocked him out but he might still be dangerous."

"The Lurker was here?"

"And Ultimate. I guess it took all of you to save the day." *Not to mention little old me*, she thought. She probably wouldn't mention that little tidbit in the article. It wouldn't be proper, having the reporter become part of the story. And people wouldn't believe a lady reporter had saved the lives of a couple of big pulp heroes.

It would be one hell of a story, anyway.

New York City, New York, October 10, 1938

John Clark answered the knocking on his apartment door and found himself facing Cassandra.

"Please come in."

The seer did. "Thank you. I am glad everything turned out all right."

"We prevented your vision from coming true, at least," John said as Cassandra found an armchair and sat down. "Several people died. None of them were what you'd call upstanding citizens, true, but I wish we could have stopped those deaths."

"You can't save everyone, John Clarke. You need to remember that, in the years to come. You aren't God. Neither am I. Using my visions to serve the greater good is a tricky process. As it turned out, you merely needed to occupy Hiram Hades' attention long enough for Linda Lamar to save the day."

"They also serve, those who stand and soak electrical bolts that might hit someone important?" John mock-quoted. Cassandra smiled. "The gentleman's last name is Horowitz, not Hades, by the way."

"You are correct. For now."

"In any case, thank you for the tip on Horowitz and his invention. If he hadn't been stopped, thousands of innocents would have died. I hope next time your premonitions will allow me to act sooner, though."

Cassandra's smile vanished. "Unfortunately, I'm here to say goodbye, John. Your path will take you through many momentous events, with so many possibilities they would drown me if I were to pry into them. I will restrict myself to smaller things, for the time being."

"I see," John said, although he wasn't sure he understood. He felt vaguely disappointed, but also relieved. He hadn't been very comfortable with the idea of being around someone who could tell the future, or even the shape of possible futures.

"I won't contact you again, John Clarke. I don't think our paths will cross for several decades, certainly not for the rest of this century."

"So not for the rest of our lives, then?"

"I didn't say that."

John decided the woman's love for enigmatic comments would have gotten on his nerves fairly quickly, so it was just was well he wouldn't have to get used to them.

"Thank you again," he said.

Cassandra rose. "I only came here to say goodbye and to take one last look at you, so to speak. I wanted to see how you'd weathered your close brush with mortality."

"I made it out alive," John responded. "The burns were all gone by the next day. There were no ill effects." The memory of the agony and the fear he had felt were still there, however. When he had embarked in his own personal crusade against crime, he had accepted the fact that he was putting his life in danger. That had been before he realized that guns and knives could not harm him. But now he had found there were things in this world that could.

None of it mattered. He could make a difference, and he'd discovered the risk of death wasn't a deterrent.

"Yes, John. Even someone like you can be killed, and in the ensuing years, you will face death many times."

"Everybody dies. I'll do what I think is right."

"That's all anybody can ask of you."

New York City, New York, December 11, 1938

Hiram Horowitz paced inside his cage and made plans.

They had given him a private cell at Rikers Island. It was a miserable place, but he wouldn't be staying there for long. Over the last two weeks since his trial and conviction, he had studied his accommodations, figured out the patterns in his jailors' routines, and put his mind to work. His escape plan was ready, and he would be free within the next two days. They might strip him of his honor and reputation, might ruin him financially and destroy his life, but they wouldn't keep him penned up like an animal.

They had called him a threat, a man who had let his ambition turn his genius into a force of destruction. Slaughter's testimony had been the final nail in his coffin, describing how, if left unchecked, the Jupiter Device could have leveled the city and killed thousands of people. As it turned out, his planned light show would have become an unstoppable storm. Hiram couldn't even argue with Doc's conclusion; the math didn't lie. He had been convicted on all charges.

All he had wanted was to help the world, and the world had spit on his face. He would escape, and then he would show them what a threat looked like.

Doctor Hiram Horowitz was dead. Soon the world would know him as Hiram Hades, and would learn to fear his name.

Hiram Hades paced in the darkness, and plotted.

The Red Baron's Last Flight

Berlin, Germany, July 1, 1944

"This is foolish," Fat Hermann said, his plaintive tone sounding almost like a wail of despair. "You will get killed, and for what? Think of the damage to morale!"

Generalfeldmarschall Manfred Von Richthofen looked at his former fellow flier – his friend, now, after all these years – with a mixture of pity and contempt. Hermann Goering had once been a powerful, decisive man, a fellow fighter ace with a sharp hunter's mind and sharper reflexes. Manfred looked at the overweight, tremulous wreck in front of him and marveled at the damage time could inflict on the mere mortal. Being exempt from such limitations did not make Manfred immune to witnessing them, if only second-hand. Hermann's physical and moral decay had matched the steady decline of the Third Reich. Years of morphine addiction and other vices had left him in as hopeless a state as the Fatherland both men served.

Eleven years ago, Goering had invited Manfred to join the rising Nazi Party. It had not been the first invitation, but Manfred had politely rebuffed all previous offers. As far as he had been concerned then, the National Socialists were a rabble of brawlers and malcontents, good enough to fight Communists on the streets but little else. By 1933, things had changed a great deal, however: the economy was in shambles, all legitimate parties had completely discredited themselves, and Herr Hitler's speeches were resonating with the discontented people of Germany. The Nazis had become a leading force in the nation. Von Richthofen had reluctantly accepted the new offer, feeling he would regret the decision but seeing no alternative, not if he wanted to join the Luftwaffe, which had been covertly growing in strength over the years. His fame had devolved into mere notoriety, and a nation without an air force had little use for the Red Fighter Pilot. He wanted to help restore Germany to its former glory, and if that meant following the lead of the brownshirts, so be it.

Following their lead had taken him to this place and time. "Hermann," Manfred said in a kind tone. "I have my orders. I did not go to war to collect cheese and eggs, but for another purpose," he mock-quoted himself.

The old joke drew a ghost of a smile from his old friend, but only briefly. "I'm still head of the Luftwaffe," Goering said. "I can talk to the Fuhrer, try to reason with him."

"He is right, Hermann." *For once*, he did not say out loud. One never said such things out loud. "We have to bring down the enemy Aesir or the war is as good as lost." The war *was* as good as lost, Manfred knew deep in his heart. The best Germany could hope for at this point was to exact a high enough price from the advancing Allies that some form of honorable surrender could be negotiated.

At the mention of the Aesir – the superhuman beings the English and Americans called Neolympians – Hermann's mood suddenly changed. "Those unnatural monsters," Goering spat out, forgetting in his sudden fury that he was speaking to one of those unnatural monsters. "Yes, if you could do for that Englishman, the butcher of Dresden..."

"Meteor, yes," Manfred said. The British Aesir was so popular for his murderous deeds that the English had named their newest class of jet fighters after him. "Twenty thousand souls, mostly civilians, burned to death by one man. I will avenge them, if I can."

Or die trying. The phrase went unspoken between the two men.

"If only the Fuhrer had let me consolidate the Teutonic Knights under the Luftwaffe..." Hermann lamented, his rage dissipating into melancholic languor once again. Manfred had to repress a sigh. Goering's deplorable love for empire-building grew tiresome rather quickly. Of course, Fat Hermann was not alone in trying to gain control over Germany's Aesir. Himmler had desperately tried to place them under the SS. Not being a fool about such matters, however, Hitler had decreed that the Knights and all Aesir of the Reich would be under his direct command. Manfred was officially part of the Luftwaffe but in effect was in two separate chains of command, always subservient to the wishes of the Fuhrer.

Manfred patiently let Goering ramble on for a while. The two men were a study in contrasts. Von Richthofen was an athletic, handsome man who most people would have thought was in his mid-twenties, unless they happened to look too closely into his eyes. Hermann looked old, tired: his formerly harsh, almost brutal features had been softened by layers of fat and assorted drug addictions. He could have passed as Manfred's father or even grandfather, despite the fact that Manfred was actually a year older than the Luftwaffe's commander. Of course, Goering was merely human.

"We could spend eternity bemoaning what did or did not happen, Hermann," Manfred said after a while. Goering subsided. Despite the fact that he was Manfred's superior, Hermann always deferred to him in private, as long as Manfred was properly respectful in public. "We have our duty. Let us carry it out. We have to deal with the Allies before they can consolidate their gains in France."

"Yes, yes. Duty," Goering said dully, deflating even further. "I had hoped to dissuade you; then between the two of us we might be able to talk the Fuhrer into reconsidering. But if you are determined to do this thing... I only wish you could keep doing your work developing strategy and tactics for our new planes. The new Me-1100 fighters are inflicting significant losses on Allied aircraft. If we had enough of them – and figure out the best ways to use them – we could sweep the Allies from the skies."

The Me-1100 had started to be produced in numbers earlier that year. They were meant to replace the Me-262s jet fighters which had nearly won the air battle over Great Britain in 1940 – if only there had been enough of them. The Reich kept developing amazing *Wunderwaffen*, wonder weapons greatly superior to anything their enemies could develop, but the amazing machines could never be produced in enough numbers to counter the hordes of lesser weapons they were pitted against. Even worse, the enemy had managed to develop their own wonder weapons. German jet fighters had been the terrors of the skies for a few months before the first American-made Airacomets (provided by the allegedly-neutral US to Great Britain) rose to challenge them. When your foe could nearly match your weapons in quality and far surpass them in quantity, the end was all but foreordained. Even more importantly, when your foe could field superhuman beings far more powerful than your own, the end was certain. Germany's only hope was that the febrile mind of Hitler's toymaker had conjured up a super-weapon able to redress that disparity.

Speaking of the hideous genius... "I have to meet with Herr Neumann later today," he told the head of the Luftwaffe. Hermann's face twisted with distaste at the name. Konrad 'the Mind' Neumann, best known in Germany as Geistesblitz, was not popular with the rest of Hitler's inner circle. "He has a new toy for me," he explained, and Goering's expression brightened up a little. Nobody liked the Mind, but everyone valued the weapons he created. "If I'm going to be hunting the American *Ubermenschen*, I will need every possible advantage."

Goering nodded in agreement, but something in his expression told Manfred Hermann did not think even the Mind's toys would be enough this time. Manfred agreed with that assessment. Neither man voiced those thoughts, however. Saying those things was not safe, not even inside the headquarters of the Luftwaffe.

"The new *Jagddrache*?" Hermann asked. At Manfred's nod, he grew slightly more animated. "If only we could have a fleet of them! Even the Mark I could put our most advanced fighter to shame. Give me a hundred of them and I could obliterate the Allies!"

"Miracles cannot be mass-produced, unfortunately," Manfred said. Some of the wonder-weapons Aesir geniuses like Geistesblitz could produce were simply advanced devices their febrile minds could conceive and design in impossibly short time spans. Others were unique marvels, creations that were not truly the products of technology but manifestations of the same unknown and possibly unknowable force that had spawned the Aesir themselves. In the case of the Dragon Hunter, that uniqueness was compounded by the fact that only Manfred could fly the damn thing. Of course, if there were a hundred pilots like him, they wouldn't need a fleet of *Jagddraches*. With his skills, he knew without any false modesty, he could sweep the sky clear of Allied aircraft at the helm of almost any aircraft, possibly even while flying Fokkers from the previous war. Such thoughts were useless, of course. There was only one Manfred, and one *Jagddrache*.

"Yes. That is a pity," Goering agreed. "Which is why I think you're wasted up in the air. You may be the best pilot that ever lived, but you are also a master tactician, Manfred. I need you to help improve our fighter doctrine."

"Fighter doctrine will not win this war, Hermann. If I can kill enough enemy Aesirs, I might just turn things around."

And if I can't the war is lost and most likely I'll be in no position to care about the war, or anything at all.

* * *

"Schnapps?" The grotesquely obese man with the oversized head was already pouring himself a drink.

Manfred shook his head. "No, thank you," he said, keeping his gaze on the inventor's desk rather than him.

It was hard not to stare at Konrad Neumann's hideous face: one eye was a solid red orb placed an inch lower than the other, and was also twice as large. It looked as if the man's features had partially melted and then congealed into a monstrous visage. According to the rumors, some accident in a laboratory during the 1920s had disfigured the man while awakening his latent abilities.

The two men had known each over for well over a decade and had worked, often closely, for nearly as long, but Manfred didn't care for Neumann. The man had no social skills or graces, and his tendency for lecturing and pontificating given any excuse annoyed the pilot. Manfred had never had much use for academics; he was a man of deeds, not words. The disregard was surprisingly not mutual, however. The Mind seemed to feel little but contempt and mild amusement for everyone who crossed his path, but he accorded Manfred a measure of respect he otherwise reserved only for the Fuhrer himself.

"Suit yourself." Geistesblitz tossed back his drink. His multiple chins quivered as he swallowed. "Panzerfaust is dead," he added casually as he refilled the glass.

The news hadn't been unexpected, but Manfred still felt a surge of shock upon hearing it. "Are you sure?" The massive Teutonic Knight had been missing since the Normandy landings, along with the rest of his unit, sent forth in a forlorn hope to slow down the Americans and their super-soldiers.

Geistesblitz finished his second drink and visibly considered having a third one before setting the empty glass on his desk. "I saw the body myself. Some poor brave souls went through considerable trouble to bring his corpse to me, in the hope I could do something to help him. I tried everything I could think of on dear Hans, but he was beyond anything I could do. He was nearly a week dead; even God could only manage his little trick after three days. Not even that ghoul Totenkopf could revive him, more's the pity. Hans is gone."

Manfred cast his eyes downward for a moment. He'd never cared much for Hans Eiffel, a.k.a. Panzerfaust; the man whose fists could batter through the frontal armor of a tank had been a bully and a blowhard. Still, he had been there from the beginning, one of the Original Twelve, the first Teutonic Knights, sometimes dubbed 'the twelve Apostles' by the sharper-tongued wits, back when having a sharp wit wasn't quite as hazardous to one's health as it was nowadays. Manfred had stood among the Knights during the 1936 Olympics, wearing his traditional World War One aviator uniform; his fame as the Red Battle Flier had helped lend a measure of credibility to the whole spectacle.

During the Great War, Manfred had been one of the heroes of the Reich, the most famous pilot of the *Luftstreitkräfte.* After sustaining a serious head wound, things had changed in strange and unexpected ways. He recovered from the near-mortal injury in less than one day, and his already sharp reflexes became truly superhuman. His amazing recovery from any injuries he received during the remainder of the war – he was shot down four more times and walked away from every crash – continued to amaze physicians, to the point that he started to outright lie about his injuries to avoid closer scrutiny. He also noticed that even old wounds that used to bother him, like a broken collarbone incurred years before, had disappeared completely. He wondered about those things, but mostly he was too busy fighting.

Manfred became a legend in his own time; his autobiography, *Der rote Kampfflieger,* written while on forced leave in 1917, had been read by millions. He kept on killing Allied pilots until Germany sued for peace in November of 1918.

The glory and renown of the Great War had faded quickly with defeat and Germany's humiliation at Versailles, however. He might have been the greatest pilot of the war, with a hundred and sixty-five confirmed victories, but all those killings had been for nothing. After the war, Manfred had returned to his family home in

Silesia, only to witness the loss of his patrimony in the chaos of the 1920s. The downfall of Germany had left him bankrupt, angry and embittered.

Manfred spent most of the ensuing fifteen years working as a civilian pilot. It was during that time that he realized he was not growing old like everyone else around him. When Goering summoned him to Berlin in 1933, Manfred was forty-one but he still looked like a man in his mid-twenties. His brother Lothar and his younger cousin Wolfram, both of whom would also join the Luftwaffe, looked like they could be his uncles or parents. That might have been passed off as simply being in good health, but his other superhuman abilities became apparent quickly enough. He was soon hailed as one of the Aesir, the Aryan demigods that would help usher a new age for Germany under Hitler's auspices.

Those had been heady times. He had stood tall and proud in the company of his fellow heroes. Donner, who could control lightning like the gods of old. Shatterhands, the deadly hero of the Condor Legion. Panzerfaust, who led the way in Poland and Norway and many other battlefields. Surtr, wielder of a flaming sword and owner of an even more fiery temperament. Freya, who could create mythological beasts with her mind and paraded the Olympics bestride an enormous glowing boar. The Aryan Super-soldier, master of all weapons. Geistesblitz, of course, although his unpleasant appearance had led to his always wearing a full face mask during public occasions. There had been four others, but they had been fakes, normal humans in gaudy costumes to round off the total number to an even dozen. Back then, they all had felt invincible, even the ersatz heroes.

Most of the twelve apostles were dead or otherwise lost. Shatterhands had died in '43 during the massive Soviet counteroffensive that had relieved Leningrad, one of the last blows the Russians had delivered before their gradual collapse. Surtr had fallen a few months later in the Ukraine at the hands of Baba Yaga. The Aryan Super-soldier had disappeared during operations in North Africa and was presumed dead. Freya lived, but she had deserted and joined the Iron Tsar's growing superhuman army. The fake Knights had all died, in some cases several times, their identities re-used and substitutes, some of them actual Aesir, replacing the deceased. And now, Panzerfaust was gone. Of the original twelve, only Donner, the Mind and Manfred remained. Donner rarely left the Fuhrer's side, his great power wasted in performing bodyguard duties. Then again, could even his mastery over thunder and lightning prevail against the likes of Ultimate? Manfred had his doubts.

"Who killed Panzerfaust?" Manfred asked, breaking the long pause.

"Who else? The American, Ultimate. He caught Hans with the First SS Panzer Division while they were trying to contain one of the Allied beachheads. The survivors said it was a good fight. Panzerfaust even knocked down the damn Ami a couple of times before Ultimate broke him over his knee like a dry branch. After the fight was over, Ultimate destroyed the whole division. Almost a thousand dead, most of the rest wounded and taken prisoner. Ultimate now has this tactic where he breaks the right leg of every man who doesn't surrender, to render them combat ineffective without killing them."

"How merciful of him."

"He still killed one in every four men in the division, give or take. He must have been in a hurry and couldn't take the time to be careful."

"As you know, I have been charged by the Fuhrer to liquidate Ultimate, Meteor and as many other enemy Aesir as I can," Manfred said, getting down to business. The Mind was looking longingly at the two-thirds empty bottle of Schnapps on his desk, and Manfred wanted to get through the meeting before the obese genius drank himself into a stupor. "You are to brief me on the newest version of the *Jagddrache*," he continued.

The Mind nodded brusquely. "Yes, yes. The Mark VIII is ready. Come with me. Might as well show you."

The two men left the office and walked through the well-guarded facility, with checkpoints and alert sentinels everywhere. An armored car drove them to the hidden airfield on the outskirts of the city. Geistesblitz remained silent during the drive, lost in thought. Manfred was glad for the quiet interlude.

The weapon testing process had become almost ritualized over the years. Given his skills and the ability to survive even a hard crash landing, Manfred had become the ideal test pilot. He'd flown every fighter and most bombers developed by the Reich during their initial trials. He'd flown Dorniers, Focke-Wulfes, Heinkels, Junkers, Messerschmitts and many others, an endless assortment of designations. He'd flown the first jet prototype in 1936, and a year later had used the *Jagddrache*

Mark I to rain death and destruction onto Barcelona. After the war began, Manfred split his time between flying combat missions and returning to the rear lines to try the new devices the Mind and other German researchers had dreamed up. His reports and recommendations had doomed many a project, often to the anger and dismay of powerful men, including Geistesblitz himself.

He'd come closer to death testing the Mind's toys than in combat, amusingly enough. The jet prototypes had been the worst: in one case the wings had been ripped clean off the fuselage and he'd bailed out too close to the ground for the parachute to do much more than mildly slow his fall to the ground. The aircraft weapon tests had also provided their share of thrills. In 1943, a light-emitter weapon malfunction caused his airplane to explode in mid-air. As it turned out, minute impurities in the crystal arrays designed to excite light into a coherent beam caused the weapon to overheat rather dramatically after a certain number of uses. The weapon, which had been tested and certified on the ground, chose to blow up when mounted on the *Jagddrache* Mark V. His report, written while in the hospital, had killed dreams of a fleet of aircraft equipped with the deadly beam weapons. The Reich simply did not have the resources to produce the light emitters in quantity, given the tolerances required. Only a handful of aircraft had been equipped with the marvelous weapons, his own included. Most light-emitters were on the ground, used as anti-aircraft and anti-armor artillery.

Unfortunately even the 200-kilowatt light-emitters of his beloved *Jagddrache* Mark VII would not be enough to perform his latest mission. He would have to hope that whatever Geistesblitz was going to show him would do the job.

* * *

The man in the colorful propaganda poster looked strong, confident, and offensively American, jaw thrust up and forward, hands on his hips, standing tall against a background of marching tanks and a swarm of stylized aircraft. The poster's slogan made a proud announcement: ULTIMATE SAYS: BUY WAR BONDS! The poster had been affixed on the wall of Geistesblitz's office. Someone, most likely Neumann himself, had drawn a target over Ultimate's face and used it as a dart board. Several darts were stuck on or near the American hero's head.

"If we can't kill this man, the Reich is doomed," Neumann said in a quiet voice.

"I still find it hard to understand how an individual can inflict so much damage," Manfred replied.

"I conducted detailed studies before the Poland campaign," Geistesblitz said in the customary pedantic, lecturing tone Manfred despised: it reminded him of his loathed instructors at cadet school. "Based on the knowledge of our own Aesir and their capabilities, and projecting estimates of similar percentages of their kind elsewhere in the world, the studies indicated we Aesir would have a relatively small strategic impact. Tactically they could be highly effective, and our experience in the Spanish War and in Poland bore this out. But strategically? Their numbers were too small, and their power, while incredible, was limited compared to the devastating nature of modern weaponry. The Britisher Meteor ignited a blaze that consumed Dresden, yes, but so could have a fleet of bombers."

"Yes, I know all of this," Manfred tried to interrupt, but Neumann was not so easily deterred.

"We underestimated how damaging they could be if not carefully monitored, however. We all remember what happened to Stalin."

"Yes." A rogue Aesir had murdered Stalin and most of the Politburo and gone on a rampage throughout Moscow that left a good portion of the city in ruins. The news had sent Hitler into a frenzied combination of elation and terror. Hopes the death of the Soviet premier would lead to victory had been dashed quickly by defeat at Stalingrad and a brutal mass tank battle at Belgorod that had ended inconclusively at best, before the Ukrainian uprising had sunk the Eastern Front into complete chaos, chaos that had swallowed all of Army Group South and most of Army Group Centre, along with untold numbers of Soviet divisions. Hitler had learned to fear his own Aesir, trusting none of them to appear in his presence again with the exception of Donner and Geistesblitz Manfred had never been part of the Fuhrer's inner circle, but even his limited access to it had been severely curtailed after Stalin's death.

"And that was just a 'common' Aesir. We never accounted for what the Americans call Type Three Neolympians," the deformed genius continued. "Mainly because we never found any of their ilk within the Reich. As things stand, neither us, the Italians or the Japanese have any of those 'Third Generation' creatures. Neither do the Soviets. The Ukrainians and the Americans have two each, and there is one in China, carving his own kingdom if the Japanese reports are accurate."

The Mind's demeanor changed. Manfred noticed an element of wonder, perhaps even of worship in the man's voice as he continued his tirade. "I was given a chance to study the initial reports from the Normandy invasion. Ultimate has perfected a number of techniques to destroy fortifications, artillery formations and large troop concentrations. He can collapse our largest bunkers at a rate of two to five in a minute, depending on how far apart they are situated. He will fly through a cannon battery and disable every single gun in it in as little as thirty seconds, often only inflicting minor casualties among the gunners, although God have mercy on the ones too close to his flight path. Of course, he has no reason not to spare the gunners' lives. Without their cannon, they are nothing but badly trained infantry. What he can do to a panzer column out in the open... Even worse, no weapon accurate enough to hit a man-sized object moving faster than a jet fighter has inflicted any noticeable damage on him. There were some reports of limited success with our special coherent light emitters, but at best they only inflicted light injuries."

Neumann's worshipful tone was tempered with dejection as he went on. "His only limitation is that he can only be in one place at a time. According to reports, some American units become reluctant to advance until their great hero arrives to soften up the opposing forces, even if other members of the Freedom Legion are available. Conversely, even rumors that Ultimate has been deployed in their area of operations have driven some of our troops into a panic. Men will face tanks and artillery and even ordinary Aesir. Against someone who can destroy them with utter impunity, however..." Geistesblitz trailed off and took a swig from a flask he'd brought along. There really was no need to complete the thought.

"How did this happen? Why did they come to possess them, and not us?" Manfred found himself speaking his thoughts out loud, not really expecting an answer. He got one in any case.

"Five people, out of a population of over two billion, comprise such a small number no meaningful statistical analysis is possible! When you have anomalies at such miniscule scales, you cannot expect anything remotely resembling an even spread. All five individuals could have been born in the Reich, or Poland, or Bolivia, and the result would have been only marginally more unlikely. As things stand, the Americans and the Ukrainians have in effect won a cosmic lottery of sorts."

"And we have lost," concluded Manfred bitterly.

"Perhaps. We are going to use a *Wunderwaffe* from the Ukraine, a creation of the so-called Iron Tsar. Perhaps it will be enough to deal with Ultimate."

"Yes," Manfred said, nodding. The Iron Tsar's super-weapons had become legendary in the last couple of years. Mechanical men who could survive everything but a direct hit from an anti-tank cannon. Death rays that could shoot down not only aircraft but even artillery shells in mid-flight. Lumbering but nearly invulnerable floating fortresses armed with a formidable array of weapons. Manfred had seen some of them first-hand, and had barely survived the experience. After years of slaughtering helpless Soviet airmen, encounters with enemies that rivaled or exceeded his capabilities had been a sobering experience.

Even if the Reich managed to wrestle some acceptable peace from the Allies, there would still be the Iron Tsar to deal with. At least it seemed the man and his equally powerful consort were content with ruling over the Ukraine and whatever pieces of Belarus, Poland and Russia they could bite off. Perhaps an accommodation could be reached with him, even if that meant giving up dreams of an empire in the East. But that would only happen if peace with the West was achieved. And that would only be possible if he killed Ultimate. Killing Meteor would be satisfying, but vengeance did nothing for the future. For the future's sake, the American hero must die.

Geistesblitz glanced over the readiness reports in the hangar's office for a few minutes while Manfred looked at the colorful poster depicting the man he must kill to save the Reich. "Everything is ready with the Mark VIII," Neumann finally said. "Let me show you the wonder of the age."

The red aircraft in the underground hangar had the familiar lines of the Mark VI and VII. The two designs had changed little in outward looks, and the *Jagddrache* Mark VIII was no different. The sleek craft had the same frame as the Messerschmitt P. 1100, with turbojets built into the swept-back wings and a sealed cockpit. There were some glaring differences, however. Two guns of some sort had been added under the wings, in addition to the standard coherent light emitter mounted on the nose. The guns made a stark contrast against the neat lines of the *Jagddrache*. The sight reminded Manfred of one of his first airplanes, which he'd fitted rather crudely with a machinegun in an improvised mount. The weapons' design looked rough and far less well-machined than what he expected from German workshops. Furthermore, he noted as he completed his first walk around the aircraft, the guns looked slightly different from each other. They were clearly of the same type, and yet...

"Those are hand-made," Manfred said, pointing at the weapons.

Geistesblitz nodded. "Some Ukrainian blacksmith put the damned things together, using components provided by the Iron Tsar himself. They were mounted on what passes for tanks in the Ukraine, more of a tank destroyer class actually. Instead of armor, it relied on an energy shield for protection. The story behind the guns' provenance could fill an entire novel. Suffice it to say, we captured four of these guns intact. I managed to master their secrets in the last two weeks. It is a good thing I can give up sleep without ill effect."

"Yes," Manfred agreed rather dishonestly. The Mind's disposition had clearly not been improved by the lack of rest, and neither had his mental stability.

"Each of those guns can burn through the entire length of a Panzer VI and destroy the tank behind it, should one be unlucky enough to be there. They can do so at ranges of over two thousand yards. The energy pulses they fire strike at the speed of light, or close to it, making them ideal anti-aircraft weapons as well, although they are rather overpowered for the purpose. These weapons are orders of magnitude more powerful than our excited light emitters, even our heavy anti-tank and anti-aircraft weapons. The Ukrainians only have a handful of them, thank Providence, or we'd be fighting them on our eastern border instead of Poland. The same system also generates a protective energy shield. As long as this shield is active, the vessel is effectively immune to conventional air defense artillery or even armor-piercing tank rounds. The Mark VIII is a flying panzer, able to destroy any man-made vehicle on the world, and to survive any conceivable conventional attack. Of course, your targets are not conventional," Geistesblitz concluded.

"What is the power source for the weapon and shield system?"

"Let me show you." The Mind took a step towards the plane, hesitated and turned to Manfred. "This is going to be rather disturbing."

Manfred tried to steel himself as the Mind carefully swung open a panel on the side of one of the guns. Its inside was filled with metal structures covered with etchings of some sort... and something else.

"Those are..." He had seen many horrible things in the wars he'd fought, but this...

"Human brains, yes," Neumann said. "Along with some nervous and connective tissue, wired into place, and surrounded by a nutrient fluid. And yes, all the biological material in there is still alive."

Manfred turned away from the sight.

"The Tsar used the brains of Aesir to power these guns," the scientist explained. "Perhaps to power all his machines, although I doubt it; there just aren't enough of us to power so many devices. You see, all Aesir are, all we are, is a living conduit to some unknown energy source. The brains of those unfortunates are kept alive somehow, and used to provide the power to fire the guns, as well as the power to protect the guns themselves and their mountings from the residual heat generated by the discharges, which by itself would be quite enough to destroy an airplane or damage a panzer. The guns in their original configuration can be discharged no more than sixty times before the biological tissue must rest for a period of no less than an hour. Or ten shots with ten minutes' pause in between, or any combination thereof. Beyond that point, the organic material may die, in a manner of speaking."

"I see," Manfred said. He still felt vaguely sick, but he was a veteran. He'd been more shocked than disgusted, he realized, and the realization bothered him more than the sight of four human brains and attached flesh and bones wired to the weapon.

"Once I understood the principles behind the guns, I was able to improve on the design. The original weapons had one brain attached. I have connected each of them to four. That provides for a larger payload, six times greater, with more intense energy discharges per shot. From the tests, at its highest safe setting each gun releases enough power to sink a pocket battleship. The payload at that level is limited to twenty to twenty-four shots, however."

"You said 'highest safe setting.' Is there a higher setting?"

"There is a third setting, yes. The resulting energy discharge will burn out all the empowering biological components," the Mind explained. "The aircraft will also be damaged and quite likely destroyed, despite its shields. I cannot accurately calculate how powerful the release would be, but it certainly would inflict enormous damage at the point of impact. Based on the initial tests we conducted on one of the weapons, possibly enough to consume an entire city, I would say."

Manfred looked at the monstrous weapon. "That should be enough," he said, and wished he sounded more certain. He would find out one way or another soon enough.

"You said the weapons were each powered by one Aesir brain. You captured four weapons. That means four of the brains came along with them. Yet there are eight in here, four for each gun."

Manfred didn't have to ask the question he was leading to. Geistesblitz understood. "We actually had three functioning brains; one of them 'died' in transit. We had to procure five more to power these systems. Three were *Juden* who were discovered to have Aesir-like abilities." The Fuhrer had declared that *Untermenschen* would not be given the honor of being named as Aesir, no matter what powers they possessed. Any such were dubbed 'abominations' or 'aberrant mutations.' "One of them was a boy with the power to manipulate metals; he caused quite a stir at one of the camps before being subdued. The others a man and woman with minor abilities. The last two brains came from captured enemies. A Russian and a Pole. We had nine enemy Aesir in our power, and now all of them serve the Reich, in their own way." The Mind glared at Manfred as he spoke, as if daring the Field Marshall to say anything. Manfred remained silent. "The others went to a similar project I'm developing for the SS. If your operation fails Himmler has his own secret program to deal with the Freedom Legion."

Himmler would probably squander any *Wunderwaffe* he got in pointless, grandiose schemes, Manfred knew, but he remained silent.

"You understand the stakes involved now," Geistesblitz said coldly. "If you fail, Himmler will try his own operation – and most likely fail. After that, there is little else we can do. Our losses on the Eastern Front have been catastrophic. Some four million men are lost, including some of our best veteran soldiers. We have little in the way of a reserve. If you eliminate enough Aesir, we might force the Allies to the peace table. If not, we will have to accept whatever terms they deign to offer us."

"The Fuhrer will never surrender unconditionally."

"If you fail, steps will be taken to ensure the safety of the Fatherland."

Manfred looked incredulously at Neumann, who was glaring defiantly at him. They were alone in the hangar, and the Mind would have made sure no listening devices were nearby. Yet, by speaking thus the inventor was putting his life in Manfred's hands. "What are you saying?"

"If you fail, the Third Reich is doomed. I will see to it that Germany is not doomed as well. If we collapse completely, the Russians might break through into the Fatherland, and they are not apt to show our people any mercy. Neither will the Americans and British, not if they have to spend too much blood bringing us down. If the Fuhrer cannot be made to see this..."

"You are speaking about committing treason. We gave our oaths, Neumann."

"I'm speaking about saving what we can! They don't listen to me! They take my inventions and waste them. We had a perfect opportunity to destroy the Soviets. The Ukraine was in open rebellion when we invaded. If we had worked out an agreement with the Iron Tsar like I suggested, we would have crushed Russia. Instead, we behaved like barbarians and the only reason the Ukrainians aren't pursuing us is that they lack the logistics to do so and because the Soviets still refuse to make peace with them. That's just one example. I warned them about my suspicions the Allies had broken our Enigma encryption systems and were reading our coded messages. I was ignored. And then there is the Fuhrer's obsession with the Jews. Do you know how many scientists we lost because of that? I was told not to waste my energy into 'Jewish science' theories like splitting the atom to release energy, and now we're lagging behind the Allies on that front as well. And now... Now our only hope is to make peace before the Fatherland is annihilated. And if that means our leadership has to be sacrificed, so be it. They should be willing to sacrifice themselves, if they truly cared for Germany and the German people."

Manfred listened in silence. Much of what his fellow Aesir was saying was true, although the Mind was omitting his own role in leading Germany to this point. The constant diversions in the search for perfect weapon designs had helped diffuse the production of enough equipment to match the Allies' massive industrial output. He'd seen it in the air, fighting through swarms of enemy fighters, inferior in every respect but their numbers, and catching up in quality without sacrificing their quantitative advantages. For all his genius, Geistesblitz had his own blind spots.

The man had also been quite willing to conduct human experiments on Jews, Gypsies and other undesirables, for all his complaints about Hitler's obsessions. Manfred had never paid too much attention to that aspect of the Reich; he'd made it a point not to delve into it.

When he was fighting on the Eastern Front, however, he had witnessed one such incident first hand. He'd gone off hunting by himself, and stumbled on an SS operation, the liquidation of an entire Jewish village. He was a hard man who had grown up under military discipline and lived through three wars and all the hardships involved, but he could not stomach such things. But if he did nothing about them, what did that make him? A coward, an accomplice, that was what.

Geistesblitz broke the awkward silence. "I've laid my cards on the table, Richthofen. If you wish to tell on me, I won't stop you, but I need not remind you that without me you may have some difficulties in learning how to use this latest wonder weapon."

"There is nothing to tell," Manfred said. "We are just two old friends engaged in some idle talk. In any case, if I succeed, none of that will matter." That wasn't quite true. He did not know if the Fuhrer would deal rationally with the Allies even if a stalemate could be achieved, or whether or not the Allies would be willing to deal with Hitler at all. The sacrifices Geistesblitz had spoken of might still be necessary. "And if I fail, I doubt I will be in any position to care about the aftermath." That was nothing but the truth.

"For all our sakes, I hope you succeed," the Mind said.

Manfred nodded, but a part of him felt nothing but near overwhelming weariness. When would this end?

It would end in death, of course. He had a brief flashback to men, women and children made to dig their own graves before being machine-gunned. His world had become a nightmare. He wanted to wake up, to be done.

He desperately wanted to be done.

Berlin, Germany, July 3, 1944

As a young child Manfred had climbed to the top of a church in Wahlstatt and watched the world from that dizzying height before tying his handkerchief to the steeple, leaving it as a marker that had still fluttered in the air ten years later when he returned for a visit. That glorious moment had been eclipsed by his first time in the air, a combination of fear and exhilaration that had been nearly overwhelming. Some remnants of that feeling were awakened every time he left the ground and felt his aircraft begin to rise. As the *Jagddrache* took off on her maiden flight, Manfred enjoyed the moment, knowing it would not last.

He was flying over Berlin. Allied daylight air raids had stopped completely after the deployment of light-emitter weapons earlier that year, so the skies over the Reich's capital were free of enemy aircraft while the sun was up. At night, things still got exciting thanks to the new American B-35 bombers. The impressive flying wings were hard to spot on radar and carried a deplorably impressive bomb load. Most nights Berlin and all German cities suffered under their onslaught, despite the best efforts of the Luftwaffe. This morning, however, he should have nothing to worry about as he tested the new aircraft.

Everything was in order. All the systems were operational. Manfred had gone over the checklist out of habit, although that was no longer necessary. He knew that everything in the aircraft was working perfectly. His Aesir gifts included a preternatural awareness of any vehicle he drove or piloted. He could control his aircraft without touching its controls, instantly knew if even a screw or bolt were loose, could perceive radio transmissions and radar signals as clearly as he could see through his eyes. That control affected the performance of anything he flew. He could make an airplane perform maneuvers that should be beyond its physical limitations. As soon as his hands touched the aircraft's yoke, Manfred became one with the newest *Jagddrache,* and he knew everything was in perfect working condition.

Manfred rose over Berlin. The test was being filmed both on the ground and by a number of camera-equipped aircraft, to be later used in a propaganda film, ideally a film that would include news of the deaths of one or more American heroes. He dutifully performed some aerial acrobatics for his audience before changing course and heading towards a practice range some miles away, an open field sown with targets. The empty hulks of antiquated Panzer IVs and Panthers were scattered through the field, alongside moving targets. The moving targets were Russian prisoners ordered to run for their lives. The casual brutality of the test bothered Manfred, but only slightly. Every night innocent German women and children were being slaughtered while cowering in inadequate bomb shelters. He would shed no tears over the poor bastards now running in his sights.

The guns performed as advertised, obliterating the target panzers even at their lowest power settings, and they were accurate enough to strike – and vaporize – a running man with a single pulse. Only a handful of Russians made it to the other end of the field, where waiting SS death squads would make sure they'd tell no one of this little experiment. The *Jagddrache* Mark VIII was ready for action.

He'd been monitoring other radio chatter while performing the tests; the ability to effectively handle multiple tasks at once was another of his Aesir abilities, one of the reasons he could fly and fight the *Jagddrache* by himself. The news on the radio weren't good. A general alert had been issued and the Luftwaffe was scrambling every available aircraft.

Ace the Boy Pilot was had been spotted over Berlin.

Manfred's pulse quickened. Here was a worthy challenge. The American flier was not as much of a threat as Ultimate, but he was a fearsome enemy, thankfully one who had until recently confined his actions on the Japanese in the Pacific theater.

The intelligence reports on Ace had included copies of the gaudy colored magazines that lovingly depicted the teenager's adventures. Both the comic books and the more sober newspaper articles agreed on the basics of Ace's story. Early in 1941, twelve-year old Arthur 'Ace' Wood had built his own airplane with the help of his grandfather, a former Great War aviator and current stunt pilot. Weeks after the Japanese attack on Pearl Harbor, the boy had flown his crate to the Pacific and proceeded to shoot down two dozen Japanese aircraft in a couple of days. In the ensuing years, the murderous child had downed over two hundred machines, gleefully slaughtering entire squadrons with impunity.

Ace's aircraft was called Lil' Eagle. It had been built out of a collection of spare parts from a dozen other flying machines. Most notably, it didn't have any engines. From all reports, the boy's grandfather had mostly helped build the cursed thing as a playground of sorts for the child. It had been never meant to fly, but with the boy at its controls, fly it did, powered by Arthur Wood's will and imagination. The boy's grandfather had been infected by the child's madness; when the war started, he'd helped install a pair of ancient water-cooled machineguns on the aircraft and sent young Arthur off to war. Manfred wondered if the old man had been punished by whatever American authorities watched over the welfare of children.

The impossible device could attain speeds in excess of 800 kilometers per hour, had withstood direct hits from 20mm cannon and even 120mm anti-aircraft artillery, and its armament would shred most machines with a burst or two, even though the weapons themselves were allegedly nothing more than a pair of antiquated Vickers machineguns. No human pilot could face the Boy Pilot and live. The only survivors from such encounters had managed to flee while he was busy with other prey. Even the Japanese Aesir, the so-called Kami Warriors, had been unable to deal with him. Ace had killed two of them in aerial duels.

With Japan largely neutralized and being slowly ground away, Ace the Boy Pilot had flown back to America for a brief triumphant celebration (and to help sell war bonds) and then turned his attention to the European theater. He had only arrived to France a week ago, and in the last five days had shot down eleven precious Me-1100s. What brought him over German airspace? Manfred wondered. Since the boy wasn't in the regular Allied chain of command or even the Freedom Legion, it could be merely a childish whim of his. Manfred smiled grimly. Time to find out what his new crate could do. If he couldn't take down the Boy Pilot, going after Ultimate would be futile.

* * *

The stage for the aerial duel was set. At Manfred's request, all nearby aircraft were grounded and anti-aircraft emplacements around Berlin instructed to hold their fire. The Boy Pilot was circling the city, looking for prey. Manfred could see the machine on his radar screen, although the image wavered and randomly appeared and disappeared. Lil' Eagle seemed to be able to absorb radar signals for brief intervals, which would make it very difficult to use radar-guided weapons against it. Thankfully, Manfred's weapons did not need radar targeting.

As he broke through some cloud cover, he spotted it. The Ami was fast, but Manfred matched his speed, and he was above him, the perfect attack position. The Boy Pilot wasn't attempting to evade, either; he was flying in a straight course, making himself an easy target.

It should have been a simple kill. He pressed the firing button on the joystick, unleashing a torrent of energy onto the seemingly unsuspecting American.

The Ami airplane changed course at the last moment, beginning to climb and shedding speed in return for altitude. The energy discharges missed it cleanly. Manfred's eyes widened as the *Jagddrache* flew past the American. It should have been impossible, but he shouldn't have been surprised. He was dealing with a fellow Aesir after all, another living impossibility like himself. Somehow the Boy Pilot had sensed his approach and set up a trap.

The American performed a high-speed Immelman maneuver, and now he was behind Manfred, firing its machineguns as it closed in for the kill. The impacts staggered the *Jagddrache* but the energy shields held. The boy's weapons could not penetrate the aircraft defenses, at least not for the few seconds before Manfred maneuvered out of the line of fire.

The fight became a duel not unlike the ones he had fought in the Great War, as the two pilots maneuvered in long circles, trying to get behind the enemy. The speeds were much higher, of course, and the stress on both men and machines commensurately so. Human pilots or normal aircraft could not have survived the deadly dance for more than a few seconds. For Manfred and Ace, the battle took several minutes.

The boy was good, a natural flier, his expected superb reflexes matched by his coolness under fire. Even as it became clear that Manfred was cutting the circles closer and closer, Ace didn't panic and kept making things as difficult as possible for his foe. It did not matter. Eventually Manfred had his shot. This time he did not miss.

Lil' Eagle had survived direct hits from most antiaircraft weapons made by human hands. The monstrous creations of the Iron Tsar tore the American plane apart in a fiery explosion. Manfred flew through the smoke and turbulence. He could see no parachute, so he most likely had killed the boy. His brief moment of triumph was washed away by the depressing realization. Just one more dead child, a little younger than most of his other victims.

The killing was reaching an end, however. One way or another, he would be done with all of this.

Caen, France, July 14, 1944

The Flying Circus went off to war.

Jagdgeschwader Richthofen consisted of sixteen pilots, each of them a multiple ace with over fifty confirmed kills. The elite unit flew the latest Me-1100 fighter jets, all armed with powerful light-emitter weapons, all painted red just like Manfred's own *Jagddrache*. The paint jobs were partly a display of pride and partly to help protect the unit's infamous leader from being singled out by the Allies. Today, the job of the sixteen fliers would be to provide cover and concealment for Manfred as he carried out his mission. The men all understood they were very unlikely to survive the mission.

France stretched out below them, the rear areas still largely pristine and untouched by the scourge of war, except for strategic targets like railroads and bridges, many of which were burning merrily. Up ahead, pillars of smoke marked Caen. The city was the focus of the latest Allied offensive. The Third SS Panzer Division was there, armed with the latest special weapons – light emitters that could destroy Allied tanks and aircraft with ease, armored suits that combined the mobility of an infantryman with the protection and weaponry of a panzer, and the dreaded *Totenkopf* units made of reanimated corpses brought to life by the monstrous Aesir of the same name. The Freedom Legion had been concentrated there to help the British and Canadian forces tasked with taking Caen. Manfred should find plenty of worthy targets for his *Jagddrache*.

His first targets were incidental. An Allied flight of B-35 bombers and their escort of antiquated P-51 fighters crossed the path of his squadron. Manfred authorized one pass as the two formations came into contact. The Flying Circus tore through the American aircraft with their light emitters, setting bombers on fire and detonating their ordinance. The prop fighters escorting the doomed mission were similarly slaughtered. *Jagdgeschwader Richthofen* went on, leaving behind the burning remains of two dozen enemy aircraft scattered all over the French countryside. All of his fliers came through unscathed. He chose to take it as a good omen.

One of Geistesblitz's newest creations spoke to Manfred through microphones built into his helmet. The Oracle Device had been described to him as a mechanical brain of sorts, designed to collate information at inhuman speeds. The machine monitored German and Allied radio traffic, searching for reports of Aesir activity. Its cold mechanical voice reported a sighting of Swift, one of the best-known Legionnaires. Manfred vectored his squadron in and started descending onto the battlefield.

The chaos of war became more detailed as one got closer to it. What had been anonymous pillars of smoke resolved into burning vehicles surrounded by antlike human soldiers. Artillery explosions erupted among the scurrying figures, creating black and red flowers of destruction. Attack aircraft swept down and rained destruction onto the infantrymen and vehicles below. A P-51 fighter-bomber came into Manfred's view, rising in the air after dropping its load on the defending German forces. He casually exploded the American fighter with a burst of his nose-mounted light emitter. A moment later, he spotted Swift.

The Fastest Man in the World scattered pieces of equipment and human bodies as he ran through a defensive trench at hundreds of kilometers per hour. Manfred overflew the Aesir and looped back, seeking a good angle of fire. A warbling sound in his helmet warned him he had been targeted by ground to air missiles. He ignored the alarm. His wingman would activate countermeasures to protect them both, and even if those were ineffective, the new energy shields protecting the *Jagddrache* should keep him safe.

There! He returned to the battle site above and behind the American speedster and opened fire. The reports claimed that Swift was impervious to most weapons while on the move, protected by some sort of energy aura. The Ukrainian death rays struck him nonetheless and turned his lethal dash into a graceless sprawl. The Ami *ubermensch* fell, his colorful costume ablaze. Manfred flew past the burning target. He would have to make a return pass and make sure the man was dead.

Two members of his squadron were down, including his wingman. Enemy missiles had hit 'Bubi' Hartmann's plane just as Manfred fired on the American Aesir. Bubi had been a good man, one of the best pilots he'd ever met. He would be missed. There was no time to mourn, however, only time to kill.

He came back from a different angle, guided by the still-glowing spot where earth had been fused into glass by the heat of his death rays. Swift lay at the bottom of a molten crater. Just as Manfred came into range to fire, however, a silver and scarlet blur dashed past and carried off the fallen American. Manfred's shots hit only the already scorched crater.

Ultimate had arrived.

Manfred flew past, seeking altitude. He distantly heard the reports as four of his fellow pilots engaged Ultimate to buy him some time to position himself. The American hero took to the air. Seconds later, all four jets had been destroyed; four more friends and colleagues were dead. He would be next.

The *Jagddrache* turned in the air, seeking its target. Ultimate was flying straight for him. Manfred fired as the two foes closed in on each other at supersonic speeds.

A blinding flash of light was followed a second later by an impact that sent his airplane spinning out of control, shaking him violently in his flight harness. Manfred tasted blood in his mouth. The collision had been brutal even through the protective shields. Alarms were blaring in his ears; multiple systems were damaged or destroyed, and he was in free fall. He fought gravity's implacable pull and managed to level off a couple of hundred feet over the ground. The *Jagddrache* started climbing once again, no longer graceful. Loose pieces of the cockpit were vibrating with painful loudness. The windshield, made of nearly impervious transparent sapphire, had a spider web of cracks at the point of impact.

It took him a few seconds to assess the damage. Nothing vital was out of commission. The *Jagddrache* was still airworthy. The protective shields were down but slowly coming back into action as Geistesblitz's ghoulish living batteries went to work. He had collided with the strongest man on Earth, and survived the experience.

One question remained, however. Had Ultimate survived as well?

The Oracle Device scanned the battlefield below and gave him a vector. Soon enough he could see Ultimate's landing site: it was a smoldering crater, larger than the one he'd carved for Swift, some distance behind German lines.

Ultimate was staggering to his feet.

Manfred raised the special weapon's power levels to their maximum safe setting and fired on the still unaware titan. Earth and stone boiled away as Ultimate was transfixed by the death rays. A massive explosion that staggered the aircraft even from five hundred meters away blotted out the target, and an instant later Manfred was climbing past the flaming pyre he'd made, turning for another pass. An unnecessary pass, he hoped. He had kept the energy beams on the American hero steady for the entire pass, unleashing incredibly amounts of heat upon him. That had to be enough.

But what if it wasn't?

Numbly, Manfred pushed the levers that set the weapons to fire at their maximum possible level. The ensuing detonation would devastate the area, possibly destroy any nearby German units, but nothing would survive it. With his aircraft damaged and the protective shields still down, neither would Manfred. But it would be worth it, wouldn't it?

The loss of their most powerful hero would shake the Americans' morale, and provide enough time for the Reich to build more super-weapons. The war would go on.

The war would go on. The idea made him want to vomit.

The enhanced viewing systems of his craft showed Ultimate crawling through the inferno below as Manfred made his final attack run. The American was gravely injured. Just as he reached the optimum firing range, Ultimate collapsed, burning and unmoving. Dead or dying? Only one way to make sure.

His thumb touched the firing button. One little push...

He never knew what made him hesitate. All he knew was that a moment later he had flown past, his weapons unfired. Through the numbness and shame, a new emotion poked through. Relief. He was done. Done with the war. Done with the killing.

Manfred ignored the threat warnings. Unheeded, the squadron of Airacomets that had been scrambled after him opened fire. A volley of missiles struck the unprotected *Jagddrache*. He spun out of control; he was surrounded by flames, burning. The aircraft became an ungainly piece of metal plummeting to the ground. Manfred didn't care.

He was done.

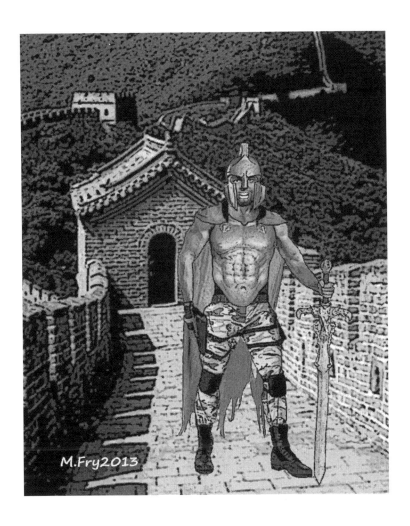

Golden Horde

Guangxi Province, China, October 3, 1968

Brickbat shouldn't have tried to fly away, but Betty Lou didn't blame him for trying. She might have tried to take wing herself, if she could fly. Brickbat had gotten killed, though.

The Moldavian Neolympian was a fast flier, faster than a fighter jet, despite his rocky reddish skin, which made him heavy and bullet-proof. He still only managed to get a whole hundred feet off the ground before being blasted by India-Charlie's triple-A firing from the surrounding hills. The Indies used the same Death Dome system as the Ukrainians. Very few things that flew could survive it.

Poor Brickbat had been torn apart by the red energy beams. Charred bits and pieces of him rained down over their position. Most of the dead Neo's petrified left hand bounced down from a trench's overhead cover and landed by Betty Lou's feet. She tried to avoid looking at it.

"Concentrate on your sectors!" Artemis shouted. Her clear voice cut through the rumbling artillery and the staccato clacking of machine guns. "Stop looking around and concentrate on your sectors!"

Freedom Legion Squad Seventeen (Foxtrot Sierra One Seven in military lingo) had consisted of ten newly-minted Legionnaires, two experienced team leaders, and a couple dozen vanilla auxiliaries. The team leaders were both dead. Betty Lou glanced nervously at the body bags piled up next to one of the bunkers dotting the hill where Firebase Enola was situated. FS-17 had been stationed at Fire Support Base Enola, well to the rear of the front lines. Their mission was to provide security for the base's artillery battery and to act as a mobile reserve. The fact that the base was surrounded by the enemy and taking fire from all directions showed just what kind of cluster-cluck this had turned out to be.

There were thirty-four body bags in the pile. The team leaders, one of the newbies, and a bunch of soldiers and auxiliaries. Betty was sure there would be plenty more. The outer perimeter had been overrun and they hadn't been able to recover the bodies of the people who had died there.

There probably wouldn't be much left to recover even if they managed to clear the perimeter. Imperial Assault troops were almost exclusively recruited from among ethnic Mongols and underwent a brutal training program that made the SS look like Boy Scouts. They were fond of collecting body parts as souvenirs.

Betty Lou Hangman adjusted the borrowed helmet on her head and rearranged the medium-length blonde hair spilling from under it. The military-issue helmet clashed horribly with her stupid pink and white costume, but she didn't care. She was mildly bullet-resistant but an extra millimeter or two of steel between her noggin and the enemy couldn't hurt. Remembering Artemis' words, she stopped looking at the body bags and kept her eyes on her sector, the area she was supposed to be watching for enemy movement. Somewhere behind her a mortar battery started firing again; the chug-chunk sounds were faint amidst all the other noises of battle. A machinegun fifty feet to her left was shooting in short, controlled bursts. Further back, the artillery battery was also opening up, slowly and steadily. So far she couldn't see much of anything, just a stretch of barbed wire and trenches out for twenty or thirty yards, clear ground except for scattered corpses for another hundred yards, and some low hills beyond that blocked her sight. An initial rush had been stopped by the mines planted all around the perimeter, but the mines were all gone now. The Chimps would be gathering behind the hills, preparing to launch another attack, she supposed.

"I wish, I wish, I wish I was a fish," she chanted tonelessly. Her little sister Mary Beth had made up that nonsense rhyme back when they'd both been children, a whole ten years ago. Betty Lou and Mary Beth had grown up in a farm in Kentucky. Betty Lou had left the farm on her sixteenth birthday, when she discovered she could throw balls of lightning whenever she got mad. The discovery had happened when Bobby Lee Hennessy, her high school sweetheart, had decided it was time for him and Betty Lou to 'go all the way' and had refused to take no for an answer. Mary Beth's last letter said that Bobby Lee still wasn't all right, between the involuntary twitching and the left eye that blinked at random all the time. "He looks pretty funny with all the blinking, he purely does," Mary Beth had written. Served him right, trying to take liberties like that. In the ensuing three years, Betty Lou had made sure anybody who tried to take liberties with her lived to regret it.

The Indies out there might want to take liberties with her. They most definitely wanted to kill her.

Her brother Tommy Dee had done one tour of duty in China and come back in '66 without a left foot and with lots of stories about 'India Charlie' – the designation for Imperial Chinese – and how deadly and vicious they could be. The Indies – most people called them Chimps, but Tommy Dee always called them Indies – were nasty; they liked to do human wave attacks, and they sometimes got back up after they were dead, because some of the Charlie Whiskeys (Celestial Warriors) could raise armies of zombies like the ones in that George Romero film her parents wouldn't let her watch because it was too scary and because the star was a Negro ("Janus is a Negro, and he's a hero," Betty Lou had replied, and gotten smacked for being a smart-mouth).

Tommy Dee's stories had been terrifying: he loved to go over all the gross stuff to scare his sisters when their parents weren't around. It wasn't just scary tales about getting blown up, or crushed by a super-strong Charlie Whiskey, or shot to pieces and left to bleed to death on some remote mountain pass. There'd been plenty of simply disgusting stuff, fungus growing on your feet if you didn't keep your socks dry, and having to eat wormy rice because the supply helicopters had gotten shot down, and going Number One and even Number Two in your pants because you were scared or just because you had to go but you couldn't stop and pull your pants down because people were shooting at you and you had to shoot them back. The worst part, though, was the stuff Tommy Dee didn't talk about, the times when his eyes got hard and bright and he stopped talking about the war or anything else.

When the men and women in the fancy outfits had shown up to take her away after the thing with Bobby Lee, Tommy Dee had looked sad and scared. The look in his eyes as she drove away with the strangers told her that the stories hadn't been horse puckey, and that she was going to find out just how real they were. She'd wanted to cry then, but she hadn't. Betty Lou never cried. Crying was for sissy girls, and she might be a girl, but she was no sissy.

She wanted to cry now. She wanted to cry for Captain Steelhead and Miss Lightning, the team leaders, who had been so nice to her and now were just two unfeeling lumps of meat inside body bags. She wanted to cry for the poor soldiers that had gotten torn apart when the Celestials crashed into the mess hall and started killing people. She wanted to cry for herself because she had killed before and in a few moments she would have to kill again. She didn't cry, though. She was no sissy.

"I wish, I wish, I wish I was a fish..."

The Indies cut loose with smoke. Mortar shells hit the dead ground in front of her and burst into thick billowing clouds. The machine gun fired into the fog, and so did everyone in the sector, but they were shooting blind. All of them except Betty Lou, that is. She concentrated and sensed the charging men leaving their positions and charging forward. She had to concentrate very hard to do it, but when she did she could see the electrical fields human beings generated. They glowed like little fireflies, each firefly a beating heart.

Lots of fireflies were coming her way.

Betty Lou let the images go. She didn't really need to see them and she had things to do. A crackling ball of electrical energy formed in front of her and she sent it forth towards the abandoned trenches. It grew in size as it moved and by the time it reached the smoke-shrouded sector it was as tall as a man and it moved a lot faster than a man could run. She directed the lightning ball to move in a weaving pattern, sideways and back and forth. The smoke hid most of it, but she knew what was happening anyway. Any Indy the lightning ball touched would be fried into a curling ball of charcoal. Their heads would sometimes explode and even the ones who were a few feet away from the ball would go into convulsions and die. She'd seen it happen, the first time she used her powers to kill a human being. This was her third time. The second time, she had killed a Charlie-Whiskey in the mess hall, about an hour ago.

A few Chimps made it out of the smoke and started scrambling through the abandoned trench line. The machinegun saw to them. One of the men who staggered into view was walking weird-like. When he turned around, Betty Lou saw half of his body was a blackened mass of burned tissue. She hadn't thought someone could get that close to her ball lightning and survive, but that man did, at least long enough to take a few more step before collapsing. Her heart and stomach lurched at the sight, but she kept moving the ball lightning in a pattern, just like she had been trained to do, back and forth in a zig-zag designed to catch as many men as possible.

No more Chimps came out of the smoke, which was beginning to thin out. Betty Lou dispelled the ball lightning and turned her special senses on again. There were a few fireflies out there, all moving back toward the hills. The smoke dissipated, revealing her handiwork. She counted the smoldering figures, because body counts were useful intelligence and she would have to include them in the after-action report. She thought there were forty-six corpses, maybe two or three more because some of the bodies were in very small pieces and it was hard to tell.

"I wish, I wish, I wish I was a fish..."

* * *

"Fuck fuck fuck."

The endless litany of profanity made Bradley Norfield (code name Mind Surge) feel a little better, but he'd started out feeling like shit, so a little better didn't cut it.

"Stop the swearing, *por favor*, Brad. It's against regulations," hissed Pedro Uzcategui, a.k.a. *El Defensor*. Pedro was all about the rules, the little Mexican prick.

"Fuck the regs, Paco, and fuck you too."

Pedro shook his head but said nothing back. Good. Bradley was too busy trying to deliver his little present to the Chimps without having to deal with Pedro's whining. "Just do your thing and keep me alive, will you?" Brad told him.

"I am doing it," the Mexican said. A greenish haze a foot in front of them showed that Pedro's force field was up and running. Every few seconds, a not-so-stray bullet hit the force field and bounced off in a shower of bright green sparks. Bradley kept flinching every time it happened. He hated himself for the flinching, but he couldn't help it. If Pedro's concentration slipped, Bradley would be stopping those bullets with his face, and unlike the other assholes in FS-17, he was a pretty frail Neo. A shot to the head would kill him just as dead as any vanilla human. Probably. Almost surely. Or he might survive and spend days or weeks feeling his brain and skull slowly growing back, which was supposed to feel worse than the worst Chimp torture techniques. He was in no hurry to find out one way or another.

They'd spotted one of the Death Domes. It was under cover behind a hill, stupidly close, which probably meant somebody'd had the bright idea of moving it into a direct fire position. When or if the Chimps got it into position, the energy beams of the Death Domes could turn all of Firebase Enola into a smoking hole in the ground. On the other hand, that meant the weapon could be attacked. His Neo power was plain telekinesis. He could grab objects with his mind, and as long as they weighed less than three of four tons he could move them at a pretty decent clip. In this case, he needed to move an improvised 4,000-pound care package – an improvised bomb made out of artillery shells – behind the hill and blow the Death Dome to smithereens, along with any Chimps unlucky enough to be in the vicinity.

Problem was, he couldn't lob the bomb very high, or one of the other AAA guns would shoot it down. He had to run it close to the ground, and that took more concentration and, worst of all, he had to keep his eyes on the bomb, which meant sticking his head above the trench, which in turn meant he was a perfect target for snipers and any Chimp in range with an AK-47 rifle and a taste for blood. That was where Pedro came in. The Mexican prick could project force fields rated to be proof against small arms and light artillery, up to and including 40mm armor-piercing shells. So far the biggest thing that had hit the force field had been rifle bullets. Bradley still flinched, and every time he flinched his control over the bomb wavered.

"Just don't drop it, okay?" Pedro said. *"Pendejo,"* he added. Bradley had no clue what that word meant, but it didn't sound very nice. Probably against regulations, too.

"Don't sweat it, Paco, I'm not going to drop it," Bradley replied through clenched teeth, and flinched again as something bigger – a burst of heavy machine gun bullets – hit the force field and sparked off like a miniature version of Fourth of July fireworks. "Fuck fuck fuck!" He almost dropped the bomb then, which would have been bad because it was still floating between the bunkers inside the firebase. He was pretty sure the bomb wouldn't go off if he dropped it from a few inches off the ground, but just like seeing if he could survive taking a bullet to the face, he didn't want to find out one way or another.

"Hijo de la chingada," Pedro muttered. Bradley was pretty sure the phrase wasn't a compliment, or regs-compliant.

"Fuck."

"I can help," said someone behind them. Bradley recognized the voice without having to turn around. It was Wesley Smythe, code name Glitch, who looked like he was a child but supposedly was twenty-one. "I can replicate Mind Surge's power and help move the bomb."

"Don't even think about it," Bradley replied. Glitch's code name was no accident. The kid – or alleged adult – could copy other Neos' powers, but his control over those powers was erratic at best. Glitch could help out a lot, sure, but he could just as easily fling the bomb back toward the firebase.

"Okay, I'll do Artemis instead," Glitch replied, undeterred. As Bradley tried to guide the bomb, he felt something grow hot behind him. Glitch must be creating one of Artemis' fire spears. The heat source vanished, and a second later the fire spear exploded on a ridge nearby, sending pieces or dirt and rock flying everywhere. "I got it! I got a machine gun," the kid said gleefully. Bradley didn't care what Wesley's papers said about his age; the kid sounded like he was twelve or thirteen, a quiet, creepy, red-haired twelve year old with solid black eyeballs and red irises, but a kid nonetheless. Still, as long as he kept throwing fire spears and kept some of the machine gunners off Bradley's ass, he was being more helpful than usual.

Bradley concentrated on moving the bomb and tried not to worry about the crazy kid behind him. If Glitch's bizarre luck caught up with him, they were all dead, but if that Death Dome didn't go away they were all dead anyway.

* * *

Hiroshi Tanaka (code name Fox Ghost) had a front row seat for the royal shit storm about to hit his sector.

The eastern quadrant of Firebase Enola had the shortest span of cleared ground, since there were hills less than fifty yards away from the perimeter. The enemy had gathered at least three or four companies behind the hills. Hiroshi had spotted them while floating above the base in his astral form. But that was only the first of a long list of bad news. The massing troops mostly wore Republic of China uniforms, not Imperial ones. The ROC soldiers were supposed to be on Hiroshi's side. The Freedom Legion was there to protect the Republic and keep the world safe for democracy and all that shit. While in his intangible form he could not feel nausea, but he experienced a spiritual version of it. The attackers were a combination of infantry troops from the ROC 5th Corps and what appeared to be two platoons of Imperial Sappers. 5th Corps were the main force protecting the Guangxi Province. If it had turned coat that meant the two American brigades and the Vietnamese regiment operating in the region were up shit creek without a paddle. Which meant FS-17 was fucked as well.

Hiroshi came back to earth with a feeling of relief. He was invisible and incorporeal in his astral form, but some sensors could spot him, and the Death Dome guns could could shred his astral form just as easily as they destroyed aircraft, artillery shells and flying Neos. Every time he took to the skies he was rolling dice with his life. Not exactly the kind of fate he'd dreamed of back when he'd been ordinary Hiroshi Tanaka of Orange County, California.

"They're coming!" he yelled to his fellow Legionnaires just as the enemy started to mount their assault. Reick and Thaddeus nodded and leaped from the trenches to counterattack, two men – and Hiroshi, for all the good he could do – against three, maybe four hundred.

Alex Marcon (code name Reick, formerly known as Dread Blade) wore a demonic-looking suit of organic metal and chitin with multiple spikes and horn-like protrusions that made him look larger than his normal six foot two height. Terence Thyr (code name Thaddeus) looked equally intimidating in his Graeco-Roman style helmet and body armor. The leading elements of the enemy saw the charging Neos and hesitated for a few seconds before reacting. Some of them went down on the ground or to one knee to open fire with their M1 rifles. The rest charged on, bayonets fixed on their rifles, or wielding satchel charges or rocket-propelled grenades. Two machine gun emplacements on the firebase trench line fired at the attackers. Moments later, two 81mm mortars started blasting the surrounding hills. That killed and wounded some of the enemy, but not enough to stop them, not enough to make the two armored figures' attack seem like anything other than suicide.

Hiroshi shook his head. "We're gonna get killed," he muttered to himself before turning astral and following his friends.

Reick reached the bottom of the hill and opened fire with the modified Browning .50 caliber machine gun he'd been carrying like an oversized rifle. He fired a long burst into the charging Imperials, walking the stream of bullets up the hill like a hose. The massive weapon should have tossed him around like a child trying to hold onto a bronco, but he kept the gun steady as if on a stabilized mount, mowing down soldiers by the dozen. He went through the two-hundred round belt in a few seconds and dropped the empty weapon on the ground; two thirty-inch blades emerged from his forearms and he rushed towards the nearest foes.

On the other side of the hill, Thaddeus picked off the enemy with his custom pistol as he closed the distance at a brisk walking pace. Every shot hit a target in the head or throat; fifteen shots left fourteen soldiers dead or dying; the one survivor fell to his knees clutching at his helmet, stunned by the grazing bullet. Thaddeus walked past the wounded soldier and casually beheaded him with the bastard sword on his left hand.

The two Legionnaires made contact with the charging soldiers. Sword and forearm blades struck faster than the eye could follow, slicing through rifle barrels and human flesh with equal ease. Enemy soldiers reeled back, some screaming and clutching at horrible wounds, others dead before they hit the ground. The Legionnaires were struck multiple times by rifle bullets and bayonet stabs as the soldiers tried to fight back. Reick's armor shrugged off the impacts. Thaddeus arms and legs bled where bullets and bayonet points found spots not covered by his breastplate and helmet, but the wounds closed seconds later. Small arms just couldn't do anything to them.

The enemy was not just armed with rifles, however.

An anti-tank team readied their RPG-10 missile launcher fifty yards away from Reick. The loader tapped the gunner on his helmet to indicate he was clear to fire. A burst of smoke marked the launch, and the missile sped through the air. Reick saw the rocket and dodged away, avoiding a direct hit, but the warhead hit the ground and exploded less than ten feet away. The explosion knocked the Legionnaire off his feet; it also killed or wounded half a dozen enemy soldiers around him. The anti-tank team reloaded. If they could score a direct hit, the shaped-charge explosion could cripple or kill Reick. Thaddeus was inflicting horrible carnage on the renegade troops, but he was too far away to even notice what was going on.

It was up to Hiroshi to save the day.

Mentally cursing himself, he swept down and became material a few feet behind the missile team. The soldiers didn't notice Hiroshi as he leveled his Slaughter-III machine pistol towards them. He fired two short bursts, riddling each man with three or four .15 caliber bullets that injected a powerful curare-based poison into their bloodstream. Death was instantaneous and painless. Hiroshi mowed down a couple more soldiers nearby and went astral again before anybody could return fire. Unlike his friends, he wasn't bullet-resistant except when he was in his ghostly form.

The assault had stalled. Between the three of them, the Legionnaires had killed or injured at least sixty or seventy soldiers, and the defenders' machine gun, rifles and mortars had taken out maybe another twenty or thirty. Those massive losses were more than enough to make the rest of the enemy turn tail and run back behind the cover of the surrounding hills. Reick picked himself up and ran back to the trench line. Thaddeus pursued the enemy for a while, catching and cutting down another three or four unfortunates before turning back.

Hiroshi materialized at the bottom of a trench and sighed in relief. They had beaten off the attack. The Imperials and the turncoat Republicans had probably thought the initial Celestial attack had killed all or most of the Legionnaires; that was the only reason Hiroshi could see for their sending unsupported vanilla troops against the firebase. Next time they wouldn't make that mistake.

"Join the Legion, see the world," Hiroshi grumbled to himself. He'd turned Neo in '65, and his choices had been simple: end up drafted into the US Army's Parahuman Operations Command, run to Mexico – Canada was sending draft dodgers back – or join the Legion. He'd figured being a Legionnaire was better than being a Papa – life in Papa Force, the Parahuman Special Forces, was no bed of roses from what he'd heard. Besides that, the Legion was an international organization, and Hiroshi had hoped he'd get less crap from people calling him a gook or chink and looking at him as the enemy, never mind that most of the people fighting the Empire were also 'chinks.'

Things had been all right at first – training and working in the Legion had kept him out of the war for a while, and he'd been assigned to a supposedly quiet sector. The Guangxi Province was as far from the main action as you could get. All the big battles were being fought in Northeast China. At least that's what everyone had been led to believe. As it turned out, the Intelligence pukes had been asleep at the switch, and Mrs. Tanaka's baby boy was in deep shit.

Reick and Thaddeus joined him in the trench. Their suits of armor were splattered with gore, but Hiroshi had learned to ignore those kinds of sights and smells. It was amazing what you got used to after a while. "Those weren't Imperials," Reick said.

"They were trying to kill us. That makes them Indies, as far as I'm concerned," Thaddeus replied.

"I think those were troops from 5th Corps," Hiroshi said. "At least two companies, fighting alongside Chimps."

"Shit," Reick said. "Were you able to identify their units? And don't call the enemy Chimps, will ya?" Reick didn't care for the shorthand term for Chinese Imperials; neither did the Legion at large. Regulations considered it a racial slur, and forbade its use. Most everybody ignored the regulation, however.

Hiroshi ignored the rebuke and thought about the stuff that mattered, like the identity of their attackers. Unlike most of his fellow Legionnaires, he'd actually paid attention to the briefings. "Yeah. They were Republican Rangers, must be from the 18th Brigade. Shit." The 18th was an elite unit, hand-picked from the local Zhuang ethnic minority. So were a large proportion of the troops of 5th Corps. "I think the Zhuang have decided they'd be better off with the Empire." The Zhuang made up over twenty percent of the province's population, and they hadn't been well-treated by the Han who ran the Republic. That wasn't good at all.

"Who are the Shang?" Thaddeus asked. He didn't sound as if he cared much one way or another. From what Hiroshi could tell, Thaddeus didn't care much about anything, not even about his own survival.

"Zhuang. The local minority here."

"If they switched sides, they're just another pack of India-Charlies. More Chimps to the slaughter."

"Stop that Chimps shit, Thaddeus," Reick said. The two armored men stared at each other for several long seconds.

"Save it for the enemy, guys," Hiroshi broke in. Whose idea had it been to put those two bull gorillas in the same sector?

Thaddeus shrugged and let it go. "It don't mean nothing."

"It means we're surrounded. 5th Corps pretty much held the border and most of the territory between the Dragon Wall and Nanning. That's the capital of this province," Hiroshi added when he noticed his friends' blank expressions. Apparently he truly was the only one paying attention during the briefings. "It means we're fucked, okay?" Worst come to worst, Hiroshi could probably get away by himself. He wasn't ready to cut and run, though, not yet at least.

It looked like he sucked at being a coward, as well as everything else.

* * *

Olivia O'Brien (code name Artemis) wanted to hover over the firebase to get a better view of the battle, but the Imperial AAA battery made that problematic, as in suicidal. There were at least four guns somewhere in the surrounding hills, and she wasn't sure she could survive more than one or two hits from them. Mind Surge was attempting to deal with one of the guns. Maybe he would succeed, but even that would leave three more emplacements to deal with.

She glanced at her wrist-comm. Seven-thirty one in the morning. An hour and a half ago, she'd been having breakfast with the rest of FS-17.

A few minutes after oh-six hundred hours, the world had stopped making sense.

No time to think about that. From the observation post, which so far hadn't been hit by anything worse than small-arms fire, she saw the battle unfolding below. Things were holding steady on three sectors, held by the Legionnaires and the remnants of Bravo and Echo Companies from the 47th Infantry, 196th Brigade. The Southern sector had been quiet so far; it was being held by a scratch force made up of a reconnaissance platoon from Charlie Company, and an ad hoc formation of odds and ends, mostly walking wounded from assorted units hastily recruited from the field hospital in the firebase. Olivia was keeping a close eye on that sector, just in case.

A massive explosion shook the very air around her and dwarfed even the sound of the big 155mm howitzers from Battery A and B firing from their redoubts. Olivia looked towards the sound and saw a burst of red light devouring an entire hill, followed by huge pillar of smoke rising from the suspected position the Death Dome. Mind Surge had succeeded. That left three energy weapons out there, but the destruction of that one would make the enemy more leery about trying to deploy the remaining pieces to rake FSB Enola with direct fire, which she didn't think the firebase could survive. So far the enemy hadn't struck with anything heavier than light mortars and a couple of machine guns, for which she was very grateful. She still didn't understand how the Imperials had managed to launch an attack on the firebase, which was deep inside a safe sector, surrounded by friendly troops. War was full of the unexpected, she belatedly realized.

Olivia hadn't seen much of the war since the beginning of her active service in the Legion, but in the last ninety minutes had witnessed more than enough to be utterly sickened by it.

An eruption of frenzied shooting brought her back to reality. An assault group was charging the Southern sector under the cover of smoke bombs even as other mortars dropped explosives on the makeshift defensive force. Olivia jumped from the observation post, flying low and fast. The Death Dome weapons could not hit her if she flew close to the ground. She darted over the trench system and into the smoke, her flame aura glowing brightly.

Olivia flew past charging enemy soldiers. She flew through them, their bodies tossed aside like broken toys, the impacts on her protective aura barely noticeable. As she moved, she left behind a burning trail of living flame that burned hot enough to soften steel and consume human flesh and bone. Olivia rushed through the smoke-shrouded dead ground, killing dozens of enemies, turning the attack into a rout. She was hit several times by rifle and machine gun fire, some of it coming from friendly soldiers behind her, but the shots were barely more noticeable than the light bumps she felt when she ran into the helpless men she turned into screaming human torches.

Killing in war isn't murder. She tried to use the words as a mantra, as a way to ignore the death cries of fathers and sons and brothers as she consigned them to the flames. It worked just well enough to keep her going.

The enemy fled. She did not pursue them but lobbed a few flame spears at two anti-tank teams as they tried to deploy rockets against her. Her spears ignited the explosive ordinance, unleashing brutal blasts on anybody unlucky enough to be near the unfortunate rocketeers. The deaths of the rocket teams turned the retreat into a complete rout. The enemy fled under the cover of more smoke. The mortar bombardment ceased shortly afterward, which might mean the enemy artillery reserves were low.

A few corpses were intact enough to identify. The dead soldiers had been wearing Republic of China uniforms, except for a black armband hastily sewn on their right arms. The sight shocked her. They were here to fight on behalf of the Republic of China. How many soldiers had turned coat and joined the enemy?

Too many had, that was the answer. Even if it was only the men she had just slaughtered, it was too many.

* * *

Betty Lou Hangman sat down and gratefully drank some water. The Legionnaires had gathered at one of the central bunkers. The Indies had withdrawn for now, and things were quiet except for some harassing mortar fire. As she drank, a nearby explosion hit the bunker walls with some shrapnel. She hoped some poor normal hadn't been out in the open and gotten hit. Too many poor normals had been hurt already.

Normals on their side, that was. She didn't feel any sympathy for enemy vanillas. They deserved whatever they got.

The other Neos looked like they'd made it okay. Mind Surge's hands were shaking a little, but he was smiling while he described – for the third time – how he had blown up the Indy Death Dome. Behind him, *El Defensor* was muttering something in Spanish; Betty Lou was sure it was an insult of some sort. Sitting by himself, Thaddeus was drinking from a flask she would bet wasn't filled with any regulation-approved beverages. On the other side of the bunker, Reick was munching on a bag of chips and playing a hand of Solitaire. Fox Ghost appeared to be taking a nap.

"Hi," someone said behind Betty Lou, startling her. It was Glitch, the little kid who supposedly only looked like he was a little kid. She had her doubts about that.

"Howdy, Glitch," she replied before taking another sip of water. She should remember to go pee as soon as she had a chance, because if the Indies attacked she didn't want to get caught with a full bladder.

"Why don't you call me Wesley?" he asked.

"We're on duty. Code names while on duty, remember?"

"I remember, but we're resting right now, aren't we?"

"We're still on call."

The kid's solid black eyes regarded her evenly. "Okay, then, Belle Lightning."

Betty Lou hated her code name. She hated puns, for one. She also didn't like to be likened to a Southern Belle, because she wasn't, she was poor white trash from Kentucky and anybody who bothered to talk to her for a bit knew it. Since joining the Legion she'd gotten as much schooling as she'd been able to, and had been working hard at not sounding like a hick from the sticks. She hoped that one day she might be able to lie about where she was from, but with a name like Belle Lightning, they were always going to think she was from the South, complete with a KKK sheet and a Confederate flag folded under bed. Oh, well, she'd have to live with Belle Lightning for now, because she'd been too timid to raise a ruckus when the Legion's PR hacks came up with the code name.

"So what's up, Glitch?"

"Things are going to get bad," he said, sounding very sure about it.

"I could have told you that. Got anything in particular you're worried about?"

"It's part of my luck powers. Sometimes I feel a big wave of back luck coming up. Like now. Bad stuff is going to happen, not very long from now. Some of us aren't going to make it."

That was not good, not good at all. Glitch's luck was... weird. The strangest things happened around him, bad luck that often turned out to be good in the end, and vice versa. One time the Jeep they'd been traveling in had sprung four flat tires at the same time – and a cargo truck that went around the Jeep got blown up by a mine that would have gotten the Jeep if it hadn't been for the flat tires.

"Thanks for letting me know," Betty Lou told the kid, meaning it. She'd be relieving herself right quick, then, and get ready for the worst.

She hoped the bad stuff could wait until then.

* * *

Before that morning, Colonel Alvin D. Poe had been a stern-looking man with flawless manners and an unflappable exterior. The Celestial attack had left him with a deep slash on his forehead that had taken twenty stitches to close up, several cracked ribs, and an acute sense of his own mortality. His left eye was twitching at random, and he was sweating a lot more than the relatively cool mountain air warranted. Olivia could sympathize. The last time an American unit had been in a similar situation, the commanding officer's name had been Custer.

"... and after the enemy retreated beyond direct fire range, I pulled out the squad to hold them in reserve," Olivia concluded the report.

For several seconds, Colonel Poe didn't say a word. He closed his eyes and appeared to be collecting his thoughts. When he finally spoke, his tone was cold as ice. "Legion Command has confirmed your authority over all Foxtrot-Lima units on FSB Enola. The disposition of your squad is in your hands, and after this meeting you are to contact Legion Command for your orders. I have been ordered to work closely with you. I cannot give you orders; I can only offer suggestions, unless Legion Command decides I'm to assume control over your unit."

Olivia remained silent.

"This is insanity," the officer continued. He reached for a folder on his desk. "I got this dispatch just before the attack on the base. It was meant for Captain Steelhead, but since he died before he could open it, I took the liberty of reading it." He flung the folder back on the desk. "Do you know what kind of people are in your goddamn unit, Miss Artemis?"

"I do, sir."

"You know shit! Your so-called Legionnaire Glitch, he is actually as old as he looks! Thirteen years old! Apparently a typo on his birth certificate allowed him to carry on with this charade, but his family just filed a complaint with the Legion and with the US Army. Then you have Thaddeus. Turns out he's a wanted criminal in three states, a suspect in four cases of aggravated assault and two murders! And of course, there is Reick, previously known as Dread Blade, a vigilante and also a murder suspect. I know he got off thanks to President Stevens' general amnesty, but that's one more loose cannon in your outfit. How am I supposed to trust any of you? A pack of children, a criminal, a former vigilante who'd be in prison if not for the war, and not a year's military experience between all of you. At least Steelhead was a veteran. I have no idea why anybody thought you could lead this unit."

"Time in service, sir," Olivia responded, keeping her cool with some effort. Poe clearly was having a hard time accepting that a woman, let alone a colored woman, could be in command of a unit, even an unconventional paramilitary unit like FS-17. She wasn't surprised. Poe was old enough to remember a time when women and blacks knew their place and kept it if they knew what was good for them. *The times, they are a-changin'*, she thought coldly. She had to admit some of the officer's concerns were valid, however.

"We are surrounded, cut off from reinforcements, with little hope of help. As long as those Death Domes are deployed, we cannot expect any air support or resupply. If I thought you were up to the job and I had the authority, I'd order your squad to take out those guns, Miss Artemis."

"We managed to disable one of them, sir. I've considered going after the others, but I was worried about leaving the base undefended."

"That should be my call, not yours. But yes, I have less than a hundred combat personnel fit for duty, and about a hundred and fifty artillerymen, engineers, pilots and medics, and they're not going to hold back an assault like the one we just lived through, not without your assistance. So what I would do is order half of your squad to remain here, and the other half to take out the guns."

"I will consult with Legion Command and if they agree with your suggestion, I will carry it out, sir," Artemis said. The trick Mind Surge had pulled would not be likely to work again. That gun had been in the open, being moved to be used for direct fire. The others would be dug in and protected; only a direct assault could destroy them. Even if they succeeded, their losses would be heavy. But if that was the price she needed to pay, she would have to pay it.

"Unity of command is essential for effectiveness," Colonel Poe grumbled. "But go ahead, consult with your superiors. Hopefully we can survive the wait. Dismissed."

Olivia saluted and left the office. She walked briskly out of the command bunker, past the still smoking ruin that had been the mess hall, and into FS-17's barracks. Captain Steelhead's private quarters also held the Legion's communication equipment. The small bunk room had a few personal mementos – a picture of Steelhead's wife and kids, another photograph of the captain shaking hands with Dwight D. Eisenhower – but was otherwise plain and undecorated. There was little in the room to show what kind of man FS-17's commander had been.

He had been a good man, Olivia knew. In many ways, he had reminded her of John Clarke, who had taken her under his wing when she joined the Legion. Just like John, the captain had been a big tough guy who could be surprisingly kind and gentle underneath his rough exterior. Both men had treated Olivia like a human being, ignoring her color and gender. Captain Steelhead had been tough but fair. And now he was gone.

The comm device was a small television console on a desk. Olivia turned it on and exchanged passwords and identification codes with the worried-looking Legion auxiliary that appeared on the screen. Shortly afterward, the screen switched and she found herself facing Kenneth Slaughter himself. Doc Slaughter was the commander of all Freedom Legion units in China. If he was taking her call directly...

"This is Foxtrot Sierra One Seven Actual," she said, naming herself as the commanding officer. "Olivia Jennifer O'Brien. Code Name Artemis."

She had only seen Doc Slaughter a handful of times since her induction into the Legion. His face seemed as impassive and collected as ever. "Acknowledged. Artemis, you are in command of Foxtrot Sierra One Seven. Please report what happened."

Olivia closed her eyes and exhaled slowly. A part of her wanted to start babbling uncontrollably, but she suppressed the impulse. She was a Legionnaire, dammit.

"Yes sir. The attack began at oh six hundred hours..."

* * *

Breakfast had consisted of the usual runny eggs and burned hash browns. The base commander had replaced the cooks twice since Olivia and the rest of the squad had arrived two months ago, but the food had yet to improve. From the look on Colonel Poe's face as he ate with Captain Steelhead a few tables away, the new cooks would find themselves a new assignment very soon.

"Did you guys listen to the Dawn Buster this morning? Man, that guy is hilarious," Mind Surge was saying.

"It's not funny when I'm trying to sleep and someone's playing the radio," grumbled Albert Bertholdt, code name Freedom Falcon. "Besides, that DJ, what's his name, Crono-something? He's kinda disrespectful."

"I only turn the radio on after reveille, man. And you can't be funny if you are too reverent toward authority. That's the whole point."

"Those cracks about President Stevens not knowing how to work a TV weren't all that funny."

"They made me laugh," said Mihai Olinescu (code name Brickbat), his soft voice always in sharp contrast with his rock-like skin. The Moldavian immigrant's English still had a faint accent. "The President thinks his TV is a radio. It's funny, no?"

"It's not true, and it's disrespectful," Freedom Falcon replied.

Mind Surge sighed. "Hey, I like the Prez, but the man grew up in the Twenties, okay? He's old."

"He can still kick your ass, and mine too. His Secret Service bodyguards have the easiest job on the planet; the Prez doesn't need protection."

"So what? Funny is funny. And Cronauer does a great Stevens impression."

"Disrespectful," Freedom Falcon said one more time.

"You are all getting on my nerves," Reick said, and the discussion came to a sudden stop. Trust Reick to put a damper on any argument. Olivia hadn't seen the man crack a smile once since she'd known him.

"Are we going patrolling today, Miss Artemis?" Belle Lightning asked her. The blonde girl looked eager to do something, anything. Olivia could sympathize. Life in the remote outpost was painfully boring.

"That's the plan," Olivia said. "Sub-Squad Alpha will head out toward the Wall. That includes you and me."

"The Wall gives me the creeps," Belle Lightning admitted.

"It is a creepy sight," Olivia agreed.

"Last time I saw it, I started figuring out how the Wall worked," Glitch said through a mouthful of eggs and bacon. "Maybe this time I can try to play with it."

"That's against orders, Glitch," Olivia said hurriedly. The youthful-looking Neo always seemed to find ways to get everyone in trouble. "Don't play with the Wall. We're only supposed to observe it." The titanic energy construct that surrounded most of the Imperial frontier was a mystery the greatest minds in the Legion had failed to solve. She wasn't about to let Glitch mess with it.

Glitch shrugged. "Okay, I won't. But..."

Pain and an incredibly loud noise washed over her, erasing all other perceptions, erasing the world.

Olivia was on her hands and knees, blood running down her nose. Her eyes would not focus at first. She blinked furiously and found herself looking at Freedom Falcon's severed head. The rest of his body was nowhere to be seen. Freedom Falcon's eyes looked at her. His mouth moved but no sounds came out. A moment later, his eyes froze, still open but staring at nothing.

Through the ringing on her ears, she could hear screams and the sounds of battle.

The mess hall had been serving the Legion detachment, a few officers, and about a dozen pilots, doctors and a couple of civilian visitors. The armored roof of the hall had been torn open. There were bodies and pieces of bodies everywhere. As Olivia tried to rise to her feet, two struggling figures rolled in front of her. Thaddeus was trying to reach for his sword, but a stocky shaven-headed man had pinned him to the ground and held him with an implacable one-handed grip on his throat while he methodically struck him. The attacker was clad in a green and gold tunic and leggings; his eyes glowed with unnatural brightness.

Charlie-Whiskey. Imperial Neolympian. Powerful. Deadly.

Olivia rushed toward the Celestial Warrior and grappled with him. The man was monstrously strong, but she broke his hold on Thaddeus' throat and pulled him off the Legionnaire. The Celestial drove his elbows into her midsection and smashed the back of his head into her face. The painful blows made her reel, but she didn't let him go. She started calling forth her flames, but the struggling Charlie-Whiskey went suddenly limp and collapsed in her arms. Thaddeus drove his blade into the dying man's midsection one more time and twisted it as he pulled it out.

Artemis let the corpse drop. There were more Charlie-Whiskeys in the mess hall, killing everyone they could reach. Two of them had grabbed Captain Steelhead's arms. Even as she started towards them, the Celestials pulled and tore the squad commander's arms off, releasing twin torrents of blood. Captain Steelhead screamed, a horrible high-pitched howl of agony.

"No!" Olivia cast a flame spear that ran one of the Celestials through, but the other delivered a double-fisted blow onto the team leader's skull. The captain's code name was blunt and to the point. When his Neo powers manifested themselves, his head had been transformed into a construct of riveted metal, a robotic visage that was highly resistant to harm. The Celestial hammering at him was strong enough to overcome that resistance. Olivia's second spear cast took the second Celestial in the face, but the damage was done. Captain Steelhead, his skull crushed, collapsed lifelessly next to the smoldering bodies of his killers.

A brutal impact struck Olivia from behind and knocked her down. She twisted on the ground and saw another Celestial standing over her. His eyes exploded with white light and she was smashed down by a torrent of white energy. Her skin bubbled and burst as it was superheated even through her protective aura. She tried to react, to do something, anything, but the pain was overwhelming, blinding, paralyzing. All she could do was scream.

The overwhelming agony ceased. She could see again. The Celestial was gone. Olivia looked around and saw her attacker crumpled against one of the walls of the mess hall. Mind Surge was holding him down with his telekinesis while Reick and Thaddeus cut him to pieces. Off to another side, Belle Lightning and Glitch were finishing off another Charlie-Whiskey with a steady stream of electricity that tore the man apart.

There had been six attackers. The last one had gone after Miss Lightning, the sub-leader of FS-17. A charred crater on the ground marked the spot where the two Neolympians had destroyed each other. Their remains were unrecognizable. Olivia couldn't tell which of the two blackened and twisted figures had been the stern but kind woman who had assisted Captain Steelhead in leading the squad.

Survivors were moving through the ruined remains of the half-destroyed structure, some screaming in agony from their wounds, others shuddering in reaction. Colonel Poe crawled out of a pile of bodies, his face covered in blood. *El Defensor* was curled on the ground, pushing his spilling intestines back into his body cavity, tears of agony running down his cheeks as he willed his healing powers to fix his injuries. Brickbat and Fox Ghost had been knocked unconscious during the first flurry of combat, but they were recovering.

Outside, gunshots and the unmistakable stutter of machine guns were ringing out. The base was under attack.

* * *

"... and after repelling the follow-up attack, FS-17 regrouped and I contacted you after a brief conference with Colonel Poe," Olivia concluded. "The Colonel wants us to go after the remaining three Death Domes while leaving a covering force behind to protect the base."

"The attack on FSB Enola is part of a general offensive," Doc Slaughter explained. "The Imperials launched three major thrusts on North and Central China in addition to the southern attack you just endured in the Guangxi Province. The enemy forces in your area appear to comprise of a single Imperial infantry division with heavy Celestial elements deployed in support of a general insurrection of the province's Zhuang minority. 5th Corps mutinied en masse sometime before dawn, murdering any loyal officers and soldiers. The only good news is that most artillery units were in the hands of loyal Han soldiers and they managed to destroy their ordinance before being overwhelmed, so the mutineers are largely bereft of heavy artillery."

Olivia silently absorbed the information. She had done her best to study the military disposition of the UN and ROC forces in the region. The units protecting the Guangxi Province besides 5th Corps weren't very powerful: a dozen or so regiments of local militia – all of them with minimal equipment and no organic vehicles, and many of them would likely join the rebellion anyway; two American brigades spread to the east of the firebase, and a motor-rifle regiment from the Republic of Vietnam, which had no desire to have the Dragon Empire on its borders. 5th Corps alone outnumbered all the other forces in the area.

"Do we have an estimate on how many Celestials are supporting the attack, sir?"

"According to the latest MK Ultra reports, a total of nineteen Celestial energy signatures have been detected since the attack commenced at 0500 hours. They were organized in three Tumen with six Celestials each, plus a commanding officer. Your squad was attacked by one Tumen, which was destroyed in the attempt; another one went after the 11th Brigade's Papa Force platoon and was also destroyed after inflicting heavy casualties. The third Tumen helped facilitate the mutiny of 5th Corps and killed the two ROC parahumans attached to that unit.

"Intelligence reports indicate the goal of the operation is to seize the province, which will provide the Empire with access to the sea, as well as cutting off the Yunnan province to the west. Once those provinces are conquered, the Empire will be in a perfect position to expand into other countries. Unfortunately, most of our resources are committed containing the other attacks. The attack on Beijing has been especially damaging. President Soong has decreed that preventing the loss of Beijing is worth any price."

"Where does that leave us, sir?" Olivia asked coldly.

"We can divert air assets to attack major enemy troop concentrations, but cannot do so if those Death Dome emplacements are operational. They need to be taken out."

"How many are we talking about, sir? There are three Death Domes in our vicinity. Are there many more?"

"A standard Imperial Assault Division has three Death Dome batteries, with three to five guns per battery. One battery has been committed to the attack on the 11th Brigade and the Vietnamese Volunteer Army, which are being pushed towards

Yunnan Province. Another was deployed against 196th Brigade's sector, which includes your firebase. The last one is somewhere to the east, covering the border with the Hunan Province. If you can take out the battery facing you, we can launch air attacks on the forces surrounding your base and the remnants of 196th Brigade before they are overwhelmed. 11th Brigade is launching an attack on the battery facing them, using the remnants of its attached Papa Force platoon. That platoon only has four Neolympians left, and their power is relatively low. General Giap of the Vietnamese Volunteers is asking his government for the assistance of their national Neolympian team, which may make a difference." Doc Slaughter looked straight into Olivia's eyes. "Can you take out the guns facing you?"

"I'll have to leave at least two people behind to help protect the firebase," Olivia demurred. "That leaves me with six team members."

"Five, actually. As Colonel Poe no doubt told you, it's been recently discovered that Wesley Smythe, code name Glitch, is a minor who joined the Legion under false pretenses. He must be left behind and cannot take part in any further operations. Is that understood?"

"Yes, sir," Olivia replied, ignoring the sinking feeling in the pit of her stomach. Glitch was unpredictable but powerful. Without him, accomplishing the mission would be far more difficult. "I think we can do it, sir. I will prepare a plan of action and inform Legion Command before implementing it."

"If it proves impossible to disable the weapons, you are ordered to hold until relieved. I am confident you will be able to do this, Artemis."

She wished she felt the same way.

* * *

Hiroshi Tanaka tried not to think of the occasional bursts of rifle fire or mortar explosions going off outside. For the time being the Indies were leaving them alone except for some harassing fire. They had lost a lot of people in the first attack, plus six Celestials. That would make anybody cautious. *You'd better be afraid of us, Chimps.*

On the other hand, why hadn't they started pounding the base with artillery?

The firebase's own artillery pieces were still keeping up a steady fire in support of the American brigade fighting it out not too far away. Maybe the Chimps were using their own arty on those targets instead.

Hiroshi shared his thoughts with Thaddeus, who had been quietly sitting on the barracks and cleaning blood off his big ass sword. "So what do you think, man? What are the Chimps doing?"

"I think we'll find out soon enough," Thaddeus replied. "This is just the calm before the storm."

"You think Artemis is going to send us out?" That thought didn't sit well with Hiroshi. Going out there meant running into Chimps in prepared positions, running into heavy weapons that could hurt him even when he was in astral form.

Thaddeus nodded. "It's better to hit them than to wait for them to hit us again."

"Stupid fucking war," Hiroshi hissed. "We're getting slaughtered, and for what? So a new set of warlords gets to rule China instead of the current one?" It wasn't as if China was a democracy in anything but name. The current president, T.V. Soong, had gotten the job after the previous one, Chiang Ching something-or-other had been overthrown in a palace coup. The freaking place hadn't held a presidential election once. But people didn't care about any of that; they were terrified of China ending up in the hands of the Dragon Emperor, which might allow the Emperor to take over all of Asia. The 'domino theory' or something like that.

Hiroshi didn't care much about politics, although politics had led to his grandparents ending up in a concentration camp after Pearl Harbor. His family had lost pretty much everything they'd had. Even after they were set free, they had to start from scratch, despite the fact that Hiroshi's father had been risking his Jap skin fighting Nazis in Europe in a US Army uniform. That little bit of his family history had also prompted Hiroshi to join the Legion instead of Papa Force. Not that it mattered. He'd ended up on the sharp end anyway.

"This war makes no sense," he said.

"Nothing makes much sense," Thaddeus replied. "I'll tell you two things that make perfect sense, though: we're here and the Chimps want to kill us. If we try to surrender, they will torture us and kill us. If you don't want to die, you fight. You fight for yourself and for the people around you, because they're fighting for you too, and without them, you're fucked."

"We could try to run," Hiroshi said, surprising himself for coming out and saying the words out loud.

Thaddeus shook his head. "We'd have to fight our way to the district capital. That's two hundred klicks, a hundred and twenty-odd miles. Artemis might make it; she's fast and she's pretty tough. Can you stay in ghost form for two hundred klicks?"

Hiroshi shook his head miserably. He could go astral for maybe ten, fifteen minutes before needing to rest for about the same length of time. Every time he had tried to push past that limit he'd been rewarded with horrible pain. Even after ten minutes it was hard to keep going.

"Besides, we'd have to leave the vanillas behind. You know, the guys without powers who are risking their ass right here with us. I'm not about to abandon them."

"Okay, okay, I hear you," Hiroshi said. He was trying to come up with a way to say something to explain himself, to make himself sound like less of a cowardly asshole, when Artemis walked into the barracks.

Everybody came to attention when the team leader walked in. The Legion was normally fairly informal about that kind of thing, supposedly, but not during times of war. Hiroshi had joined in the middle of a war, and he was hoping he'd have a chance to experience the Legion in peacetime. Or that he'd have a chance to experience anything after the next day or two.

"At ease," Artemis said. She went over the situation; it was just as bad as Hiroshi had feared. "The bottom line is, we have to take out the Death Domes or we won't get any air support."

"The one Death Dome we took out was close by and in the open," Mind Surge said. "The other three are at least three miles – sorry, five klicks – away. They are going to be dug in and well-defended. We'll be able to hit the first one, sure, but then the Celestials are going to scramble and intercept us. We can't handle Celestials and the Death Dome defensive teams at the same time. Not while leaving two or three people behind to cover the base. It'' a suicide mission."

"If we can take two of the Death Domes, the flyboys can handle the last one," Reick said. "We can do it."

"If we hadn't lost Freedom Falcon and Brickbat, yeah, it would be doable. Not a cake walk, sure, but doable," Mind Surge conceded. "But now? Artemis, you are the only fast flier left. We are going to have to attack one target at a time."

"I have a plan," Artemis replied. She went on to explain it.

Mind Surge wasn't happy with the plan. Neither was Hiroshi, to be honest. Artemis idea sounded damn close to a suicide mission. Reick and Thaddeus were wholly committed, of course. They weren't afraid of getting killed. Everyone else looked resigned to following Artemis, who was like nineteen years old and was the leader only because she'd been a Legionnaire a few months longer than anyone else. Hiroshi thought about speaking out and joining in with Mind Surge to argue for a different plan, but in the end he just shrugged and kept quiet.

He was pretty sure people weren't going to come back from that mission. The question was whether or not anybody would come back.

* * *

"Glitch, come with me."

"Yes, m'am."

Olivia led the kid to Captain Steelhead's office – her office now, she realized. This was insane. She wasn't ready for any of this. The office, the responsibility, having to decide whether to take FS-17 into danger or to cower in the bunkers until someone rescued them. She wasn't ready, but she'd been handed the responsibility and she'd have to make the most of it. Even if it meant following stupid orders, like leaving behind one of the most powerful members of the squad on account of his being a few years younger than the rest of the team.

"I know you're only thirteen years old," she told Glitch was soon as they were behind closed doors.

"I didn't want to lie, but they told me I needed to go into the Legion, and that meant I had to lie."

"Who told you that? Not your parents. They've reported you missing since before you joined up."

"That was my mother, and my stepfather. They don't really know about me.

About my powers, I mean. Dad knew, he sent me to my uncle to train me. Dad didn't want me registered, was afraid they'd put me away. So he sent me to this uncle, not a real uncle, but that's what I call him."

"Why was your father afraid? Did anything happen?"

Glitch looked worried, even a little scared. "Stuff... stuff happened. Bad stuff. Some people got hurt, not hurt bad, but it could have been real bad. My uncle tried to teach me, he's also a Neo, knows a few others. They tried to teach me, but things kept going wrong. That's why they named me Glitch. They told me I had to join the Legion, that there would be people able to help me in the Legion. But I had to lie about my age. They gave me the fake papers with the fake age. I guess Mom finally found out and now she's told on me."

"I've been ordered to leave you behind, Wesley."

"You should call me Glitch, we're on duty."

Olivia sighed. "You're not on duty anymore, Wesley. You are too young to be here. You cannot fight and put yourself in danger. When this is over, I'll make sure you get a full scholarship at the Freedom Institute. You can finish school, learn to control your powers, okay?"

"You guys are going to need me. I can't abandon you, you're my friends. Bad things are going to happen, and without me they are going to get worse."

"You have to stay, Wesley."

He didn't say anything, but he stopped arguing. Olivia decided to take that as a good sign.

* * *

This is going to be bad.

Bradley Norfield couldn't shake the feeling. He tried to set it aside. Worry too much and you'd be as likely to get killed as if you didn't worry enough.

He looked at the rest of the strike team. Artemis was in her golden outfit, looking grim and ready. She might be a girl, but there was nothing girlish about her right now; she looked deadly and inhuman, just like the mythological goddess she'd been named after. Reick's pseudo-organic armor of chitin and spikes made him look like some sort of alien creature. He was gung-ho and ready to go. Fox Ghost's costume covered most of his face, so Bradley couldn't tell much about his mood, but his guess was that the Japanese guy was crapping his pants. Last but not least, Thaddeus looked calm and detached in his Greek-style battle armor. Bradley wished he could look detached. Oh, well, that's why they paid them the big bucks – five hundred a week, to be exact.

Belle Lightning and *El Defensor* would be staying behind, along with Glitch. The news that the creepy kid had turned out to be just as old as he appeared to be hadn't really surprised anybody. The Legion was probably going to get sued for sending a minor into combat – that kind of shit might have happened a lot back during World War II, when a bunch of teenage Neos had marched off to fight the Nazis and the Japs, but not anymore. That really sucked; Glitch was pretty powerful in his own bizarre way. Bradley wished the discovery of the kid's real age had waited until after the mission.

"Ready?" Artemis asked. Everyone nodded. They had gathered between two bunkers, out of sight from outside the base. Legion Command had given them a rough estimate of the location of the Death Domes, courtesy of some US Air Force surveillance satellites and MK-Ultra, the CIA program that used (and some said created) assorted psychics and clairvoyants. Hopefully the intelligence reports were right and they wouldn't have to loiter around looking for targets while getting their asses shot off.

Artemis hovered a few feet off the ground and floated over Bradley. She grabbed him by the retractable hand holds built into his costume and lifted him up. Okay, time to get to work. Bradley concentrated and reached out with his mind, picking up the other three Legionnaires. He arranged them in a triangular formation behind Artemis. "We're a go," he said into the small microphone in his mask.

And just like that, they were off.

Encased in a bright flaming aura that glowed without burning – Bradley didn't even feel the temperature go up around him – Artemis accelerated to jet fighter speeds in the span of a couple of seconds. She stayed fairly low to the ground, no more than fifteen or twenty feet high, and rushed out of the base. At those speeds, everything became a blur to Bradley. He caught brief glimpses of enemy troops sitting behind hastily dug trenches, but they flew past before the enemy could react to their presence. This might just work, just might. Hit them fast, hit them hard, and blow up the fucking Death Domes before the enemy figured out what was going on. Unfortunately, the return trip depended on almost everything going right. He was pretty sure that wasn't going to happen

"Dropping off," Artemis announced; a hill grew in size as they approached it. The squad leader slowed down to a mere hundred mph or so before releasing Bradley and the rest like so many missiles. Then Artemis was gone, soaring off to attack the second Death Dome emplacement by herself. It was the only way they could hit both of them before the Chimp reactions forces were able to counterattack. After Artemis was done, she would come back and pick up the rest of the squad. If she got killed, Bradley would have to fly them back, much more slowly. Wonderful plan.

Up to him now. He kept his telekinetic grip on the gang and took over flying duties, guiding them around the hill, slowing them down a little more and finally letting everyone go as they came into view of the other side of the hill, where the first Death Dome was supposed to be.

It was there, surrounded by sandbags and a shield projector. And further surrounded by machine gun and rocket emplacements and Imperial Guards in their insanely colorful suits of green and gold scale armor.

Mind Surge let out a primal scream of terror and fury as he and the rest of the squad charged the enemy.

* * *

The impossible accuracy of the Death Dome system came from its simplest component. A human 'operator' was linked to the deadly machine. The unfortunate human didn't operate anything; the Death Dome used his brain as a processing system that analyzed the information gathered by its sensor systems to aim the fire of its particle beam generator. The operators suffered severe neurological damage within a few days of being linked to a Death Dome, damage that became fatal within three to nine months of constant use. Death Dome operators were usually convicted criminals, political dissidents or prisoners of war.

Olivia flew a little too high after dropping off the attack group, and one of the Death Domes acquired her as a target. Guided by a doomed man's brain, the weapon fired, launching a packet of charged particles at eight tenths of the speed of light in her direction.

The direct hit swatted her out of the sky with the suddenness of a lightning bolt. She felt bones break. One second she had been flying. The next she was deep inside a crater she had created after crashing through several trees. A small section of forest had been shattered and set on fire by her arrival.

She was hurt, but she was alive, and that was all that mattered.

Olivia struggled to her knees, ignoring the pain as her broken ribs snapped back into place and started knitting themselves. The agony turned into an almost unbearable itching sensation that made her want to reach into her flesh to scratch the healing bones. She ignored that as well. She'd learned to tolerate many things since joining the Legion.

Three years ago she had been a happy child, listening to her Chuck Berry 45s and hoping that cute boy Leonard Howard would ask her out to Junior Prom. Three years ago she had been normal, as normal as the child of a colored woman and a white man could be in America, where those things were looked askance, but fairly normal nonetheless. Now she waited for her vision to clear while she crouched on a burning patch of forest in a foreign land, on her way to kill or be killed. Funny how much the world could change in three years.

Olivia rubbed her eyes, wiping tears away. Tears caused by physical pain or by sorrow for the happy child she had been? She didn't know.

Her injuries were gone, even the memories of the brutal blow and the agony that followed fading away like a bad dream. She took to the air once more, staying as low to the ground as she could. She weaved her way between trees and hills, at one point running into an enemy foot patrol and scattering the shocked men like so many ninepins.

Her wrist-comp had survived the hit; its armored casing and her own defensive aura had protected it from both the explosion and the electro-magnetic pulse that would fry unshielded electronic components. She slowed down for a few seconds as she flipped the wrist-comp case open and checked her position on the map on the screen. Her target was about a mile away. From the looks of it, it had been the very gun that had shot her down. Time to return the favor.

She reached the position a few moments later. By itself, the Death Dome looked like a featureless red egg, nine feet tall, crackling with energy. The weapon was in a deep trench surrounded by defensive works, only the tip visible above them. As soon as she saw the weapon, Olivia cast a flame spear at it.

The fiery missile exploded in a shower of flames six feet short of the target. A protective force field was revealed, its coruscating energies shining brightly as they deflected the attack. A machine gun team had been too close to the explosion, and three men leaped from the entrenchment, enveloped in flames and screaming. Olivia flew past, throwing two more spears. The force field held, but it was weakening.

The Imperial defenders scrambled into action like the warriors of a kicked anthill.

As Olivia circled the position, staying low enough to avoid being engaged by the Death Dome, a storm of rifle and machine gun fire followed her. Most of it fell short, but she was still hit by dozens of bullets, the impacts shed by her protective aura, doing no damage. Some of the men around the emplacement were dressed in medieval-style armor and held spear-like weapons: Imperial fire lances. The seemingly primitive weapons spat balls of plasma moving at supersonic speeds. She flew in a tight circle, avoiding most of them, but a couple of hits burned her even through her defenses. Enough of those would whittle her down.

There was no choice. Olivia let loose with her fire once again, a superheated trail that consumed everything within a dozen yards of her flight path. She charged the Imperial Guards in their colorful costumes and deadly weapons.

The Guards' body armor contained a personal force field that was proof against small arms weapons and artillery shrapnel. Against her flames, the energy shields only prolonged their final agony.

As she slaughtered the soldiers, Olivia continued striking the Death Dome's defenses. If she could break through, if she could unleash the caged energies contained within the deadly egg-shaped device...

Something slammed into her from one side and turned her graceful flight arc into a short straight thrust into a nearby hill. She and the attacking Celestial struck the hill with a thunderous crash. Her attacker was unaffected by the collision. He kept hitting her with sharp quick punches and elbow jabs, expertly delivered and powerful enough to puncture the armor of a battleship.

Olivia had been trained by some of the best hand to hand fighters in the planet. She blocked some blows with her forearms while she created a shield of flames that blocked further attacks and burned hot enough to sublimate hardened steel. The Celestial recoiled, singed by the flames. His retreat unmasked her to the fire of his two companions. Laser beams and a stream of pure kinetic energy hammered into her shield and aura. She twisted and rolled before the attacks could pierce her defenses, fired back at her enemies.

The Celestials had arrived, and the surviving defenders were rallying.

Olivia gritted her teeth and fought against the seemingly impossible odds.

* * *

"Here they come," *El Defensor* said. "*Putos chingados de mierda*, here they come."

Betty Lou could see that. She and her Pedro were on top of the command bunker, behind a barricade of sandbags with a metal and wood roof; they had a great view of two thirds of Firebase Enola. The vanilla soldiers were mostly concentrating on defending the remaining third of the base.

The attack had started a few minutes after Artemis and the rest of the Legionnaires had left. Bad news travels fast, and the Chimps must have been ordered to attack as soon as they heard FS-17 had left. When the Neos are away, humans will play. Of course, not all the Neos had left.

She sent out three lightning balls, one for each sector she could see, and the energy spheres darted back and forth, killing again and again. Machineguns and mortars also hit the attackers. Dozens, maybe hundreds fell. The enemy was coming in dumb, not bothering to jump from cover to cover. Their only hope was to get through the open ground as fast as possible, get close enough to hit her with grenades or satchel charges. They had to get to her, and she had to kill them before they could do it.

Concentrating on three lightning balls was hard. She was sweating under the helmet and biting her lips hard enough to draw blood. People were shooting at her, too. Snipers on the hills had figured out where she was. *El Defensor*'s defensive shield glowed brightly and bullets bounced off it, making pretty sparks on the greenish energy wall.

Something big went boom on the defensive shield, blinding her for a few seconds. When she could see again, she noticed several sandbags and some of the overhead protection had been blown off. "Anti-tank rocket," Pedro explained. Blood was running down a pressure cut on his forehead. He wiped it off absent-mindedly. "That almost got through. I cannot take too many more hits like that."

"Okay." She tried to look for the rocket teams. She spotted one and sent the closest lightning ball in their direction. Men screamed and died and their rockets blew up, killing more people. One team down. She found two more, and dealt with them the same way. More dead Chimps.

Was there no end to them?

* * *

Alex Marcon cut loose with his shoulder-mounted gyrojet guns. A swarm of 15mm mini-missiles flew in guided paths towards the enemy soldiers a hundred yards away. Each rocket found a target, and the high-powered explosives tore huge wounds or ripped limbs off. The gyrojets were pretty useful, but the shoulder mounts only held thirty rockets each. Alex fired them dry in less than a minute while he closed into hand to hand range, forearm blades ready. It was too bad that his .50 caliber machinegun had been destroyed by a mortar round in the previous fight, but he had plenty of other weapons.

He had lots of toys to play with, and plenty of targets.

Chung-chung, went the spring-loaded throwing stars on his wrists, and four more Imperials were down, clawing at the mortal wounds on their throats. By then Alex had reached the trench line. He kicked a soldier in the head, crushing his skull, and jumped in. At close quarters it was like a fight between a tiger and a flock of penned sheep.

All in all, he'd rather be in Philadelphia, Alex decided. But he hadn't been given much of a choice. His activities as Dread Blade had attracted too much attention. If he hadn't accepted the general amnesty the president had offered, he would have been hunted down. The offer also took him away from a rather awkward situation involving him, his father's second wife and a fairly sordid affair that had begun when he was sixteen; he'd been glad to leave that mess behind. Alex had chosen the Legion rather than become a 'Papa' in the Army. It was a job. He didn't mind it, but he didn't love it. He would be far happier going after criminals than the poor bastards who were there mostly because they'd been told to do so or else.

The last of the poor bastards tried to run. He mowed them down with one of their own AK-47s. None of them mattered. He needed to get to the Death Dome.

A human-sized force of nature landed in an explosion of dust and shattered stone, barely missing him. Reick rolled away from the impact. The new arrival was in the same outfit all Celestials wore to battle, but had a few personal touches that made him stand out. For one, his skin was grayish-blue. For another, a long bone spike protruded from each middle knuckle in his hand. The Imperial grinned at Reick, revealing sharp, shark-like teeth. *Great, a freaking werewolf*, Alex thought.

The Celestial rushed after him. Alex emptied the AK-47 on the charging man, which did nothing, then clubbed him in the face with the gun, which staggered him back a step but didn't do much else. Most Celestials were super-strong and very hard to kill. The blue werewolf lashed out with his talons. Reick dodged back, but a near miss cut through his armor and drew blood.

Things were going to get interesting.

* * *

Terence Thyr – he mostly thought of himself as Thaddeus– spun through the Imperial Guards, lashing out with his bastard sword. The Keshig had personal force fields and their fire lances could burn through his body armor, so he had to be nimble and quick, or soon he'd be dead. Dying wasn't much of a problem for him, but failing and letting the squad down was.

The elite soldiers were good and well-trained, but they still moved painfully slowly compared to him. His sword cut through their defensive shields and their antique scale armor with equal ease. He left a trail of twitching bodies in his wake as he reached the Death Dome.

He'd killed before – he'd done many things he regretted before joining the Legion – but never like this, never in these numbers. He'd joined up in an effort to redeem himself, but he was beginning to believe he was turning into a monster He didn't know what he would become after this was over. That was one reason death didn't bother him all that much.

The Death Dome was just ahead. Thaddeus vaulted over two Imperial Guards who, in their rush to impale him with their fire lances, ended up spearing each other. He fired his gun at the Dome as he moved. The emplacement was shielded, but every weapon he fired ignored most defensive systems; his powers somehow negated force fields and protective auras. The enhanced .60 caliber bullets hit the top of the glowing egg-like structure. Bright cracks appeared around the points of impact, spreading through the Death Dome's surface. Would that be enough? He decided to keep firing to make sure.

There was a loud metallic sound behind him, and he felt a cold impact on his back and chest. A burst of blood – his blood, he realized dully – splattered onto the body of one of the men he had killed. He tried to turn around, had to turn around, but his legs weren't working. He dropped to his knees, dully realizing someone had stabbed him from behind hard enough to pierce the front and back of this breast plate. The blade was pulled back, grating on bone and sending an agonizing spasm through him. Thaddeus dimly felt a kick that sent him sprawling on his back. A Celestial stood over him, a glowing sword in his hands. *That would have been a good fight*, Thaddeus thought, if only the Chimp bastard hadn't hit him from behind. The wound wasn't mortal, but it would take him a few moments to bounce back, and the Celestial clearly wasn't going to wait for him to recover.

Thaddeus looked unflinchingly into the eyes of the man who was about to kill him.

* * *

They weren't going to make it.

Too many India-Charlies between them and the fucking Egg Foo Young of Doom. And too many of them were Keshig, Imperial Guards, with spear-like weapons that could burn Hiroshi in his astral form. During the initial attack he'd followed his much tougher friends and shot down any stragglers that got through them with his machine pistol, but now they were getting down to brass tacks, or decisively engaged if you wanted to get technical, and things were going to get bad. Off to his right, he saw Reick explode out of another trench, and a blue-skinned Charlie-Whiskey leap after him. *Better you than me, buddy*, he thought.

But then another Celestial flew down into the trenches and skewered Thaddeus from behind. It was a big Charlie-Whiskey with an even bigger sword, and he raised it to deliver the coup de grace onto the fallen Legionnaire.

Hiroshi acted without thinking. If he'd given the matter any thought, he'd have done the exact opposite of what he did.

Ghost form. Rush through the Celestial's body, the weakly-interacting particles of the two bodies delivering a cold shock through the Chimp that staggered him for a second. Still in astral form, grab Thaddeus and turn him intangible as well. Drag him to safety.

A fairly simple move. With one simple problem that made it a fairly – no, a completely – stupid move. He couldn't carry other people while going astral. Not really. Not without risking massive physical and psychic feedback. The bad kind of feedback. The kind of feedback that could kill you.

He did it anyway.

Hiroshi reached for Thaddeus with his ghostly hands and willed the astral transformation to spread onto the armored man. For a few seconds, everything went okay, and he dragged the now invisible and intangible guy through a corner in the trench system, out of sight of the Chimp.

A few seconds later, the feedback hit him.

They both became solid. His ghost powers never let him materialize inside an object, so they became solid on the trench floor and not *in* it. At the moment, wracked by agony as he was, Hiroshi couldn't have cared less if they had become solid halfway inside the dirt floor. At least he would have died quickly.

He was bleeding from his mouth, nose and ears; blood was running down his eyes like tears. He could tell that some of his internal organs had ruptured, had died. The places that did not hurt as if he'd been stabbed with barbed knives felt oddly, scarily numb, as if there were no live nerves there to report back on how bad the damage was. Neos could heal from almost anything. He might recover from this, given time, given weeks or months, but not anytime soon. All he could do was lie down and wonder if the vomit rushing out of his mouth was just ordinary puke or bits and pieces of stuff he needed to live.

Hiroshi dimly noticed that the Celestial was coming around the corner. If Thaddeus was as messed up as he was, all Hiroshi had done was to extend his life by a few seconds.

* * *

Bradley lashed out with his mind, and men's heads exploded like so many cherry bombs.

He flew forward, killing as he moved. The only way he could live through this was to kill them before they could kill him. The fire lances of the Keshig warriors he was facing would take him out in one shot. Luckily Thaddeus had charged ahead and taken out most of the special troops defending the Death Dome emplacement. Bradley saw the armored Legionnaire reach the dome and fire a few shots into it. Maybe he'd damaged the damn thing; Bradley was too far to see what was going on. He floated down in the trenches, which for the time being were only filled with the dead. If he could get a little closer...

Multiple powerful impacts made the entire trench system shudder. Big heavy hitters had landed. Celestials. Reick and Thaddeus' positions disappeared in clouds of debris marking two spots where the Charlie-Whiskeys had struck. Bradley looked around and saw a figure head toward him. Same uniform, same bald head, same glowing eyes and glowing tattoo on the chest. The man rushing him looked almost identical to the ones who had torn Captain Steelhead apart with their bare hands.

"Fuck!" Bradley unleashed a telekinetic wave that struck the charging man and stopped him in his tracks. By rights, the Chimp should have been smashed back at bullet speeds, but instead the Celestial staggered back a couple of paces, braced himself and started walking forward, pushing against Bradley's power and winning. The Chimp was stronger than him. "Fuck."

Strength wasn't going to do it. Time to get tricky. Bradley kept trying to push the advancing Celestial away while he reached behind the enemy. A fire lance wasn't too far away, its tip dull and dark. Bradley grabbed it with his teke and sent it flying into the Chimp's back; the weapon bounced off. The Chimp got closer. A few more steps and he'd be at arm's length.

Bradley ignored the gibbering part of his mind that just wanted to turn tail and run in pure mindless terror. He would never be able to outrun the Celestial. Instead, he concentrated on the fire lance. The damn things usually self-destructed a few minutes after their wearers died, so nobody had been able to study them. How the hell did ordinary India-Charlies operate them? There were no triggers, no levers, no moving parts he could sense. His telekinetic grasp allowed him to feel the entirety of the weapon, but he couldn't find any physical control. He picked up a psychic aura coming from the lance, though, and he figured it out. The lances were activated through mental commands.

The Celestial was three steps away. One more and one of his outstretched arms would reach Bradley. He tried to connect with the fire lance. His telepathic powers were rudimentary at best; he could send simple messages if he was touching somebody, and that was about it. He sent a thought into the lance through the telekinetic link, a desperate, urgent thought.

The lance's tip glowed brightly. An instant later, a burst of plasma struck the Celestial in the back. The man grunted, more in surprise than in pain, and he started to turn around. Bradley thrust the spear into the Celestial's face with all his mental strength even as he willed the weapon to unleash all its power.

The world was washed away in yellow-white light.

Bradley woke up and found himself lying against a dirt wall, half buried in it. His face felt like the time he got badly sunburned on a family trip to Florida when he'd been eight. He really couldn't feel much of anything from the neck down, though. One of his eyes wasn't working, either. He opened the other one and saw the Celestial's headless body lying few feet away. *I won*, Bradley thought triumphantly. *I beat the fucking Chimp!*

The feeling of triumph only lasted until he looked down and saw a long piece of the fire lance protruding from his abdomen, still glowing faintly with residual energy. His body from the chest down looked shriveled and blackened. He didn't feel any pain, just incredible thirst and a distant, draining sensation. Things were going dark, his vision rapidly narrowing into a tunnel that became a fading point of light.

This can't be happening. I won! I fuc –

* * *

Thaddeus struggled to his feet, ignoring the nausea that had wracked him when Ghost Fox dragged him away. He wasn't operating at a hundred percent, or even fifty percent, but he could move and if he could move he could kill, and the Celestial swordsman was coming for him. Do or die time.

He didn't have his sword or pistol. But the human body has plenty of weapons, if one knows how to use them.

The Celestial could have played it smart, used his sword carefully in the cramped conditions of the trench, and easily won the fight. The attacker was overconfident, however, and went for an overhead slash, trusting his inhuman speed would let him strike before Thaddeus could react. He was almost right – Thaddeus barely had time to get in close before the attack connected – but almost right is another term for wrong.

Index and middle fingers struck like a knife point. That close up, the Celestial couldn't dodge, and Thaddeus' outstretched fingers struck the swordsman's left eye, piercing his protective aura and the eyeball behind it. The Indy screamed. The two men wrestled. Even dealing with the sudden agony of his destroyed eye, the Celestial was stronger than Thaddeus. An attempt to break the Imperial's neck failed, and the Imperial tried to shift the grip on his sword to stab or slash his tormentor. Thaddeus turned and twisted, delivered a stunning head butt into the enemy's bloody eyes socket, and grabbed the man's sword hand. The Imperial was stronger, but his strength could be turned against him.

The two Neos struggled for a few seconds, the only sound a couple of grunts of effort. Something nearby exploded, shaking the trenches and making the combatants stagger for a second. The brief interruption came at just the right time, and the Celestial's stabbing attempt became his own undoing. Thaddeus broke free and pivoted away. The Charlie-Whiskey started in shock at the sight of his own sword, driven into his stomach. Thaddeus kicked the sword's hilt, driving it deeper into the Celestial's body, then grabbed it in his hands and used it to disembowel the wounded Charlie-Whiskey. It took a couple more slashes, but the Imperial finally went down.

Thaddeus recovered his weapons. He left the Celestial's sword by the body of its wielder. A few strides down the trench led him to Fox Ghost's body. Hiroshi Tanaka was still alive, but barely conscious. "You get him?" he asked Thaddeus between gasps of pain.

"I got him."

"Good."

"Time to go," Thaddeus said, picking up the injured Legionnaire. "I think the Death Dome is done, too."

"Yeah? Shit, I hope it doesn't blow..."

Thaddeus felt a sudden, massive change in air pressure and saw debris and small objects fly overhead, all heading in one direction – the Death Dome. He threw himself down on the bottom of the trench, hoping it would be deep enough.

"...up," Fox Ghost finished before the world turned red.

* * *

It had been a little too interesting.

A fight with blade weapons at close quarters was never a pretty sight. The old joke about knife fights was that the loser went to the morgue and the winner went to the emergency room. You couldn't avoid getting cut; your only hope was to cut up the other guy badly enough that he was the one to go down first. When two

Neos got into that situation, things got even uglier.

Reick had used every weapon in his arsenal against the rampaging Celestial. He'd broken one of his forearm blades; half of the blade was embedded in the blue man's skull, looking like an antenna. Alex had tried to jam the blade all the way into the man's brain, but he'd only managed to get it stuck into the Imperial's super-dense cranium. Bullets, poison darts and organic metal spikes had inflicted dozens of wounds, but the Imperial hadn't gone down. Alex was bleeding profusely, his armor punctured in several spots. He rolled with a kick that could have taken his head off if it had landed squarely, spat out a mouthful of blood, and got up again.

The Imperial was stronger and about as fast, but the main problem was his invulnerability. Nothing was getting through to him. Reick tried to keep the blue man from grappling, punishing the enemy with a constant barrage of kicks and slashes, but finally the Celestial got a grip on him and took him down. The enemy Neo grinned triumphantly as he started stabbing Reick repeatedly with his fist spike. His organic metal armor deflected some of the stabs, but others went through. Too many were going through.

The ground shook violently and a continuous wave of red energy flashed overhead. The Death Dome had been destroyed, releasing enormous amounts of energy.

With a last burst of strength, Reick pushed the Celestial off him, just high enough for the man's head to protrude above the trench, right into the path of the energy release. The Imperial didn't even have time to scream before his skull burst open under the massive burst of power from the exploding Death Dome. The headless corpse collapsed over Alex. He pushed the dead man away just as the trench crumbled over them both. He could feel the mound of dirt on top of him was getting hot, very damn hot. It was going to turn into lava if it kept getting hotter.

There was no enemy to fight, only agony to endure. He would have to find out if he could survive being encased in molten rock.

If he couldn't, he'd at least have a lot of company in hell.

* * *

"You can't ever give up, girl." Her mother's voice, sweet and sorrowful, the voice of a woman who has suffered much, endured much, and moved on.

"Everywhere you go, they're going to expect you to give up, to make up excuses to give up, to list all the reasons – and there will be plenty of good reasons, child – to give up. And no matter what your reasons for quitting are, they are going to smirk and look at each other, and believe you gave up because you're not as good as regular people, because of the color of your skin or because you're a girl, or both. So don't give them the satisfaction, child. Be stubborn. Be stubborn as hell, and don't ever give them the satisfaction of seeing you give up."

Mama, I can't do it.

"No shame in losing if you did everything you could, child. But you have to do everything you can first."

The endless barrage of bullets and energy beams had turned the surrounding hills into pock-marked sculptures, blasted down to bedrock which bubbled merrily after being superheated by forces beyond science and nature. Olivia bled and burned and fought on. One of her arms hung down limply from her shoulder, broken in three places after a devastating attack tore through her fiery shield and scored on the flesh beneath. Two Celestials had fallen, along with hundreds of regular soldiers and Imperial Guards. Two Celestials remained, however, moving in for the kill. One was the lone survivor of the group of three that had attacked her, but he had been joined by another, a Mongolian Noyan, an Imperial Knight, one the leaders and elite warriors among the Celestials.

The Noyan wore a golden suit of stylized armor, complete with an elaborate helmet that looked like a dragon's head, decorated with blazing ruby eyes and a gaping mouth. He had flown into battle just as Olivia had killed the second Celestial, and his arrival had turned the tide. The armored man had endured everything Olivia had thrown at him. His counterattacks had been blasts of white light; one of those blasts had broken her arm. She didn't think she could beat him in a fair fight, let alone the current circumstances. But she wasn't going to give up. She was going to fight until she died.

"No worries." That wasn't her mother's voice in her head. It was a radio message coming through her implanted communicator. Olivia rolled away from a fusillade of energy blasts as she tried to identify the voice. "It took me a while to sneak out, and a while to find you, but I got lucky," the voice continued. It was Glitch. "Don't worry, Olivia. I'm going to save you. And then I'm going to ask you out."

She didn't have the breath to tell him to go away, and the truth was she didn't want to tell him to go away. If she died, the base and everyone in it, Glitch included, were as good as dead. She grunted something that might have been taken as a sign of encouragement or assent, and fought on. Her flame spears forced the Celestial Warriors back, which bought her a few seconds for her broken arm to regenerate into some semblance of functionality. Olivia created a flaming shield again. The golden Noyan advanced confidently towards her. They would duel, she would lose, and the man would take her head as a trophy.

Another golden figure entered the fray.

The golden armor was a smaller version of the Noyan's but identical otherwise. The newcomer struck his larger twin from behind with the same white blasts, staggering him, then followed up with a barrage of electrical attacks that Olivia recognized: Glitch had somehow not only reproduced the Noyan's armor and powers, he had also copied Belle Lightning and Miss Lightning's abilities. He had copied everyone's powers, she realized in shock as Glitch produced Thaddeus' sword and drove it into the Noyan's back. The sword burst into flames while inside the Imperial Knight's torso even as Mind Surge's telekinesis burst the man's armor open. The Noyan came apart in an explosion of metal and flesh. When the smoke cleared nothing remotely human remained.

The remaining Celestial did not run away, which would have been the only wise thing to do. Glitch became a humanoid tornado of elemental power. It wasn't a fight, merely an execution. Even as the last Celestial crumpled to the ground in two separate pieces, Glitch flew towards the Death Dome. He flew high enough for the device to target him, however, and he was hit with several blasts. Olivia heard him cry with pain, but he never changed the course of his flight.

"I'll bust it open and get away," he explained. "I can handle this."

He should have. He launched a multicolor spear made up of every power he had copied, pushed forward with telekinesis, and sheathed it with Thaddeus' armor-piercing aura. It struck the egg-shaped Death Dome and burst it open. Glitch turned in midair, and started to accelerate away at incredible speed.

That's when his powers disappeared. That always happened to Glitch, often at the worst possible time.

Less than a hundred yards away, the golden warrior wreathed in incredible power was replaced by a slender figure in a grey and black costume. Glitch, no longer able to fly, fell to the ground

An instant later, the Death Dome exploded in a blast of red.

Olivia did not have time to scream his name before she was swept away by the conflagration.

* * *

Betty Lou staggered out of the ruins of the command bunker. The Chimps had finally started using artillery against the base. One shell had burst right on top of her position. She was only alive thanks to *El Defensor*, thanks to Pedro, who had gotten killed saving her.

She limped towards the front lines. One of her legs wasn't working right. She didn't know what had happened to it – machine gun bullets or a mortar blast or shrapnel, something had made it hurt and bleed and stop working right. She didn't care. She limped out and cut loose with her ball lightning whenever she saw any India-Charlies. The enemy was all over the place. They had overrun the interior trench lines, and were fighting between the bunkers. Another bunker had been blown up with satchel charges. The only good news was that the enemy artillery had stopped hitting them to avoid killing the attackers.

The lightning spheres zipped back and forth and men screamed briefly before turning into twisted blackened figures. Betty Lou cleared the area around her and she reached the outer defenses. The dead ground ahead of her was covered with charging enemies. She would get some of them, and then they would shoot her or blow her up and it would be over.

Jets roared overhead. The Chimps had no air force to speak of. That meant the swift aircraft swooping down had to be friendlies. As if to confirm her thoughts, a series of fiery blasts walked across the dead ground, sweeping the incoming India-

Charlies with a torrent of fire. The napalm bombardment stopped the attack dead in its tracks.

Betty Lou fell to her knees and started crying.

She cried for a long time.

Guangxi Province, China, October 8, 1968

CASUALTY REPORT

Albert Bertholdt, Code Name Freedom Falcon – KIA

George Eisenberg, Code Name Captain Steelhead – KIA

Miranda Esposito, Code Name Miss Lightning – KIA

Bradley Norbert, Code Name Mind Surge – KIA

Mihai Olinescu, Code Name Brickbat – KIA

Pedro Uzcategui, Code Name *El Defensor* – KIA

Elizabeth Hangman, Code Name Belle Lightning – WIA, prognosis good.

Alex Marcon, Code Name Reick – WIA, prognosis good.

Olivia O'Brien, Code Name Artemis – WIA, prognosis good.

Hiroshi Tanaka, Code Name Fox Ghost – WIA, condition critical, prognosis unknown.

Terence Thyr, Code Name Thaddeus – WIA, prognosis good.

Wesley Smythe, Code Name Glitch – MIA, presumed KIA.

Olivia went over the report one more time and signed her name on the dotted line. Later today she'd be writing letters to the families of the KIAs. As the commanding officer, it was her duty.

She had read some of the other reports that one day would comprise the story of the Battle of Bama Yao. Four Vietnamese Neos had joined forces with the remnants of the Papa Force platoon and taken out the other Death Dome battery without taking any casualties. *Of course not*, Olivia thought bitterly. Unlike her team, they didn't have to fight any Celestials. Reinforced by the Republican 7th Corps and a Marine Expeditionary Unit staging out of Beihai, the Allied forces had swept away the Imperials and the mutineer ROC soldiers. Very few enemies had managed to retreat behind the Dragon Wall. The Imperial attack had turned into a complete disaster. Olivia had the feeling that the Zhuang were going to have plenty of time to regret their rebellion. The Legion would have to do something about the inevitable human rights abuses that would follow.

There was still fighting up north, on the other side of China, but it wasn't going well for the Imperials, either. The war was far from being won, but it had not been lost.

Did it matter? Did any of it matter?

Olivia moved the reports aside and looked at the single-spaced letter she had typed earlier. It was a politely-worded missive regretfully offering her resignation from the Freedom Legion. If she sent the letter, she would be repatriated to the States and assigned some new duties by the Parahuman Operations Command. Her active service should qualify her for a rear-echelon position, away from combat, especially if she was prepared to make a stink about it. She had seen enough death. She had dealt enough death.

Someone knocked at the door.

"Come in."

The man in the blue costume with the yellow lightning pattern looked indecently clean and spiffy. He was handsome, with blonde hair and green-blue eyes, a square jaw and the looks of a Hollywood leading man. He wasn't smiling, but Olivia had seen plenty of pictures of him with his trademark impish grin. Larry Graham, Code Name Swift, the Fastest Man in the World according to his comic books and trading cards.

They saluted each other and shook hands. She had met Swift a few times during her training period. He had been pleasant enough, although a few of his double-entendres and jokes had made her feel uncomfortable in his presence. At least he hadn't been all roving hands with the women around him – she'd had plenty of bad experiences along those lines.

"I was sent here to supervise cleanup operations and take over the squad," Swift explained. "I wanted them to let you keep command of SF-17, to be honest – you did as good a job as I could have."

"Half of the squad is dead. Most of them died after I took over. You call that doing a good job?" Olivia said. Was he mocking her?

"You led a team that destroyed two, count them, two Celestial Tumens, not to mention a couple of battalions of Imperial regulars and ROC renegades, and took out three Death Domes. By rights, your entire command should have been killed, Artemis. Can I call you Olivia, by the way?" The charming smile made a quick appearance. She nodded.

"Listen, Olivia. You kept things together. Your team mostly consisted of newbies, including yourself, with minimal training. We would have never deployed FS-17 if we weren't so desperate for warm bodies, and we put you in a quiet sector that nobody expected would be attacked. The enemy was well-briefed; they went after your team leaders first, knowing that without them the unit would probably rout and would almost certainly not be fit for anything but conduct a static defense. You proved them wrong."

"We all did, sir."

"Can you skip the sirs and call me Larry? Might as well keep it informal." The grin came back for a moment, and she felt the beginning of a smile forming in her own face.

"We all did, Larry. Everyone did everything they could. Nobody gave up."

"Fair enough. But a team can only be as good as their leader. You did great, Olivia. You and your team won this battle. Believe me, nobody's going to forget that."

"Thank you, Larry. By the way, when do you want me to turn the office over to you?"

"You can keep it. We're probably going to move soon. FS-20 is going to replace us at Guangxi Province in a week or so. We'll get reassigned to Hong Kong for some R&R, get a few replacements, then go through some more training before we get deployed back to the front lines. I'm looking forward to working with you." Had that been a come on? His expression seemed guileless enough, so she wasn't sure. "Let's have lunch and talk shop some more, what do you say?"

"I'll see you at the mess hall in a minute."

"See ya then." Larry left.

Olivia took the resignation letter and tore it up. Was that all she needed to stick it out? A pat on the head and a charming grin from a good-looking boy? *That boy's almost fifty years old*, she reminded herself. She didn't know. Maybe being in the Legion wouldn't be about death all the time. Maybe there would be more to it after the war was done. And if there wasn't, she could always type out another letter.

All she knew was that she wouldn't be quitting the Legion today.

* * *

Wesley Smythe floated up from beneath the ground. He'd been able to copy Fox Ghost's powers and dive deep into the earth just before the explosion, but then he'd become trapped in his astral form for several days. His powers worked in mysterious way.

He considered his options. If he returned to the Legion, they would send him to school. He wasn't sure he wanted that. Maybe he could sneak out of the country and go rogue. Of maybe he could hang around and secretly help the Legion whenever he had the chance.

A world of possibilities awaited him.

Tripping

San Francisco, California, May 20, 1969

"They broke the dialectic, man," Mouse said before taking a long toke of the joint between his fingers. He kept the smoke in as long as he could before coughing and exhaling. "Fucked it up all too hell. Fucking Neos."

"Not all Neos are bad," protested Hank. Mouse was harshing his mellow with all his dialectic bullshit. All Hank wanted to do was to lay back, listen to Hendrix and enjoy his smoke-out, but Mouse had gotten all didactic and shit on him. "How about Ironik right here at San Fran? He's a righteous dude. Or Janus? The first Negro superhero. He's done more for civil rights than anybody. Okay, maybe anybody besides Reverend King."

"You don't know shit," Mouse said sourly. He was a big, hairy man, his long blond curls framing a broad face dominated by a prominent nose and generous lips and surrounded by a thick beard. His eyes were bright, their fire undiminished by the epic amount of primo Afghani Skunk the two of them had consumed. Mouse wasn't handsome by any definition of the word, but he never had any trouble getting laid. It was his passion that did the trick. Chicks – the right chicks, the smart college chicks – dug that passion. Hank envied his best friend for that, something he would only admit to himself, and only when he was drunk or stoned.

The envy made him more belligerent than he normally was. "I don't know shit? Why don't you enlighten me, Professor?" Lotus and Rainbow should have been here by now; if they had been around, Mouse wouldn't have gotten all maudlin and depressed and shit. He always cheered up when the girls were there.

"Oh, I'll enlighten you, my man," Mouse said, his deep baritone echoing in the confines of the VW van. He rearranged his considerable bulk on the mattress as he spoke. "First of all, Neos aren't black, or white, or anything, no matter what they look like on the outside. They aren't human, man, don't you get it? Secondly, Neolympians are living embodiments of the Fascist Ideal. They represent the triumph of the individual over society. They mystify the people with their stupid costumes and the comic books and the movies and all that neon and glitter bullshit. They are the new opiate of the masses, better than the old religions, man. Living gods for the proletariat to worship so they can be distracted from their plight. We're fucked."

"Aw, come on, Mouse," Hank replied, his burst of pique dissipating. Mouse was really upset. That brightness in his eyes could even be tears. He might envy his friend, but he didn't like seeing him like this. "Things aren't so bad."

"They aren't? The fucking war's been on for five years now, man. We've had the draft for four years. Chuck's dead, in case you forgot."

"You know I haven't," Hank said. Chuck had been Mouse's cousin. Hank and Mouse had managed to keep their grades up and avoided the draft, but Chuck hadn't been so lucky. He ended up wearing a uniform, got sent to China, and got killed the year before.

"Five years of war, and nobody gives a fuck."

"We give a fuck, man. We're doing that peace rally next Sunday, remember?"

"Yeah, us and two dozen other assholes. We ain't even gonna make the papers. People are too busy listening to The All-American Asshole with his square jaw and baby-blue eyes. Motherfuckers. They killed Kennedy."

"Kennedy's still alive, Mouse."

"They killed his dream, man. Killed his presidency. Killed our last chance to have some meaningful reform in this fucked up country of ours. Now the rich will get richer and young kids like Chuck will get shipped to the other side of the world to get killed in the wars between Neolympians. Fucking modern day gladiators. *Morituri te salutamus*. Let the motherfucking games begin. All Hail Caesar!"

Hank lit a new joint, puffed on it and offered it to Mouse. "Okay, so maybe we are fucked," he said while Mouse toked away. "So what's the point, then? Do we give up and go get a job and a haircut?"

Mouse coughed hoarsely. "Fuck that. 'Get a job, Hepster?' Fuck that."

Hepsters. Yeah, that's what they were. Most of the world thought they were just a pack of losers, but what the fuck did they know? Miserable squares. They just didn't get it. Hank took the joint back from his pal. Hank and Mouse had turned on, tuned in and dropped out, just like The Doctor had told them to do in '66. He remembered that glorious day in San Fran. There'd been a good three, four thousand Hepsters that day, protesting the Asian War, celebrating change, espousing hope. Doctor Leary's speech had moved Hank deeply, and it had driven Mouse into an exhilarated frenzy. They had...

A sudden pounding on the side of the van derailed Hank's thoughts. He and Mouse froze at the sound.

"We've got you surrounded! Come out with your hands up, potheads!" The voice was trying hard to sound harsh and authoritative, but Hank relaxed when he recognized it. Those weren't the pigs.

"You'll never take me alive, pigs!" Hank shouted back mockingly as he opened the van's side door. Lotus and Rainbow grinned at him, two heavenly visions of resplendent womanhood in tie dye shirts, cutoff jeans and sandals. Lotus was tall, slender and platinum blonde. Rainbow was short, dark and voluptuous. They were smart and pretty and quite willing. Hank's mood brightened. Even Mouse looked a little happier as Lotus cuddled up next to him.

He hadn't cheered up enough for Lotus not to notice something was wrong, however. "What's got you feeling blue, Melvin?" Hank knew Mouse's real name, but only Lotus ever used it without risking Mouse's wrath.

"He's off on his usual rant about Neos is all," Hank said as he gathered Rainbow under his arm. Her pleasant warm presence got Hank all worked up. Oh yeah, this was the life. So what if the rest of the world thought Hepsters were the scum of the earth? They were having the time of their lives.

"It's just so messed up, man," Mouse said. "I can't believe they re-elected that Stevens asshole in '68. Fucking Neo Fascist So-Called Patriot. Shit."

"I know, baby," Lotus said soothingly. "That old warmonger has no business leading America. People are just being stupid, but they'll wake up soon enough. We'll all wake up soon enough."

Lotus sounded like she had something specific in mind, and that got Hank worrying again. Mouse liked to bitch and moan and rant. Lotus was a lot quieter, but when something got her going, she didn't talk about it. She did something about it. Lotus was a doer, and doers will get you in trouble a lot more often than talkers will.

A few months back a local pig had made it a hobby to harass them. He hadn't caught them holding, but he'd written them up for loitering, trespassing – they'd been at a public park, for Christ's sake! – and assorted other bullshit. Lotus had done something about it. Hank didn't know the details, but it had involved her, someone with one of the new wrist-comm cameras Kodak was pushing out, and some very racy pictures of Lotus getting naked with the very married cop. The pig was leaving them well enough alone nowadays. Those wrist-comm cameras were something else. Expensive, and the pictures were grainy as fuck and you could only hold like twelve of them in the memory transistor or chip or whatever, but now it was as if the whole world was watching. Lotus was a doer.

She would let only Mouse see the pictures after she got them developed at one of those do-it-yourself Kodak kiosks. That kinda bummed Hank out.

"Pass me that joint, willya?" Rainbow asked him. Hank started to, realized it had gone out and fumbled around for his lighter. Lotus leaned forward with her own, an expensive silver-plated Zippo she'd stolen from her previous boyfriend, an asshole square who'd fucking *volunteered* to go get his ass shot off in China. The Zippo produced a jet of flame that almost singed his eyebrows as he puffed on the joint. "Easy with that thing, Meteor Lass," he said as he passed the lit joint to Rainbow.

"Don't start with the Neo stuff again," Rainbow said after she exhaled. "You'll get poor Mouse all riled up again."

"It's not just the Neos," Mouse said, beginning to get all grumpy again. "It's the war. Fucking Gallup poll says sixty-nine percent of America thinks the war is quote the right motherfucking thing to do unquote."

"Is that how Gallup put it?" Hank asked. "The right motherfucking thing to do?"

"Yeah, real funny, man. Ninety thousand dead American kids ain't laughing just about now. Only CBS still has the balls to keep listing the casualty lists in the news. Everyone else dropped them. 'It was in poor taste,' some asshole TV exec said the other day."

"I know, Mouse," Hank said. "I watch the news too, okay?"

"Do you? 'Cause sometimes I wonder."

"Stop it, you two!" Lotus broke in before Hank could come back with something that might really get Mouse riled up. "Scratch a male and all you find is a bull gorilla thumping his chest and playing silly dominance games. You're supposed to be better than that, Melvin."

"Ook-ook, baby," Mouse said, mellowing out a bit. "Watch out or that tree-swinging asshole in Rhodesia will take control of my mind and add me to his ape army."

"Well, stop it. Lotus and I came here bearing gifts, but if you and Hank don't stop monkeying around you aren't getting them."

"I love your gifts, my lady," Mouse said gallantly while clumsily groping her.

"Not that, you silly," she said indulgently and slapped his hands away. "This." She reached into her bag and came out holding... something Hank hadn't seen before.

"What's that?"

'That' was a long shiny green strip that looked a bit like a Twizzler twist, except it was smooth and green. The color and texture made Hank think of gummy bears, and thinking about gummy bears made him immediately hungry. "Is that shit edible?" he asked.

"It's not candy, if that's what you mean," Lotus said. "Well, I guess you could call it candy for the soul."

Candy. For the soul. That had a nice ring to it. "Groovy. Give me some."

"Wait," she said, pulling away. She waved the gummy string or whatever it was like a wand as she explained. "This is some new stuff I scored in Chinatown. It's called Dreamtime. There's this new guy selling it."

"Chinatown? What were you doing in Chinatown, Lotus?" Mouse said. "It's not safe for a girl to be there by herself, you know."

"Firstly, I wasn't there by myself. Secondly, none of your beeswax. Anyways, I got this stuff in Chinatown. It's supposed to be better than acid. Better than anything. Rainbow and I tried a little bit of it. It's gonna change the world, I think."

"It was incredible," Rainbow confirmed. She casually stroked Hank's crotch with one hand as she went on, smiling at he rose to the occasion. "We could see auras and everything. I could see what Lotus was thinking, and she could taste my feelings."

That sounded great to Hank, although with Rainbow hand working on him it was hard to concentrate on much of anything. "Sounds great. Give me some." He ran the tips of his fingers down the curve of Rainbow's neck, and she shivered at his touch. She was still high on that stuff, he realized. Rainbow had never been shy, but she'd never been this hot to trot before.

"Hold on just a sec more," Lotus said. She and Mouse were made for each other, Hank thought sourly. They both loved to lecture people. "Like I said, we only did a tiny little bit. You're supposed to start out slowly, okay? OD'ing on this stuff is supposed to be downright nasty."

"Neo shit," Mouse said in a low voice.

"What?"

"Don't you see, Hank? That's some Neo shit she's got in her hand. Some concoction one of those freaks cooked up using his alien abilities."

"Not aliens again, man," Hank said. Mouse was convinced that Neos were not just fascist inhuman monsters, but that their super-powers were the result of extraterrestrial intervention, meant to keep humanity ignorant and enslaved. That theory had been going round for a while. There'd even been a whole TV show based on the idea a couple years back. *Star Trips* had been a fun show, depicting a future where Neos and their alien creators had been cast out of the planet after the Olympian Wars; hundreds of years after that, heroic Captain Pike and his crew battled the exiled Neolympians and assorted aliens to keep the United Galactic States safe and sound. Neat shit, sure, but that was made up shit, and the show had been canceled after two seasons anyways. "Please don't start with that Captain Pike crap again."

"I'm right, aren't I?" Mouse told Lotus, ignoring Hank. "Tell me the truth, Lotus."

"Okay, okay. The guy, his name is the Soul Seeker, and yeah, he's supposed to be a Neo."

"And you want us to defile ourselves with that shit?" Mouse was really getting angry now. Nobody liked Mouse when he got angry. Rainbow stopped playing with Hank, which pissed Hank off, and that might have started a fight if Lotus hadn't saved the day yet again.

"Take it easy, Melvin," Lotus said. "It's good stuff, okay? Like I said, we did a little bit, and it was great. It's great. Don't be afraid."

"I'm not afraid," Mouse grumbled.

"I can see what you're feeling, Melvin. I dig it, being afraid of Neo shit, but you don't have to worry. It's okay. It's really okay."

"Give me some, willya?" Hank broke in. "If Mouse doesn't want any, I'll take his share too."

Lotus tore off a little piece of the stuff, about the size of a gummy bear, and handed it to Hank. Mouse looked like he wanted to slap the stuff off Hank's hand, but he just sat back with his arms crossed in front of him, glaring.

"Here's looking at you, kid," Hank said in a horrible Bogart impression, and popped the piece into his mouth.

It tasted sweet and a little tangy – a little too sweet, actually, like an overripe piece of fruit. It wasn't entirely pleasant, but he swallowed it and down it went. "Flavor ain't too bad," he commented, waiting for something to happen. "You sure that's enough to get me off?"

"You just wait a bit," Rainbow said, and started nibbling on Hank's neck. "It's going to feel so good, Hanky-Panky. You just wait."

If given a choice between being called Hanky-Panky and scooping out his own eyeballs with a rusty spoon, Hank would normally have had to sit down and think about it, but he didn't bitch about Rainbow using the nickname, for the same reasons Mouse didn't bitch about Lotus using his Christian name. It still normally annoyed the fuck out of him, but this time he didn't mind. Rainbow's little kisses on his neck were distracting him. Usually he didn't care for them – being kissed on the neck just felt wet and annoying – but now the sensation was... interesting. Rainbow's tongue glided over his skin, and he could feel a tingling feeling wherever it touched him. He looked at her. She was glowing faintly with a light the color of a peach, a sweet Georgia peach, and she tasted like one too. He was tasting her with his eyes.

"I'm feeling it," he whispered, and Rainbow giggled. Her laughter was like soap bubbles rushing out in waves and tickling him. Hank giggled back.

Lotus handed Rainbow a piece of the stuff and popped one herself. "Feels good, doesn't it?" Her smile was warm and bright like a sunset at the beach, but with dark clouds in the horizon, warning of an approaching storm. Lotus was happy, but she also was a little scared. Hank didn't know why he was so sure of that, but he was.

"It feels like..." Words failed him. Rainbow giggled again, enveloping him in bubbles of mirth, tickling him. The bubbles smelled like fresh baked bread, warm and inviting.

"Fine," Mouse said. He reached out and grabbed the strip of Dreamtime off Lotus' hand. "I'm not afraid," he muttered and bit off a big chunk of it, almost half of the remaining strip, and swallowed it convulsively.

"Mouse, don't!" Lotus yelled.

"What? You wanted me to take it, so I took it."

"Too much," Lotus whispered, her eyes wide. The sunset was gone, and she looked now like dark waves during a night storm, cold and terrifying. The fear washed over Hank and made Rainbow's happy bubbles disappear. The fear felt like sandpaper on bare skin, and it stank like roadkill three days dead.

"Fuck it." Mouse stuffed the rest of the strip into his mouth, chewing it down. "Might as well go for broke, right?"

Hank could see Mouse was afraid and pissed off when he took the Dreamtime and started eating it. He was glowing like Rainbow, but his colors were dark red and green and had that fear-sandpaper feel. It hurt just to look at him. And something worse was happening. Hank felt it build inside of Mouse like a monster wave rolling towards land, an upswell of destructive power. "Not good, man," Hank said in a low voice. "Not good at all."

Mouse opened his mouth like he was trying to say something, but no sounds came out. The upswell grew inside his head and Hank knew it was going to explode, it was going to go off like a bomb, like those atomic bombs the Army kept testing out in the desert, it was going to be big and it was going to kill them all. "We gotta get out of here, man!" Hank said. Rainbow gave out a panicked shriek that drove needles into Hank's head, needles that stank like the grave. She was seeing it too, and her fear hurt Hank as much as seeing Mouse had. Lotus just looked at Mouse, her eyes incredibly wide, frozen with terror. Hank started to crawl towards the van's side door. He didn't make it.

The universe exploded.

* * *

At precisely 9:17 p.m. Pacific Time, over eight hundred thousand people – all the residents of San Francisco and neighboring counties – were struck by a mental scream. Most people suffered the loss of all motor control for several seconds, followed by a severe headache lasting anywhere from a few minutes to several hours. Four hundred and fifty-eight people were killed instantly by brain aneurysms. Over two thousand more died as a result of a variety of accidents related to the incident – unfortunates fell down, crashed their vehicles or suffered from a myriad other vicissitudes. Another hundred and sixty-seven victims fell into deep comas; ninety-three of those never recovered consciousness.

The incident came to be known as the San Francisco Shriek. A sizable minority referred to it as the 'San Fran Mindfuck.'

San Francisco, California, May 21st, 1969

Jason Merrill adjusted the oversized goggles that covered his eyes and a good portion of his forehead. He hated the contraption, hated the necessity of having to wear it whenever he went out in public, hated the fact that without them he didn't dare look anyone in the eye. The dark lenses were as much a part of his identity as his code name: Mesmer, Master of the Human Mind. His loathing was tempered by resigned acceptance. One could get used to hanging, if one hung long enough.

The press had been waiting for him even as the Freedom Legion's jet plane taxied to a stop at SFO Airport. There were plenty of reasons for the gathering of journalists, photographers and cameramen. The San Francisco Shriek had plenty of people scared, and the arrival of the proverbial cavalry in the form of one Freedom Legionnaire was great news fodder. Also, with the war in Asia still in full swing, any sighting of a costumed superhero had become a minor event in itself. There would be plenty of reporters itching to ask some uncomfortable questions that had nothing to do with the San Francisco situation.

Jason went down the stairs leading from the jet to the ground, ignoring the relentless storm of flash photography and the shouted questions.

"Is the Empire behind the Shriek?"

"Do you have any suspects?"

"Why is the Legion involved in this case?"

This wasn't the time or the place for a news conference. He paused briefly and started speaking. "I am here to act as a consultant for the FBI and the San Francisco Police Department. There will be a press conference this evening, and I'll be happy to answer your questions then. Have a good day."

The reporters started shouting questions again, but he walked towards the waiting limo without saying another word. Public relations weren't his kind of thing, although he had been forced to undergo training in how to deal with the press. He probably could have been smoother, but, frankly, he didn't give a damn. Jason stepped inside the luxury vehicle and shut the door on the shouts and camera flashes with a grateful sigh before turning to the other passengers.

The portly black man in the business suit was Chief of Police Howard T. Young; Jason recognized him from the files he'd read on the flight over. Young had started as a beat cop and earned his way to the post the hard way, aided by a sterling record and surprisingly effective political skills. At the moment, the top cop looked like a general on the losing side of a war: harried, worried and exhausted. A surface scan of his thoughts would reveal more, but Jason abstained, as he usually did.

The other man sitting in the limo surprised Jason by his presence. The blue cape with the peace symbols the shirtless man in the faded blue jeans wore was unmistakable. Jason was in the presence of Ironik, San Francisco's most notorious Neo. The use of the peace sign in his costume was just as ironic as the man's name – the symbol had been first used by an anti-nuclear and anti-Neo organization which made no distinction between weapons of mass destruction and parahuman powers.

"Welcome to San Francisco, Mr. Merrill," Chief Young said, shaking Jason's hand and introducing himself before indicating his costumed companion. "And this is Ironik. He offered to assist in the investigation and the Mayor agreed. He insisted on it, as a matter of fact." Young didn't sound very happy about that.

Jason kept his face impassive. Politics. It always came down to politics. Ironik was very popular in the city, despite his vocal opposition to the Second Asian War, and to any war in general. He was also a competent crime fighter, using his superhuman senses to ferret out thieves and murderers, which he would then subdue with his 'peace rays.' Mayor Dobbs must be trying to score points by recruiting him.

Oh, well. Might as well be friendly. He extended his hand toward Ironik. "Pleased to meet you."

Ironik shook hands with him, but his light brown eyes did not show much warmth. "Mesmer. Your reputation precedes you. Hopefully you won't have to infringe on anyone's civil rights during this investigation."

And there it was. Mesmer was a full telepath, with the power to read thoughts and emotions, implant hypnotic suggestions, and a great deal more. A lot of people didn't like the idea of having a mind-snoop around. There were huge legal complications involved in using telepathic readings as evidence. The Fourth and Fifth Amendments applied, according to the latest Supreme Court ruling, and in any case the testimony of telepaths was by and large considered hearsay evidence and thus not admissible in court. The whole thing was a mess, and it made Jason glad he didn't usually deal with criminal matters.

He contented himself with a wry smile and a calm response. "I am here only to help find out what happened last night. I won't be tearing people's innermost thoughts out of their heads, I promise you that."

Ironik's expression showed he didn't believe a word Jason was saying, but he didn't say anything.

"You read the files we sent, Mr. Merrill," Chief Young said, switching subjects deftly. "Any initial thoughts? We should get to the epicenter shortly, but maybe you have some theories. We have almost three thousand dead and thousands of injured; we really could use some answers."

"Yes, I've gone over all the initial information. The event appears to be a very powerful psychic explosion. It was very intense, and it dissipated quickly. The most likely explanation is that a Type Three Telepath caused the event – and died shortly thereafter."

"Died?" Ironik asked. "How do you figure?"

"Mind to mind communication is a two-way street," Jason explained with heavy patience. Even the comics got that kind of stuff right most of the time nowadays. "The psychic backlash caused by affecting that many minds at once would be fatal. Hell, reaching that many minds at once would have driven any telepath insane, even if the contact had been minor and harmless." On his best day, Jason could safely link with a hundred, hundred and twenty minds at once. He could probably send out something like the Shriek to ten, twenty thousand people, as long as he didn't mind dropping dead a few seconds later. "I'm sure the body of the perpetrator will be found at the epicenter."

"There were some bodies there," Chief Young admitted. "We're not sure how many, and it'll be hard as hell to identify them."

"There you go. If I had to guess, I'd say some poor unfortunate Neo had his or her powers manifest for the first time, unleashing a psychic event that proved deadly." If that was the case, Jason could be on his way back to Washington in a couple of hours, and damn the press conference. He had to make sure, however, and the only way to be sure was to conduct a thorough scan of the epicenter.

"If we can confirm that to the press, that will really help calm people down," Chief Young said with a hint of relief. "We've had thousands of people fleeing the city already. There's traffic jams on every road leading out of town. People are scared."

"With good reason," Ironik said. "I was nearly overwhelmed myself, and I have some decent psychic shields."

Not as decent as you think, bucko, Jason thought. Even without performing a scan on the local hero, Jason could sense the outline of Ironik's psionic defenses. They were hard but brittle, much like the man behind them, and tinged with some form of old mental trauma. Child abuse, Jason guessed. If he wanted to, he could finesse his way past the shields, unleash some repressed memories and have Ironik convulsing on the ground. He could do all that, of course, at the price of inflicting that trauma on his own psyche. Violating another's mind always exacted a terrible price. Jason had paid that price before, and would again, but only if there was no alternative.

"If my theory is correct, this will be the last time we'll hear from the perpetrator," Jason said reassuringly.

"And if it's not?" Ironink asked.

"If it's not – we have a big problem." A Category Ten Disaster kind of problem. A psychic able to assault hundreds of thousands of minds without getting killed by the inevitable psychic backlash would be a threat orders of magnitude greater than the Dragon Emperor.

Jason was ninety-nine percent sure about his initial theory. He would feel a lot better when he reached a hundred percent.

* * *

The Feds were crawling all over the epicenter by the time the limo and its police escort arrived. "I was wondering why the FBI had not sent somebody to join the welcoming committee," Jason muttered.

"I guess the Legion and the Federal Burro of Investigation don't get along, uh?" Ironik said sardonically; he clearly wasn't a fan of the FBI, either.

Jason grinned ruefully and shook his head. "No, we really don't," he said, a more honest response that he would have given if he hadn't been suffering from a severe headache. The dislike went back a long ways. J. Edgar Hoover had been a notorious Neolympian skeptic and hadn't taken kindly to being proven wrong. To the Feebs, every Neo was a potential criminal, and they treated even the Neos in their own agency with thinly veiled suspicion. It was no wonder that most Neolympians working for the US government were either in the military, the CIA, and the Secret Service. You could count the number of Neos in the Bureau with the fingers of one hand.

All of the serious-looking men in suits wandering around the epicenter site were human, as far as Jason could tell. He could normally pick out Neos at a glance. On the other hand, it would be hard to pick out anything against the psychic background of the epicenter.

The vacant lot overlooking the city was a seething cauldron of psionic fire.

Jason had been feeling a steadily growing pressure inside his head that had triggered a migraine by the time the limo came to a stop. The residual energies triggered by the event coated the entire area like the radioactive aftermath of a nuclear explosion. Whatever had happened there had involved incredible levels of power.

The event had also left behind physical signs. Most of the FBI agents were congregated around a small crater in the vacant lot, a crater covered by the remains of a vehicle of some sort. As he walked towards the crater, Jason saw a few agents taking pictures of a scorched and half-melted wheel rim lying a hundred feet away from it. Other bits of debris littered the area.

A tall and slender woman in a pantsuit was walking around the edge of the crater. Her raven-black hair was tied back in a severe bun, and much of her face was hidden behind dark sunglasses that reminded Jason of his own trademark goggles. She walked determinedly towards Jason and his two companions. "Special Agent Benson," the woman introduced herself, firmly shaking Jason's hand. "I'm in charge of the investigation. I'll be glad to hear your insights on this matter, Mr. Merrill."

Benson. Jason was familiar with the name. Alyson Benson was an expert in parahuman crimes with an impressive track record in the detection and capture of Neo criminals, especially given the fact she was a normal human, not to mention a woman in a male-dominated agency; the FBI had only started letting women in after Hoover kicked the bucket back in '63, and female agents were only slightly less uncommon than Neos in the agency. Agent Benson's accomplishments made her special regardless of her gender; she had even taken down a Neolympian serial killer by herself a couple years ago.

"I will do everything I can to help, Agent Benson," Jason said. "I'd like to start by conducting a psychic examination of the site."

"Do you need me to have my men evacuate the area?" Agent Benson offered; the offer to help put her head and shoulders above most Feebs Jason had worked with.

"No need. I should be able to get a good read despite their presence. And I promise you it won't affect them in any way."

"Sounds good." Again, her attitude was unexpected. The FBI was even more paranoid about Neos with mind-reading abilities than it was about Neos in general. Mind-snoops ended up in the NSA or MK-Ultra and were most definitely not welcome in the Bureau. Agent Benson was either unusually open-minded, or she was playing a game of her own. Jason quickly repressed an impulse to try and find out one way or another and got down to business.

He kept the goggles on. The device had been developed by Doc Slaughter, and it protected both Jason and those around him from the full scope of his powers. The goggles served to protect him from the lingering psychic emanations permeating the crater and its surroundings. Jason closed his eyes and concentrated, extending his senses outward, past the goggles and into the world on the other side.

He looked at the crater with his mind's eyes, and he nearly fell to his knees.

Power. Enormous power. Jason had been in the presence of the likes of Ultimate and Janus. Whoever had caused the Shriek was – had been, hopefully – someone on the same scale as them. The Neo's powers had unleashed a wave of psychic energy as well as enough residual physical energy to consume the vehicle he had been in. Jason's mind caught flashes of the past: two men and two women inside a van, and a maelstrom of strong emotions just before the psychic eruption. Along with the emotions there had been something else. For a few moments, the four people had become linked to each other, and to something else, something far bigger and more powerful. A gestalt of minds.

The gestalt had been injured by the Shriek, but it hadn't been destroyed. It still existed somewhere in San Francisco, and it was potentially as dangerous as the Shriek itself.

Jason realized someone had been holding him steady while he was lost in his mind. He saw Agent Benson standing close, steadying him with a firm hand on his shoulder. She was a tall woman, and strong. The close contact let him sense her inner strength, and a mind well-trained in ways to avoid psychic intrusions. Jason could also sense a measure of concern coming from her. "Are you all right?" she asked him.

"Not really," he replied honestly. "None of us are going to be all right."

* * *

"Hank! Hank, wake up!"

"Go 'way," Hank muttered. He'd never been so tired before. All he wanted to do was to sink into slumber and let the world disappear.

Come to think of it, the world *had* disappeared, hadn't it? Or something worse than just disappear. It had exploded. Memories of an intense burst of a light and an overpowering flash of pain rushed into his head, forcing him to wake up. He opened his eyes.

The last thing he remembered was trying to escape from his van. He wasn't in the van anymore. Hank was lying on a couch in a large living room that felt familiar and strange at the same time. The fireplace to his left looked exactly like the one in the house he had grown up in, down to the cracks on the brickwork, but above the mantelpiece was a stuffed moose head he'd never seen before. He'd never seen it, but he'd heard Mouse describing a mounted head just like it, from *Mouse's* childhood's home. Mouse had been terrified of the moose's dead eyes looking at him. There were pictures on the mantelpiece: two young girls and their parents, and one of the girls looked exactly like a younger version of Lotus; next to that picture was a shot of Hank taken after his First Communion; next that that, a picture of Rainbow during her nineteenth birthday party, a picture that Hank himself had taken nine months ago.

Rainbow was kneeling next to Hank. She was trembling and tears were running down her face. "Hank," she said again. "Thank God, you're awake. You're alive."

Hank sat up. "What's going on? Where's Mouse? Lotus?"

"They are looking around. We all just woke up in this house. It's so weird! Parts of it look just like places where I grew up, or even my college dorm, and some of it is stuff Lotus remembered, and Mouse."

"Bad trip, man. It's got to be that stuff we took," Hank said. Except the couch he was lying on and the floorboard beneath felt perfectly real, as did the smell of air freshener and Pine-Sol in his nostrils. Every detail on Rainbow's worried face looked exactly as it had before, from her slightly crooked teeth to her full lips to the pimple on her left cheek. This couldn't be a hallucination. All his senses were engaged. If anything, everything felt somehow more real than normal.

Mouse and Lotus walked into the room, holding hands. They looked scared.

Hank rose to his feet and greeted them. "Hey, man. What's going on?"

"Nothing that makes sense," Mouse replied curtly. "The house is huge, it goes on forever. It's my parents' house and that cabin near Portland where we stayed last summer, and our crummy apartment, and places Lotus grew up in, and more. It goes on forever, and the only thing we didn't find was a door leading out; every door takes us to another room. We got worried about getting lost, so we decided to come back."

"Fucking weird, man."

"It's that Dreamtime shit," Mouse said, glaring at Lotus. "It's doing something to us, a shared trip, something."

"It's not supposed to be like this," Lotus said. The bleak expression in her face was new; so was the tentative way she spoke. The self-assured, bossy girl Hank knew and sort of loved was gone. "I don't know what happened."

"This can't be real. I know that much," Mouse said. He was angry and scared, Hank could tell, but he was also thinking about things, and if anybody could think his way out of this situation, Mouse was the one. "My parents' house got plowed under when they built a new highway over it. It doesn't exist anymore. Neither does the house Lotus grew up in. This place is like a jigsaw of places we remember, Ergo, it can't be real."

"But it feels real, man," Hank replied. "I've never had a trip that felt this real before."

"We never took some Neo super-drug before, either," Mouse said. Lotus hung her head. "But that doesn't matter now. If this is a trip, some sort of shared hallucination, we just got to keep our shit together until we come down."

"Sounds good to me, man." Hank felt relieved. For a second he'd thought he'd died and this bizarre room was some form of Limbo, or even Hell. They were tripping, that was all.

"I told you trying that Neo shit was a bad idea," Mouse groused.

"You're the one who OD'd on it," Lotus countered. "We were fine before."

Mouse opened his mouth to answer just before the house started to shake. Stuff fell off the walls and tables. "Earthquake!" Hank shouted. He'd been in San Diego during the big quake in '68, and this felt just as bad if not worse.

"It's not real," Mouse reminded them all, but the house was shaking badly enough to make it impossible to stay on their feet, and man, it felt real enough. Hank helped Rainbow to a nearby entryway – shaped exactly like the one in his dorm room on his first year at USF – and cowered there, hoping the roof wouldn't collapse on their heads. He glanced towards Mouse to yell at him to get a move on, but the warning froze in his throat.

Mouse was glowing.

"Not real," Mouse muttered and closed his eyes, his thick brows furrowed in concentration. The light surrounding him flared up for a moment, and the shaking stopped as suddenly as it had begun.

"Fuck, Mouse!" Hank said. The glow surrounding his friend vanished. "What did you do?"

"Dunno." Mouse looked confused and scared at the same time.

"Neo," Rainbow whispered.

Lotus' eyes widened. "You took too much stuff, Melvin. You should be dead, but you aren't. Ergo…"

"He's a Neo," Rainbow said, more loudly this time.

"Bullshit. It's all a fucking trip," Mouse said, but he sounded a lot less sure than he'd been before.

Somebody knocked on a door that hadn't been there a moment ago.

Hank was sure of it. For one, the door was large and solid black, and just looking at it made him scared. He would have noticed it if it had been there before. The dark door was on one of the walls of the living room. The knocking started again, making the whole house reverberate with it.

"Let me in," someone said from behind the door in a cold, angry voice. "Let me in, or I'll kill you all."

Something about the tone of the words made Hank sure that what the stranger meant was more like 'Let me in *and* I'll kill you all.' "Don't do it, man," Hank said.

"Wasn't planning to," Mouse replied, then, turned to the door and spoke in a louder voice: "Who the fuck are you?"

Silence for a second, then: "I'm the Soul Seeker, little Neo. And you are making a mess of my home. Now let me in before I get angry."

"Don't let him in, Melvin," Lotus said, holding onto Mouse's arm. "He wants to hurt us." Hank nodded in agreement.

"Sorry, man," Mouse told the man behind the door. "You ain't welcome here."

The Soul Seeker or whoever it was began pounding on the door, and the whole place started shaking again, just like before. "LET ME IN! LET ME IN OR DIE! I'M GOING TO KILL YOU ALL!"

The words were loud enough to bring Hank to his knees. He dimly sensed Rainbow screaming in agony and convulsing on the floor. "Make it stop!" he begged Mouse.

There was another burst of light, and the pounding and the screaming stopped. Hank heard a surprised cry of pain coming from the other side of the door.

Mouse was standing in front of the door, glowing like a human spotlight. "You cannot pass," he said. "Go back to the Shadow! You cannot pass." Hank realized Mouse was quoting from *Lord of the Rings*. Far fucking out.

"You think you know what you are doing, little Neo? I'll huff and I'll puff and I'll murder you and your friends. You'll see. You'll see."

Silence followed, and the oppressive presence on the other side of the door disappeared. Rainbow grabbed at Hank and started sobbing hysterically. Lotus held on to Mouse, but instead of crying she gave him a hard, considering look. "I think you just saved our lives, Melvin," she said calmly.

"This is crazy. I didn't do anything," Mouse said, but the denial sounded weak.

"You stopped him, man," Hank said while holding onto Rainbow. "You held it at fucking bay, Mouse."

Of course, that left them trapped in God-knew where, with their only protection a newly-minted Neo who hated Neos.

Far fucking out.

* * *

The San Francisco Police Department refused to use the term 'paramilitary unit' for their Special Enforcement unit, but that's what it was. The heavily armed officers in the van were all Asian War veterans. Jason Merrill could feel their bad memories from that conflict, little flashes of violent remembrances going off like fireflies in the dark. Jason, Ironik and Special Agent Benson were in the van with the eight-man team. Agent Benson had changed into black fatigues worn under body armor and helmet, and was toting a Thompson .50 Cal submachine gun. Jason wondered idly if the agent knew how to handle the gun – the heavy cartridge made the big Thompsons buck like wild broncos. He'd been fairly impressed with the woman's quiet confidence, however, and trusted her not to start spraying heavy-caliber bullets all over the place if things got violent.

Agent Benson was engaged in conversation with the SE team leader, a gruff police lieutenant who clearly wasn't happy to be working with Neos and the FBI. "I don't like it," he was telling Agent Benson as the van entered Chinatown. The police vehicle was disguised as a delivery truck, to help avoid spooking their prey.

"You don't have to like it, Lieutenant," Benson said icily. "You have your orders. The only reason the FBI isn't handling the entire operation is that we are short on time. You and your men will provide perimeter security. Mr. Merrill, Ironik and I will make entry into the premises. Your job is not to storm the drug den, it's to make sure nobody gets away. Is that understood?"

The SWAT leader nodded reluctantly. Benson turned to Ironik. "Remember, there is at least one parahuman in there, power level unknown. Don't take any chances."

"I rarely do," Ironik replied with a smirk. Jason wished he could feel so confident. Going after a powerful Neo with unknown abilities was a nightmare, about as safe as juggling hand grenades. Going in with a makeshift group comprising the FBI, the local police, an independent Neo and a Legionnaire – the operation had all the makings of a disaster.

It was the war's fault, like so many other things. Ordinarily this case wouldn't have involved the Legion at all; the situation would have been handled by the California Angels, the state's licensed and bonded Neo team, backed by the FBI's Special Response Team. Most of the Angels were in China after being drafted into service by the US military, however, and the ones who remained were mostly only good for making public appearances, not bearding a Neo in his den. The Lost Angeles

Capes, whose ranks were also thinned by the war, were being assembled as a backup, but it would take time for them to get their stuff together.

Time was a luxury they didn't have.

The SFPD and FBI had handled the investigation quickly and efficiently, the urgency of the situation pre-empting the usual posturing and turf wars. The remains of the van at the epicenter had turned out to belong to one Henry Castellano, senior at USF, no criminal record except for a few citations and misdemeanors. A dead end. The break in the case had happened by accident – while meeting at a police station, Jason had sensed two minds touched by the gestalt, which in turn had led him to a couple of locals being held on drunk and disorderly charges. The man and the woman's minds had been affected by the same process Jason had felt at the epicenter of the Shriek. A quick scan of their minds had revealed the existence of a new drug called Dreamtime. The SFPD had already been looking into the drug, a form of hallucinogenic similar to LSD which had started showing up in Chinatown.

One look at some Dreamtime samples had been enough for Jason. The drug was somehow allowing its creator to form a link with the minds of its users. Jason had to stop the dealer, the so-called Soul Seeker, as soon as possible. If it was possible. If the drug allowed the Neo to somehow tap into the minds of hundreds or thousands of users, there was no telling what he could do next. A bigger Shriek, perhaps. Best to take him down quickly.

If the raid failed, the next step would be to call in as many Neos as possible and send them into the city. San Francisco could be laid waste in the ensuing fight. Jason hoped it wouldn't come to that.

The van rolled to a stop. They were there. Agent Benson glanced at Jason, who nodded and, careful not to look at anybody directly, sent out a mental command to the goggle system that lifted the protective lenses that kept his senses locked in.

He was immediately flooded with a Babel of stray thoughts: Agent Benson was reciting a mantra to herself (*You can do this, you can do this, you can do this*); Ironik's shields grated with psychic static; the police officers in the van chorused in a myriad voices (*Please God, not today/I'll waste all those fucking Chinks/Oh, man, there's gonna be so much paperwork after this is over*). Jason pushed through the mental cacophony and reached out towards the building's basement nearby, where people with the right password were let inside to buy the newest thing on the streets: colorful strings of Dreamtime at a hundred bucks each, good for a dozen doses. There were six armed men in the basement, bored but still attentive. They were members of the local Triad gang, which was getting a cut of the action in return for protection. Half a dozen customers were making purchases; another half dozen were trying the merchandise in a few rooms set aside for that purpose, and their minds were being linked into a monstrous network Jason could see more clearly because he was close to its point of origin.

The Soul Seeker was at the center of the network, in an office in that basement. Jason could sense a dark and powerful mind, a psychic with a power to rival his own even without the augmentation provided by the gestalt. Fortunately, the Soul Seeker was distracted, wandering inside his mental network, searching for something. They had arrived at a perfect time to strike.

Jason lowered the goggles back over his eyes and gestured to Agent Benson. "Six armed guards. The Seeker is also there," he told her.

She nodded. "Let's go."

The van's rear doors opened and Ironik jumped out, followed by Jason and the agent. They rushed towards the basement door while the SWAT team fanned out; nearby police cruisers would arrive soon to provide more manpower. Jason hoped they wouldn't be needed.

Ironik vaulted the staircase leading to the entrance. A man standing watch barely had time to gape at the sight of the caped superhero before a beam of orange light emanating from the Neo's left hand struck him. The guard collapsed against a wall, a beatific smile in his face. Jason could sense that Ironik's 'peace beam' had caused the man's neurons to fire up in an orgasmic burst of pleasure, overwhelming him.

Confronted with the locked metal door, Ironik went on to show his abilities went beyond the power to knock people out by overloading their pleasure centers. The hero spun on one foot while delivering a sharp kick with the other, aiming at the door's lock and shattering it. The door slammed open, knocking another guard aside. Ironik blasted him into blissful ecstasy as he rushed inside. Jason followed.

A short corridor led from the door to a large waiting room. The other four guards had enough time to draw their weapons. Ironik dropped one with another peace beam. Jason dealt with the rest. Even through his goggles, his mind reached out and made contact with theirs. He waded through the guards' consciousness streams and sent forth one irresistible command: sleep. The three men went down like puppets with their strings cut. Their guns clattered on the floor, along with their limp bodies. Psychic feedback struck Jason with the same urge to fall asleep, but he resisted it. He could handle three targets. Five or six would be tricky; seven or more and chances were he'd knock himself out right along with his targets.

There were other people in the room, mostly young men and women, all white and looking fairly prosperous, even the ones in affected hepster clothing. They froze in terror at the sight of two costumed Neos. One of the men burst into tears. "We didn't do nothing, man!" he blubbered.

"Shut up," Ironik said in a stern tone. "All of you, go stand against that wall and stay out of our way. Move!" Move they did.

Another locked door yielded to another super-strong kick from Ironik. According to his files, the San Francisco Neo could bench press a couple of tons; mere locked doors were no impediment to him. The door led to another corridor with doors along its sides, and a final door where, Jason sensed, the Soul Seeker awaited. He followed Ironik towards it, with Agent Benson bringing up the rear.

Ironik crashed through the last door as if it wasn't there. Jason followed him into the room. The former office's décor was anything but businesslike. The floor was covered with colorful rugs dyed in an assortment of patterns, and instead of a desk and chairs there were dozens of large pillows and cushions scattered on the rugs. Ritual symbols belonging to a dozen cultures from around the world hung from the walls; Jason recognized Native American dream catchers side by side with West African religious masks and European hex signs, along with others he'd never seen before.

In the center of the room, the Soul Seeker slept.

As Neos went, he wasn't a very imposing man: medium stature and build, mixed Asian and Caucasian features on a handsome face seemingly belonging to a man in his late twenties, with long hair but otherwise clean shaven. He wore silk trousers and slippers and nothing else. His eyes were closed and he was lying on the cushions, eyes closed. Their loud entrance didn't stir him from his slumber.

Jason's psychic senses were overwhelmed as soon as he his psychic senses touched the Soul Seeker's aura. He staggered and fell to one knee.

Ironik extended a hand towards the sleeping figure. "You have the right to remain unconscious," he said, and shot the man with his peace beams. Jason tried to shout a warning, but he was still dazed from the psychic backlash. It all happened too fast in any case.

The peace beams hit an energy barrier of some sort and dissipated away. A second later Ironik grunted and collapsed as if he'd been poleaxed. To Jason's telepathic senses, the counterattack was a bright explosion of red light, although there were no physical signs of it. Ironik's psychic shields collapsed under the onslaught like a glass plate struck by a cannonball. So did the mind behind them. The San Francisco hero twitched feebly for a few seconds and lay still.

Agent Benson leveled her submachine gun at the Soul Seeker.

"Don't!" Jason shouted before she could squeeze the trigger. She frowned at him but held her fire. "You probably won't hurt him with that thing, but he can kill you."

She shrugged and knelt down to check on Ironik. "He's still breathing."

"Good. He might even wake up one of these days," Jason said out loud, although he didn't think the Neo's chances were great. The attack had been brutal and had shredded Ironik's mind like so much tissue paper. Neolympians could recover from all sorts of injuries, though, so there might be a chance.

"What about him?" Agent Benson pointed at the Soul Seeker. "I'm loaded up with two-stage penetrators," she added, patting her weapon. "They should punch through his shields and put a few holes in his head." She didn't sound at all worried about summarily executing the sleeping Neo. Legally, the Soul Seeker was a dangerous unregistered parahuman with active abilities, so he was fair game.

Jason shook his head. "Even if you hurt him, the backlash will likely kill you. Even worse, he's not alone in there."

"What do you mean?"

"The Soul Seeker has created a telepathic network. Users of the drug he was peddling, at least a couple thousand people; their minds are linked to his. If he dies, he may take them all with them. Even worse, his death might trigger another Shriek, or maybe something worse."

Agent Benson was biting her lip as she considered the possibilities. "We could put him on a boat, take him out into the open ocean and blow it up."

"That might prevent another Shriek, although it won't help the people in the gestalt. And provided he doesn't wake up and decide to do something about it. I don't think we can count on that."

"Crap. Is he really sleeping?"

"In a way. His mind is wandering the mental network he's created. What happened to Ironik was an automatic reaction. He is unaware of what is happening here for the time being, but I have no idea how long that's going to last."

"Can't kill him, and he took down a Type Two Neo while he was taking a nap." Agent Benson said with a frustrated tone in her voice. "So what's the plan, Mesmer?"

"I'm going to have to go in there after him."

* * *

Something was happening on the other side of the door.

Hank had not fucking idea what it was, but he was certain it couldn't be anything good. The hammering had stopped, but after a blessed but interlude of peace it had been replaced with a slight scratching sound and something else. The closest Hank could come to describing it was an increase in air pressure. Whatever was on the other side of the door was pressing on it, on the very air inside the room.

"He's trying to break in," Mouse said, confirming Hank's fears.

"What are we going to do?" Rainbow asked in a pleading voice. She held onto Hank with hysterical strength.

"Mouse will stop him," Lotus said. She was terrified too, but hiding it well. Her calm presence was keeping Hank from blubbering and pissing his pants, and it helped quiet Rainbow down as well.

"I can't be a Neo," Mouse whispered. "I hate those fascist fuckers."

"It coulda happened to anybody, man," Hank told him in a commiserating tone. "You didn't choose to become a super-fascist."

"It's not what you are, but what you do, Melvin. What you choose to do with your powers."

"You don't get it, Lotus. Yeah, I'll try to do the right thing, but in the long run, it won't matter. As long as Neos exist, there is no hope for equality. You see…"

"Mouse?" Hank broke in.

"Yeah?"

"Shut the fuck up for five minutes, okay? In the long run, we're all dead, and right now your fascist powers are the only thing keeping whatever is out there from coming in here and killing us."

"Okay, I hear you." Mouse touched the door. "He's trying something else. I think we should go."

"Go where, man?"

Mouse pointed towards a doorway on the other side of the living room. "This way, for starters." They headed out, going through several rooms and corridors, all cluttered with things from their past. Hank walked past a stack of *Shadow Terror* comics: his personal collection, long lost when his mother had finally gotten sick of the mess in his room and thrown them away. The sight brought back the anger and betrayal he'd felt when he'd come home and discovered his beloved comics were gone. Each object of his he saw affected him that way, and he could see he wasn't alone. Rainbow's mood picked up when she spotted her prom dress lying on a bed.

"We're in some sort of mental construct," Mouse explained as they walked on. The Soul Seeker's presence was gone, at least for the moment. "It's big. I think it has hundreds of minds linked together, but this particular corner belongs to us, and it's made up of our thoughts and memories. And no, don't ask me how I know all of this. I just do, okay?"

"All part of your Neo charm," Hank chided him.

"Don't start, man. You still don't get it. Now I remember what happened to us." Mouse stopped speaking after he opened a door. On the other side was the inside of the van, the place where all this insanity had started. Unlike the other rooms, the van was occupied – by replicas of themselves. Hank watched himself scrambling towards the sliding door, trying to escape, while Lotus and Rainbow stared at Mouse in terror. "Watch and learn, man," Mouse said, pointing at his memory-self. The phantom Mouse's head flashed brightly. The van, and everything inside it, flared up like a pool of gasoline touched off by a match. "Watch," Mouse said again, and the images moved in slow motion. Hank saw Lotus' hair catch fire moments before the rest of her was consumed by white flames. Rainbow turned into a blackened skeleton an instant later; Hank was the last one to go as the energy wave that rushed from Mouse reached out and obliterated him.

Mouse slammed the door shut on the conflagration. "Did you see? The fucking Dreamtime activated my Neo powers, and when those powers woke up, the first thing they did was kill you. They killed me too, I think. I killed us all."

"If we're dead, is this heaven? Or hell?" Rainbow asked. Hank had expected Mouse's statement to drive her into another bout of hysterics, but she spoke calmly.

"No idea," Mouse said. "Neither, I think."

Hank didn't know what to think. He felt fine. Sure, the house of memories was clearly not real, but he felt perfectly real. How could he be dead?

"It's my fault," Lotus said numbly. "I gave you the Dreamtime and it triggered your powers."

"People, it doesn't matter whose fault it is," Hank said. So maybe his body had burned to a crisp. He was still around somehow, and he intended to stay around. "We need to figure out..." A loud crash somewhere near interrupted him. "Fuck! It's that Soul Seeker guy, isn't it?"

"He's catching up with us," Mouse said.

"We'd better scoot."

They ran through the maze of memories.

* * *

"You might want to join your colleagues," Jason told Agent Benson. The feds had cleared the building and the surrounding block, just in case. The only people inside the perimeter were the Soul Seeker, Jason and Agent Benson. Ironik had been wheeled out and was on his way to a hospital, for all the good it would do him.

"I think I'll stay," she said. "If he wakes up and tries anything, I'll shoot him in the head."

Jason sighed but didn't say anything. Hopefully Agent Benson wouldn't get the chance to try her version of a plan. Without further ado, Jason turned to the Seeker and triggered the mental command that raised his protective goggles for the second time that day.

He rarely got the chance to look at the world with his naked eyes, because they saw too much. At a glance, he could reach inside people's minds and see their deepest thoughts and memories. Even worse, people would feel their secrets being exposed, and Jason would share their outraged feelings of violation. Unprotected contact with other minds was excruciating for everyone concerned.

Unfortunately, for something like what he had to do here, it was the only option.

Jason looked at the Soul Seeker with his unobstructed senses. The Neo's mind was protected by powerful shields, but Jason pushed through them as if they weren't there. He saw the huge mental network centered on the sleeping man like a glowing spider web, each strand representing a human mind. His mind reached out towards it.

Displacement.

He no longer stood in the grungy office in Chinatown. He was in a large nightclub, tables arranged around a dancing area, with an open stage where a band was playing. Men and women in outfits from the 1940s danced merrily around the stage. Or not so merrily, Jason noticed after taking a second look. All the dancers and performers had equally blank and unsmiling expressions, their eyes staring at nothing in particular while they went through the motions of dancing like automatons. This was a mental construct at the center of the psychic network, and each person here represented one of the linked minds. Those people were unaware of the link or their virtual presence there. For the time being, they weren't being directly affected, although Jason suspected they were experiencing assorted side effects, anything from fatigue and short-temperedness to headaches and temporary memory loss.

"I don't think you have an invitation to this little shindig."

Jason turned towards the sound of the voice. The Soul Seeker stood in the center of the dance floor, dressed in a formal suit. "I've always loved big band music," he explained. "Love Glenn Miller. Gotta hand it to him, that tough bastard's still going strong; pushing seventy, and still doing concerts. I'm going to try and have him join my Gathering one of these days."

"This needs to stop."

"Why? Is this about the Shriek? Not my fault, pal. Someone OD'd on my stuff, and it happened to be a Neo. What are the odds of that happening? The stupid bastard almost destroyed my Gathering. He's still somewhere in here, and when I find him I'm gonna make him pay. Him and his little friends," he muttered.

"You are forcibly linking people's minds to your own," Jason said. "That's assault with parahuman powers, at least several hundred counts."

"You have no idea, man. More like two thousand, and that's just the beginning. I've finally figured out a way to produce a water-soluble form of Dreamtime. It will work at five parts per million. All I need to do is get enough of it in the San Fran water system and I'll bring a few hundred thousand people into the Gathering, and then it's all over."

"It's all over now. The police has your body in custody. The only reason nobody's put a bullet in your head is that I asked them to wait while I tried to get you to surrender."

"I'd like to see them try. You don't get it. They can't hurt me. I've got the power of two thousand minds at my disposal."

"A thousand vanilla minds," Jason replied.

"How racist of you, sounding so contemptuous for our less privileged brethren. What you don't realize, Mister Super Neo Man, is that vanillas can also access Spooky Energy."

"What?" Spooky Energy was Albert Einstein's term for the mysterious source of Neolympian powers. By definition, only Neos could make use of it.

"Yep. It surprised me, but I was able to feel it was soon as I brought the first people into the Gathering. I thought if I could link into people's minds, I could use it to learn their secrets and maybe mind-control them. The mind control didn't work, it hurts too much to force someone to do something. But I found my powers got stronger, way stronger, even when I linked up with a few dozen minds. Each human can only channel a tiny amount of power. I have no idea what use they get from it. But when you chain-link them, the effects is magnified. I've put that energy to good use. Anybody tries to mess with my body, they're gonna die. When I link to a hundred thousand minds, I'll be able to kick Ultimate's ass.

"Even if they manage to destroy my body, who gives a shit? I'm spending most of my time here, inside my Gathering. The real world, it plain sucks; it's so… disappointing. Here, I can make my own reality."

"Hard to keep your mental construct going if you're dead," Jason pointed out reasonably. Out in the disappointing real world, agent Benson was probably gathering some high-power artillery in case she had to put down the Soul Seeker. Jason was sure he didn't want to be inside the so-called Gathering when that happened.

"Don't be so sure, man. There's a few dead people here already. I think as long as my will is strong enough, I can continue to tap into the Spooky Energy and keep the Gathering alive, with me at its center. I'll be immortal, like."

"Nice theory. Even if that's the case, you're missing one thing."

"Oh, yeah?"

"I'm here, inside your defenses," Jason said, and cut loose with a psychic attack. Inside the Soul Seeker's construct, it looked like a blast of purple fire that washed over the mad Neo.

"Fuck!" the Soul Seeker screamed. "That hurt!" The fire had singed his clothes and skin, but he didn't look terribly injured. He looked a lot angrier than hurt, as a matter of fact. "You shouldn't have done that, pal." His eyes flared with bright pink energy.

Jason raised his mental defenses, shields of purple flames that met the pink light beams the Soul Seeker launched in his direction. The shields held off the first impact, but only barely. The second strike made his shields crack and buckle; he didn't think he was going to survive the third.

Laughing maniacally, the Soul Seeker gathered his power for the killing blow.

* * *

"He's not chasing us anymore," Mouse said.

"How can you tell? We've been wandering in this fucking acid trip for like forever, man!"

"I just know, all right?" Mouse replied in a defensive tone. If Hank had been in a more charitable mood, he'd feel sorry for the big guy. Unfortunately, he'd seen too much disturbing shit in the past few… hours? Days? He had no clue.

At first their wanderings had taken them through times and places from their lives. The jail in Tijuana where Mouse and Hank had spent a night until Mouse's father had shown up to bribe the local pigs. The Catholic school Lotus had attended until she got kicked out for getting caught smoking. The Nebraska farm Rainbow had left when she was fifteen, fleeing into the dark with dark bruises on her face and her father's curses ringing in her ears. All those places had been devoid of life, but they had evoked powerful feelings, feelings they all experienced, not just the person whose memories had created them.

Hank had learned things about his friends that he never suspected, things that he now wished he could forget. He now knew that Mouse had accidentally killed a younger boy when he was nine. He now knew that Lotus and Rainbow's virginities had been taken by force early in their lives, by trusted family friends, in two incidents that had been eerily similar and so heartbreakingly painful all four of them had broken down in tears when they relived them.

And all the while, they had felt the presence of the Soul Seeker, hunting them, full of claws and teeth and bloody thoughts. Hank knew exactly what the Soul Seeker wanted to do to them, and the knowledge was like rats gnawing at you from the inside, like having battery acid poured over open wounds.

Hank still wasn't sure this was Hell, but he was beginning to suspect Hell couldn't be much worse than this.

Mouse was right, though. Hank couldn't feel the Soul Seeker anymore. He hadn't felt his presence since they had come to the auditorium in Hank's high school, where Ray Stevens, a.k.a. the Patriot, a.k.a. the Fascist Pig President of the U.S.A. had given a speech when Hank had been sixteen. Echoes of the awe and pride Hank had felt that day triggered a burst of anger from Mouse and contempt from Lotus. *I was just a kid!* Hank's mind had protested, but neither of his friends had bought it.

Only Rainbow had been sympathetic, but only because she'd had a crush on the Patriot when she'd been younger. Hank had been glad to leave that room behind.

"Let's take a breather for a sec, all right?" Mouse said. He'd really picked a great spot to stop, Hank thought bitterly. They were in the funeral parlor where Hank's family had said goodbye to Uncle Dave. It had been the first time Hank had seen a dead body, an experience that he had no desire to relive. "I really don't want to hang around dead Uncle Dave, man."

"Dave's not here," Mouse replied, and yes, that was technically true, the place was as empty as all the other locations they had wandered through, but the feelings were there, alive and well.

"Yeah, nobody's here. Not even us."

"Except we are. I'm beginning to figure out what all of this means."

"Mind sharing with the rest of the class, Melvin?" Lotus said. "Our bodies are dead, destroyed. How come we are still around?"

"It's like this: our bodies are like a radio speaker. We use them to communicate, to deal with the world. But we – our consciousness, memories – are like a radio signal. We exist with or without a radio."

"You are talking about souls, Melvin. Souls? You're an atheist!"

"Hey, none of this shit needs to be metaphysical, all right? Just because our consciousness may exist without a physical body doesn't prove there's a soul. Maybe the universe can store information in other forms. It could just be a perfectly natural thing, like gravity or electro-magnetism. Just 'cause we haven't figured it out yet doesn't mean it's souls and ghosts and superstitious claptrap like that."

"That's all wonderful, Professor," Hank broke in. "Have you figured out anything useful?"

"The fucking Neo that did this must be using his drugs to capture the minds of everyone who takes them. I think we're inside his mind, or at least we can get to it from where we are."

"What's so good about that?"

"He's stopped chasing us because he's probably busy doing something else. So we go take the fight to him, man. It's better than waiting for him to get back to hunting us down. Running away isn't going to do anything. We're trapped in here with him."

"Can we fight him?" Lotus asked.

"I don't know. We can try and kick the shit out of him and see what happens. It's gonna happen sooner or later. We might as well try to hit him first, instead of waiting for him to start chasing us again."

"We're supposed to be pacifists," Rainbow protested weakly.

"You've felt the Soul Seeker, Rainbow," Lotus said. "Do you think we can talk him out of killing and torturing us?"

"No," Rainbow admitted.

"Do you want to be tortured to death? Assuming we can even die here, which means we could be talking about an eternity of suffering?"

"No."

"Then we fight," Lotus concluded. She turned to Mouse. "Can you find him?"

"I think so."

"That was pretty convenient, you getting mind powers just in time to deal with some sort of mind-fucker," Hank commented.

"I don't think luck had anything to do with it. I think I can do this stuff because I became a fucking Fascist super-dude while I was being mind-fucked by another Fascist super-dude, if that makes any sense. Action-reaction. Thesis, antithesis."

"'Sometimes, you get what you need'," Hank quoted.

"Something like that. Now shut up for a second and let me concentrate."

They all did, although Hank kept wishing they had picked a different place for their pit stop. Every few minutes, he could feel the growing dread he'd experienced as a child when his mother made him walk up to the open casket, the fear and disgust and *Oh shit, that's gonna be me someday* realization that had crept up inside him, leading to the final shock of seeing Uncle Dave – the man who'd laughed and drunk a little too much every Thanksgiving, who was always ready to regale his audience with stories about being a grunt in France during the war, who'd been friendly and funny and so very much alive – cold and dead inside an upholstered wooden box. The whole thing washed over him like a cold wave, and like a wave it receded for a bit, gathered momentum, and hit him again.

Rainbow put a hand on his arm. "This is pretty awful, isn't it?"

Hank had experienced her version of awful, and it had been much worse. He couldn't imagine spending any time inside one of her dark tableaus. "It's okay, I can deal," he told her. For a little while, at least. If they spent enough time in the funeral parlor he might start doing something crazy.

"I got it," Mouse finally said. He pointed to a new door, one that – surprise, surprise – hadn't been there a moment ago.

They went in and walked into a playground. Nobody recognized it, but its emotional impact was painfully clear: they all felt it going in. This was where a half-Chinese, half-white child had been beaten to within an inch of his life. Hank felt the child's pain, heard the shouted slurs *("The Chimps killed my Dad, you fucker! Go back to China!")* and the shame and rage and impotence the child had felt.

He also realized the memory belonged to the Soul Seeker. They were in his head, or his personal space, or whatever.

"We're getting closer," Mouse said. "There." Another door across the playground. They walked through the pain-drenched scene and made it there.

The next room, unlike all the previous ones, had a lot of people in it. An old-fashioned nightclub, with a large crowd of people standing around like mannequins, except for two figures. One of them was a costumed hero Hank identified as Mesmer from the Freedom Legion. The other was the Soul Seeker; Hank recognized him despite never having laid eyes on him before. His presence was like the smell of blood or a threatening growl; it instilled fear and anger immediately.

To make matters worse, the Soul Seeker was kicking Mesmer's ass.

* * *

Jason Merrill didn't notice the newcomers until a large long-haired man smashed into the Soul Seeker from behind. The pink blast that would have destroyed Jason's defenses exploded harmlessly against the ceiling.

"You fucking bastard!" the big man roared as he punched the fallen Neo again and again. "You fucking Neo piece of shit!"

The attacker was joined by three other people, two women and a man. They laid into the Neo with savage gusto, kicking and punching him. For several seconds, the Soul Seeker huddled in a ball and submitted to the beating. Just as Jason recovered enough to rise to his feet, the Seeker flung his attackers away with a flash of energy. The newcomers flew in all directions, crashing into furniture or bowling over the mindless dancers on the nightclub floor.

It was Jason's turn.

The brief breather the stranger had provided had given Jason a chance to study the connection between the Soul Seeker and the two thousand minds he had invaded. Instead of attacking the renegade Neo directly, Jason struck at that connection, trying to sever it. The attack caused the mental network to become visible. It manifested as a bright pillar of light emanating from the Soul Seeker's head. A web of tendrils spread from the pillar and touched every patron within it, as well as Jason himself and the four newcomers.

Jason hit the connection over and over, trying to sever it. The Soul Seeker screamed in pain, but the energy pillar survived. *This is going to get interesting*, Jason mused a moment before he was blasted to his knees, his defenses strained to near their breaking point once again.

"Kill you all," the Soul Seeker growled.

"Not if I kill you first."

The large man had risen; he was surrounded by a bright yellow aura and held a sword in his hands, a long silver blade with mystic runes inscribed along its length.

"All right! It's fucking Anduril! You go get 'im, Mouse!" shouted the other man.

"Not Anduril, *Glamdring*!" Mouse shouted back. He charged forward, enduring an energy attack from the Soul Seeker without flinching, and struck at the energy pillar with his conjured blade. The sword bit deep, scattering energy in all directions, and the Soul Seeker screamed again. Jason hit the pillar a moment later. *We've got him on the ropes*, Jason thought. *Just a little more and...*

The Soul Seeker exploded, blinding everyone in flash of light. When Jason could see again, the Neo was gone, along with the crowd in the nightclub, except for the four newcomers. They rushed towards each other and hugged.

"You got 'im, Mouse! You and your magic sword."

"My wizard's sword, just like Gandalf's. Glamdring." Mouse kissed one of the women, long and hard. Jason gave them several seconds before he politely cleared his throat to get their attention.

Mouse turned towards him. "You're Mesmer, aren't you? Why aren't you in China, destroying villages to save them from tyranny?"

Jason rolled his eyes. *One of those.* A hepster had saved his life. He would never live it down. "That is my code name," he said neutrally. "And I appreciate the assist."

"I didn't do it for you," Mouse replied. "I did it because he was a worse Fascist than you, and because he killed us."

"What happens now?" one of the women asked. "Is the Soul Seeker dead?"

"I think he's dead," Jason said. "The mental network he created is beginning to fall apart, at least." Even as he said the words, he saw the nightclub waver and become less substantial with each passing second.

"What's gonna happen to us?" the other man said. He turned to Jason. "You gotta help us, man! If we're inside the dead dude's head and he's dead, then..."

Jason tried to come up with something, anything. If these people were Henry Castellano and his unfortunate friends, all that was left of their bodies were charred bones in a San Francisco morgue. They had no place to return to. There was nothing he could do for them.

"I'm sorry," he finally said.

"We'll figure something out, Hank," Mouse said. He glared at Jason one final time. "We don't need your help. We don't need..."

There was a disturbingly long moment of discontinuity. Jason blinked. He was back in the real world, lying next to the Soul Seeker's body. Agent Benson was kneeling over him. "Good to see you back," she told him. "The Soul Seeker stopped breathing about thirty seconds ago. Did you take care of him?"

Jason nodded. Agent Benson grinned grimly, turned and fired two shots into the Soul Seeker's head. The enhanced rounds made quite a mess.

"That was a bit over the top, Agent," Jason said, wiping blood and chunks of brain matter from his face. There wasn't much left of the Soul Seeker from the neck up.

"It's the only way to be sure," Benson replied unapologetically.

Jason sighed. Under the circumstances, summarily executing a Neo prisoner wasn't even illegal, and the man was probably already dead. "Guess this case is closed," he said.

"More or less," Agent Benson said. "I've got a metric fuckton of paperwork to fill out, and after that I'm taking a couple of days off" She gave Jason a speculative glance. "If you don't have any plans, I could buy you dinner."

Jason considered the offer while looking into the soft, seemingly guileless eyes of the cold-blooded Fed. He smiled. "Sure, why not?"

Everyone loves a happy ending.

* * *

"Where are we?" Rainbow asked.

At first glance, the answer was obvious. They were back in the van, the air thick with the smell of the Afghani Skunk they had been smoking, Hendrix playing on their little portable mini-record player. For a brief and poignantly hopeful moment, Hank thought the whole thing had just been a really weird trip, and he was now back in Kansas jawing it up with Aunt Em and Uncle Henry and the Professor. Then he saw Mouse's expression and his hopes washed away.

"It's going to be okay," Mouse said.

"It wasn't a dream, was it?" Lotus asked. Mouse shook his head. "So where are we, Melvin?"

"Well, it's kinda complicated," Mouse said, and then paused for several seconds.

"Just parse it for us, Professor," Hank told him.

"I, uh, sort of grabbed ahold of the Soul Seeker's network. It was coming unraveled, but I managed to keep it together, more or less. It's not like what it used to be, that dude was powerful, like, and evil, he could do things to everybody in his web, nasty stuff. I sort of fixed it so we're, uh, hitching a ride. A ride inside all the heads of the people in the network. It's over a thousand people, and we are taking a bit of space inside each of those heads, all spread out among their brains."

"Far fucking out."

"I don't know what all the rules in this place are, but I guess we'll figure them out. I think we could make our own little reality here."

Rainbow had a lot more questions. As Mouse tried to answer them, Hank considered the situation. They were trapped with each other in some sort of dreamland, for who knew how long. Was that better than being dead? Hank guessed he always had the choice to drop out and find out.

Until then, he might as well enjoy the trip.

Hungry Love

Newark, New Jersey (Earth Prime), May 11, 1991

Patricia Dark was drunk and stoned, but not so drunk or stoned she didn't notice the two guys that were following her.

Uh-oh.

Marty's party had been fun, but she'd had enough of Marty's loser friends hitting on her, and rather than wait for someone to give her a ride, she'd figured she could just walk home. Her crappy little apartment was only four blocks away and it was a nice enough night. Except that now, two blocks into her walk, she'd happened to look behind her and noticed the same two guys she'd seen a block back still walking behind her, getting closer and closer to her. They were walking fast and with purpose, way faster than she could ever move in her freaking four-inch heels, and they were going to catch up to her any second now. Patricia was pretty sure they weren't looking for directions or looking to ask her to accept Jesus as her own personal savior.

Let's see. Options: none too good. The most dangerous thing in her purse was a can of hair spray, which if she had a lighter could be turned into a nifty personal flamethrower but she'd lost her lighter earlier than night, which sucked. She could just start screaming at the top of her lungs, which might scare the guys away or get someone to call the cops. Or she could ditch the heels and start running. Back in high school she had made the track team, except she usually wasn't drunk like a skunk when she ran track.

Even through the clippity-clop clatter of her heels, she could hear them catching up. Oh, shit. She stopped and turned around. They were close. She opened her mouth to scream.

They were too fast for her. A rough hand smacked her in the mouth and closed over it, breaking her upper lip and muffling her scream, and the guys picked her up and half-carried, half-dragged her into an alley between two buildings despite her kicking and trashing around. She ended up with her ass on the cold ground, the stink of urine and garbage of the alley burning her nose. One of the guys was on top of her, still covering her mouth with his hand. She bit his foul-tasting palm, hard enough to draw blood. "You bitch!" the guy hissed and raised his other hand, clenched into a fist.

Someone grabbed the guy's hand. His weight came off Patricia as he was bodily yanked off her, and his startled yell was cut short by a sound like an ax handle hitting a side of beef. From the ground, Patricia saw a short guy standing over the would-be mugger and/or rapist he'd just decked, facing would be mugger/rapist Number Two, who was now brandishing a big-ass knife, a *Crocodile Dundee* 'This is a knife' knife, the kind of knife you could use to chop up firewood. Patricia feared the worst.

"I'm gonna mess you up, motherfucker," Big Ass Knife guy said and took a slash at the little guy. There was a flurry of motion too fast for Patricia to see clearly, and Big Ass Knife guy started screaming. His big ass knife was nowhere to be seen, and the arm that had been holding it was bent in a decidedly unnatural way. The little guy stopped the screaming by the simple expedient of punching the former Big Ass Knife guy in the throat, and that quieted him down right quick. He went down and assumed a peaceful prone position next to the barely twitching mugger/rapist Number One. Little guy had game, for sure.

Her rescuer leaned over and offered her a hand, which she gratefully took to help her get to her feet. The little guy was fairly old, at least thirty, which made him almost ten years older than her. He had red hair and a rough expression; if Clint Eastwood and Carrot Top had a love child, it'd look just like him. The thought made her giggle, despite her close brush with death and/or fate worse than death or whatever. The pain on her upper lip cut the giggle short, though.

"Are you all right?" her rescuer asked her. His voice was rough, too, the rasp of a two-pack a day smoker. If her inappropriate giggling bothered him, he didn't show it.

"Yes! Thank you so much!" She looked at the unconscious mugger/rapists. "Uh, I guess we should find a phone and call the police?" Patricia wasn't all that keen on that idea, mainly because she had two joints stuffed with Hawaiian Gold goodness in her purse. And still no lighter.

"No need. They won't be bothering anybody else tonight."

"Oh, okay. And thank you again. I'm Patty, by the way. Patty Dark."

"Damon, Damon Trent," he said, shaking her hand.

"Thank you, Damon-Damon Trent." Poor impulse control or sheer whimsy made her add "Do you think you could walk me home, Damon?"

He smiled at her, and his grin softened his features and made him look a little younger. "It would be my pleasure," he said.

One thing led to another, as such things often do.

Newark, New Jersey (Earth Prime), August 3, 1991

Damon Trent looked at Patricia Dark's unsmiling face and felt a stab of regret. It had been a pleasant few months, far more pleasant than he had expected, but his job was nearly done.

"What's wrong?" he asked her, the words sounding hollow in his ears. He knew what was wrong.

"The rabbit died."

"What do you mean?"

"As my friend Cindy would put it, I'm totally preggers. Just peed on a stick this morning. Three sticks, actually, just to be safe. I shoulda known, being over a month late, but I really didn't want to know. Knocked up. Love, marriage, baby carriage, except no marriage, unless you've got a ring in your pocket you'd like to have me try on for size? Sorry, not trying to pressure you or anything. I know I'm babbling, but I can't stop."

"It's okay," he said.

'I'm keeping it," she told him. "Guess that's it for my love-hate relationship with booze and pot. Bummer. I don't know how it happened, we were so careful!" She looked at him. "Listen, I'm not trying to entrap you or anything, okay? We had fun, even if I still know next to zip about you, but we never said this was going anywhere and if you want to walk, that's fine. It's my problem." Tears started running down her face. She wiped them off with a furious gesture. "Fuck. It's the freaking hormones is what this is. Shit, now I'm blubbering like a... like a fucking baby, and I'm going to have a fucking baby. Something's wrong with this picture."

"It's going to be okay," he said, extending a hand towards her. She grabbed it convulsively and squeezed it tightly, crying in earnest now. Regret became pain. He'd thought he had been beyond such things, but seeing this beautiful, vibrant woman cry hit him like nothing had before. The thought he was going to hurt her even more was almost too much to bear. And yet...

He couldn't stay. He had already tarried for too long in this world. Given enough time, his Adversary might be able to track him there, or worse, whatever version of his Adversary dwelled in this universe might. He would only be able to come back sporadically and for short periods of time, until it was time to bring his child back. That had been the plan all along.

It hadn't been supposed to hurt like this, however.

"I have money," he said. "You and the child will never lack for anything."

"Thank you," she mumbled through the tears. "Thank you, I thought I was going to have to do this alone. Thank you."

She had misunderstood him, but he didn't correct her. Let her think he would be with her for a little while longer. There would be a letter explaining things as best he could, followed by checks every month through a trust fund he had already set up. She would be sad, and she would be angry. She was strong and she would recover from this.

He would not, he realized as another bit of humanity was chipped away.

* * *

"I'm keeping it."

Violet's normally friendly face looked sour and tense, her lips drawn together tightly, her eyes glaring under her furrowed eyebrows. "I thought you were pro-choice."

"I am pro-choice," Patricia replied evenly. "I made my choice. I'm keeping it. Him. Her. Whatever."

"So you're going to let one mistake fuck up the rest of your life," Violet said in an incredulous tone.

"If that's what happens, I guess so." *I could really use a drink and a smoke just about now*, Patricia thought, and had to suppress a surge of bitterness. No pot and booze for now. Maybe not ever. Mommies-to-be aren't supposed to party.

"What did the guy say?" Violet asked, moving onto a different part of the argument, switching gears in her relentless campaign to change her roomie's mind. Patricia looked at her best and oldest friend and felt a sense of foreboding. *This is the last time*, she thought. The last time they were going to speak as friends, as real friends.

"Damon said he'd be there for me."

"Whatever *that* means. He didn't go and propose, did he?"

"I'd have said no if he had." Would she, though? She wasn't sure. Getting married because a guy she'd spent a whole dozen – okay, maybe two dozen – hours with had gotten her preggers struck her as a singularly stupid thing to do. But if he had asked her, she might have gone along. For Baby's sake. Baby should have a father, shouldn't it? Her, she decided. *I'm not going to call my child an 'it.'*

Violet rolled her eyes and leaned back on the kitchen chair. Patricia looked down and absentmindedly picked at the plate of spaghetti and meatballs in front of her. The smell of cooling Italian food made her queasy. Morning sickness had already made a couple of appearances; she hated, hated, *hated* throwing up.

"Pat, you're not being rational. You were going to go back to college next year. You are finally bouncing back after, you know, your Mom, and now this? The guy's probably lying through his teeth. You don't know anything about him. Chances are he'll bail out on you and then you'll be stuck handling this alone. *Murphy Brown* is a great show, but even if she keeps the baby next season, her character has plenty of money to hire nannies and day care services, and it's a TV show and not real life. You're going to end up on food stamps, and that's if the fucking Republicans don't manage to abolish welfare."

"I have a job."

"Yeah, bartending at that shithole. You think they're gonna let you work there when you're seven months in and have ballooned up like the Goodyear Blimp?"

"I'll get another job."

"You're going to change your entire life because a clump of cells is growing inside of you," Violet hissed. "Don't do it. Get rid of it."

Patricia felt an almost irresistible urge to grab Violet by the ears and smash her face into the kitchen table until she shut the fuck up. She controlled herself – barely – but something must have shown up in her expression because her friend recoiled in surprise. "Jesus, Pat!"

The feeling of fierce protectiveness shocked Patricia. She'd never felt this strongly about anything. Must be love. A quote from her favorite Stephen King book sprang into her mind. *'Love is insectile; it is always hungry…. It eats friendship.'* Her friendship with Violet was being eaten away in front of her eyes. She loved Baby, but a part of her hated Baby too. No, not Baby; she hated herself for her feelings. That was when she decided to name her daughter after the haunted car in that book. A little reminder of the price her love would exact from her, and maybe a reminder that she would pay that price gladly, regardless of what it was. Yes. If she had a daughter, Christine would be her name, a bitter joke about the situation. She was going to do what she had to, but would she have regrets? Oh, yeah. Plenty of regrets.

"Violet," she said mildly, looking at her friend without rancor or anger. This was going to suck, but at least she could be civil and cool about it. "It's going to be okay. Our lease is up next month, so the timing is actually pretty good. I'll pack up and leave this week, but I'll still pay for next month's rent, and you can keep the security deposit."

"Pat, you don't have to leave," Violet replied, but she sounded half-hearted at best. Patricia's cynical side knew that at least some part of Violet was worried about how the pregnancy would affect *her* life. She couldn't even blame her friend; Violet hadn't placed an order for this shit sandwich. Patricia hadn't, either, but she was choosing to eat it anyway. Enter freely, and of your own free will, and don't bitch about it if it turns out to be a rough ride. Because love is always hungry. "Where will you go, Pat?"

"I'll talk to my father." Mom had passed away a bit over a year ago. Cancer had snuck up on her and by the time the doctors had discovered it, there was nothing to do but wait for the end. Patricia and her mother hadn't been particularly close – they had been as different as two people in the same nuclear family could be, and Patricia had often delighted in seeing how far she could push her oft angry, ever disappointed mother – but her death had left her shaken up. She'd dropped out of school, moved to Newark, and partied like it was 1999. Her mother's death had sent her off into a meaningless spiral; it seemed fitting that a new life would snap her out of it. *You're gonna be a grandma, Mom*, she thought, and felt tears forming in her yes. Patricia realized she was going to be disappointed if Christine turned out to be a boy. She had a feeling she was carrying a girl, though. Hey, she had a fifty-fifty chance of being right. She'd made bets on far worse odds.

"It's going to be okay," she repeated, more to herself than to Violet. Her friend opened her mouth, closed it without saying anything, and started eating, leaving Patricia with her thoughts.

Her father would help. Brandon Dark had been a bit of a wild child in his youth, a roadie for such luminaries as Bruce Springsteen and Bon Jovi who even now would occasionally grab his old Gibson and join forces with the rest of The Innocent Bystanders, a cover band that played in assorted lesser venues around the tri-state area. He and Mother had been an odd couple, and since her passing he'd been unfurling his wings and letting his freak flag fly proudly again. Yes, Dad wouldn't judge her, wouldn't try to talk her into anything. He'd welcome her to the old homestead, and between the two of them they would make it work. He loved her with all his heart, and he would feed that love, feed it well.

Patricia realized she'd dismissed Damon Trent from her calculations. Violet's words on that subject, if not on any other, had sunk in. She could not count on a man she'd barely known. He might have been a white knight for about five minutes on their first night, but she didn't have a lot of confidence in him.

Lost in thought as she was, it took her a few seconds to realize Violet was crying quietly while she ate. Patricia wanted to join in, to shed her own tears and hug her friend and make it all right, but she knew now that Violet would never understand, would never accept her decision. Her eyes remained dry, and she set aside her feelings, like so many other childish things she must set aside now that she was with child. "It's going to be okay," she said soothingly and held Violet's hand. "You'll see, it's going to work out."

Violet nodded, accepting defeat.

Things did work out. Her father took her in, and between the two of them they made it work. Damon disappeared, leaving her with a lame Dear Jane letter and a monthly stipend; the money helped a lot, but she never forgave him. That was fine. Baby turned out to be a girl just as she'd hoped, and Christine-O was her name-O.

She saw Violet a few times over the next couple of years, lost touch with her for well over a decade, and reconnected through Facebook long after partying like it was 1999 had come and gone and become classic rock. Violet had been married twice, divorced twice, had no kids and was living happily with her fiancée of five years. They exchanged greetings and likes and commented on each other's updates. Their former friendship was gone, largely unlamented.

Love must be fed.

Freshman Class

Liberty Hall, Freedom Island, January 10, 2008

When you gathered this many Neos in one room, the air seemed charged with potential energy, and the world felt heavier, like a supersaturated solution, or a near-critical mass. Power and danger hovered above the gathering like dark storm clouds.

Jake Duchamp tried to count how many people were in the auditorium, and came up with thirty, give or take. That was a lot more than he'd expected. Before this morning, he'd never seen more than five or six Neolympians in one spot. This was Freedom Island, though, with a permanent population of eighty or ninety Neos, plus another fifty or so students at the Institute. A crapload of Neos, in other words.

Everybody in the auditorium had spent months or years of training on how to control their powers, but there was always some energy leakage. Static electricity, for one: Jake noticed a few people's hair standing on end, and smiled before looking around himself to make sure he wasn't sending stray photons everywhere. He wasn't leaking, but the momentary worry made his smile vanish. The dreams he'd been suffering couldn't be real – he had checked – but the feeling that he was a ticking time bomb still haunted him. He wondered how many other Neos in the room felt like they were on the verge of losing it and having to be put down like rabid dogs. Hopefully he was the only one.

A few latecomers scrambled to find open seats in the small auditorium. There was an empty one next to Jake, in one of the rows in the middle, and a short woman half-walked, half-ran towards it. She was slender, with tan skin and dark brown hair and eyes. Her smile was nice. "Mind if I sit here?" she asked, the question aimed at Jake and the person on the other side of the seat, a stunningly beautiful woman with black hair, brown eyes and possibly Native American features. Jake had been too intimidated by her looks to do more than nod politely at her.

"Go ahead," Jake said even as the beautiful girl said "Of course" with a dazzling grin, the kind of grin that would make grown men change tires and donate their kidneys without having to be asked twice. Maybe being gorgeous was her Neo power.

The newcomer sat down with a sigh of relief. "Thank you. I thought I was going to be late when my flight was delayed, and I really didn't want to sit down there." She gestured to the front row, where most of the remaining empty seats were. Jake could understand that. He had picked the middle row himself, just in case the little ceremony included some form of audience participation. Jake didn't like standing out. He supposed he would have to get used to standing out, just not yet.

"My name is Susannah, by the way. Susannah Martinez." She shook hands with both of them. Jake felt a little tingle at the touch, a tingle that wasn't physical: he'd learned to tell the difference. Susannah Martinez was a psychic of some sort. He almost recoiled at the touch. What if she could sense his fears, or worse yet, his nightmares? He controlled himself, however, and she didn't seem to notice anything.

"Pleased to meet you, Susannah. I'm Aurora McCrary," said the gorgeous woman.

"Jake Duchamp," he said, trying to relax and think of something witty to say. He came up with nothing. He'd come up with something good in a couple of hours, probably.

"And I'm Jorel Levenson," the guy on the other side of Jake said, reaching over to shake hands with Susannah. Jorel had long hair and a full beard and mustache. "Pleased to meet all of you."

"This isn't a meet and greet," someone muttered a couple of rows above and behind them. Susannah blushed and looked down. Jorel and Jake both shrugged. It couldn't hurt to be friendly, now could it? Maybe the mutterer was from some country where speaking out loud was considered rude.

The thirty-odd candidates came from all over the world, although over half of them were from the US and Western Europe. Jake could pick out the Americans because most of them were dressed casually, typically in jeans or slacks and t-shirts. Most of the non-Americans were wearing their Sunday's best, business suits or something even more formal. A few were in dress uniforms from countries he couldn't readily identify. Nobody was in costume. That had been made clear in the acceptance letter welcoming them into the Freedom Legion Candidates Program: they were supposed to show up in regular clothes (military uniforms were allowed but discouraged) or not at all. Only one person wasn't wearing anything normal, and that's because he couldn't. He was a short but massively wide man whose skin was made of bright orange metal. The metal man was sitting on a special chair, probably because he weighed several hundred pounds. Jake recognized him.

Susannah noticed Jake looking at the metal man. "He looks familiar," she said. "You know who he is?"

"His code name is Orange Crusher," Jake replied. "He's a solo operator, works out of Detroit. Fully licensed and bonded," Jake didn't mention he'd collected all thirteen issues of *Orange Crusher Comics* until the book was discontinued in 2006. Apparently the deeds of a metal fireplug with legs hadn't been very popular. The hero's brief run as a spokesman for a line of orange-flavored soft drinks hadn't lasted very long, either.

"Oh, I remember him now. He was in those pop commercials."

Jake nodded. "That's him." Someone shushed them from behind, probably the same idiot who'd spoken earlier. "Guess we're not supposed to talk while we wait," Jake grumbled.

"My fault," Susannah whispered.

"Well, I saw plenty of 'No Smoking' signs but not any 'No Talking' signs, so someone is being a jerk," Jorel said from the other side, looking back to see if he could spot the jerk. Jake did too, and caught a thin-lipped guy in a suit glaring in their direction. He was tempted to do something, but he couldn't think of anything that didn't involve using his powers, and that was even more of a no-no than wearing costumes at this gathering. 'Power usage is strictly prohibited except during a life-threatening emergency.' All part of the candidate rules: they were being scored as much for their ability to maintain control of their powers as for anything else.

Jake and the complainer traded stares for a second. "It doesn't matter," he said with a shrug, turning his back on the jerk. "Looks like things are getting started."

One of the doors behind the auditorium's central stage opened, and Artemis walked in. She looked magnificent in her golden costume, breast plate, boots and tiara all polished brightly enough to reflect the lights of the auditorium; she looked just the way a Neo superhero was supposed to look. The crowd felt silent for a second before someone started clapping, triggering a wave of applause. Jake found himself joining in. Artemis was one of the top members of the Freedom Legion, a true hero. Her being there was a big deal.

Artemis stood behind the podium at the center of the stage and waited for the applause to die out. "I just wanted to welcome all of you to Freedom Island and to the Legion's Candidate Program. We are honored by your desire to join the Freedom Legion. There is always more work that needs to be done around the world than hands available to do it, and we need all the help we can get. Thank you for your willingness to help, protect and serve the planet and all who dwell there."

The speech went on for a few minutes. Jake listened to some of it – there were some interesting bits about the history of the Legion – but his mind wandered after a while. It was all stuff he'd heard before, mostly from his father. His father had always been fond of giving speeches about heroism and responsibility, until the day he had died.

Great. The idle thought sent a wave of depression coursing through him. It had been eight years since Jake's father had died, but sometimes it hit him as if it had happened yesterday. His mind flashed back to that day, to the two men and the woman in their colorful costumes knocking on the door of his home. Jake had been behind his mother when she opened the door. He'd recognized the heroes – the Shadow Terror in his black costume with the white skull and crossbones, and Stars and Stripes, the brother-and-sister team, wearing their signature flag-inspired outfits. He'd read all the comics about them, and had met them in person because his dad was one of them, was a hero like them. Was...

"Dead," his mother had said before they could speak. "That's what you're here to tell me, aren't you? Daniel is dead."

Jake didn't remember what they had said, only the sound of her mother crying. She had never been that upset, before and since. Well, not until she heard the news Jake had developed super powers. There'd been plenty of tears on that day, too.

"You're going to get killed, Jake, just like your father."

He shook his head, dispelling the bad memories. Artemis was finishing up her spiel to another roar of applause. She wished them the best of luck, and walked out. The next speaker was far less appealing, a broad-shouldered medium-sized man in a plain red costume. Jake recognized him. Scott Palter, code name Red Rhino. A Neo with a strange combination of high resilience and strength and precognitive powers.

"I hope you all enjoyed Artemis' speech," he said without preamble. "I'm here to fill in the blanks and give you the less than rosy details. Every year, we receive about a hundred applications to the Legion's Candidate Program. This year, we accepted thirty-seven candidates from one hundred and six applications. Our selection criteria includes experience in law-enforcement or the military, actual or potential power level, and extensive background checks. You are the ones who met the initial requirements. Congratulations." His dry tone didn't sound very congratulatory.

"Every year, an average of nine candidates from that pool become Legionnaires. This is an average based on the last twenty years since we established the program. Twice during that time period, nobody made the cut. One time, we inducted all twenty-nine candidates. Most of the time, between half and one third of all candidates were accepted. Make of that what you will. My personal prediction for this year is eleven. I'm right about these things a good eighty percent of the time.

"Being a Legionnaire is not very much like what you read in comic books, even the Legion-approved comics. Most our active duty time is spent sitting around waiting for something to happen, not unlike firemen. When we are not on call or training, we spend our time helping out in humanitarian projects around the world and doing public relations work, basically parading around in our costumes, giving speeches, and looking pretty for the cameras. And once every two to three months, on average, we have to deal with something real, something where lives are at stake. We train long and hard so that when those calls come in we are ready to handle them. In return, you get a nice salary, shares in any licensing deals involving your Neolympian costumed personae, and assorted other benefits. You also will have law enforcement duties and privileges valid in most nations around the world. On the down side, you will become public personalities. That means the press will dig out any dirty secrets you or your family might have and put them out there for everyone to see. If you can't handle that, the Legion is not for you. Any questions?" A few hands went up. "I was just kidding. You can ask your questions to whoever the Legion puts in charge of answering them. That's not my job. Have a nice day!"

* * *

Jake walked into his dorm room, suitcases in hand. The candidates were housed a few miles from Liberty City, in a small complex out by the beach. He didn't know if the clump of buildings had a name, but he thought that if it did it'd probably have Liberty or Freedom in it. Freedom Hamlet or Libertyville or something like that. He'd only been on the island for a whole three hours or so, and he was already getting sick of how everything in the damn place was freedom-this or liberty-that. *I get it already*, he thought to himself. Not to mention that, for an organization that was all about freedom, it sure had a ton of rules and regulations. He had an electronic copy of the Legion's Handbook stored in his wrist-comp; the dead-tree version was about two thousand pages long, covering everything from the rights of prisoners (during times of peace, war, and other circumstances) to what pets were allowed inside Legion residences (lions, tigers and bears, amazingly enough, were only allowed if 'considered integral to the usage of Neolympian abilities'). Oh, well, he'd eventually get used to it all, hopefully.

This dorm room was a lot nicer than the one he'd had at Yale on his freshman year, before his powers had manifested themselves and he'd dropped out. It had a much nicer view, for one, being on a hill overlooking the ocean. The building itself was no great shakes. It was a three-floor structure built like a bunker, with thick ferroconcrete walls and bulletproof windows. In other words, the dorm was built to minimize the damage a Neo might do if he screwed up. It was the same reason the dorms were a ways away from other inhabited areas. Inexperienced Neos were very much like explosives, best kept far away from everyone else.

The common area of the room was spacious enough, featuring a couple of worn but nice-looking couches, a coffee table, and a brand-new 60-inch screen built into a wall. Nifty. There were four bedrooms, two on each side of the central living room and two bathrooms, one between each set of bedrooms. He'd be sharing the accommodations with three roommates. The bedroom doors had numbers; he'd been assigned Unit Number Two.

Jake walked over the bedrooms to the right of the entrance, where Number Two would be located. The door to Unit One was open, and as he walked there a guy with very short hair and a long braided soul patch came out. He was wearing jeans, a t-shirt, and flip flops, and looked like he was in his late twenties.

"Howdy," Jake said, extending his hand. "I'm Jake Duchamp. I'm in Unit Two."

"Ben Barton," Soul Patch replied. His handshake was firm but not hand-crushing, so he wasn't one of those people who turned casual greetings into tests of strength, which was fine with Jake. He hadn't been into throwing his weight around before his powers showed up, and now that he could bench press a hundred tons or so, it just wasn't a safe game for anyone involved.

Jake opened the door to Unit Two, revealing a fairly narrow room with a bed, a desk, a closet on one wall, a flat screen hanging from the wall where the desk was placed, and two rows of shelves on the opposite wall. The place was somewhere between 'cozy' and 'cramped.' Jake casually tossed his suitcases onto the bed. That was going to be his home for the next year, assuming he didn't wash out before the candidacy term ran its course. "Not bad," he said.

"I've lived in worse," Ben agreed.

Another roommate showed up. He was about five eight, mid-twenties, with dark brown hair and a mix of Western and Asian features. "Hey," he said.

Jake and Ben introduced themselves. "I'm Paul Singleton. Code name Biomancer."

"That's cool," Jake said. "Some sort of healer?"

"Yeah, kind of."

"Good deal. Healers are always good to have around," said someone from the front door. The newcomer was the long-haired guy Jake had met at the auditorium.

"I'm Jorel, Jorel Levenson," he introduced himself. "Code name Dread Beard," he added with a smile.

Jake grinned at that. "Not bad. Better than Captain Something or Other. Everybody likes to add Captain to their name nowadays, it seems like." He turned to Ben Barton. "Uh, unless you're a Captain Something or Other, in which case, no offense meant."

Ben shrugged. "Not a Captain. I'm Dream Termite."

"I guess we'll be part of the same training unit," Jake went on.

"That's right," Paul said. "Us four and two ladies; their room is next door. Aurora and Susannah."

"Jorel and I met them at the opening ceremony," Jake said. "Funny coincidence."

"If it was a coincidence," Paul said. "Neos seem to be synchronicity magnets, to the point they sometimes appear to violate causality."

"You just said a mouthful there," Jorel said.

"I used not to believe in fate, or much of anything," Paul went on. "I was an atheist until I decided I lacked the empirical data to prove or disprove God's existence. Neos, however, seem to attract fate and destiny like a dog attracts fleas. Coincidences involving us usually mean something."

Ben and Jorel looked skeptical but didn't say anything.

"Anyways," Jake said. "How about we go say hi to our teammates and maybe check out the local diner?"

It'd be nice if the team was destined to get along, but it looked like they'd have to work at it.

Liberty Hall, Freedom Island, January 17, 2008

Elizabeth Hangman (code name Brontes) leaned back on her chair and went over the report on the computer screen. This year's candidate crop was particularly interesting. If Red Rhino's predictions turned out to be as accurate as usual, the Legion would be adding almost a dozen members to the roster, and a number of them would play a major role in some future crisis. She hated it when precogs announced something was destined to happen, but she'd do her job and let fate take care of itself.

The intercom on her desk buzzed. "Artemis is here to see you," her assistant said, her voice betraying a hint of nervousness.

"Send her in," Elizabeth replied, a frown on her face. A Legion Council member didn't usually drop by unannounced; she hadn't seen Olivia in almost a year except during public occasions. Something was up.

Olivia O'Brien walked in, dressed in a pantsuit outfit, just as she usually did when not clad in her trademark golden costume. This particular version was a somewhat somber dark navy blue suit that didn't compliment her light mahogany skin or green eyes, in Elizabeth's opinion, but nobody had asked her for fashion advice and she wasn't about to volunteer it. She got up from the chair to shake Olivia's hand. "Been a while, Olivia," she said.

"Don't I know it?" The two women smiled at each other, and Elizabeth was pretty sure they were both thinking about their first meeting back in 1966: a black woman and a Kentucky hillbilly weren't expected to get along, but gotten along they had. They had become friends in the way only people who have shared the horrors of war can. Their friendship had grown distant over the years, as often happened to incredibly busy people who don't have too many opportunities to work together, but it was still there, evidenced by the warmth in Olivia's eyes.

They went to sit down on the comfortable armchairs on one side of the office. "How have you been, Betty?" Olivia asked her.

Very few people called her Betty these days. Elizabeth's smile wavered a little. "Could be better, could be worse. I could complain, but who'd listen?"

"I would."

"We've got an interesting candidate class this year," Elizabeth said, setting aside the offer to listen to her troubles. "I just kicked out three people, and it's just the first week. They were infiltrators: CIA, MI-5 and Mossad, respectively. I sent them packing and ordered a bug sweep just in case they left some presents behind. My guess is that there's at least a couple other covert agents with better cover stories. I'm keeping an eye on one Erik Fischer from Germany, who I'm fairly certain is either a BDN agent or a mole for the Grey Army Faction."

"I do read the memos you send to the Council, Betty," Olivia replied with a gentle tone. "I was asking about you, personally. We really haven't talked much since the divorce."

"Well, if you read my Facebook page you know all there is to know," Elizabeth said with a shrug. "Turns out the second divorce is a lot easier than the first. Kinda like riding a bike, you could say." Elizabeth's first marriage had been the endpoint of a whirlwind romance back in the 1970s, starring one Betty Lou Hangman and Hiroshi Tanaka, fellow Legionnaire and teammate. That one had lasted all of five years before their differences became irreconcilable. Her second turn at a Vegas wedding chapel had involved vanilla human billionaire Demosthenes Onassis, a charming younger man who in the end had found their lifestyles to be wholly incompatible. He'd thought he could eventually talk her into quitting the Legion, and after eight years of trying he'd quit her instead.

It had been fairly amicable as such things went, though. Her marriage with Hiroshi had ended amidst a great deal of drama and tears; the second divorce had been a quiet and subdued process, mostly involving lawyers. As far as Elizabeth was concerned, there would be no marriage number three. "Poor Demosthenes was a sweetheart, all things considered. He even offered me a settlement well above what our prenup stipulated. I turned him down, of course. I didn't marry him for the money. Anyway, it's over, and I'm over it," she said, making it clear she wasn't going to go into any further details. "How about you, Olivia? How's Larry?"

"He's, well, Larry. We don't spend as much time together as we'd like," Olivia said casually, making it clear she wasn't going to go into any further details, either. Their friendship did not extend into certain areas, Elizabeth realized ruefully. There were plenty of rumors Larry Graham, a.k.a. Swift, had been running around with assorted women whenever he wasn't right under Olivia's nose, but Elizabeth wasn't going to bring that up while making small talk with her wartime bestie. "How's everything else?"

Olivia's grin became a little sad. "Ultimate is still grieving over Linda's death, but he's recovering. Other than that, most everyone is doing well. The Legion keeps getting caught in political battles within the UN, but that is unavoidable. Luckily there hasn't been a Class Six or higher disaster in a couple of years, which means we can keep up with all the meetings and paperwork."

"Yes, I wish the comic books showed us conducting meetings or filling incident reports, instead of traipsing around in the fancy outfits and blowing things up all the time. Might give the fans some perspective," Elizabeth commented. The two women chuckled and sat in companionable silence for a few seconds. "So what brings you here, Olivia?"

"Mr. Palter's visions brought me here," Olivia said, getting down to business. "Red Rhino's predictions are fairly accurate, so when he says something is up, we all listen, even if the man is as cheerful as an Italian funeral."

"Yes, he told me a few things too. Anybody in particular?"

"He gave me a list. Can you pull their files so we can go over them, one by one?"

"Of course." Elizabeth flipped open her wrist-comp and did some finger-tapping on the screen. A holographic screen came up over the coffee table between the two armchairs. "Who do you want to check out first?"

"Might as well go in alphabetical order. Benjamin Barton."

Elizabeth brought the file up on the screen and read the information out loud. "Barton, code name Dream Termite. Age twenty-nine, no criminal record, no law enforcement or military experience. Psychic powers which appear to activate only when he is in a state of REM sleep, and which mostly involve lucid dreaming and entering the dreams of others. Initial PAS score is 1.3, well below average for a candidate for the Legion. I figured he'd end up in the Intelligence Section with all the spooks and snoops, if he can pass muster, that is. He's somewhat marginal."

"Red Rhino's visions have him in an active team, though," Olivia said "There must be more to him than meets the eye."

"We'll see, I suppose," Elizabeth said before opening the next file. "Jake

Duchamp. He was already in my sights. Age twenty, no criminal or service record. Dropped out of Yale University at age nineteen when his powers turned up. The son of Daniel Duchamp, code name Sun Knight, one of the better-known Texas Rangers before dying in the line of duty in 1999. Jake applied for the same code name as his father: his family state held the code name rights, so he got it without any problems. Has the same powers – very high physical abilities plus photon-emitting abilities, including Type Three defensive shields. Overall Parahuman Ability Score of 2.8. An obvious up-and-comer, not to mention a very interesting case – there haven't been many Neos with identical powers as their parents."

"A grand total of eleven known cases, as a matter of fact," Olivia said. "In every case, the powers developed after the death of the parent with said powers. The prevalent theory is that the powers are handed down from parent to offspring somehow. The whole thing will definitely merit some study. He's definitely an unusual candidate."

"I'm sure he'll love all the extra attention."

"There's more to it than that. Seven of the eleven known 'legacy' Neos developed severe mental problems over time, including erratic, violent behavior. We're talking about a very small group, of course, so it's hard to tell if there is a pattern. Maybe Jake Duchamp will be fine, but we have to be careful."

"Lovely. I smell a cluster-cluck coming up. Okay, next. Jorel Levenson, code name Dread Beard. Age 25; has a couple of misdemeanor criminal convictions in the US – reckless endangerment, destruction of property. That makes him a borderline candidate at best." Somebody with that kind of record got the basic 'zero tolerance' treatment – one screw-up and you're out. "Powers-wise, he controls sound waves in a variety of ways. Initial tests give him a PAS of 2.5. Some potential, as long as he manages to keep his nose clean." Usually Neos with shady pasts tried to join the Legion for two reasons: to get a second chance and a clean start, or to try to make up for past misdeeds by going into public service. It'd be interesting to find out which of those two categories Mr. Levenson belonged to.

"There's no particular reason to think Levenson is particularly important," Olivia commented.

"I can't think of one. Next: Susannah Martinez, code name Psi-Cat. Age twenty-one, dual Mexican and US citizenship. Born *Susana* Martinez, changed her name's spelling when she moved to the US, probably so people would pronounce it correctly. Served in the Mexican Federal Police's *Fuerza Especial* from ages seventeen to twenty under the code name *La Gata Fantasma*, Ghost Cat. Was dishonorably discharged for 'cowardice in the face of the enemy.' From the looks of it, she refused to take actions that might have harmed innocent civilians. Immigrated to the US and applied to the Legion shortly thereafter."

"The Mexican authorities tend to be fairly callous when it comes to collateral damage," Olivia noted with a trace of bitterness in her voice. "I read the detailed case files before coming over. Ms. Martinez was in the right."

"I'll take your word for it. Let's see – some telepathic abilities, but her main power is the creation of thought forms, psychic projections that can affect the real world. Mostly in the shape of cats of assorted sizes, so I guess she's not a dog person. A 2.6 PAS score. Definitely Legion material here. Nothing particularly weird stands out."

"There is a chance the dishonorable discharge is a cover story and that she's a covert agent working for Mexico's intelligence agencies," Olivia suggested.

"True enough." Mexico, under the fifty-year rule of *El Presidente*, had gotten into more than a few tussles with the Legion, often playing the US off against the Legion and vice versa. This wouldn't be the first time that country tried to bring a spy into Freedom Island. "Okay, I'll launch a deep background check on her, just to be safe."

"Sorry to throw more work your way."

"If I'm not overworked, I worry that I'm missing something. Next on the list we have Aurora McCrary, code name Luna Amirah, age twenty, of mixed Cherokee and white extraction. Attended the Freedom Institute from ages eighteen to twenty. She was recommended for the Legion by her instructors. Genius-level intelligence, Type Two levels in agility and weapon skills, specializing in archery and martial arts. All of her teachers plain loved her and gave her very high marks. She could be sitting in the Legion Council in a couple of decades."

"Good. We could use more new blood there."

"That is a problem with an organization run by immortals," Elizabeth commented wryly. "Promotions are very hard to come by."

"We do try to rotate people in and out, but yes, that is a problem and it's only going to get worse."

"Not my problem, thank you Jesus. Anyway, no problems with Ms. McCrary, she seems like a perfect candidate. That leaves us with the last name on the list. Paul Singleton, code name Biomancer. Age thirty-one; his powers manifested relatively late in life. Grew up in a very dysfunctional family environment but bounced back and became a productive member of society before he gained Neo powers. Has a great deal of control over biological organisms, used mainly for healing, although he has the potential to become quite deadly. His PAS is at least 2.5, quite possibly higher. Nothing stands out with him either."

"Other than being in the same prophetic vision as the other five candidates," Olivia said. "You need to keep them under observation and see how they do."

"Now, does this mean I can't wash them out because they might turn out to play an important role down the line?" Elizabeth asked, feeling some trepidation. She'd been in charge of the candidacy program for almost ten years. It was a job she enjoyed, helping choose and train future Legionnaires, and she didn't want some precog's vision messing things up.

"Visions of the future are notoriously unreliable," Olivia noted. "They represent probable outcomes, not exact predictions. If you have to disqualify any or all of them, do it. The Legion doesn't have room for people who can't do the job. At most, give any reviews a second look, and if it's a tossup, give them a chance to redeem themselves. Major infractions or breaches won't be tolerated, however."

"Fair enough," Elizabeth said, although it really wasn't. If she tossed out any of those six, her actions would be carefully examined by her higher-ups, so she would have to think twice or even three times before doing so. She was going to have to cut those kids more slack than she normally would, just because Red Rhino had dreamed about them. The added complications annoyed her, but she'd do her job one way or another. "They are on the same team, and so far they are doing all right. I'll keep an eye on them."

* * *

Aurora McCrary's drew and loosed three arrows with sinuous perfection, her movements so quick that to a normal human and even your average Neo it seemed as if the arrows magically disappeared from her quiver and hit the target two hundred yards away.

A couple of her fellow candidates had looked dismissively at her choice of weapon. After a few demonstrations, however, everybody had been impressed. The arrows were sunk to their feathers into the distant target, arranged in a perfectly symmetrical triangle. Aurora drew and fired another volley in under a second. The next three arrows made an overlapping triangle, also perfectly spaced, creating a six-pointed star on the center of the target. A couple of the candidates watching her clapped their hands. Aurora ignored the praise just as she had ignored the jokes at her expense.

A group of twelve candidates were undergoing physical tests in a big open-air field. Each candidate was supposed to show off what he could do while the rest of the group watched. Before Aurora got to show off her skill with a bow and arrows, a guy from India had shattered blocks of concrete with his fists, and an Australian girl had performed some serious acrobatic moves and demonstrated her ability to climb walls like a lizard or spider.

Jorel Levenson was next. For a few seconds he stood on the target range, concentrating. A buzzing sound grew around him. He gestured, and the sound changed, became a burst not unlike a gunshot, and a hole appeared in one of the targets. Not bad, Jake thought. Precision and power, and that was just a crude use of Jorel's sonic powers. The guy could generate all kinds of sounds, including music. Dread Beard was a walking one-man orchestra. Jorel proceeded to destroy all the targets he was presented with, and ended the show with a rousing rendition of Beethoven's Ninth Symphony. Not too shabby.

After Jorel was done, Jake stepped up to the notional plate as a new set of targets came on line. Time to show everyone what the new Sun Knight could do. He felt the power coursing through him as he gathered it around himself. The first time his powers had manifested he'd almost blown up half of New Haven; ever since then, he'd summoned his powers slowly and carefully. That probably wouldn't work if he was facing some clear and imminent threat, but for now he was going for safe over sorry.

He started glowing as he called forth his photonic aura. Time to start using up some energy. Jake made a thrusting motion with his right hand and a blast of pure yellow-white light flashed forth and made one of the targets explode. Unlike the comic books, his energy blasts did not leave a colorful trail behind; the energy flash was visible around his hand and at the point of impact, with nothing in between. It didn't look all that impressive unless one knew he had generated an explosion equivalent to a thousand pounds of TNT.

He fired a few more blasts as the energy continued build up inside him. So far so...

Murderer.

His sight wavered, and for a second he found himself somewhere else. An abandoned building. A still-smoldering body lay at his feet.

Murderer. Killer.

"No!"

The shout was accompanied by a bright flare around him. The ground melted beneath his feet, and he felt a brutal wave of heat even through his defensive aura.

"Holy crap!" someone shouted from the stands. Some of the nearer candidates recoiled from the sudden flash of heat. A Burmese girl nearby generated a protective field around Jake, which probably saved several people from a severe sunburn at the very least.

Jake's legs fell wobbly. The power within him ebbed away and finally disappeared altogether. The instructor of the day – the notorious Swift – rushed towards him in the blink of an eye, clearly ready to pound Jake into unconsciousness if the uncontrollable power release continued.

"Are you done, Duchamp?" Swift asked him in a stern voice. Jake nodded weakly. "You are dismissed."

Jake hung his head and walked away. He could have hurt someone. Most Neos with his power level knew instinctively how to control their abilities, but not him. If he showed he couldn't control his powers, he wouldn't just wash out of the program, he'd be in deep trouble.

"Epic fail, Duchamp," one of his fellow candidates said. Jake recognized him; it was the same jerk who had shushed him on his first day. His code name was Diamond Drill, and he enjoyed pushing people around.

Jake didn't say anything back. HIs shame at knowing he was a failure was much worse than anything anybody could say to him.

Liberty Hall, Freedom Island, April 3, 2008

Susannah Martinez looked at his teammates, trying not to let her nervousness show. It was funny that she should be so worried, since she had more experience in this kind of operation than anybody else in the team, but her last time out in the field had not gone well. If things went badly here... She couldn't go back to Mexico; she didn't know where she would go if the Legion rejected her.

No seas idiota. Calmate, she admonished herself. The whole exercise was a simulation using psychic illusions created by Panorama, a powerful Legionnaire with telepathic powers. The simulation felt almost perfectly real, but nobody could get hurt in it, other than their feelings, of course. She just needed to do her job and everything would be all right.

She looked at Aurora – no, Luna Amirah, she was supposed to use code names now – and the tall archer gave her a reassuring smile. Luna was in charge of the team in this exercise. Four guys rounded out the group: Biomancer, Dread Beard, Dream Termite and Sun Knight. Sun Knight worried Susannah the most, and not just because he wasn't in full control of his powers.

Murderer. Foreign memories from the powerful Neo had been seeping through in her mind, memories of Sun Knight killing several people. She wasn't sure if the memories were real or some sort of waking nightmare, however. Her telepathy was erratic at best, so she couldn't swear the visions were accurate. The thought that one of her teammates could be a murderer horrified her, however. Jake was one of the nicest guys she had ever met, and she couldn't reconcile those visions with the person she knew.

Sun Knight looked perfectly calm at the moment. His white and gold costume was perfectly tailored to fit his muscled frame, and his stylized helmet hid most of his face, but he looked calm and ready for action.

"Any changes to the plan, fearless leader?" Dread Beard asked Luna Amirah. He also looked willing and eager. His skull-face half-mask looked intimidating, with fake long mustaches that matched his beard. His grin was open and friendly, in contrast with the cloaked outfit with its skull motifs.

"We have an unknown subject in the building across the street, a male Neo with unknown powers," Luna summarized. "According to the reports, he broke into a local boxing gym, took hostages, and holed in. He hasn't made any demands; he might have a personal issue with one of the hostages in the warehouse, but that hasn't been confirmed. We need to take him down and save all the hostages. Let's go over each team member's role." She nodded towards Biomancer first.

The Healer was in black body armor and a helmet that completely covered his face. He was all business now. "I will hang back and provide support for the strike team. My secondary mission is to keep any injured hostages alive."

"Good. Dream Termite?"

"Since I'm all but useless in a stand-up fight, I will stay with Biomancer and try to pull any hostages out of the line of fire if at all possible." Dream Termite's powers only worked when he was asleep. He'd been undergoing training in meditation methods that would allow him to enter a dream state voluntarily, but he still couldn't pull it off. His full face mask concealed any disappointment he might be feeling.

"Even without your dream abilities, you are still strong enough to lift three hundred pounds. You can carry any injured civilians out of harm's way, and that can be important," Luna said before turning to Susannah. "Psi-Cat?"

She tried to keep her voice steady as she went over her mission. "I will scout the area and report. Once we know where the target is, I will engage him with one of my cats."

"Keep in mind that the hostages' safety is the most important thing."

Susannah nodded. "I know." She briefly thought back to her last mission with the Mexican Federal Police – the safety of innocent civilians hadn't been of much concern then.

"Sun Knight?"

"I will make an entrance as close to the target as possible and engage and subdue him."

"And Dread Beard?"

"I will follow Sun Knight and assist in subduing the target."

"And I," Luna concluded, "will follow Dread Beard and act as a tactical reserve. I will also signal Biomancer and Dream Termite to join us when they are needed. Any questions?"

Nobody said anything. Luna nodded to Susannah.

She mostly preferred to create illusionary cats with her powers, and that's what she called forth. A small kitten appeared in front of her, indistinguishable from a real cat except for the fact that it was made up of semi-transparent reddish-pink energy. The tiny feline meowed and set off towards the building at a fast trot. When it reached the warehouse, the cat crouched behind some discarded cargo pallets and fragmented into a dozen spider-like creatures.

Controlling the much smaller spiders wasn't pleasant; they felt cold and alien to Susannah, unlike the warm furry presence of her cat creatures. Cats were too large for her current purpose, however. The energy spiders crawled along the walls and sneaked into the gym through windows and cracks in its walls. Seeing through their alien multi-faceted eyes was very uncomfortable, but Susannah had trained herself to assimilate the multiple visual inputs. It took her a few seconds to process the information but soon she had a clear picture of what was going on inside the building.

The gym had been a warehouse or factory in an earlier life. The place had a thirty-foot ceiling, and was dominated by a boxing ring. Most of the space around the ring was filled with assorted training equipment: free weights, punching bags and other athletic paraphernalia. Nine men and a woman were huddled the wall closest to the boxing ring. Five of the men were clearly injured; someone had bandaged their wounds, which included several broken and sprained limbs and two head injuries. Pieces of broken gym equipment littered the floor, as if a tornado had run rampant through the building.

The perpetrator stood on the boxing ring, facing the hostages. He was a medium-sized man, bare-chested, with a crew-cut and goatee. His chest was covered with an assortment of tattoos, in both regular and prison varieties, depicting assorted mythological beasts. The tattooed man was screaming at the hostages.

"You still think I'm a loser, Joey?" he yelled at an older, tough looking man in the group; the old guy was among the injured, with an arm in an improvised sling. The solitary female hostage was clinging to him. "You gonna try to kick me out again?"

That didn't sound good. Susannah described the scene to the rest of the team. "I think he's working himself up to do something bad," she concluded.

"Very well," Luna Amirah said decisively. "Psi-Cat, engage him. It's a go, everyone!"

Susannah turned her attention back to her pets. The spiders coalesced into one large creature, a huge lion that took shape near the boxing ring, between the target and the hostages.

"What the..?"

She spoke through the lion: most people found a large predator speaking with a pleasant female voice to be both distracting and disturbing. "You are under arrest for assault with parahuman powers. Surrender peacefully and you won't be harmed."

"Oh, yeah? You and what army, kitty-cat?"

Sun Knight smashed through a wall and charged the assailant. Susannah gathered herself for a leap.

Things happened very fast.

The tattooed man raised his hand. A torrent of silvery energy slammed into Sun Knight with a thunderous explosive impact and sent him crashing back the way he'd come. Susannah's leap carried her lion form into the ring, barely avoiding a second energy blast. She pounced and struck with enough power to shatter concrete or tear through steel, sending the man reeling away. He recovered quickly, however, too quickly. A familiar nightmarish feeling came back, a feeling that things were spiraling out of control. She tried to overpower the man, but he raised his hand and more silver energy rushed forth, blinding her.

There was a burst of pain, and Susannah's senses snapped back to her physical body. The lion thought-form had been destroyed. Her head was pounding with a blinding headache. She could hear the sounds of battle erupting from inside the gym; she had to get back there and help. Fighting through the pain, she sent forth another cat form, a smaller but faster panther. She had to see what was going on.

It was over by the time the panther made it back inside. The tattooed man was down, struck down by Dread Beard's sonic blasts and Sun Knight's solar rays; the hostile Neo was dead.

So were most of the hostages. Biomancer was among them, using his healing powers, but only three figures were still moving. The others, including the old man and the young woman, had been hit. They had been hit by the silver energy that Susannah had dodged. Instead of protecting the hostages, she had drawn the tattooed man's fire in their direction.

"Simulation over," a godlike voice said over their heads.

Susannah blinked. She and the rest of their team were no longer in the gym. They were sitting in a row of comfortable armchairs, wearing the psychic linkage helmets that allowed Panorama to create mental simulations that felt indistinguishable from the real thing. It had felt real. Much too real. Susannah could still smell the blood of the dead victims.

"Nice going, Cat Gurl," someone said mockingly behind her. She turned and saw Ginsu and Diamond Drill standing over her chair. Ginsu (real name Scott Coady) could turn his middle fingers into deadly metallic blades that could cut through almost anything. He had attempted to parlay his abilities into a gig with a Japanese knife manufacturing company, but neither the Ginsu knives nor Ginsu the hero had been very popular. The chastised would-be advertising star had ended up trying to join the Legion while keeping the name in return for some meager endorsement royalties. Susannah had met him a few times; he wasn't a bad guy, but he sometimes followed the lead of some complete idiots.

Diamond Drill was a perfect case in point. Leonardo Jimenez was a Chilean-born force projector whose specialty attack was a thin armor-piercing energy beam. He liked to pick on people he deemed to be unworthy of the Legion. Ginsu thought Leonardo was a friend, so he backed Drill's plays more often than he should.

During the first week of the program, the Chilean Neo had made a pass at Susannah. She had politely turned him down. He'd kept pushing, growing less pleasant after each rejection, until she'd threatened to report him. That had stopped the seduction attempts, but they had been replaced with underhanded attempts to undercut her.

"You got half the hostages killed, *Senorita*," Diamond Drill said. He and Ginsu must have been monitoring the training exercise. "*Muy irresponsable.* But it's not the first time something like that has happened, hasn't it?"

He was talking about the incident in Cancun. She had refused to launch a frontal attack and been relieved from duty; all the hostages had been killed when the frontal attack had been performed by the rest of the Special Force. The nasty reminder of that failure, combined with the shock from the simulation, almost brought her to tears. Diamond Drill kept pushing her, sensing weakness. "I don't think you're cut out for this kind of work, Susie. What do you think, Ginsu?"

Ginsu clearly wasn't enjoying being dragged into the argument. "Dude, we all make mistakes," he said half-heartedly.

"She's supposed to have law-enforcement experience," Drill replied. "There is no excuse for her carelessness."

"It was my fault."

Everybody turned toward Sun Knight, who had stood up from his chair and walked up to them. "I should have contained the target," he went on. "Psi-Cat was standing between the perp and the hostages in case he charged them, and it was my job to keep his attention. He managed to knock me away, which he shouldn't have, and that gave him a clear shot at Psi-Cat and the hostages. It was my fault."

"Sounds to me like your entire assault team was at fault," Drill replied. "Crappy planning and execution."

"If the planning was a problem, it was my fault," Luna Amirath said, joining the argument. She and the rest of the team were there, surrounding Drill and Ginsu. Susannah noticed that Biomancer was quietly recording the conversation on his wrist-comm. "We will go over the after-action report, watch the video of the simulation, and learn from our mistakes. I'm sure your opinion will be valuable to hear, Diamond Drill, but I don't think you need to browbeat a fellow candidate right after the simulation."

Drill still had a contemptuous expression on his face, but he also looked disappointed. Even without looking into his mind, Susannah could tell he had been hoping to provoke a violent reaction, which would have gotten anybody who overreacted in trouble. One of the points of candidacy training was to help Neos learn to control their tempers. People with super-powers just couldn't afford to lose their cool, not when they were an angry thought away from unleashing havoc.

"I'll be sure to write a full report of what I observed," Drill said after an awkward pause. "So long." He walked out.

Ginsu looked around uncertainly. "Sorry, guys," he said. "Drill can be a jerk sometimes."

"He can be a total d..." Biomancer started to say, then caught himself.

"Everyone can be reasoned with," Dreadbeard said. "We shouldn't let him get to us."

Susannah nodded distractedly. She was less worried about Drill than she was about Sun Knight. When he'd claimed it was all his fault, she had caught more stray thoughts from him. More guilt, and a couple of horrifying images of men and women writhing and burning under Sun Knight's energy beams.

If those images were real, her teammate was a murderer.

She didn't know what to do. Nobody liked a rat, and that's what she would be if she reported what she'd seen. But she couldn't let it go.

Liberty Hall, Freedom Island, April 6, 2008

Susannah and Luna – Aurora now, since they were off duty – shared a double suite. Their small living room was pretty crowded with the rest of the team in it. The rest of the team minus Sun Knight. Jake Duchamp was the reason Aurora had called for the meeting. Susannah had explained her psychic flashes about Jake. "I just don't know what I should do."

"It's none of our business. We shouldn't meddle in this," Ben Barton said in a firm tone.

"We just can't do nothing," Jorel Levenson replied. "Listen, I know about making mistakes, okay? About having to live with those mistakes. And if we do nothing, do you really want to have somebody on the team who could be a murderer? Wouldn't you rather know one way or another?"

"What's the protocol for this kind of situation?" Paul Singleton asked in a reasonable tone. "I know that in the US, telepath testimony is inadmissible in court, but it can be used as probably cause for search warrants and the like. I haven't memorized the Legion by-laws yet, but if I remember correctly, they are similar."

"I have memorized them," Aurora said, surprising no one. Her mental capabilities were every bit as amazing as her physical prowess. "Susannah has enough information to go to one of the instructors, or even Ms. Hangman herself. That's what I advised her to do."

"I don't want to just rat him out, though," Susannah said.

"Yeah, that's kind of rough, reporting the guy like that," Jorel agreed. "I think we should try to learn more before going official. An investigation might ruin Jake's chances to join the Legion."

"We should just leave it alone," Ben repeated.

"We're supposed to be a team," Susannah replied. "If we just report Jake without giving him a chance to explain himself, he's never going to trust us. And it's going to be hard for the rest of us to trust each other, knowing that if we are in trouble we'll just do nothing or go report on each other. What do you think about that?"

Everyone fell silent for several moments. "We should go talk to the guy," Jorel said. "And find out one way or another."

Ben sighed. "I don't like this, but if you have to do it, maybe I can help. If Jake agrees."

"I was hoping you'd say that," Susannah said. "Your help would be invaluable here, I think."

"I'm not going to enter his dreams without his consent, though."

"I wasn't going to ask you to do that." Susannah looked at the rest of the group, looking for an answer.

"I guess trying to learn more could be a good idea," Aurora said. "But if he's not willing to cooperate, we must report this."

"I second that motion," Paul added. "Jake's okay, I guess. But remember, he's very powerful. If he goes rogue, it could be dangerous for all of us."

"I think it's worth the chance," Susannah said. Nobody replied, and she chose to take the silence as agreement, or at least acceptance.

* * *

Jake sat down on the couch and looked at his teammates. They all looked concerned, some more than others. Aurora and Jorel seemed a bit more sympathetic than the rest. Susannah looked anxious but determined. The rest just mainly seemed worried. He briefly thought about denying everything. Yeah, that would go over well.

"Okay, I've been having some weird flashbacks and nightmares," he admitted after Susannah told him everything she had found out. "They started when my powers showed up. In the dreams, I killed some people. Maybe a lot of people. The first time I had them, I searched the web, but found nothing that matched the dreams. No burned corpses turned out anywhere near me, at least. There were disappearances, but there's always people going missing. So I don't know. If I did kill the people in my visions, I somehow managed to make the bodies disappear. Except I don't remember ever doing anything like that."

"They could be false memories," Susannah explained. "Or maybe they belong to someone else."

Jake could only think of one person. "It couldn't be my father," he said firmly. "He was a hero. I know some Neos who inherit powers sometimes get their parent's memories as well. But my father never murdered anybody. He was a hero."

"Maybe we can find out one way or another," Jorel said. "Susannah has a plan."

"Dream Termite could help," Susannah said. "If you let him."

"I could try to go into your dreams," Ben said. "I'd rather not get involved, but I guess I can give it a try. And only if you're okay with it."

"The alternative is, you could turn yourself in," Peter added. "It would look better than having us turn you in. But then you would have to agree to subject yourself to a full telepathic scan, and if you refuse, you will be expelled and you'll have a yellow flag in your record as a potentially dangerous Neo. And that's what will happen if an investigation doesn't link you to any murders. If it does... well, you know the routine."

Jake nodded. Just about everywhere in the world, a Neo that was found guilty of murder faced the death penalty after a very fast trial. If significant mitigating circumstances were found, the sentence could be commuted to life in exile in one of the handful of penal colonies set around the world for Neos deemed too dangerous to live among humanity. Those colonies were in small islands far away from civilization. The inmates at those places had their powers constantly suppressed and could be summarily executed if they ever got out of control. Nobody who went there ever came out, unless they managed to somehow break out, and escapees were hunted down without mercy.

The two 'Neo Allocation Centers' the Freedom Legion ran were fairly nice places. One was only a hundred miles from Freedom Island, as a matter of fact. The other was in another island in the Pacific. They both had plenty of amenities and were run more like resorts than prisons. But you still couldn't wake up one morning, decide New York was nice that time of year, and walk out. Jake didn't want to spend his life in one of those places. But if his nightmares were real, that was the most he could hope for.

"Okay," he said. "Let's try to find out what's what."

Susannah nodded to Ben. "I'll do it as soon as you fall asleep," he told Jake.

"Yeah, 'cause that's going to happen anytime soon."

"Not to worry. I know some relaxation techniques, a bit like hypnosis, that will get you there."

"Sounds terrific," Jake said resignedly.

* * *

The nightmare was always the same. It started with the running man and it ended with the burning crowd.

The running man was terrified. He stumbled through a forest of some sort, tripping on fallen branches, running into shadowy trees, being chased relentlessly until he was finally cornered with nowhere to go. The man fell to his knees, pleading, begging, although Jake never actually made out the words. It didn't matter anyway.

The dark forest was briefly illuminated by a photonic blast, and the man was torn apart.

More death always followed. The faces and places changed, but the end was always the same. The last one was the worst. A meeting room, where a dozen men and women sat and talked until something made them turn around in terror. Jake set them all on fire, using just enough photonic energy to ignite everything flammable in the room, making sure their deaths were slow and agonizing. He watched them die, and a part of him felt a surge of joy and pleasure.

He was a monster.

"Wrong," said somebody next to him. Jake turned and saw Dream Termite standing by his side. "Look," Ben continued, pointing to a mirror in the burning room. Jake did and saw himself, in his Sun Knight uniform. He wasn't wearing his helmet, so he could see his features clearly, and he finally understood.

The face in the mirror wasn't his.

He was watching his father commit murder.

Jake screamed.

He woke up with a start, the scream still echoing in his ears. Susannah was sitting next to him. "It's okay, Jake. It's all over."

Jake sat up and held his head in his hands. "It's not over. My father was a murderer, and he's inside my head." He looked at the rest of the team. "I'm in deep doo doo, aren't I?"

Ben looked concerned as he spoke. "There is somebody in there. It's not just memories, there is a separate personality lurking inside Jake's mind."

"Great. I guess I'm off to a Neo Reallocation Center, then."

"We now know what the problem is," Aurora said reassuringly. "That's half the battle right there. I think if we work together we can find a solution."

"It's not your fault you had a messed up father," Paul added without looking up from his wrist-comp. He'd been working on it while Jake was off having nightmares. "I'm running a search on missing person reports at times and places where your father was around. Maybe we can identify the people he killed in your dreams. It might help make some sense out of this."

"I've done some research on inherited Neo powers," Aurora said. "This kind of thing has happened before. Apparently if powers are passed on from a dead parent to a child, memories and personality elements can manifest in the new Neo's mind."

"Nice to know I'm not a complete freak," Jake said. "Or at least, I'm not a unique complete freak."

"We can try to work things out," Susannah said.

"Or we can go to the Legion so they can figure out how to work things out," Paul said.

"That might be the best thing to do," Aurora agreed.

Jake looked around the room. Susannah and Jorel seemed willing to help him try to work things out by himself. Everyone else was somewhat dubious. He thought about it. If he was wrong, if he couldn't control whatever was happening inside him, people could die. He couldn't afford to take the chance.

"I'll turn myself in," he said.

Most of his team mates seemed relieved at his decision.

"I think..." Jorel started to say when the alarms began blaring.

They had heard them in training simulations, but this was the first time the alarms had gone off for real. The sirens were loud and accompanied with flashing lights as every light fixture in their rooms, hallways and external lighting began blinking on and off.

"Oh, crap," Jake said.

"We'll have to deal with this later!" Aurora said, already on the move.

They had all drilled for this. The alarms meant they had to suit up, grab their weapons and equipment, if any, from the lockers located on their dorm floors, and get to the parade ground outside their building, as fast as possible. Everyone rushed off. Jake did as well.

I guess I can turn myself in after this is over, whatever this is, he told himself.

* * *

"We have a situation," Ms. Hangman said to the gathered candidates. "Earlier tonight, a giant creature was reported approaching New York City. The Empire State

Guardians have engaged it, but they cannot contain it. The Legion has been asked to assist by the US government. We have already sent all available Legionnaires except for the mandatory reserve, but it looks like it may not be enough. Accordingly, I'm asking for volunteers from the candidate pool; you guys, in other words. Any volunteers will be granted a brevet Legion membership for the duration of the emergency. I myself will lead one of the teams."

There were fourteen candidates left, divided into three teams. Only two people declined to volunteer, Jake noticed, both low-power Neos who were on the verge of washing out anyway. He couldn't even blame them; they were clearly not ready to participate in a dangerous mission. Of course, he wasn't sure he was ready, either, but he couldn't just hang back, could he?

If you screw up and the ghost inside your head messes things up, people will die, he told himself. *Maybe even your friends*. He looked at his teammates. This was their chance to tell on him and get him off the team.

Nobody said anything. He didn't know whether to feel proud they trusted him enough to go into harm's way with him or terrified that they were all making a terrible mistake.

Don't worry, Jake, Dream Termite said inside his head. *Now that I've established a link with you, if you go crazy I'll just put you in a dream state*.

Well, that was a relief. Jake felt better about volunteering knowing there was a fail-safe of sorts around.

"Thank you," Ms. Hangman said to the volunteers. "Luna Amirath, you will command your team, now designated TFS-35. The rest of you will be with my group, designated TFS-34. Let's move!"

* * *

The Legion's transport shuttles covered the sixteen hundred mile trip from Freedom Island to New York City in a little under twenty minutes. The team spent the flight largely in silence, watching the reports of the action on a central screen. From what they could see, things weren't going well.

The first sightings of the creature – of the freaking giant monster – had occurred at around six in the evening, when a cargo freighter had made an emergency call and gone silent. A Coast Guard ship had been next; it had managed to radio a brief description of the creature before it too went off the air. Both ships, along with another half dozen vessels, were presumed lost with all hands.

Members of the Empire State Guardians had met the creature when it was a few miles away from the city, half an hour after the first report. They had not been able to stop it. Footage from news choppers and police drones showed glimpses of a gigantic mass of tentacles and claws, being blasted ineffectually by Star Eagle and Justice Princess, two of the more powerful Guardians. A shaky shot from one of the news chopper cameras caught Justice Princess, surrounded by the bright blue nimbus of her personal force shield, just as a lashing tentacle as thick as a city bus struck her in mid-air and blotted her out of the sky.

The creature had reached the southern end of Manhattan, where it had proceeded to damage the Statue of Liberty before making its way onto the city itself. The Freedom Legion had arrived just in time to hold it at bay, but not before the monster had severely damaged several buildings. The confirmed death toll was already over a hundred. Even worse, the creature had begun releasing smaller versions of itself that were running rampant on the streets.

Jake and his friends were about to join in the madness.

Their shuttle made a turn over the city below, and Jake saw fires raging unchecked and a gigantic mass of writhing limbs tearing into a building, mere blocks away from the World Trade Center. The monster had to be at least three hundred feet tall. It was an impossible sight: nothing that big had any business existing. It violated just about every law of physics and biology, and yet there it was. As he watched in fascinated horror, something *shoved* the creature away from the building, moving its kilotons of mass for at least a hundred feet. That had to be Ultimate.

The shuttle turned away from the battle as it prepared to land.

"Attention, Team 35!" Artemis voice filled the shuttle's cabin. "You are being deployed to Greenwich Village. Protect civilians and help contain any creatures there, in conjunction with local police."

The shuttle slowed down and started a vertical descent onto the chaos below.

Luna Amirath looked pale under her ninja outfit, but her eyes were set and determined. Everyone else looked tense but ready, even Dream Termite, who Jake thought should have been left behind – his dream abilities would be useless in the current situation. He hadn't backed out, however, and Jake was the last person to tell someone else they shouldn't be there. Besides, the dream psychic could shut Jake down if he lost control of his powers.

Dread Beard played a riff of *Ride of the Valkyries* as the shuttle made its final descent, drawing some chuckles from the team. Then the drop doors fell open and Team 35 leaped into the night. The shuttle rose, the roar of its engines diminishing as it moved away. With it gone, Jake could hear what was going on in the ground.

The night was alive with screams of terror and inhuman roars and growls.

People were running everywhere, some following the instructions of a dozen harried-looking city cops, the rest milling around mindlessly; some actually headed south, right where the monster was. Traffic had become hopelessly snarled; dozens of crashes had made driving away impossible. As the team gathered, something flew over their heads and crashed into the street near them. Several civilians were knocked off their feet, but luckily nobody was struck directly by the flying object.

By the flying Legionnaire, that was, Jake realized as the fallen figure picked itself up from the hole it had carved on the sidewalk. It was Brass Man, his suit of armor dented and battered.

"Are you all right?" Luna Amirath asked Brass Man.

"All systems are nominal," Brass Man replied. "Carry on with your orders, Legionnaire." Without further ado, the man in the powered armor jumped up and away, flying back toward the main action. Jake itched to take flight and follow him, but he had his orders.

"Attention New Yorkers!" Dread Beard used his powers to amplify his voice to loudspeaker levels. "Follow the instructions of the police and calmly walk, don't run, in the direction they indicate. Stay calm and win valuable prizes, like your lives!" Underneath his voice there was another sound, a calming vibration that helped mitigate some of the panic, and people stopped running in all directions and actually did as they were told.

Biomancer and Dream Termite were administering first aid to several injured people. Most victims were suffering from sprains and bruised limbs, but a few unfortunates had broken bones, inflicted when the panicked crowd had trampled them. Luna Amirath was talking to the cops and having Dread Beard convey their instructions. Jake and Psi-Cat moved two bodies off the streets, an older man who'd apparently suffered a heart attack and a young woman who had broken her neck somehow. They placed their bodies out of the way and used two tablecloths from a nearby restaurant to cover them up.

"This is totally useless," Jake grumbled as they finished up. "We should be over there doing something."

"We are helping," Psi-Cat said. "Besides, Artemis said there were other creatures…"

A deafening roar silenced her, silenced even Dread Beard's enhanced voice. The ground beneath their feet shook. Something huge had landed nearby.

"Go, go, go!"

Jake took to the air and rose high enough to spot the creature. It had landed around the corner from where the team was working, right in the middle of a crowd, crushing several people. The creature was as big as an elephant, a shapeless horror of barbed tentacles and multiple fanged mouths. It reached for the people around it.

Jake struck.

He didn't dare use his photon beams, not with so many people around, not when his powers could go out of control. Instead, he flew right at the creature, smashing into it at the speed of a bullet. He crushed the monster and smashed his fists into it, tearing it apart. A few seconds later the creature shimmered briefly and disappeared, leaving nothing behind except the bodies of the three unfortunates it had killed.

There was no time to consider what the disappearance meant. New screams erupted from a block away. Jake flew up and headed towards the sounds.

His teammates were already there. One of the monsters, a smaller version of the one Jake had destroyed, was blown apart by half a dozen explosive arrows. Luna Amirath loosed one more arrow, ducked under the tentacles of a second monster, and slashed its limbs off with her sword. Dread Beard finished off Luna's attacker with a concentrated sonic beam.

Two monsters were down, but half a dozen more had arrived. Psi-Cat had called forth a gigantic saber tooth tiger; the massive feline pounced from one target to the next to keep the creatures distracted. Jake unleashed his photonic blasts when he saw nobody living was between him and the attackers. The intense stream of coherent light obliterated two of them, but the rest scattered in different directions.

There were too many of them.

Only one way to get them all. He started gathering power, glowing like a humanoid star. He would vaporize everything in a five-block radius. That would take care of them.

He was halfway through the process when sanity reasserted itself. What was he thinking? He'd been about to kill everyone in the area, including his teammates!

It hadn't been him. The ghost of his father had triggered that murderous thought.

But he was a hero! The protest was weak. Something had been wrong with the original Sun Knight, and it had affected Jake as well.

While Jake hesitated and did nothing but hover in the air, the creatures had spread out. Three charged the rest of the team, and two fell under a barrage of arrows and sonic beams. The saber tooth pounced on the last one and savaged it until it dissolved away.

A few blocks away, another fight had broken out. Team 34 had been placed there, led by Bronte (Ms. Hangman's code name). Bronte's electrical powers accounted for most of the creatures. But several more came crashing down onto the streets, in the space between the two teams. Clearing the much larger monstrosities took both groups. Jake flew overhead, saw Ginsu riding one of the creatures while slashing it apart with his claws. He finished it off with a carefully-aimed photonic blast. Not too far away, Orange Crusher bludgeoned another monster with a light pole. Jake took that one out as well.

Diamond Drill was using his energy beams with wild abandon, inflicting a lot of damage, but he neglected to watch his back, and the largest creature yet rolled up behind him. Luna Amirah covered fifty yards in a single bound and shoved Drill out of the way of a falling tentacle that would have crushed him like a bug, and Psi-Cat's saber-tooth provided cover for them while they rose to their feet. Diamond Drill looked somewhat chastised as he helped his rescuers put the monster down.

A pair of even bigger creatures landed, smashing huge holes in the sidewalk. They were being thrown or spit out like living cannonballs. Jake wanted to blast them, but there were too many civilians nearby. He flew overhead, looking for a safe angle of attack, while Luna Amirah and Psi-Cat ran to intercept. They weren't going to make it before the monsters reached a group of people. Jake prepared to fire, grimly realizing he would be killing innocents. Somewhere inside his head, his father exulted.

Biomancer made a sweeping gesture with his arms, and the two monsters came apart like exploding water balloons. The leathery skin and flesh that resisted bullets and all but the most powerful energy blasts were liquefied by the will of the healer. "I finally figured out their biology," Biomancer called out through their radio implants. "Their cellular structure is like nothing I've ever seen before, but I can destroy it now. They're..."

"They're dreams," somebody else said, cutting him off: Dream Termite. "All of the creatures are dreams made real! They're kinda like Psi-Cat's constructs, but they aren't a conscious creation. They are nightmares come to life."

Jake distantly heard the exchange while he searched for more creatures. It looked like the sector was clear for the time being, but out in the distance, near Wall Street, he could see flashes of light and pillars of fire and smoke rising into the night. He caught a glimpse of lashing tentacles the length of commuter striking in different directions.

"Bio, Termite," Jake called out on the radio. "Do you think you guys can take out the big monster?"

"I should be able to disperse much of its mass," Biomancer said. "But if it's a thought-form like Termite said, its creator can probably conjure more mass as fast as I can destroy it."

"I think the dreamer is inside the creature," Dream Termite said. "If I can get close enough to him, I could reach out and try to deal with him."

"Or her," Luna said.

"No, it's a guy. I can tell that much from the mental impression. A young guy with some serious issues."

"And a Type Three or maybe even a Type Four in power," Dread Beard said. "I've been monitoring the strike team's radio traffic. They are barely slowing it down. They've poured enough energy into the critter to turn Manhattan into a glowing crater, and it's still alive and kicking."

"I've got an idea," Jake said. He outlined his plan in a few terse sentences.

"We have our orders," Luna Amirath said doubtfully. She looked around for Bronte, but she and her team had moved away to cover more ground. "I'll try reaching her or Artemis." She subvocalized a call for a few moments before giving up. "Too many people are trying to contact her at once. The monster took out two of the shuttles, including one tasked with coordinating radio traffic. There's too much going on."

"We have to try it," Jake said. Luna thought about it for a moment, then nodded. He turned to Biomancer and Dream Termite. "You guys ready?"

They nodded; both had put on a body harness with handles on the back that would allow Jake to carry them in flight.

"We'll keep this sector covered," Psi-Cat said.

"Yeah, we can handle it," Dread Beard said confidently, although Jake knew that their chances to handle another dozen of the creatures at once weren't all that good. He'd better be right about his plan.

He grabbed his two teammates and took off. As he rose above the intervening buildings he got a good look of the battle ahead.

One skyscraper had collapsed completely and several others were burning. Jake could only hope the buildings had been evacuated in time, or the death toll would be in the thousands. More creatures had spread out onto the financial district. The Condor Jet was hovering there, which meant New York's other superheroes were on the job. Jake silently wished them luck as he flew on.

The Legion and the Guardians created a dazzling lightshow as they fought, its beauty belying their destructive power. A figure surrounded by a deep crimson aura of light marked the position of Nebiru. The Iraqi sorcerer fired off a dozen eldritch bolts that vaporized huge chunks of flesh from the monster. From below, laser beams, lightning bolts and thrown chunks of concrete and other improvised missiles struck it. From above, Ultimate plummeted towards the creature at such speeds he left a glowing contrail and sonic shock wave behind. When he hit it, the impact shattered windows all around and made Jake's flight path waver for a second.

Nothing living should have survived that, but as Jake flew closer he saw that the football field-sized crater Ultimate had carved into the creature was already closing. The dream-entity healed damage almost as quickly as it was inflicted.

"Artemis to Sun Knight!" blared Jake's comm implant. "What do you think you are doing? You are not cleared to engage the creature!"

"I have a plan!" Jake replied. "Repeat, I have a plan!" He switched the comm off and kept flying. "I'm the man with the plan, you can call me Dan, and I don't give a damn," he muttered to himself. Either he was getting high on adrenaline or he had finally lost his mind. He wasn't sure which.

Artemis tried to raise him on the radio but he ignored her. He accelerated to his maximum speed – a paltry four hundred miles per hour or so – and charged the monster that had withstood the most powerful beings on Earth, carrying his friends right into the multiple maws of the monster.

Biomancer cut loose just before they hit it. The monster's flesh turned into flowing protoplasm and boiled away, thousands of cubic feet gone in an instant. Jake plunged into the gaping wound, extending his protective field to guard his teammates. They were inside the creature, inside a nightmarish jelly-like mass of ichor that surrounded solid connective tissues the thickness of redwood trees. Jake felt lethal levels of pressure pushing on his defensive field. The creature's flesh was pressing on him and his companions from every direction, generating enough force to crush a main battle tank into a lump the size of a subcompact car. His shield held, at least for the time being. His flight speed slowed to a crawl, however.

"Keep going!" Dream Termite called out. "We're getting there!"

Biomancer unleashed more of his anti-healing force and managed to relieve the pressure around them by vaporizing a huge volume of the creature's spongy insides. Even through Jake's shields, the heat and stench were almost overpowering. They pressed on, but the passage they had carved into the monster closed behind them almost as quickly as it had been torn open. They were inside the monster while the most powerful Neos of the free world pounded on it from the outside. Would the Legion pause their attack because he and his friends were in the line of fire? Jake doubted it, not with a city of millions on the line.

As he slowly flew/swam towards the creature's center, Jake started feeling as if something was scratching him from inside his head, a different kind of pressure that evolved into pain, as if thousands of tiny needles were slowly pressed into his skull. They were getting close to the heart and mind of the monster, and its psyche was a thing of mental fire that burned those who approached it.

His friends were feeling it too. Biomancer grunted and started shaking his head wildly, as if trying to dislodge whatever was hurting him. Dream Termite didn't make a noise, but pressed his hands over his ears. "Too much," he said in a low voice, but kept concentrating.

They were still well over a hundred feet away from the dreaming figure, but Jake could sense his presence with something other than his eyes. He didn't understand what was happening at first, until he remembered the connection between him and Dream Termite. His teammate had made contact with the Dreamer, and Jake had a front row to the spectacle.

The Dreamer Within had grown up poor and hungry in some unidentified country, a country without the things Americans took for granted, things like having enough food to eat, running water, electricity and basic safety. The child who had led a life of privation and casual brutality had grown up into a young man and had secured employment in a tramp freighter, working long hours for little money, teased and brutalized by the older and more experienced crewmen.

That was fine with the man. He was relatively happy until the dreams started. They evolved into nightmares, manifestations of fear and rage. One of his more abusive shipmates disappeared one night, and the other sailors on watch reported hearing inhuman roars mixed with terrified screams the night of his disappearance. More dreams had led to more disappearances, acts of vandalism, terrifying sights and sounds. The more superstitious sailors had started talking about witches. A likely suspect had disappeared one night, the victim not of a nightmare but rough vigilante justice. The Dreamer eventually came to suspect the truth, but he had been too scared to speak out. A new nightmare confronted the would-be vigilantes, and as the ship approached its final destination – New York City – it did so with less than a third of the crew remaining.

The vessel's captain had been reluctant to contact the authorities; not all the cargo in the ship's hold was legal. Things had gone too far, however, and the commander had forced the surviving crewmembers into their quarters at gunpoint, locked them in, and sent out a mayday call. Trapped in his cabin, the Dreamer had been scared. He had gone to sleep dreading what was to come.

He had never woken up. His new nightmare was even now destroying the city he had longed to see.

Jake saw all of this even as the psychic echoes of the dream-made-flesh tore at his mind, protected only by the intervention of Dream Termite, who was desperately trying to wake up the monster's creator.

It wasn't working. The Dreamer wasn't waking up, and they were running out of time.

The part of him that spoke with Daniel Duchamp's voice stirred eagerly. Daniel – Jake's father – had started out as a hero, but in his last years had found himself solving more and more of his problems with the liberal application of Neo powers. Like the old saying went, if you think like a hammer all problems start looking like nails. Daniel's power had corrupted him in the end. The people he had hunted down and killed were not innocents; they might have even deserved death, but Daniel hadn't even bothered to consider alternatives. He had merely burned them down, singly or in groups. In the end, he had even turned against his friends and partners.

Jake realized that Daniel Duchamp had not died at the hand of Neo criminals. He had been put down by his fellow heroes.

Killing had been solved by more killing. And now the ghost of his father urged Jake to kill as well. To kill for the first time. He had felt like a murderer before, but those had been fake memories, the sins of his father being passed on. If he did what he voice in his head wanted, he would be a killer in truth.

The creature shuddered as it was struck again by one of the Legion's powerhouses, Ultimate or Hyperia or maybe the Myrmidon and his endless arsenal of weapons. The Dreamer didn't even notice, letting his subconscious rage and destroy. There was no time.

Jake could do what he had to, and live with the consequences, or do nothing, die and let thousands more die with him. He really had no choice.

He normally directed his photonic blasts with his hands, but he was holding his friends with them. His father had controlled his most powerful attacks with his eyes, however, turning his gaze into an instrument of destruction. Jake gathered as much power as he could. "Make a hole!" he yelled at Biomancer while the energy he called forth built up inside of him, burning him until the agony of the Dreamer's mental attack was eclipsed by it.

Biomancer grunted again and tore a huge tunnel through the creature's flesh, a tunnel aimed at the Dreamer like the barrel of a gun. The opening started closing almost immediately, but Jake only needed a moment or two, and that much he got.

The universe became light that washed all other things away.

* * *

They were losing.

After Sun Knight left with Biomancer and Dream Termite, more monsters had shown up. Luna Amirath had run out of arrows; she fought on with grim determination with her sword and dagger, a whirlwind of motion that slashed tentacles and clawed limbs and dodged attacks like a ghost, but the creatures took a lot of killing, and she was getting tired. Dread Beard's sonic attacks had proven deadly, but a glancing blow from a dying beast had sent him sprawling to the ground. Susannah stood over him while he recovered, shielding them both with a pride of psychic lions that bought them some time while the monsters tore them apart. There were too many of them, and the reduced team just didn't have the damage output to take them down in those numbers.

At least they had managed to save most of the civilians. The police had evacuated the area, risking and in several occasion losing their lives to keep the people of New York safe. Susannah's heart went out to them. Soon she and her friends would join those fallen heroes.

The last of her lion constructs let out a defiant roar a second before it was torn in half and disappeared. Dread Beard, bleeding profusely from a scalp wound, tried to sit up and failed. His eyes weren't focusing right. "What's happening?" he said.

"It's okay," Susannah lied as three of the monsters rushed them. In between the lumbering figures, she saw Luna Amirah surrounded, with no escape in sight. "It's going to be..."

All the monsters vanished abruptly, leaving nothing behind but loud popping sounds as air rushed to fill the space they had left vacant.

"... all right."

Dread Beard shook his head. "Holy crap. Is it over?"

"It's not over," Luna Amirah said as she limped towards them. One of her legs had been slashed open, and she was using one of her sword scabbards as an improvised crutch. Susannah rushed to bandage the wound. "Jake's plan worked, I think. Or someone else's did. The creature is gone. But our jobs aren't over."

"Yes, there's plenty more we need to do," Susannah agreed. "Search and rescue; who knows how many people are trapped under collapsed buildings? Help the police keep order. Assist the wounded. Recover the dead. It's going to take a good long while before this is over."

"This is the kind of thing comic books never bother to write about," Dread Beard complained as he struggled to his feet.

"We may dress up like cartoon characters, but yes, life is not a cartoon," Susannah agreed.

"Yeah. Too damn bad."

Liberty Hall, Freedom Island, April 12, 2008

Elizabeth Hangman glanced at the report one more time. "Well, this is one for the history books," she concluded as she looked at the members of Temporary Freedom Squad 35, all lined up in her office, all looking mildly anxious. "The Board of Inquiry will render its verdict in about a week or so, but I can unofficially tell you that your actions will be deemed appropriate and justified, Mr. Duchamp," she told Sun Knight. No sense keeping the poor kid in suspense, not with all the guilt he was clearly feeling for killing the still-unidentified Type Three who had created the monster.

"There is still the issue about my father's psycho-psyche stuck in my head,"

Duchamp said. He was definitely Legion material, Elizabeth thought, never letting go of any problems until they had by God been solved, one way or another.

"Well, that is under review, and you will probably be undergoing a great deal of counseling, both psychic and mundane. Mr. Barton should be very helpful in that matter.

"I guess I'll be spending a lot of time inside Jake's head," Barton said dryly. "Awesome."

"Hey, it's not like I enjoy having people inside my head," Duchamp grumbled.

"Pipe down, you all," Elizabeth said gruffly. The six candidates – the six Legionnaires, as soon as the formalities were taken care of – quieted down. They all looked tired, which was natural after spending the better part of a week helping New York get back to its notional feet, but also more confident. Their doubts were mostly gone, along with their innocence, unfortunately. What was that phrase Ultimate liked to say? They had seen the elephant. A damn big elephant in this instance. They had been tested, and not found wanting. Red Rhino's vision had been right on the money.

"You are on leave until the final review at the end of the month," she went on. "And if I catch any of you bragging or throwing your weight around, all bets are off, but I think I can let you in on the news: you are all on the fast track for acceptance to the Legion. You still need to go through the full candidacy program, of course, but if you don't screw that up, you're going to get the invitation to join, assuming you still want to."

Elizabeth saw a glimmer of doubt in the eyes of a couple of them, but she was pretty sure they would all accept the offer after giving it some thought. Joining the Legion was not to something to accept lightly, after all.

"Dismissed."

They left quietly, but she was certain that as soon as they were out sight the laughter and hugs and backslapping would start. They deserved that.

Elizabeth smiled and turned back to her computer. She had new profiles to evaluate.

Next year's candidates looked to be another interesting bunch.

Death At A Con

New York, New York, October 7, 2010

Artemis was dead. The Myrmidon stood alone, facing the boundless might of the Doomsday Devil. The fight seemed hopeless.

Drake Mackowski glanced at the cards in his hand one more time. It didn't look good. Losing Artemis had hurt. He didn't want to play his special card this early in the game, but if he didn't the Doomsday Devil card that Josh had just deployed was going to take out Drake's Myrmidon and be three points away from winning the game.

"What's the matter, Drake?" Josh Stefano said triumphantly. "The Devil too much for you?"

"I don't know about that," Drake replied with a grin, setting Hyperia's card on the table. Her impish grin and killer bod were perfectly captured by the glossy photo in the center of the card, surrounded by her impressive stats. With a 3.2 PAS rating, Hyperia was the clear winner over the Doomsday Devil's paltry 2.9, especially when Drake tapped a *Here Comes the Cavalry!* Circumstance Card to increase her power by one extra level.

"Ooh, when did you get a Purple Hyperia?" Marion Lopez asked, sounding impressed as hell; his pudgy cheeks actually flushed with excitement at seeing Hyperia's card. "That's a super-rare card, the special purple costume one with the extra attack!"

"Opened a couple of starter decks couple days ago, and there she was," Drake said modestly before continuing to play. "Okay, I've got enough Energy Points for both attacks, and the both get a plus one for *Here Comes the Cavalry!* That's going to be eight damage points to your Devil, Josh." Josh dejectedly tossed the defeated Doomsday Devil card into the discard pile.

"Man, I didn't think anybody ever got super-rare cards from starter packs, like ever," Marion commented. Drake's pal wasn't very good at playing *Neo: The Gathering* but he made a great one-man peanut gallery.

Drake nodded. It was the first time he'd gotten one of those cards. Rumor was that distributors opened all the card packs they got and grabbed the rare and super-rare cards so they could sell them separately. They then filled the packs with regular crap and resealed them. Those thieving bastards. People accused stores of doing the same thing, but Drake worked at one such store, and in all his years at Whirligig Periodicals he'd never witnessed that kind of stuff. Supposedly the new seals BC-Topps was putting on the card wrappers made it a lot harder to pull off those shenanigans.

"If I didn't know you, I'd think you went on E-Bay and plunked down a couple hundred bucks for that Purple Chick," Josh said sourly. "Freaking pay to win, man, it's gonna ruin the game."

"It's not pay to win. I got lucky. Just opened an ordinary pack and there she was."

"Oh, I know you wouldn't do that. You're too broke to pay to win anything," Josh conceded, poring over his hand. Drake knew what would come next. Josh would launch a number of sacrificial attacks using weak Neos supplemented with Artifact and Circumstance cards to whittle down Hyperia until one of his remaining heavy-duty Neos could take her down. Drake wasn't sure he had the cards to counter Josh; he'd have to hope to get lucky on the next draw. If he could pull his Ultimate card (not a super-rare, but still a damn good card for any Freedom Legion Deck), he might have a chance. Josh was using a Blackguard Deck, and the black-rimmed cards included some very nasty tricks and critters. This was going to be a tough game.

"Guys..." Marion said in a funny voice.

"Keep it down, Mar," Josh cut him off, glancing back and forth between his hand and the cards on the table. "I'm trying to think here." He smiled. "Okay."

Drake winced as Josh set down a Gunsel Gert alongside a Silveryte card. Not enough to take out Hyperia, but Gunsel Gert's special skills and the Silveryte's ability to neutralize Neo powers were a nasty combination. Hyperia would lose her next action and would take double damage this turn. Crap.

"Guys..." Marion repeated.

"Not now, Mar," Drake said as he thought of a counter. Marion was a good guy, but he geeked out too much sometimes. Hmm. Doc Slaughter's Heal Pack Card would counteract the Silveryte, wouldn't it?

"Yes, now, guys!" Marion said almost yelling, something so unlike him Drake finally turned his attention away from the game. He looked up and saw her.

"Holy shit."

It *was* her, walking across the gaming area of the convention floor, making the noisy crowd of gamers and fanboys fall silent with her mere presence. Drake's heart jumped in his chest. He'd known she would be at the convention, but he'd never expected to see her in person like this.

"Holy fucking shit."

Drake glanced at the card on the table and back at the tall figure a mere fifty feet away. The picture on the card hadn't done her justice.

Hyperia was tall, six feet two in her knee-high boots. She was in her silver and red costume, not the purple outfit in the card; the silver and red bodysuit with the long red cape looked a bit like Ultimate's outfit and had led some dickheads in the press to dub her 'Ultimate Girl' back in the day. She had switched her hair color from brunette to blonde as she was wont to do: her hair was pure golden glory, shoulder-length, with the new bangs he'd seen in the latest e-tabloid pictures covering her forehead and hanging above her huge deep blue eyes, pixie nose, pursed lips with just a hint of gloss, the beautiful face Drake had fantasized about all his life...

She was walking through the convention hall. The fans were too intimidated to rush toward her; Neos did that to people, unlike other types of celebrities. You could muster the courage to crowd a movie star or a singer, to the point they needed a horde of bodyguards to stave off fans, but Neos were like tigers or bears, dangerous and scary as well as fascinating and beautiful. Hyperia could casually drive a finger through a human skull; a slap from her would send a human flying a hundred yards to land as a bag of broken bones and dead meat. You only approached someone like that with caution, even when you knew she wouldn't dream of hurting an innocent like that.

"Where are you going?" Josh said. Drake was only vaguely aware of the words, just as he was only vaguely aware of the fact that he was rushing towards Hyperia, his super-rare card in his hand.

A woman in a business suit was walking alongside Hyperia, looking tiny next to the statuesque Neolympian. She moved deftly to cut Drake off. "Sorry, kid, she's not signing autographs right now."

"Oh, I guess I can do one," Hyperia said. Her voice was sweet and lighthearted, making her sound like a teenage girl. She gently took the card from Drake and produced a fancy pen from a pocket in her cape. "Your name, kid?"

"Drake. Drake Mackowski."

"To Drake, for having *cojones*," Hyperia said as she wrote. She handed the card back, and his fingers brushed hers. Her skin felt warm, almost hot.

"Thank you," he heard himself said. He might have been drooling a little.

"Gotta go now," she said.

"Thank you."

He watched her walk away, a big foolish grin on his face.

* * *

"Uh, oh, we'd better get moving," Laura Herschel said.

Alessandra 'Ali' Fiori, a.k.a. Hyperia, nodded. Her business manager was right. Seeing her pause and sign the fanboy's card had encouraged several dozen people at the gaming room to follow suit. If she didn't get going, it was going to get very crowded, very quickly. Trying to cut through the open gaming room had been a mistake, but she'd been trying to avoid a gaggle of press critters waiting for her on the main concourse. She wasn't in the mood to deal with the paparazzi. She didn't want to start an autograph feeding frenzy, either.

If you didn't want the attention why did you arrive in costume? Ali chided herself. The truth was, she'd been in a lousy mood that morning, and she'd thought basking in some public adoration would help lift her spirits. The adoring look in the fanboy's eyes as she handed him the signed card had made her feel better, as a matter of fact. She was constantly on display; she might as well enjoy the perks that went along with the crap.

"Meet you at the hotel room, Laura, okay?"

"Lucky you," Laura grumbled.

Ali smiled apologetically and took flight. There was enough clearance in the large convention hall for her to rise a couple dozen feet off the ground, as long as she was careful not to fly into one of the dozens of colorful banners for assorted gaming companies and comic book publishers hanging from the ceiling. Some of the approaching fans booed when they saw her escape, but most contented themselves with taking pictures or shooting video of her as she hovered over the convention floor. She paused in midair and waved to the crowd.

She used her camera implant to take several shots of the crowd and automatically post the pictures and video in all her social media spots, along with the message 'Hello fans! First Day at #HeroiCon2010!' Just about every person in the crowd below would be personally tagged in the picture, thanks to the new face recognition app one of her genius super-pals (Smith or Slaughter, probably, or maybe Cyber Punkette; she could never keep track of who invented what) had come up with last year. Her Hypernet profile score would go up a few dozen points, which would translate into a couple hundred grand in merch sales over the next twenty-four hours. Not that she needed the money, but it really wasn't about the money. It was about the recognition. Whoever dies with the most fans wins.

She could have just flown out of the convention center and to her hotel room's balcony, but instead she did a few slow-motion aerial acrobatics for the folks below, letting them get a little more footage of her T-and-A. The people at *Maxim* had been clamoring at her for another interview-and-cheesecake feature, and this would only add fuel to the fire. One would think she would have become jaded to the whole fame and fortune bit, but a part of her continued to crave it. A part of her would never be sated.

In 1981, she'd been a nineteen year old wannabe star, alone in L.A. looking for her chance. There'd been headshots and auditions in between waiting tables and working in strip clubs. There'd been dates with producers and production assistants and screenwriters and casting directors, a few one-night stands with some of the above, and dozens of promises that turned out to be pure bullshit. The closest she'd been to the spotlight had been a couple of movies shot on VHS where she'd been strung up by her wrists while a masked man beat her naked back and buttocks with a belt; she'd been paid a whole seventy bucks an hour for those adult-only screen gems, and she'd spent the money long before the bruises had faded.

Four years later she'd crawled back to Newark and her on-and-off boyfriend, a tough guy who worked for the New Jersey Sanitation Department and liked to show her off to his mobbed-up pals. A year after that they'd gotten into an argument, and he'd won it by using his fists; lying on the floor, unable to see out of one eye and bleeding from a nasty cut in her lower lip, she'd felt a surge of power and become the World's Strongest Girl. Things hadn't turned out well for the now permanently ex-boyfriend. He'd chosen not to press charges when he regained consciousness a few days later; by then she'd finally become the star she'd always felt she was destined to be.

Ali hid her reminiscing behind a big fake smile as she kept on waving to her fans.

At first it all had been glamour and glory. She'd registered and gotten tested, only to find out she wasn't just your run-of-the-mill, one in a million Neo, but a Type Three, one in *two hundred million*. Type Three Neos were big news, and she hadn't been shy when the press came knocking on her door. The offers had poured in. One of them had come from a nondescript middle-aged woman in a dour business outfit, representing the Freedom Legion. The offer had been simple: there were things that needed doing in the world, and Ali was one of the few people with the power to do them. The woman's spiel hadn't been particularly stirring, but the words had reminded Ali of how she'd felt lying on the floor with her boyfriend looming over her, fists clenched and a sneer on his face: she'd felt helpless and trapped and afraid. She didn't want to feel that way. She didn't want anybody to feel that way, and she had the power to stop people like her boyfriend and the lying producers and the porn moviemakers – and she knew there were people out there much worse than anybody she'd encountered.

She accepted the offer, went through candidacy training, and endured her baptism of fire in Haiti, facing Papa Doc and his Bogeymen. Since then, her life had consisted of facing super-powered lunatics a handful of times a year, doing public service about one week a month, and being a celebrity the rest of the time. There'd been comic book and movie deals, magazine articles and pictorials, endorsements, interviews. She donated half of her yearly income to assorted charities but she still had made it to the Forbes' One Hundred Wealthiest Women of 2010 list (number eighty-two, to be exact; number thirty-five if she'd kept it all). She was doing good and doing well.

Life was good. Or should be. She didn't feel as happy as she should have been. Maybe she was getting bored.

Maybe she still hadn't bounced back from breaking up with Jason Merrill., which was ridiculous. It had been over ten years.

Maybe I just need to get laid, she told herself. Conventions were always good for that, if for nothing else. She could meet up with a discreet fellow Neo, or give a fanboy the thrill of a lifetime. If things went well, it would help her relax for a few hours. If things went badly, she'd have plenty of drama and troubles to distract her from her sense of dissatisfaction. Win-win, in other words.

Ali flew away and left her adoring fans behind.

* * *

Drake's eyes followed the flying figure until she left the auditorium. The crowd started dispersing, people heading back to their game tables or checking out the vendor booths. Most of the gawkers looked just like him, typical geeks in t-shirts or sweatshirts with colorful geeky designs, guys who could use some time out in the sun and a diet-and-exercise program. Drake was your standard-issue nerd, five eight, clocking at two-thirty, wearing an official XXL Ultimate Tee which probably should have been replaced by an XXXL several pizzas ago.

Two people nearby stood out, however, enough that he noticed them despite still being star-struck.

One was a tall blonde guy with the build of a martial artist or pro athlete, dressed in a casual suit that looked pretty expensive. He had been looking at Hyperia with interest rather than the worshipful awe of most of the people in the crowd. The other one also wore a suit but was far older, like fifty-something, and far less physically imposing; he had greying brown hair and looked like he'd be more at home in a courtroom or Wall Street than at a comic book convention. He had been glaring at Hyperia with a very unfriendly expression. As the crowd dispersed the old guy had walked past him with a leering expression that made Drake want to call security. The old dude had 'super-villain' or at least 'crazy stalker' written all over him.

Drake thought about following the old man, but Josh was waving impatiently at him from the table and, let's face it, he liked comic books but he was no comic book character, and following some old guy just because his face looked funny wasn't heroic, just creepy and stupid. He went back to his game.

"Good going," Josh said; he sounded like he was trying to sound sarcastic but couldn't quite pull it off. "You almost started a stampede there."

"I wasn't thinking," Drake admitted. He put the autographed card on the table and started digging in his backpack for a vacuum-seal holder. That card wasn't going to be exposed to air ever again. "But I got her sig on the card, so I don't care."

"An ultra-rare Hyperia card with her autograph. You could sell it on E-bay and pay off your student loans," Josh said.

"Drake would never sell that card," Marion said. "He's been into Hyperia since forever."

"Well, if my mother needed a kidney, I might think about selling the card to buy her one. But other than that, nope."

"What if I needed a kidney?" Josh asked.

"It would suck to be you." Drake put the card in the holder, and the holder in his backpack, which he now would keep next to him until he could go back to his hotel room. Did the room had a wall safe? He'd have to check.

It had been awesome, talking to Hyperia face to face. Drake figured that was going to be the high point of the convention.

Drake figured wrong.

* * *

"It's good to see you again, Ms. Fiori."

The line was good enough to make her stop despite Laura's exasperated sigh.

This had already been an unusual con. Usually vanilla humans gave her a wide berth, even fans, but it was only Thursday and she'd already been stopped twice by strangers. Or alleged acquaintances in this case. She looked at the tall guy who'd intercepted her as she walked to the big auditorium for the big 'Superhero Q&A' event of the evening. He was in this thirties, blonde and green-eyed, built like a Ninja assassin, and his general posture and demeanor told Ali the guy had been in the military and probably still was, even if his haircut wasn't regulation length, which might mean he was Special Forces or part of the CIA's 'Army of Northern Virginia.'

"Do we know each other?" Ali replied, looking him in the eye. She fired off her implant with the face-recognition system, and did a background check on the guy while they talked.

He was relaxed and confident. "My unit worked with you in Madagascar back in '07."

Madagascar. That brought back memories she'd rather forget. "SEAL Team Five? Or was it Seven?" Ali asked. She'd worked with both teams, if by working you meant flying in to rescue the squids after they had been cornered by a powerful and murderous Neo. SEAL Team Five specialized in fighting Neolympians, but even their special weapons and tactics couldn't handle anybody with a PAS above 2.4, not really, and the Neo involved had been a 2.8 at least. The dickhead had given *her* some trouble.

He nodded without specifying which unit. SEALs tended to be cagey about sharing information. She considered him. He was the right age and build, and he could have been any of the dozen figures in body armor and full battle helmets she'd rescued. The two SEAL units had lost over half their personnel in the brutal firefight, after a simple scouting mission had gone very, very wrong.

"Madagascar was a hot mess," she said. The blonde guy nodded. A Neo gang led by a wannabe warlord with more power than sense had seized control over the island nation following a disputed election. Over a quarter of a million people had died before a joint UN-US operation spearheaded by the Legion had put a stop to it. The SEALs' involvement hadn't made the news, so the guy was probably legit. A few seconds later, her implant confirmed it. His records were sealed, but he'd been in the Navy at the time.

"Go Navy," she told him. "You want an autograph?"

"I want your phone number," he replied with a relaxed smile.

Ali snorted. "Tell you what. Write down your number for me, and if I feel like it, I'll give you a call."

"Works for me," the ex-SEAL said and handed her a printed card. She glanced at the name – Jason Patrick Tudor – and confirmed it was the same name that had popped up during the background check before putting the card in one of the pockets sewn on the inside of her cape, about the only thing the damn things were good for. The last time she'd gone for a Jason hadn't ended well, though, so Mr. Tudor had already a strike going against him.

"We're running late," Laura said to Ali, which wasn't true but was Laura's way of telling her she was wasting too much time interacting with the little people. Not only that, but more and more passing fans were stopping and gawking at her, which meant the hallway was getting crowded. She really shouldn't linger in a public spot for very long. Costumed Neos were people magnets, even if most people would just stare and take pictures rather than try to pick them up.

Ali started walking past Jason. "See ya later. Maybe," she said.

"Looking forward to your call," he called after her, and Ali paused for a couple more moments.

"Just don't hold your breath; it's a fifty-fifty chance, and it's going to be a busy four days. Semper Fi and all that," she added, ignoring his grumbled "I'm not a jarhead" as she walked on.

"Handing out autographs and dates, Ali?" Laura said after they left Mr. Tudor behind. "If word gets out they're going to have to evacuate the hotel. You'll get marriage proposals and have your name scribbled on restroom stalls all over town."

"Okay, okay, I get it," Ali relented as they walked into the auditorium's back entrance. Even with the delay, they were early and the place was empty except for the special guests. Hercules Eight of the Empire State Guardians was already on the stage, his massive physique straining his chair as he gave his lion-head helmet a final going over before plopping it over his head. Hercules wasn't a bad guy; he did his job, never acted like his shit didn't stink, and, unlike a lot of other strongmen, he didn't find Ali threatening despite the fact that her bench press was a couple orders of magnitude greater than his.

Next to him, Shadow Terror was casually reading something on his wrist-comm screen while he waited for the show to start. His shiny black latex costume with his trademark skull and crossbones and red cape was just for show. Ali knew that when the guy went into action he wore a costume that used a much duller and tougher material, and he didn't wear a cape. The man had been in the superhero business for as long as Doc Slaughter; he knew the distinction between show business and parahuman law enforcement. He also rarely did public appearances, spending most of his time running the Texas Rangers' Special Team. Ali wondered how they'd roped him into showing up at HeroiCon.

The three of them made up what Ali considered the legitimate portion of the panel. There were two other panelists, and they were genuine Neos, but that's about all they had in common with the rest.

Captain Combat was on his wrist-comm as well, his face mask pulled up to reveal a handsome sandy-haired man with a nasty glint in his eyes that he took trouble to conceal while in view of the general public. The original Captain Combat had been a minor Type One Neo who'd showed up just as World War Two was winding down. The guy had never accomplished much, and had ended up getting murdered by Hiram Hades a few years later. The name had been appropriated by the current holder, one Tom Enfield, during the early 1990s. Enfield was another Type One Neo much like the original Captain Combat. He also happened to be a comic-book artist who specialized in over-the-top drawings of characters with grossly exaggerated and impossible anatomies (his women consisted mainly of gigantic tits and asses; his guys had utterly out of proportion limbs and torsos). As soon as he'd gotten himself registered, Enfield had proceeded to write and draw comics about his own (wholly fictional) adventures, which somehow became one of the most popular titles of the decade.

Enfield invented such tricks of the trade as producing multiple variant covers for the same comic book issue, so collectors would buy the same book five or six times. By the time the boom-and-bust comic book frenzy was over, Captain Combat had launched his own publishing house (IconiComics), three cartoon shows, and a 1997 movie he wrote, directed and starred in. That flick, *Captain Combat Extreme*, had bombed so badly at the box office that it was hard to find anyone who'd actually watched the damn film. It didn't help that a slew of lawsuits had led to the movie never being distributed on tape, LaserDisk or any other format, although bootleg copies sometimes showed up at conventions. Still, not bad for a 'hero' who hadn't thrown a punch in anger since the seventh grade.

None of which terribly offended Ali's sensibilities except for the fact that the man was also an absolute pig who'd only escaped half a dozen sexual harassment charges by paying off victims and having an army of lawyers that threw money or legal briefs at his problems until they went away. The only reason nobody had beaten the crap out of him is that his army of lawyers was also there to sue and press charges against any Neo that did anything to him. Ali had met him in San Diego a few years back; he'd had the sense not to say anything untoward around her, but his creepiness had bubbled to the surface quickly enough. She'd been dreading sharing space with him when she'd read the con schedule, mainly because she'd have to resist the urge to squish him like a grape.

And last but not least, there was Kestrel.

The Kinky Kestrel, to be exact, not that her real code name was in the convention brochures. The woman bothered Ali in many different ways. She was an illegal, for one: Kestrel had refused to register in the National Parahuman Database, and her identity remained a closely-guarded secret. While non-compliance with the Parahuman Registration Act (signed into law in 1964) was not a crime, a non-registered Neo who used his or her powers in any way could be prosecuted for unlawful use of said powers. Kestrel was a suspect in several assaults, but since the victims had all been hardened criminals and none of them had ever been willing to testify against her, she remained free as a bird. Ali found that offensive: there were rules, and those rules had good reasons to exist. She hated to see anybody breaking them and flaunting the fact.

That was just the tip of the iceberg, however. Kestrel happily pandered to the lustful fantasies of the teenaged (actual or in spirit) males that made up a bit over sixty percent of the convention's attendees. She'd traded her usual latex bodysuit for a dark purple outfit that was made of three or four square inches of material and covered just enough naughty bits to avoid an indecent exposure charge, as long as none of the material shifted by more than a quarter inch in any direction. Other than the barely there outfit, Kestrel was wearing her traditional helmet and high-heeled boots, which should have clashed with the micro-bikini but somehow didn't.

Ali had heard plenty of rumors about the Kinky Kestrel, including stories about the woman's alleged side job as a pro dom in the S&M circuit. There were children at the convention, for God's sake! Although in all fairness the Q&A session was restricted to people over thirteen.

Oh, well. Ali walked up to the table, exchanged pleasantries with Hercules and Shadow Terror, and sat down, pointedly ignoring the other two Neos. Kestrel was at the other end of the table, which was just as well. Unfortunately, Ali was sitting right next to Captain Combat. He'd spread out on his chair while he rambled on the comm, taking up enough room that he'd be invading her personal space if she sat down next to him, but when he saw her coming he shrank back from her, which made him smarter than she'd given him credit for. If he accidentally-on-purpose brushed up against her, she was going to accidentally-on-purpose punt him into the East River.

Shadow Terror was sitting on the other side. He noticed the tension between Ali and Captain Combat. "They'll invite just anybody to these things," he said, loudly enough for the Captain to hear. The comic book creep didn't react to the put-down.

"Tell me about it," Ali replied, sending a pointed look at Kestrel. The near-naked vigilante was talking to Hercules Eight, though, and she missed it. "So what are you doing here? I didn't think you were the convention type."

"I'm not," Shadow Terror said with a rueful grin. "You should hear my agent going on about it. I was going to be in town anyway, however, so I got talked into it."

"Is there anything going on?" Ali was genuinely curious. She'd checked the threat boards before heading for the Big Apple, and the world was fairly quiet at the moment.

"Nothing major, not really." The Texan superhero looked faintly embarrassed, but kept talking. "At least, nobody thinks so, except me. There's been a string of unusual deaths, from San Francisco to New York. Bunch of them in Texas. One of the victims was a colleague of mine from the Rangers."

"Ironik," Ali said. She'd read about the death of the hero a couple of months ago. "I thought nobody had figured out who or what did him in."

"I never cared much for the man, but he'd been a Ranger for two decades, ever since he got thrown out of San Francisco back in '89, and I won't rest until I figure out who did him in. Something burned out his brain. I've been doing some checking, and found a number of similar cases. The victims – all vanillas – went into comas and never came out. Most of them had been filed away as simple brain aneurisms. The trail of unusual deaths – six so far – led me here, so I booked myself into the convention as a cover."

"Interesting. Have you found out anything?"

"Nothing so far, but I just got here. I'm meeting with the NYDP and the Guardians' liaison officer tomorrow morning."

"Best of luck," Ali said, and meant it. Covert Neo killers were bad news for everyone. When their crimes inevitably became public knowledge, they usually stirred a new spate of anti-parahuman rage and paranoia from the usual suspects.

Shadow Terror nodded. "Thank you kindly."

"Let me know if there's anything I can do." Ali doubted Shadow Terror would take her up on the offer. The Freedom Legion only got invited to help during mass disasters nowadays, at least in the US. Only if the local cops and Neo teams, and the Feds and their Neo teams couldn't handle something would they design to involve the upstart international organization. Politics, she thought ruefully.

Oh well, the Shadow Terror's case didn't involve her, she thought, having no clue how wrong she was.

* * *

Drake shut off his wrist-comm screen after he was done reading his just-purchased e-copy of *New Legion #1*. "How did you like it?" Josh asked him; he'd been reading the printed version of the same comic. Drake's hard copy was still in its plastic wrapper, to preserve its collectible value.

"Meh," Drake said. "What about you?"

Josh shrugged. "It was okay, I guess. The art was pretty good. They made lots of changes in the storyline."

"Lots of bullshit," Drake replied. "They're just making shit up to sell comics. Ultimate is not off in outer space searching for Janus, for one. Hyperia is not hooking up with Mesmer, not anymore. They've been broken up for like ten years. And Doc Slaughter hasn't been arrested for murder. It's all bullshit!"

"Take it easy, dude," Josh said, tapping a finger on the comic book. "It says it right here on page one: 'this story is based on characters owned by Freedom Legion, Inc. It does not portray actual events.'"

"I know, but they could at least try to, I don't know, stay within the lines."

"They've got *Legion Tales* for the real stuff, you know that. But they only release four issues a year unless something big happens, because most of the time life in the Legion is boring as shit. You want more real crap, you can read People.net like everyone else."

Drake sighed. He knew all of that, but he'd expected more from the new shiny comic book he'd purchased. At least he hadn't splurged and bought all five variant covers of *New Legion*. There were still suckers out there collecting every version of the first issue of a comic, expecting it would go up in value in a couple of years. Problem was, with a few million people doing the exact same thing, those bagged comics ended up being as worthless as used toilet paper. He didn't know why he kept storing bagged issues of comics he was never going to sell in his apartment/converted garage. Maybe a part of him hoped some Neo Apocalypse would wipe everyone's collection but his. "Freaking waste of money," Drake grumbled.

"Come on, guys," Marion said. He collected comics but didn't read them, so he didn't have a dog in that fight. "We should check out the *City of Heroes* demo."

"Yeah, we might as well," Drake said. He'd really wanted to go to the big Q&A panel, but he hadn't been able to get tickets for it. Too bad. Hyperia was going to be there.

Speak of the devil... Drake spotted a familiar face walking past him. Not Hyperia, but the woman who had been walking by her side earlier that day. She must be her agent or bestie or whatever. She'd been smiling then, but she had a tense, bleak expression on her face now.

A man in a rumpled business suit was walking with her, holding her by the arm, and none too kindly by the looks of it. Drake recognized him as the strange old dude who'd been staring at Hyperia. The way the two were walking didn't look right to him. It was as if the old guy was forcing himself on her.

Drake looked around for any convention personnel. HeroiCon had very strict rules against harassment, and if the old guy was bothering Hyperia's friend, he would get thrown out. All he saw was assorted comic book geeks and cosplayers. He saw the old guy all but drag the woman across the vendor area, and nobody noticed or cared. Somebody needed to do something.

For the second time that day, Drake acted without thinking and started walking after the old dude and the woman.

"Hey! Where're you going?" Josh called after him. Drake ignored his friend and picked up the pace, weaving his way through the convention crowd. He was in no shape to be fast-walking, and he was wheezing and gasping for breath in no time at all, but he managed to keep an eye on the woman and the guy that was strong-arming her.

He had no idea what he would do when he caught up to them.

Drake followed them as they made it to the hotel lobby and the elevators. A bunch of people were waiting for elevators, evenly divided between conventioneers and regular guests. Drake saw the woman looking around, clearly scared. She seemed to be considering doing something, maybe calling for help. The old man leaned close to her and whispered something in her ear. They turned away from the elevators and instead went through a door leading to the stairs.

Drake paused by the door. Should he follow them? Almost nobody used the stairs; the old guy would hear the door opening and would realize someone was following him. Then what? Maybe he should just call the police, except he didn't know what he would say to them. Maybe…

Somebody shouldered him out of the way, almost knocking him off his feet, and went into the staircase. Drake recognized him as well: the blond guy in the nice clothes from that very morning. Drake followed him before the door to the staircase closed.

The blond guy stared at him for a second. "You don't want to be here, buddy," he said.

Drake hesitated. "That old guy," he said. "I think…"

"He's taken Hyperia's assistant hostage," the blond guy cut him off. "He's got a gun. Call the police." As he spoke, he reached behind his back and pulled out a gun of his own. Drake's eyes got wide and his jaw dropped. Shit had just become way real.

Someone screamed up the stairs. The blond guy started rushing up. Drake followed even as he flipped up his wrist-comm cover and started dialing 911.

The blond guy made up one flight of stairs before he froze and dropped. He rolled down the stairs to land at Drake's feet, where he twitched a couple of times, and went still.

Drake looked up at saw the old guy, the woman hanging limply in his arms, just as the 911 operator picked up the call. "What is the nature of your emergency?"

Drake tried to speak. His eyes met the old man's, and time froze in its tracks.

He dimly realized he was falling as everything went dark.

* * *

Captain Combat droned on about his plans for IconiComics. Ali had to suppress a yawn for the third time. A part of her was glad that Tom Enfield was getting the bulk of the questions from the gathered geeks in the auditorium, despite the boredom involved in just sitting there. Unlike Enfield, she dealt with real life, so her answers tended to be disappointing. Even worse, a lot of the questions she got referred to the wholly fictional storylines in her licensed comic books, comic books she didn't even read. Too many fans just didn't get that those stories were fake. Some people just couldn't distinguish between reality and fantasy. Granted, the lines between reality and fantasy had grown rather blurry in the past eighty years or so, but still…

The Shadow Terror's wrist-comm beeped, interrupting Captain Combat in the middle of his spiel. Nodding apologetically at the audience, the Texan superhero checked his e-mail. Ali saw his eyes widen and his face become noticeably paler as he read the message. "The killer is here," he muttered.

"In New York?"

"At the convention," he clarified. "One dead body and two comatose men were found a few minutes ago, right on this hotel. Same symptoms as the other victims. I need to try and find him."

Most people knew the Shadow Terror as a lesser version of Ultimate, or Hyperia, for that matter. He was super-strong, nearly invulnerable to injury, and could fly, although all his powers were several notches lower in the PAS scale. Besides those flashy abilities, however, the Texan hero was also utterly immune to mental powers and had the ability to recognize psychic signatures. "This is the first time I'll be able to examine a recent victim," he continued. "This time he won't get away."

"I'd help you, if I had the right skill set," Ali said. The Shadow Terror probably didn't need more muscle.

"Much obliged for the offer. I'll be in touch," he said as he rose, interrupting Captain Combat a second time. "My apologies, but I have to go. There's been an emergency." He walked out while some of the crowd applauded and cheered him on. If there was something comic book fans understood was Neo heroes having to deal with emergencies. Ali almost followed him out, but like she'd said, she wasn't the right Neo for the job, and the show must go on. She had to remain in the auditorium for another fifteen minutes. Not surprisingly, most of the questions were about the Shadow Terror's emergency.

"Do you know where the Shadow Terror went?"

"I'm not going to comment on an ongoing investigation, sorry," Ali responded to the third fan to ask the same question. She wasn't about to tell people a murder had been committed at that very convention center. That would be a disaster all by itself, with people either trying to flee in panic or rushing to catch a glimpse of real Neo violence. She hoped that the police and the Guardians would handle things discreetly. Ali noticed that Hercules Eight had discreetly checked his wrist-comm. If he wasn't rushing out, that meant other Guardians were on the case, leaving him to continue doing public relations work.

Who the hell was crazy enough to kill people at HeroiCon? There were about three dozen Neos in the guest list alone, and even if half of them were about as useless in a fight as Captain Combat, that still left a lot of firepower available to quash any incidents, not to mention that New York City had one of the highest concentrations of Neos in the planet, right behind Freedom Island and the Dragon Emperor's Court. Somebody was convinced he could get away with it, which made whoever it was either incredibly stupid, incredibly powerful, or both.

The panel finally came to an end. The moderator thanked all the panelists, there was another round of applause, and they were finally free to go. Ali headed for her hotel room to change into civvies, which would afford her a measure of anonymity. She'd have dinner with Laura, and then if she felt like it she might give the SEAL a call and meet him for drinks and whatever.

There was a crowd of lookie lous by the elevators, along with cops keeping people away from the stairs going up, yellow crime scene tape and, as she reached the area, paramedics wheeling a covered body away. Ali spotted Shadow Terror talking to a plainclothes detective, and mentally wished him luck as she took an elevator up to her floor. She should probably skip drinks tonight, just in case she was needed.

She opened the door of her room, saw Laura sitting on her bed, and immediately sensed something was wrong. Her friend's body language looked wrong. So did the expression in her face.

"Hyperia," Laura said, a malicious leer disfiguring her features. "We..."

Ali didn't bother responding. She was in motion by the time the Laura-that-wasn't had said 'Hyperia.' She punched her friend just hard enough to knock out a normal human and sent her rolling off the bed. She had to knock her out fast, if she was dealing with what she thought she was. You couldn't give this kind of Neo a chance to...

Her eyes met Laura's. She could have hit Laura again, a killing blow this time, but she hesitated a moment too long. Her psychic defenses flared up; pain shot up through her head when her mental blocks crumbled under the attack.

Darkness overwhelmed her. The last thing she was aware of was mocking laughter coming from inside her own mind.

* * *

He was in a purple room with the screaming corpse of a woman.

Uh, what? The question flashed briefly through his mind and then was gone and forgotten.

He was in a purple room with the screaming corpse of a woman.

That's how it was. He didn't remember waking up, really didn't remember much of anything. The only things that were clear in his mind were the big purple box filled with purple light and the screaming dead woman in the center of the box. Every once in a while he tried to think, to understand what was going on, but those two facts kept overwhelming him. Purple room. Screaming corpse. He knew the screaming woman was dead just as he knew that somebody had made her scream in agony and despair until she died, and the torment had been so overwhelming her dead soul was screaming even as it slowly dissolved away. All he could do was experience the fact that he was in a purple room with the screaming corpse of a woman. He was in a purple room...

Somebody slapped him across the face.

"What..?"

Another slap, and he realized someone else was in the purple room with him. It was the blond guy in the nice suit, and he was getting ready to slap Drake a third time. That was his name, wasn't it? Drake Mackowski, that's who he was. For some reason, he had forgotten who he was, and everything else other than the fact that he was in a purple...

Slap.

"Hey!" Drake said, rubbing his face. The slaps had hit him pretty hard. They managed to make him think, actually think instead of experiencing things. The dead woman in the room kept screaming, but somehow the terrifying sound became something like background noise instead of the only thing he could hear. Drake didn't think the volume of the screaming had changed, but he could somehow hear other things. The blond guy was talking, for one, and he didn't have to shout for Drake to hear him.

"Have you snapped out of it?" The guy spoke calmly, but he was pretty tense underneath the calm, and that probably meant that if Drake didn't snap out of it there would be plenty more slaps in the near future.

"Snapped out of what?"

"The trance state you were in."

"Is that what it was? The whole thing about being in a purple..?"

Slap. "Don't dwell on it or you're going to fall back into the trance."

"Okay, I won't." Drake forced himself to think about something, anything. The screaming dead woman looked familiar. Think about who she was, he told himself. "That's the woman the old dude was dragging around!" As soon as the thought became complete, Drake's mind felt clearer. He remembered things now: following the old guy to the stairs, and then falling and passing out.

"He killed her," the blond guy said. "And we're next, if we don't figure out a way to escape."

"Where the hell are we?" Drake said.

"Mental construct," the blond guy said, sounding very sure of himself.

"What?"

"Neo psychic creation, a sort of illusion. Our consciousness have been trapped here."

"Shit. You mean the old guy was like Doctor Occulus? Or Mesmer?"

"Something like that, except the old man did something to the woman, changed her somehow, and then he died. I think he's a body jumper."

"Oh, shit, like the Parasite! He has no body, so he has to kill the mind of whoever he wants to possess. Shit, that's what he did to that poor lady!"

"Yeah, that's what I figured happened to her. And probably us."

"Is she really dead? I mean, she's still screaming, but I know... I mean, I think she's dead."

"She's dead," the blond guy said. "She was Hyperia's personal assistant, so I think Hyperia is the ultimate target. The body-jumper is trying to take over Hyerpia's body."

"Jesus! That would be... Wait, Hyperia is a Type Three, they are like immune to mental attacks, aren't they?"

"You do know your Neo facts, don't you?" Blond dude said, in not-really approving tone. "That's true for the most part," he went on. "The tango in question seems to disagree. I'm Jason Tudor, by the way."

"Drake Mackowski. So, uh, how did you escape from that trance stuff?" Even as he spoke, Drake could feel the lure of the purple room trying to drag him back. He managed to resist it, mostly because he was getting tired of being slapped around.

"I've had some training in counter-psi," Jason explained. "I can't get out of here, though. That's why I woke you up. I need your help."

That sounded a bit like Jason would have left Drake to rot in the purple room if he didn't need his help, but Drake decided not to think about that for now. "How can I help?"

"SOP when trapped inside a construct is to find and engage the controlling element," Jason explained. "Visualization can be very effective in this kind of environment."

"Visualization?"

"Once you are aware you're inside a mental construct, you can try to affect its notional reality. It works a bit like lucid dreaming."

"Okay..." Drake said. Jason turned away from him and faced one of the walls in the purple room. After a few seconds, he spun and kicked the wall. The kick sent shock waves through the room, actually rocking Drake almost off his feet, and cracks formed on the point of impact on the wall. A second later, however, the damage repaired itself. Jason concentrated for a few seconds more, and a freaking rocket launcher appeared in his hands. He fired a shot point-blank into the wall, and the explosion knocked them both off their feet, but the wall repaired itself yet again.

"It's been like this ever since I snapped out of the trance," Jason said. "I was hoping maybe the two of us working together might break out."

"I see." Drake did see, finally. For the first time in his misbegotten life, he had a chance to be a hero. He imagined himself with the strength of Ultimate, the speed of Swift, the destructive power of Atomic Annie. He walked up to the wall and punched it. Pain shot through his knuckles, but the wall remained unharmed. Crap.

He tried again. Nothing. Visualization, Jason had said. Okay. He brought memories of comic books, movies, TV shows. He'd wasted thousands of hours on them, on the costumed heroes he had dreamed of becoming one day. The problem was, he could picture them clearly, but he just couldn't see himself inside one of those costumes, doing those things. He was just Drake Mackowski, comic-book nerd, who had been bullied and intimidated all his life, a failure in every sense of the word. He was a failure, and the knowledge he was a failure filled him with impotent rage.

Rage. That was it! Emotions helped Neos transcend their limits. What if it worked the same for him? Drake punched the wall again. It hurt, but he didn't care. He concentrated on remembering all the things that made him angry. The first time he'd had his nose broken, in fourth grade, the pain and humiliation as he felt his blood running down his face and heard the other kids laughing at him. The day a bunch of guys from the Varsity Football team had thrown him into a garbage dumpster for the crime of crossing their path the day after they lost a big game. The time he'd asked the biggest loser-girl in school to go to the prom with him, and she'd laughed in his face.

Drake punched the wall again, and it cracked under the impact. He dimly noticed Jason was hammering at the wall with a variety of weapons, but most of his concentration was on reliving the past. He reminded himself of more angry moments. The rejection letters from assorted colleges. He'd barely made it to a local community college, because his grades had been shitty and his extracurricular activities had sucked. The job interviews that had left him feeling inadequate and pathetic. Six years working at a comic book store and he'd never even made it to assistant manager. He was living in his parents' converted garage and paying them half of what he made at the store for rent. He hadn't gotten laid in almost a decade.

"I've... wasted... MY LIFE!" Drake roared, and he punched the wall with the strength of a hundred thousand angry nerds.

The wall collapsed. Yellow light poured through the opening. "Come on!" Jason said as he made his way through the hole.

Shaking his head, Drake followed.

***

Ouch.

She was in pain. That didn't happen often, not since she had become a Neo.

Even her monthly cramps, once a source of much agony and torment, had disappeared after her ascension to near-godhood. There were still plenty of things that could hurt her, but since most of them were military ordinance or fellow Neos' powers, they didn't figure all that often in her life. She was most definitely hurting at the moment, however.

Ali kept her eyes closed. Someone was likely to be around, and she didn't want whoever it was to know she was awake until she had a chance to assess the situation. Her wrists and ankles were manacled, and her limbs had been pulled into an X shape, stretched painfully apart. She was lying on a table of some sort. And she could sense somebody looking at her.

"Welcome to my world, Hyperia," someone said. A man's voice. She opened her eyes.

The room was a featureless grey box. The only furnishings were the metal table she was chained to, and a smaller table holding a combination of surgical instruments and old-fashioned torture tools. Standing over her was the man who'd spoken to her. She'd never seen the guy before, which was disappointing. Most of her nemeses were dead, but it would have been nice to run into one of the few survivors and add them to the dead list. Instead, she was facing a new threat, with unknown capabilities.

The stranger was a tall, athletic Asian man, likely Chinese, with long unkempt hair, clean-shaven, wearing only a pair of silk trousers. His bright, hateful stare and his nasty leering grin were identical to the expression Ali had seen on Laura's face back at the hotel room. He looked silently at her for several seconds, clearly expecting her to say something, maybe something pathetic and victim-appropriate like 'Where am I?' or 'What is happening to me?' Ali didn't say anything; eventually the creep would start talking. Creeps like him always loved to hear themselves talk.

It only took a few seconds. "Nothing to say? I expected better from the World's Strongest Girl," he said, using the long-forgotten but still despised nickname the dickheads at Buck Comics had used back in the day. That was before she'd gotten an agent and gotten some respect. "You aren't going to ask me what I want? Or what I'm going to do to you?"

Ali ignored him and tugged on the chains binding her. She should have been able to snap any earthly material without any effort, but the chains resisted her efforts. Either her powers were being suppressed or...

"You can't escape me, you little bitch," the man hissed when he saw her struggle. "This is my realm and I make the rules here."

There we go. She'd figured if she let him ramble long enough he would give something away. 'Realm' could mean a few things when dealing with a Neo, but the most likely possibility was a mental construct, an illusion of the mind. She'd been trained against that form of mental attack and had sparred with one of the foremost telepaths on the planet long before she'd started dating him. Her odds weren't great, but she had a chance.

"What do you want? What are you going to do with me? You'll never get away with this, you meanie," Ali said in a deadpan, reading-off-a-checklist tone. "There. Do you feel all manly and validated now?"

"You don't know who I am, do you?"

"You are the dickless wonder who's been killing people from San Francisco to New York."

"I'm the Soul Seeker, back from the dead," he said, and paused, no doubt to give her a chance to gasp in amazement and terror.

The name sounded vaguely familiar, but Ali kept quiet and let the back-from-the-dead Neo continue his rant. He sounded like he needed it.

"Yes, my body was destroyed, but my mind lived on in my network of minds, even after some miserable hepsters stole it from me! It took me a long time to escape, but I'm free now, free to avenge myself. I killed Ironik, and after I've wiped out your mind, I will take over your body and hunt down Mesmer." He leaned over her threateningly. "Where is Mesmer? Tell me!"

Jason Merrill and the new wife and kid were on station in Vietnam, at least until the end of the year, when they were going to be reassigned to Freedom Island. Ali had been dreading that transfer. She didn't say any of that, of course.

The Soul Seeker smiled, and Ali realized by the change in the man's expression that he had heard her thoughts.

"I knew I'd smelled his presence on you," he said. "I would have attacked any Legionnaire, but I'm glad it was you. I'm sure Mesmer will be hurt by your demise."

"Jason could care less," Ali lied while she concentrated.

"You can't hide the truth from me," the psychic said gloatingly. "I'm the Soul Seeker. I am a true Master of the Mental Arts, unlike that charlatan that got me stranded in Limbo."

Ali finally remembered Jason Merrill talking about the Soul Seeker. That had been a while back – she'd been six or seven years old at the time – but Jason had told her the story about the drug dealer who had built a mental gestalt and accidentally triggered the San Francisco Shriek. The scumbag had supposedly died: his mind was allegedly destroyed and his head got blown off by an overeager Fed who'd ended up becoming Jason's first serious girlfriend. That wouldn't be the first time a Neo's death report had turned to be an exaggeration, though.

"I can sense you care about each other a great deal," the Soul Seeker continued. "So what happened to cut your romance short? Let's find out."

Her vision wavered for a second, and next thing she knew Ali wasn't chained to a wall anymore. She was in the apartment they'd shared at Legion Hall, glaring at Jason as he glared back at her.

"Why did you do it?" she said. She was reliving that horrible night back in '98, and the worst part was that she knew what was going to happen but was unable to do anything but say and do the same things she'd done then. "Why did you take Hiram-Fucking-Hades' side against John's? Are you out of your mind?"

Jason looked unrepentant. "I read John's mind, that's why. I did my job, that's why. It almost killed me to get inside Ultimate's brain, but I managed it. I saw what was going on in John's head when he killed Hiram-Fucking-Hades. So yeah, I had to testify against him. He acted out of anger. What he did was wrong, and it doesn't matter that the Legion acquitted him. He told me as much after the hearing was over, and he isn't holding any grudges against me, either. The question, Sandy, is why are you?"

"Because we don't turn on our own," Ali snapped back. Only Jason called her Sandy; it was his special nickname for her. At the moment, she hated the sound of it in her ears. "Because John Clarke is like a father to me. He may be too nice to notice the knife you stuck in his back, but I'm not."

"I told the truth."

"You could have told the truth without making John look like a psycho."

"John lost it that day. Not that I'm blaming him. Hiram Hades always knew how to push his buttons, and turning Linda's niece into a cybernetic killing machine turned out to be the last straw. Hiram would have gotten the death penalty in either the US or Peruvian courts; US probably, since the Peruvians would have handed him over like a hot potato. But John killed a helpless prisoner in cold blood. It was wrong, Sandy."

"I don't care. John's family. You turned your back on family." That really was it, as far as Ali was concerned. John Clarke might have been acquitted at the hearing, but Jason's testimony had been a betrayal. She could never forgive that.

"There's no point in hashing this over," Jason said after a few moments of silent glaring. "I'm going. I got plenty of leave time saved up; I was hoping maybe we could take a vacation together, but maybe we need some time apart."

"We need more than that, Jase."

He didn't say anything, but she could see the hurt in his eyes, could see he knew what was coming. She knew he couldn't read her mind, not without her noticing it. He didn't need telepathy to see what was in her mind, though.

"We're done, Jason." The words hurt her almost as much as they hurt Jason, but she could never be with him after he had gotten on his high horse and denounced the best man – the best person – Ali had known.

"I guess so," he said softly, and left. After that, they had only spoken while on duty, and, after he got reassigned to the Pacific contingent, they hadn't spoken at all. There hadn't been anybody after Jason; nobody that counted anyway, nothing more personal than one-night stands or fun weekends. Sometimes she wondered about her and John, but that just wasn't in the cards, not now and probably not ever. Linda Lamar might be dead, but John was still married to her in his heart, and would likely stay that way for years to come.

She relived the hurt of that day, and it was just as painful as it had been then.

The scene from her past vanished; she was back in chains in the featureless room.

"Nice," the Soul Seeker said. "We have plenty of regrets and broken hearts here. I can't wait to see Mesmer's face when I tell him I killed you, just before I use your body to kill him."

"Good luck with that, asshole," she growled just as she pulled at her chains and snapped them. Broken metal links flew apart with a shriek of overstressed metal.

The Soul Seeker's eyes widened in shock. "How..?" he started to say before her right fist shut him up and sent him spinning into a wall.

"Visualization, dickhead," she answered, kicking him on the side. It had taken her a while to use her imagination to restore her super-strength, but it had finally paid off. She felt bones break under her foot. Ali had to keep pouring it on, kill him before he could react, before he could...

Pink light blinded her; she felt her skin burn. Ali fell to her knees as bands of reddish energy forced her arms behind her, tethered her by her limbs and her neck, immobilizing and inflicting overwhelming pain on her. It took all her willpower not to scream.

"You really, really shouldn't have done that," the Soul Seeker said. His bloody lips and all other injuries were healed away with a wave of his hand. "It's going to cost you."

"By the time I'm done, you will beg me for death."

How trite, she thought, but he picked up her thoughts and made her pay for them.

* * *

"This sucks," Drake said as he and his new bud faced yet another locked door.

They had spent who knew how long traipsing down a bizarre sort of Memory Lane, areas littered with objects from their past. Drake had spotted his garage-apartment, his collection of Freedom Legion Bobbleheads, and his first computer, an ancient IBM back from when a 2-terabyte hard drive was the wonder of the world. Jason had identified his first car, his first hunting rifle, and a bleak landscape from someplace he referred to as The Suck. "That's where I learned to embrace the suck," Jason had said. "Embracing the suck is helping me keep my shit together here."

There was other crap in the seemingly endless succession of rooms they were walking through. Drake spotted pictures of the dead woman and other stuff that was beginning to grow translucent with every passing second. Her memory-things were going away now that she was dead, he realized. *That's what's going to happen to us.*

Every once in a while, they entered a room and found all the doors locked, including the one they had used to enter. It was some sort of trap or security thing, Drake guessed, probably to keep them trapped until the Neo who'd kidnapped them could deal with them. Each time, they had been able to smash through the doors. Well, Drake had. Apparently his imagination was a lot better at conjuring super-powers. His new bud could probably snap his neck like a twig in the real world, but here Drake was a Neo, and Jason wasn't, although he could conjure up plenty of fancy weaponry.

During their wanderings around Memory Lane, Jason had revealed he was ex-military but little else. Drake suspected the guy was Special Forces or something like that, which was funny, because at conventions and similar geek gatherings there were always a couple of clowns wearing Army Surplus clothing who'd happily tell you they'd been Green Berets many years and about a hundred pounds of beer gut ago. The fact that Jason wasn't bragging made him more likely to be legit. He also seemed to know a lot about Neos, but very little about Neo comic books and movies, which he largely dismissed as garbage. To Drake, that meant Jason had studied Neos in a tactical way rather than for entertainment purposes.

"Fuck," Jason said after he tried unsuccessfully to kick the door down. "You're up, Mackowski."

"No problem," he said. After the first couple of times, he didn't need to work himself into a berserker rage. He concentrated and called forth the powers of one of his heroes. This time he used Meteor's flames. His hands were surrounded by fire and he used it to burn through the door. It would have been a lot cooler if he hadn't known he was just dreaming things.

The burned-down door led to yet another chamber; this one looked like a room in a luxury hotel, with expensive-looking carpeting and furniture. It was vaguely familiar to Drake, although it took him several seconds to recognize it. "Hey,

I think this is one of the residential suites in Freedom Hall! At least that's the way they show it in the comics."

"Yep, that's it," Jason confirmed. "I've seen pictures."

"Military briefings?"

"*Good Housekeeping*, actually. What? I was at a doctor's office, and I'd already read every issue of *Soldier of Fortune* in the waiting room. Anyway, this must have come from Hyperia's memories. We're getting closer to her."

"About time," Drake grumbled. Jason had been following some sort of gut feeling as to what direction to follow. It was nice to see that they were on the right track.

There was (surprise, not) another door in the room, one that looked completely out of place in the suite. The door was massive, a thing of metal and rivets that looked like it belonged in a bank vault or a prison cell. It also had a sinister... vibe was probably the best word for it. Just by looking at it, Drake knew whatever was on the other side wasn't good.

"She's there, along with whomever did this to her. To us," Jason said.

"So what you're saying is we're about to go after a Neo super-villain. A guy who created all of this. Who can basically dream up his own reality."

"Mental construct, but yeah, it's close enough to reality. Our only chance is to kill him before he can obliterate us. Inflict enough trauma here, and it will kill him just as it would in the real world."

"I wonder why he hasn't killed us already."

"It takes time to destroy a mind, and he needed to go after Hyperia. From what I've read, it actually takes a great deal of effort to snuff a human mind, a lot more than to kill someone physically. He killed Hyperia's friend so he could possess her body, but didn't have enough time to kill us, that's my guess. He probably figured we'd be trapped in that trance-inducing room until he could come back and deal with us."

"At least that means he can't just wave his hand and make us go 'poof' or 'boom.'"

"True. On the other hand, that means he won't go down easy, either. It's going to take a lot to kill him." Jason concentrated and a big-ass gun appeared in his hands.

"Our chances aren't great, but it's all we can do."

"They sure don't have a positive attitude in whatever secret military organization you work for."

"Oh, I have a positive attitude. This situation positively sucks shit."

"Okay, you have a point." Drake turned to the door. It looked more solid than anything they had encountered so far. No matter what cool powers he could manifest, knocking that door down was going to take time. Time for the super-villain on the other side to prepare a nice reception for them. "This is a job for Fox Ghost," he muttered to himself.

"What was that?" Jason asked.

"Fox Ghost. You know, he can walk through walls and stuff. Goes intangible and invisible. I can take us through the door without busting it open, maybe take the guy by surprise."

"I've read the official files on Hiroshi Tanaka, a.k.a. Fox Ghost. His so-called astral form can go through solid objects, but certain energy fields can affect him in that form. If the enemy has placed countermeasures on the door…"

"We're positively fucked?"

Jason grinned. "Something like that. It's also supposed to hurt like hell when he carries a passenger through solid objects."

"I guess that falls under 'embrace the suck.'"

"Not bad, Mackowski. You're beginning to get it."

"Yeah, I'm getting a clue I never stopped to think about the stuff they don't put in comic books."

"Don't think about it too much. Your ability to live in your own dream world is the only thing allowing you to do the stuff you do."

"Awesome. Being delusional is my pseudo-Neo power," Drake muttered. *Okay, let's think about Fox Ghost.* He'd never been one of Drake's favorite Legionnaires, and the guy mostly did secret-agent stuff that nobody was supposed to know about, so there wasn't a lot of coverage about him. His entry in the *BC Universe Encyclopedia* had covered all his powers, though, and Drake had obsessively memorized every entry in the Encyclopedia, the better to engage in detailed online arguments with other Neo fanboys. He concentrated and tried to translate the power descriptions into something real.

He was positive he was about to embrace some serious suck.

* * *

The torture was bad. The humiliation was worse.

One of the things Ali truly hated about comic books with her name and face in them was all the times she ended up a helpless captive waiting for one of the big tough macho men in the Legion to come and save her. Since BC Comics had the license to her character, they could make up entire storylines about her. In theory, she had a say in what went into the four-color funnybooks, but in practice that meant long sparring sessions between her attorney and agent and their attorneys and creative directors and assorted sexist bastards. Most of the time she ignored the whole thing, but she hated the stories where she was a damsel in distress. She particularly hated them because she had only been held captive once, for about fifteen minutes, during a botched operation involving the Dragon Empire, and she'd broken through her captors pathetic restraints and proceeded to maim and kill them all as soon as she recovered consciousness. Nobody rescued Hyperia. She did the rescuing. She'd once rescued the fucking Patriot, good old Mr. President himself, for God's sake!

Not this time. Ali knew the energy bonds holding her down weren't real, and neither was the agony coursing through every nerve ending in her body, but they felt real enough. They were real enough, in that sooner or later the pain would break her will to live. The Soul Seeker had made her scream. She would die before he made her beg, but her death would satisfy him. Once she was gone, he would be able to take over her body like he had Laura's. Ali would join her dead friend soon if she couldn't break free. She kept trying to, but the Soul Seeker was stronger than her in this dream-world.

"In the real world, there are limits. Eventually the pain receptors shut down, unless you are very skilled in the arts of torment. It takes a real artist to keep the agony going for as long as desired." To add insult to torture, the Soul Seeker loved to talk while he did his thing. "In my realm, there is no such escape, other than the ultimate escape. When you finally break, your spirit will vanish, will dissipate into oblivion. And you will welcome that fate."

He took a break from the pain-inflicting bit, just so she could say something back. Can't have a Socratic Dialogue without a Hippias or Ion or some other Greek moron whose job is to tell Socrates what a wise dickhead he is. Not that Soul Seeker was anything like Socrates or any philosopher. Still, she might as well say something, if only to break up the routine a little bit. It already felt like she'd been tortured for decades.

"I am going to kill you for this, you know," she said, as steadily as she could, which wasn't as steadily as she wanted. "If you had any brains, you'd have killed me already."

"I wish I could, my dear. Unfortunately, Neos take a great deal of killing in the incorporeal dream. Even Ironik, who had a fraction of your power, died slowly; in the end, I could not even get the use of his body. Fortunately, I've learned from my mistakes since then."

Ali was still baffled. How had this little shit managed to overcome her psychic defenses, or Ironik's? She didn't voice her thoughts out loud, but the Soul Seeker heard them anyway.

"I met a teacher, the first time I was able to create a meat puppet," he said. "A very creepy and disturbing little man, to be honest, but very knowledgeable. He taught me a few new tricks, and he promised to teach me more when I'm done getting revenge." His grin widened. "But I think you've had enough respite. We have miles to go before you sleep."

She closed her eyes and tensed up in anticipation of more pain and more screaming. Instead, she heard a surprised grunt from the Soul Seeker. Ali opened her eyes.

Somebody was behind her tormentor and had just stabbed him in the side of the neck, at just the right angle to completely cut through both carotid arteries and his windpipe. The Soul Seeker made a hideous gurgling sound as the attacker pulled the knife out and then struck another killing blow, this one aimed to his right temple. The knife crunched through the thin skull bone there as it was driven into the Neo's brain. The Soul Seeker slumped, and Ali recognized his attacker. The tall ex-SEAL, which explained the knife work, if nothing else. What the hell was he doing there?

Either of the two knife strikes would have been fatal on a normal human, or even on a low-power Neo. They weren't in the physical realm, however, and the Soul Seeker wasn't a typical Neo.

A blinding flash of pink light obscured the two men for a second. When Ali could see again, the SEAL was crumpled against a wall, his clothes and hair on fire. "How the hell did you get here?" the Soul Seeker asked the fallen soldier. "It doesn't matter, I guess. I'll..."

A metallic, riveted fist the size of a medicine ball appeared out of nowhere and hit the Soul Seeker right in the face, with enough force to catapult him into the opposite wall – and through it. A moment later the body attached to the fist resolved into an overweight young man with an intent expression in his face. She vaguely recognized him as the fanboy who'd gotten her autograph earlier that day. The gigantic metal thing that had replaced his right hand was also familiar: it was the signature power of one of the most ridiculous Neos in the biz, the man they called Mega-Fist. Mega-Fist had the most ridiculous, cartoonish power, but she had to admit it could come in handy, pun intended, and Mega-Fist packed a wallop that could knock *her* down.

The fanboy – she'd completely forgotten his name – turned towards her. The gigantic fist disappeared and was replaced by an ordinary hand as the kid reached for the energy bonds holding her. "Are you all right? Here, let me..." When he touched the energy tendrils, there was another flash, albeit a smaller one, and he recoiled. "Shit, those things burn!"

"Among other things," she said, trying to break free. The damn things were still stronger than she was. Which meant...

Twisting bolts of pink energy lashed out at the fanboy and sent him twitching to the ground. The Soul Seeker reentered the room, surrounded by a glowing aura of the same hue. "Is this for real? I'm being attacked by *comic book fans*?"

The fanboy struggled to his knees, protected by the mystical shields of Nebiru, Master of the Secret Arts. "A comic book fan," he said. "And a Marine."

"I'm not a jarhead!" Jason Tudor shouted as he opened fire with a conjured rocket launcher, one of the new barely man-portable models that fired enhanced explosive breaching charges meant to blow up tanks, bunkers, and Neos. Firing one of those things indoors would have been suicidal in the real world, but here, directed by the soldier's imagination, the weapon's back blast didn't fill the room with flames. The missile flew true and the ensuing explosion knocked the Soul Seeker off his feet. The fanboy followed Jason's lead and hammered the Neo with Nebiru's mystical blasts.

The two humans were holding their own, but the Soul Seeker was still in the fight. Ali pushed against her bonds, pitting her will against his. If her two new pals could distract him enough...

The energy tendrils holding her arms behind her back snapped, and she was free again, just as the fanboy's defenses collapsed and the Soul Seeker began roasting the kid alive. The evil prick didn't see her coming until she grabbed his head in both hands and literally ripped it off his shoulders.

"You bitch!" the disembodied head screamed at her. A moment later, his headless body tackled her. She dropped the head while she wrestled with the unattached body. The situation had gone from the ridiculous to the sublimely ridiculous.

"Get the head! Kill it!" she yelled at the fanboy, who was dazedly struggling to his feet. He reached for it, but the Soul Seeker's head floated away and unleashed red energy beams from his eyes that sent him sprawling back onto the floor, screaming in agony. The SEAL conjured another gun, a heavy caliber assault rifle, and sent a stream of bullets after the flying disembodied head. They were hurting the Soul Seeker, but it wasn't enough.

"KILL YOU! KILL YOU ALL!"

The headless body was clumsy but monstrously strong, stronger than Ali. It forced her back until she twisted and flipped it over her shoulder, an old martial arts trick Doc Slaughter had taught her. She broke free from the body and rushed toward the head. She would gouge his eyes out, bash him against the floor until his brains were leaking out of his ears, whatever it took to just *kill* that bastard!

Another flash of light filled the room, and the Soul Seeker's head and body were reunited. "It's all over," he hissed at her. "It's..."

A bearded blond giant wielding a colossal flaming sword came behind the Soul

Seeker and smote him in mid-rant.

The brutal, unexpected blow split the screaming Neo down the middle, from head to crotch. It wasn't a neat bisection; the sword kind of slanted a bit to the left, so the two pieces that collapsed in opposite directions weren't exactly symmetrical. But neither piece even twitched after hitting the floor.

Even better, the bastard was silent. The bastard was dead, had to be dead.

"That was a long time coming, man," the hairy man told the unmoving pieces of the Soul Seeker as they started to dissolve into the ground. The newomer was tall and broad shouldered with an impressive pot belly and the physique of someone who worked with his hands rather than body-sculpted himself at the gym. His long unruly blond hair and beard covered most of his face, and he was wearing a sleeveless denim vest over his otherwise bare torso, wide-bottomed jeans, and open-toed sandals. He smelled of patchouli and marijuana, and if it wasn't for the impressive smiting with the glowing sword, he could have passed for one of those hepsters you still saw in select parts of California, the ones where people were still stuck in the 1960s.

He looked at her, and at the soldier and the fanboy, who were picking themselves off the floor, hurt but alive. "I'm sorry, man," he said. "I wish I could have dealt with him sooner. He was a tricky one, and if you hadn't weakened him, I couldn't have gotten to him."

"No problem," Ali said. "And you are..?"

"Oh, sorry. My name is Melvin Finney, but everyone calls me Mouse."

He grinned, softening his coarse features. "Welcome to Comatown."

* * *

The food wasn't real, but it tasted delicious.

Hyperia (she wanted him to call her Ali, but he hadn't been able to bring himself to do it) had wanted to return to the real world ASAP, but the big hairy hepster had told her that returning their minds to their bodies was going to take some time. "I'm gonna have to restore your connection to the real world," he explained. "I will work on it while you take a load off, okay? We just want to thank you for helping us deal with that fascist asshole."

After some grumbling, Hyperia had relented and Mouse had led them through the maze of memory rooms to Comatown proper, a bizarre and clearly drug-influenced magical mystery tour kind of place, an organic tie-dyed collection of dwellings, sculptures and other works of art, full of music and dancing. The 'town' sprawled under open blue sky and glowing sun that seemed to be a little closer to the ground than in the real world. There were about a dozen inhabitants there, people who had fallen into permanent comas when the Soul Seeker's network was damaged during what became known as the San Francisco Shriek, and people whose bodies had died and somehow managed to make 'the transition' into the mental network they now called their home.

A beautiful hepster babe by the name of Rainbow had answered their questions during the feast, while Mouse went off to do 'prep work' for the trip home. "We thought the Soul Seeker was dead, back in '69," she explained. "We didn't even suspect otherwise for years, decades even. It's hard to keep track of the real world, you see. We get bits and pieces from the minds of the people who make up the network, but unlike the Soul Seeker, we never went prying into their heads. And we hear stuff from the new citizens, you know? But most of the time we're too busy exploring this world here to pay attention to the world outside. We had no idea the Soul Seeker was around, let alone reaching out into the physical world."

"So how did the Soul Seeker escape?"

"He must have been hiding somewhere in the mind network, biding his time. He figured out a way to take over the minds of people connected into the network, and from there jump into other people's heads. By the time we learned of it, he had locked out us of entire sections of the network. Mouse was only able to break through when you weakened his defenses."

Mouse, as it turned out, was a Neo whose powers had manifested when trying a drug created by the Soul Seeker. He had helped Mesmer defeat the Soul Seeker the first time around, and this time he'd taken him out permanently. Well, hopefully, Drake amended. He had felt the Soul Seeker's mind go 'poof' when Mouse had cleaved (Cloven? Cleft? Something like that) him in two with his kickass magic sword. So that probably meant he was wherever you went when you died for keeps.

But when you're dealing with Neos and mental realms, 'for keeps' might turn to be an exaggeration. Also, Hyperia had mentioned the Soul Seeker had learned some of his tricks from an unknown teacher. Nobody at Comatown had any idea who that might be, but he sounded like bad news.

Rainbow did her best, but by the time food was served and people were stuffing their imaginary faces, Drake still had more questions than answers. He enjoyed the food, though. Mouse joined the group just as the meal was done. He didn't look terribly happy.

"You are ready to return to your bodies, but there's been, uh, complications," he said.

"What do you mean?"

"It's you, man," he continued, looking at Drake. "It looks like you suffered a stroke when the Soul Seeker ripped your mind out of your body. Things don't look good."

"I'll have the best Healer in NYC look into it," Hyperia said. "Brain damage is tricky, but I've seen people bounce back from it. I'll do it as soon as we're back."

"That means bumping me up the line, which means some other person probably will die waiting for a Healer to be available." Drake had read about that sort of thing. There just weren't enough Neos with healing powers, even in New York or Freedom Island. "Screw it. I'm staying."

"Are you serious?"

"I was thinking about it even before I knew about the stroke. Here, my fucked-up mind actually counts for something. I'm... I'm a Neo in here. If the Soul Seeker comes back, or his teacher shows up, I can help stop him here. Out in the real world, I'm..." *I'm nothing. I'm a fat loser who works at a comic book store and lives in his parents' garage.* He didn't say the words out loud but some of it must have shown in his face, or maybe Hyperia was picking up his surface thoughts here in Mental World, because her expression got very sad all of a sudden.

"What you are is up to you, you know, here and in the real world," she said, and maybe she even meant it. Drake wasn't sure. A part of him wasn't sure he wouldn't be a loser here, but at least he'd have a better chance.

"It's okay. Just have them turn the machines off. If you can explain to my parents that I'm not really dead, that'd be cool. And you can tell my friend Marion he can have my stuff, even signed Hyperia card. He'll appreciate it."

Mouse had been following the conversation with a frown on his face. "Are you sure, man? I mean, you'd be welcome here, but it's pretty isolated. We've got a whole seventeen people here, eighteen with you."

"That's about fifteen more friends than I've got out there," he said. "I'm sure. I'd rather be here than have to deal with a brain-damaged body, I'm sure of that."

The super-hepster nodded.

Hyperia gave him a parting hug and a kiss on the forehead, which was pretty awesome. "Thanks for helping me, kid. I may have Mesmer check up on you."

"Cool. I always wanted to meet him."

Jason shook his hand. "You kicked some righteous ass, Mackowski. Enjoy dreamland, but watch your six."

"Thanks, dude."

Then they were gone, and Drake started figuring out how to lead his new life.

He probably could alter his mental avatar into something the ladies could appreciate, for one.

O', brave new world.

New York, New York, October 9, 2010

Ali got a text on her wrist-comm when Drake Mackowski was declared dead on Saturday afternoon. She was at a panel ('Sexism in Pop Culture') at the time, and she made a note of it but kept answering questions. The con must go on.

The rest of the weekend had been fairly tame, except for the severe beating of Tom Enfield at the hands of an unknown Neo; rumor had it that shape-shifting crime-fighter Face-Off had been the perpetrator. Ali didn't think Face-Off did conventions, although another rumor had linked the vigilante with the notorious Kestrel, so it was plausible, if you believed the rumors. Enfield could use a good beating, so she didn't care either way. Plenty of bad stuff had happened to good people during the damned convention.

Calling Laura's family with news of her death had been heartbreaking. Her friend had never married, but the Herschels were a big family, and the news had been devastating for many good people. Working with Neos could be dangerous; even business managers were at risk. Knowing that didn't make the foreseeable consequences any easier to bear. Ali had set her emotions aside for the time being; there were precious few shoulders to cry on in her life. She'd had drinks with the Shadow Terror to celebrate the end of the Soul Seeker. He had understood she was in mourning, and had helped her get through it the old fashioned way, by drinking and talking about absent companions. It was a good thing Neos didn't get hung over. The con must go on.

Ali felt bad for Drake Mackowski. He wasn't really dead, but he had pretty much written himself off from the rest of humanity. Telepaths weren't going to make contact with the mind network every day, although she would get Mesmer to visit it every couple of months or so. She and her ex really needed to work things out now that they were going to be stationed on the same side of the world. Maybe talking about his unfinished business regarding the Soul Seeker would be a good ice breaker.

Speaking of unfinished business... Ali fished out Jason Tudor's card from her cape pocket. The SEAL had saved her life, more or less. That didn't mean Ali owed him any sexual favors, but she could buy him dinner and let him try his charms on her. It might be a good time amidst all the crap. Or just more crap, of course. Maybe she should just lose the card. As she walked through the convention floor, smiling at the adoring Neo nerds and the paparazzi and all the other reminders of her glamorous life, she decided she would call Mr. Tudor.

Everyone was entitled to a shot at a happy ending.

New Olympus

What if people with superhuman abilities existed as depicted in pulp magazines, comics and movies? How would the course of history have been changed by these extraordinary individuals? The world of New Olympus explores those questions.

The year is 2013. For almost a century, Neolympians have helped shape world events. Costumed heroes are a common sight in the skies over major cities (as well as war zones and disaster areas). Several heads of state (including the US president) are super-powered men and women. And the world will never be the same.

Neolympians

"The origins of Neolympians remain a baffling mystery. There may be a genetic component in the development of superhuman powers, but even after the Human Genome Project was completed in 1971, the 'Neolympian gene' has continued to elude the greatest minds of the 21st century. There is also no apparent answer as to why these extraordinary men and women started to appear sometime in the early 20th century, growing in numbers with every succeeding generation.

"A more important question, of course, is what the future of the world holds in store for us, with an ever-growing number of seemingly immortal beings with godlike powers who have reshaped the world in their image, for good or ill. Is there room in this brave new world for us mere humans?

"I cannot help but wonder what the world would have been like if Neolympians had existed only in our imaginations, if the words 'normal' and 'inferior' had not become synonymous – if our destiny had been left in the hands of ordinary men and women."

- Art Blood, *Mortals in Olympuis (1992)*

Neolympians (Neos for short), also known as "parahumans" and "neohumans" are men and women gifted with extraordinary powers. They are all stronger, faster and more capable than normal humans, and the most powerful among them can literally move mountains and survive direct hits by nuclear weapons. By 2013, there are over five thousand Neolympians on the planet, and they have left indelible marks on it.

All Neos have a few things in common. The weakest of them are as physically capable as Olympic-level athletes. Their powers seem to develop during their late teens or early adulthood on the average. They don't age, or at least do so very slowly: no Neolympian has aged appreciably in the past century. On the other hand, most of them seem to be "adrenaline addicts," and almost invariably end up engaging in risky behaviors, so their mortality rate is fairly high. Neolympians are never happy leading normal lives and almost all of them seek excitement in some way.

Somewhat more worrying, a significant number of these men and women are sociopaths, lacking a conscience or empathy, and a smaller but still high percentage have severe mental problems. This accounts for the great number of "super-villains" who cause as many problems as their more benign counterparts solve.

So far, no scientific explanation for Neolympian powers has been found. All Neos seem to draw energy for an unknown source, energy which powers all of their abilities, starting with cellular regeneration (all Neos will recover from any non-fatal injuries) and ending with the ability to manipulate and release enough energy to rival nuclear weapons. Whatever this source of energy is, it allows its wielders to routinely defy several physical laws.

Neolympian Power Levels

In an attempt to measure the power of Neolympians, a rough classification level was developed. Power Types made their appearance during World War Two, when a number of comic book publishers started classifying their characters (real or fictitious) in this manner. Type Ones had few or no abilities beyond above average athleticism or smarts; they comprised most of the so-called First Generation

Neolympians and initially were thought to be extraordinary humans rather than superhuman beings. Type Twos clearly had abilities beyond human limits, with powers like flight, inhuman physical attributes, or control over elemental forces like fire or electricity. Type Threes were Neos whose powers bordered on the godlike. Ultimate the Invincible Man and Janus were the first heroes to be classified as Type Threes.

During the post-war years, US scientists developed the Parahuman Ability Score (PAS), scaled to work with the pre-existing 'Type' classification. The PAS is a logarithmic ranking system that ranges from 1.0 to 4.0, with each integer representing roughly ten times as much raw power as the one before (i.e. a 2.0 Neo would in theory be ten times as powerful as a 1.0 one). The PAS system is not very accurate and is often misleading, but is widely accepted as a measure of power. Most Neos try to learn what their PAS number is and they often bandy it about; many exaggerate or outright lie about their power score.

Type One Neolympians are the most numerous, comprising roughly 55% of all known parahumans. Most of them (those with PAS rating of 1.0 to 1.5) have no abilities beyond above-average physical and mental capabilities, the ability to recover from injuries at an accelerated rate, and immunity to the aging process. At the higher end of the spectrum, Type Ones may have some special powers, but their variety and scope are relatively limited. While some Type Ones go for the flamboyant "super" lifestyle, many eschew the code names and gaudy costumes favored by their more powerful counterparts, in no small part because such notoriety can be dangerous for Neos who don't have the sheer power to defend themselves.

Type Two Neos comprise about 44% of the parahuman population and make up the vast majority of the costumed superhero (and supervillain) characters made popular by comic books, television shows and movies. Their powers are incredibly varied, and mere mortals have little chance of stopping or destroying them. Most Type Twos can be killed with military weapons, but only with great difficulty, even with the advanced weapons and armor developed through parahuman-enhanced science.

Type Three Neolympians are the rarest and most feared parahumans. They are men and women with truly godlike powers. During World War II, only five Type Threes made their public appearance. Janus and Ultimate from the US wiped out most of the Axis' Neolympians. The Iron Tsar and Baba Yaga in the Ukraine reshaped the course of the war on the Eastern Front. The Dragon Emperor conquered most of China's interior provinces. Each new Third Generation Neo has either made a huge impact in the world or has died (or more accurately, been killed) relatively quickly. About forty-five Type Three Neos have made public appearances since the end of World War Two. Of those, some two dozen remain alive.

Neolympian Inventions

A large number of Neolympians are "geniuses" capable of incredible mental feats, including the invention and production of amazing devices. Some Neo creations are real technological breakthroughs, the product of their inhuman intelligence levels. Their discoveries may also be the result of some form of extra-sensory perception that allows them to "guess" correct hypothesis and paths of research and experimentation. Many other inventions are simple extensions of their powers, no more technological than the ability to fly or to throw fireballs. Actual technological creations are known as Gadgets, while power-based devices are called Artifacts. Artifacts cannot be mass-produced; each of them is a hand-made creation. A handful of Neos (the Iron Tsar among them) have shown the ability to create large numbers of Artifacts, but they are a dramatic exception to the rule.

Code Names and Costumes

When the first extraordinary criminals and vigilantes started appearing in the 1920s, the criminal underworld came up with colorful nicknames for them, much like they did for any notorious members of their community. The press adopted those names, and public interest in them grew. In 1930, *The Lurker* magazine started featuring stories about the masked crime-fighter of the same name. Even early Neos who didn't conceal their identity (like Kenneth "Doc" Slaughter) ended up being given those nicknames.

The practice of matching colorful names and titles with even gaudier uniforms and costumes was started by Nazi Germany's Teutonic Knights. The combination of superhuman powers and iconic identities captured the imagination of the world; within a matter of months, the first costumed hero made his appearance in the US, and within a year, the first comic book about him came out. By the 1940s, the tradition of dressing up and adopting an evocative code name had become ingrained among the Neo community and that of their followers. Tradition became a business almost immediately, and famous Neolympians quickly discovered that their name and likeness were marketable commodities.

In the US, Neo code names are trademarks managed by the Parahuman Code Name Registry. Any Neo who registers into the National Parahuman Database can apply for a code name, and once the application is accepted, has the right to license that code name for assorted commercial purposes (and to sue anybody making unlawful use of it).

With thousands of costumed Neos running around, most of the good names have already been taken. The PCNR allows people who want to adopt mythological names to use a number to distinguish themselves from other similarly-named characters. The code name Hercules is a typical case: in the US there are twelve heroes with that name, Hercules One through Hercules Twelve, with the number assigned based on their first reported appearance.

A Brief History of Earth Alpha

The world of New Olympus is an alternate Earth where history started diverging from our own during the early years of the 20th century. Outlined below are some of the most notable historical changes in the timeline.

The Post-War Era: The First

Generation

World War I went on as scheduled, and remained the same horror-filled event that reshaped the world. A handful of extraordinary individuals were reborn in the blood-filled trenches of France and the battlefields in the East, but their contribution did not change history, not until years later.

During the 1920s, the first "mystery men" appeared, men and women with unique abilities and powers. For the most part, these early Neolympians did not play much of a role in historical events. Neos became involved in the rise of organized crime in the US following Prohibition, both as ringleaders and crime-fighters, but the press by and large discounted the stories of people with extraordinary abilities. The truth was too hard to accept, and the evidence of their existence remained ambiguous at best.

Technology and Daily Life

For the most part, the 1920s were indistinguishable from our timeline. Neos had an interesting effect in the world of genre fiction, however. As tales of mystery men performing heroic deeds became more common, magazines and later on radio programs started chronicling their deeds.

Authors Robert E. Howard and H.P. Lovecraft wrote the earliest accounts of Neolympian adventures. Howard's *The Shadow Terror* (1928) detailed the early deeds of the Texan crime-fighter of the same name; it was later revealed the Shadow Terror was a personal friend of Howard's and had provided the writer with detailed first person accounts of his actions. H.P. Lovecraft's *Rise of the New Gods* (1929) was a compelling tale wherein the world was destroyed by the actions of a handful of people with godlike powers, powers that were granted by dark and monstrous entities from beyond our reality.

Lovecraft and Howard's friendship was destroyed by their disagreement on the role of Neolympians in the world. To his dying day in 1947, Lovecraft insisted Neolympians constituted a mortal threat to human civilization. Howard was a staunch Neo supporter and went on to become one the most popular American novelists of the 20th century, writing over a hundred novels before his death in 1963.

The 1930s: Neolympians Go Public

As the Great Depression shook the world, Neolympians started making their presence known. Stories about the deeds of masked vigilantes began to appear in reputable newspapers. Pulp magazines and radio shows featuring real or fictional mystery men became hugely popular. In 1933, genius adventurer and crime-fighter Doc Slaughter ended up on the cover of both *Time Magazine* and *Weird Tales*. The lines between reality and fantasy began to blur.

Stories about strange individuals and incredible feats spread around the world. A flying man surrounded by flames was sighted over London in 1935. An invisible thief wreaked havoc in Paris throughout the decade. Every month or so, some impossible event happened in front of too many witnesses to be dismissed.

A number of national governments started taking a serious look at the growing list of unusual occurrences. In 1933, an informal group led by former US Attorney William ("Wild Bill") Donovan started reaching out to some of the better known mystery men, especially those based in New York City, which seemed to have a particularly high concentration of extraordinary individuals: those efforts led to the creation of the Freedom Legion a few years later. Other countries were far more proactive in their efforts: Nazi Germany was particularly successful in locating and recruiting Neos into its service.

In 1936, Adolph Hitler introduced the Teutonic Knights to the world during the Berlin Olympic Games. He called them the Aesir, in reference to mythical Norse and Germanic gods, but the Western press used the term "New Olympians" (eventually compressed to "Neolympians" or "Neos") instead. The scientific community coined the terms "parahuman" and "neohuman" but they never became as popular or widespread.

During the opening ceremonies of the Olympics, eleven men and one woman with superhuman abilities were paraded in front of the world, clad in colorful costumes. Newsreels showed impossible footage of a flying man, a woman who could create monsters with her mind, people lifting impossible weights or bending solid steel bars with their bare hands. Later that year, Italian dictator Benito Mussolini unveiled his own super-powered Praetorian Guards.

Even as the world struggled between disbelief and acceptance of the events of the Olympics, the course of history started to diverge noticeably from our own.

In the Ukraine, the Man in the Iron Mask led a rebellion against the forced farm collectivization being imposed by the Soviet government. The rebellion started with the murders of hundreds of government officials and led to pitched battles between Communist forces and partisans armed with energy weapons and other impossible devices. By 1939, whole swatches of the country were ungovernable. Ironically, the rebellion actually ameliorated (although it didn't completely prevent) the mass starvation of millions that occurred in our timeline during that time. The Ukrainian rebellion continued into World War Two and would play a crucial role in the wider conflict.

Nazi and Fascist Neolympians also played a major role in the Spanish Civil War. Hitler sent several of his Teutonic Knights and Mussolini dispatched the entire Praetorian Guard in support of the Nationalist side in Spain. The super-soldiers quickly showed their value on the battlefield, helping rout entire armies and ending the war a year later with the Burning of Barcelona (causing over 10,000 deaths) in 1937.

Technology and Daily Life

Neo geniuses like Daedalus Smith, Doc Slaughter and *Geistesblitz* (roughly translated as "mind-flash," the nickname of the Third Reich's famed genius) started filing hundreds of new patents during the 1930s. Many of these inventions were nothing but extensions of Neo powers and were thus impossible to mass produce or even replicate, but many others led to breakthroughs years or decades ahead of their time. Jet engines, for example, were developed and refined early in the decade, and the first military jet fighters saw action during the Spanish Civil War. Antibiotics entered the mass market in 1932, when Doc Slaughter developed a process to purify and mass produce the newly-discovered penicillin. The first solid-state transistors were built in 1936, over a decade ahead their time, and were being used by some devices by the time World War Two started.

Nazi Germany's expansive weapons development program was an early adopter and beneficiary of these technological breakthroughs. By 1939, the Wehrmacht's Panzer III was about as advanced as the best version of the Panzer IV of our timeline, with sloped armor and a 75mm gun that was the terror of the battlefield. The venerable Mauser rifle was in the process of being replaced by a "storm rifle" capable of automatic fire (the term "storm rifle" continues to be used as an equivalent or substitute of "assault rifle") and mobile mortar and artillery vehicles were used in the Poland invasion. The Luftwaffe had deployed radar systems ahead of the British and Americans. The effects of these developments would impact the coming conflict.

Popular culture was deeply influenced by Neos. In the US, they adopted colorful nicknames and costumes: pulp magazines, comic books, radio shows and movie serials lovingly followed their adventures, gleefully mixing fact and fiction. Buck Comics (which eventually became BC Comics) became the leading chronicler of Neolympian heroes, beginning with *Action Tales* (1938), a four-color comic book detailing the exploits of Ultimate the Invincible Man. *Action Tales* quickly became a best-seller, sparking the Golden Age of Comics.

The 1940s: Neos At War

The decade was dominated by the most destructive war in history and the widespread influence (some would say dominance) of Neos in world affairs. By 1950, two countries were ruled by Neolympians, and a Neo independent organization held a vote in the United Nations Security Council. Nazism and Fascism were dead, Communism was dying, and the world was a very different place.

The Opening Moves (1939-1941)

By 1939, the world had changed radically. In addition to the Teutonic Knights and the Praetorian Guard, several countries sponsored teams of Neolympians: the Freedom Legion in the US (informally; the group would be officially named in 1940), the Kami Warriors in Japan, and the Heroes of the Revolution in the Soviet Union. Parahuman geniuses like Daedalus Smith, Doc Slaughter and the Mind developed new weapons. When Nazi Germany invaded Poland in 1939, it did so with advanced tanks and aircraft; the attack was spearheaded by the Teutonic Knights.

Germany conquered Poland in less than a month; unlike our timeline, the Soviet Union played no part in the invasion, being too busy with events in the Ukraine. The Nazis absorbed Poland in its entirety. In 1940, German armies conquered Denmark, Norway, Belgium and the Netherlands. Blitzkriegs led by the Teutonic Knights overwhelmed the Allies, leading to the fall of France later that same year. The only bright point of the campaign was the evacuation of Allied troops at Dunkirk, made possible by a group of British and American volunteer Neos who fought the Teutonic Knights and the Luftwaffe to a standstill for several days.

The Battle of Britain saw the deployment of jet aircraft on both sides (albeit in small numbers), and the use of radar, mid-air refueling, air-to-air missiles and other advanced technologies. German heavy bombers and the Teutonic Knight known as Donner inflicted a great deal of damage during the London Blitz, leading to some 120,000 civilian deaths (three the number of dead in our timeline) and the devastation of the country's infrastructure. The brutal air campaign ended indecisively, however, and the Nazis abandoned plans to invade Great Britain and turned their attention east, toward the Soviet Union.

In the Mediterranean, Italy launched an ill-advised attack on the British that was repulsed and also led to the deaths of most of the Praetorian Guards. The collapse of the Italian campaign showed that Type One and Two Neos could be killed by mere humans, especially if they could be caught in the open and targeted by heavy weapons. When the Germans sent forces (including several Teutonic Knights) to rescue the Italians, they applied the lessons the Praetorian Guard had learned the hard way, and were far more successful.

The Far East remained dominated by Japan, which continued its campaign of conquest in China. The Soviets were beset by another Neo-led rebellion, this time in the Mongolian Soviet Republic, in 1940. The leader of the rebellion, known only as the Dragon Khan (later to become the Dragon Emperor), single-handedly destroyed several Soviet Army units, secured the loyalty of the native Mongolians, and proceeded to launch raids against China early in 1941. The Mongolian army was small and ill-equipped, but it was led by dozens of Type Two Neos which the Dragon Khan allegedly could create by gifting promising warriors with superhuman abilities.

While the Axis ran rampant in Europe, Asia and Africa, the US remained neutral, at least in theory if not in practice. President Roosevelt was openly sympathetic to the Allied cause, and did his best to help through programs such as Lend-Lease. The Freedom Legion was founded in New York on April 15th, 1940 (leading to the celebration of Legion Day on that day of the month, which unhappily coincides with tax day in the US). Its founding members included notorious adventurer Doc Slaughter, inventor and industrialist Daedalus Smith, Ultimate the Invincible Man, media darling Lady Libertas, and the Texan hero Shadow Terror.

The Legion had strong ties to the US government through a special agency led by Wild Bill Donovan, but unlike the Teutonic Knights or the Heroes of the Revolution, it remained a private organization, in no small part because that status allowed its members to render assistance to the Allies without directly involving the US. Several Legion members volunteered to help the United Kingdom, where they participated in the Dunkirk evacuation and the Battle of Britain. The most powerful Legionnaires remained in the US for the time being, however, dealing with local spy rings and saboteurs, including a group of Teutonic Knights that secretly deployed to the US in the aftermath of Pearl Harbor.

Tipping the Balance: 1941-1943

"They can't even suppress the Ukrainians! We only have to kick in the door and the whole rotten structure will come crashing down."
- Adolph Hitler

On June 1st, 1941, Germany launched Operation Barbarossa, the invasion of the Soviet Union. The multi-pronged attack caught the Soviets completely by surprise, leading to numerous defeats and the loss of millions of troops, killed, wounded or captured. The attacks were particularly effective in the Ukraine, where Soviet troops were spread out and engaged in anti-partisan operations, which made them easy prey for the Wehrmacht. Most Ukrainian resistance forces initially stood aside and did not engage the Germans; a few joined forces with the invaders against the hated Soviets. The Nazis' brutal behavior would soon change that.

By December 1941, the Germans reached the outskirts of Moscow before winter stalled the offensive. The drive to Moscow also featured one of the most spectacular duels between two high-powered Neolympians. The Teutonic Knight Donner battled the Hero of the Revolution General Winter (both Neos had an estimated Parahuman Ability Score of 2.7 or 2.8). The fight took place over the city of Vyazma in October: over 20,000 soldiers on both sides and about as many civilians were killed as the thunderbolt-hurling Donner and the ice-controlling General Winter unleashed their powers on each other and any unfortunates nearby. Donner killed the Soviet Neolympian but was severely injured and nearly killed himself when a Soviet armor division and other Heroes of the Revolution launched a counterattack. A couple of months after that battle, the drive to Moscow came to an end, as nature's own "General Winter" made further advances impossible.

As the invasion of Russia reached a standstill, Japan launched a surprise attack of its own. The attack on Pearl Harbor, spearheaded by the Kami Warriors, inflicted devastating losses on the US Pacific Fleet. The Japanese Neos rampaged unopposed throughout Hawaii, killing US Admiral Husband E. Kimmel and thousands of soldiers and civilians. The final death toll in the attack was close to ten thousand dead, much higher than in our timeline. Hitler declared war on the US shortly after Pearl Harbor, bringing the country into the European war. At the same time, Japan mounted assaults on numerous European colonies across Asia.

The day after Pearl Harbor, a soft-spoken African-American man teleported into the Freedom Legion headquarters on the Empire State Building and volunteered to join under the code name Janus. A few days later, the most powerful Neo in the US Army, the Patriot, also joined up. The relationship between the Legion and the US remained informal and undefined, much to the consternation of many military and government officials. Generals found it hard to work with beings of incredible power who would obey orders only if they agreed with them. President Roosevelt received numerous demands to put all Neos in the US under military discipline. He demurred, possibly because he was worried trying to do so would be counterproductive, or perhaps because the president had fallen under the influence of Doc Slaughter, who had become a personal friend and advisor earlier on.

While the US geared for war, the Japanese and Germans remained on the offensive. Japan won a string of victories throughout the first half of 1942. Only in China, where clashes with the Dragon Emperor continued, did Japan suffer any reverses. The tide turned later that year, however.

The Freedom Legion concentrated most of its efforts on the war against Germany. Only one Legionnaire, the newly-appointed Janus, volunteered to go to the Pacific. Janus attached himself to the Navy and proved his worth at the Battle of Midway (June 4-6 1942). During the battle, Janus killed three Kami Warriors and sank two aircraft carriers, half a dozen other vessels, and the battleship *Yamato*, killing Admiral Yamamoto. Japan's navy was all but crippled after the battle; Janus went on to destroy dozens of Japanese vessels the rest of the year.

The Germans resumed their advance on the Soviet Union in the summer of 1942 after defeating several Russian counterattacks. The offensive reached a climax in the city of Stalingrad, where a brutal siege ensued. During the siege, an overzealous political officer ordered the arrest of the Hunter, one of the Heroes of the Revolution, allegedly for defeatism and seditious talk. The Hunter resisted and died in the ensuing firefight. Upon hearing the news, fellow Hero of the Revolution Medved (the Bear) went on a vengeful rampage that ended in Moscow, where the powerful Neo killed Stalin, several members of the Politburo and the Communist Party, and thousands of soldiers and civilians, laying waste to much of the city before being driven away.

Stalin's death was a severe blow to the Soviets, but the Nazis did not enjoy much success from it. An uneasy troika led the Soviet Union after Stalin's demise; it comprised of surviving Party members Vyacheslav Molotov and Mikhail Kalinin, as well as renowned general Georgy Zhukov. The Soviets fought on, and the siege of

Stalingrad ended up disastrously for the Nazis. By 1943, the Germans and their allies were on the defensive and had suffered terrible losses.

The End: 1943-1945

Soviet counter-offensives at the beginning of 1943 pushed the Nazis back. Massive battles in Kursk and Belgorod led to further German retreats. It was then that the Ukraine exploded. During the German occupation of the Ukraine, the Iron Tsar had been secretly stockpiling weapons and taking control of the diverse partisan groups in the area, killing most Communist and nationalist leaders and replacing them with his own men. When he struck in March of 1943, attacking both Nazis and Soviets, he led over a hundred thousand partisans. This was a small force compared with the massive German and Russian armies in the area, but the partisans entered the conflict armed with energy rifles that could cripple or destroy a tank or shoot aircraft from the sky, were supported by hundreds of humanoid automatons that could withstand anything short of direct artillery fire, and wielded a myriad other super-weapons of the Tsar's creation.

The Tsar and another Neo, the "Witch of Pinsk" which the Russians would later refer to as Baba Yaga, single-handedly massacred entire armies. After the first few slaughters, the Tsar or his terrible consort would offer enemies from both sides two options: join the rebellion, or die. Thousands of Axis and Soviet soldiers, especially those of non-Russian and German extraction, ended up turning coat and joining the Tsar's growing army. Even one of the Teutonic Knights, the pseudo-goddess Freya, switched sides, as did several members of the Heroes of the Revolution; the ones that didn't fell in battle against the more powerful Ukrainian Neos. The rebellion also gained mass support by dismantling the collective farm system wherever it had been instituted.

By 1944, the Ukraine had become a death trap for Soviets and Nazis alike. After suffering massive losses, the Germans withdrew from the region completely, as well as Belarus, and signed a truce with the Iron Tsar shortly after Operation Overlord. The Soviets, unwilling to accept Ukrainian independence, kept launching futile attacks there as well as on German-held Poland. In October, two Ukrainian flying fortresses, gigantic destroyer-sized vessels, reached the Soviet oil fields at Baku and destroyed them, crippling Soviet logistics for the remainder of the war. The Russian counteroffensive stalled on all fronts; the Soviets never made the territorial gains they did in our timeline. General Zhukov was forced into a humiliating surrender on November 1944, and shortly afterwards the two remaining members of the Soviet troika turned on each other. Molotov emerged triumphant, but assumed power over a weakened Soviet Union wracked by rebellions, starvation and chaos.

After the dreaded flying fortresses bombed Moscow a few weeks after Molotov had won the power struggle there, the Soviets had had enough. In violation of the Casablanca Declaration of 1943 (where all members had pledged to stick together in demanding unconditional surrender from the Axis), Molotov signed a ceasefire agreement with the Germans and the Ukrainians on December 3, 1944, removing the Soviet Union from the war. In retaliation, the US suspended any further shipments of war materiel to Soviets, further wreaking havoc on the coutry's devastated economy. The Nazis' earlier truce with the Iron Tsar had given up all of the Ukraine and parts of Poland, Romania, Slovakia and Hungary. Under the new agreement, the Soviets surrendered parts of Belarus, Russia and all of Moldavia: a new nation, the Dominion of the Ukraine, had been born.

In conquered Europe, resistance to the Nazis continued, with varying success, often involving Neolympians from several countries. The most notorious resistance fighters were the Scourge and the Golem, two Jewish concentration camp victims who used their powers to escape and reveal to the world the truth about the Holocaust. The Scourge, a powerful teleport, rescued tens of thousands of victims from several extermination camps and killed hundreds of prison guards, concentrating his efforts on camp commanders and "researchers," including such notables as Theodor Van Eupen, Rudolf Hoss, and Josef Mengele. Even with Neo support, however, none of the partisan movements accomplished much more than diverting some of the Nazis' resources into keeping them suppressed.

Meanwhile, the Western Allies continued to make gains against the Nazis. Victories in Africa, Sicily and mainland Italy paved the way for Operation Overlord in June, 1944. The invasion of Normandy should have been an impossible undertaking under the circumstances. The Germans, despite heavy losses on the Eastern Front, were not under as much pressure from the Soviets even before the ceasefire in December, thanks to the Iron Tsar's rebellion. They were able to place many more troops in France, where the Allies were expected to invade. The operation was nearly scrapped (the British in particular were extremely pessimistic about it) until a Freedom Legion delegation convinced the Allied High Command to proceed by promising full cooperation during the invasion. The Legion played a crucial part in Operation Overlord: Ultimate alone cleared four of the six beach landings during D-Day. Allied casualties were far lighter than expected, although losses would be heavy in the ensuing months of fighting.

As the Allies relentlessly advanced towards Germany, the Neo Geistesblitz organized the assassination of Adolph Hitler in an attempt to secure a better peace for Germany. In November 11, 1944, the German dictator burst into flames in mid-rant during a late night meeting with his staff. The case of "spontaneous combustion" led to a brief power struggle and the rise of Heinrich Himmler as the new Fuhrer. The Mind was unmasked as the killer: his collaborators were captured and executed, and he fled to the Ukraine, where he was welcome by the Iron Tsar and went on to become a leading advisor. Himmler tried to negotiate a peace accord but the Allies remained firm in demanding an unconditional surrender.

In the Pacific, Janus and US Navy destroyed the last Japanese carrier vessels in a battle off the coast of the Philippines in June 1944. By November of 1944 the Philippines were in American hands. The ability of Janus to destroy any concentration of enemy troops radically changed the course of the Pacific War. After the fall of the Philippines Janus was essentially directing the strategic moves of the US armed forces. By December, the Japanese islands of Iwo Jima and Okinawa had fallen, and every city in Japan's main island had been bombed into ruins.

On February 1945, the Allied leaders held the Paris Conference, which was attended by President Truman (Roosevelt had died in January, and the Vice-President elect was hastily sworn into the job), British Prime Minister Churchill, Free French leader De Gaulle and Chinese Premier Chiang. Soviet leader Molotov declined to attend when he discovered a Ukrainian delegation had been invited, sending instead a delegation of his own. The discovery a few months prior of extensive Soviet spy rings in both the US and UK, and the Soviets' separate peace accords with the Nazis had completely soured their relationship with the other Allies. The Paris conference outlined the surrender terms expected from both Germany and Japan, as well as the fate of liberated territories. Soviet demands and claims were bluntly denied, leading to the Soviets' exit from the talks in protest.

On February 24, 1945, Janus killed the last of the Kami Warriors and confronted Emperor Hirohito, who agreed to the formal surrender of Japan, accepting the Paris Declaration terms. A few weeks later, Ultimate defeated the Teutonic Knight Donner over besieged Berlin, precipitating a coup in which most prominent Nazi leaders were killed; the highest-ranking German commander left alive, Grand Admiral Donitz, unconditionally surrendered on March 29, 1945.

While World War II saw horrors aplenty, the intervention of superhumans prevented some of them. The Manhattan Project was completed successfully, but no nuclear devices were used in the war. Strategic bombing was not as severe as it was in our timeline, since Neos could target military targets more accurately. Millions still died, and Germany and Japan were utterly devastated nonetheless. A firestorm in Dresden that killed thousands was caused by Meteor, a British Neolympian, instead of by Allied bombers as in our timeline, but the death toll was just as high.

The Post-War Years

The second half of the decade was spent dealing with the consequences of the war. In many places, fighting would continue for years, or even decades, to come.

The first issue the nascent United Nations had to face after the surrender of Germany was the growing power of the Dominion of the Ukraine. Two Freedom Legion powerhouses, Janus and Ultimate, traveled to Kiev and confronted the Iron Tsar. This led to a duel between the Tsar and Ultimate, fought over the Sea of Azov, with the Tsar agreeing to hold general elections if the American superhero could best him. Flashes of light and blasts of thunder from the battle could be heard on every shore bordering the sea, which ended in a draw, despite Ultimate's best efforts. After the spectacular fight, the Tsar demonstrated several weapons of mass destruction for the benefit of the Legionnaires, along with the threat to use them if the West tried to interfere with "Ukrainian domestic issues."

Facing a threat that Neo powers could not easily overcome, and exhausted by the war, the United States and Great Britain formally recognized the new borders of the Dominion in return for a pledge from the Tsar not to seek further territorial gains. The Soviet Union, facing chaos and starvation, was powerless to intervene as the Ukrainians backed independence bids in Belorussia, Estonia, Latvia and Lithuania that led to the expulsion of the Communists and the establishment of governments friendly to the Dominion. The Soviet Union was cut off from Central and Western Europe by these developments. Attempts to retain control of the regions by force resulted in the "fraternal assistance" of Ukrainian troops and their fearsome weapons. The mysterious death of Premier Molotov in 1948, shortly after such an attempt, was the first demonstration of the Dominion's policies toward Russia: support for any subversive and independent movements in Russia's sphere of influence, backed by the assassination of any leader who threatened to lift the Soviet Union from its weakened state, or of any Neo who grew powerful enough to pose a threat to the Dominion and its growing ring of puppet states.

Propelled by Neo super-science, the Ukraine became the major power of the region by the end of the decade, a major food producer and an industrial giant that attracted migrants from all over Europe. The country remained a strict autocracy where the dictates of the Tsar or his ministers were the law and no political opposition was allowed. Most of the Ukraine's "allies" ended up as parliamentary democracies, but most of their leaders didn't hesitate to obey the Dominion's every request; the exceptions to the rule came to an assortment of bad ends.

While that Neo-ruled nation rose to power, a Neo organization broke its ties with all national governments. On April 10, 1945, some two weeks before the UN Conference on International Organization began in San Francisco, the Freedom Legion officially reconstituted itself as an independent international body, officially severing its ties to the US or any members' country of origin. Ten of the thirty-eight Legion members, including the Patriot and Shadow Terror, resigned from the organization in protest. The Legion moved its headquarters from New York City to an uninhabited island in the Pacific (an Atlantic Headquarters was established in 1954). A Legion delegation attended the UN Conference and successfully lobbied to become the fifth member of the UN Security Council (the other four were China, France, Great Britain and the US).

The surrender of Japan did little to stop the bloodshed in China, where a three-way war continued between Chiang Kai-Shek's Nationalists, Mao Zedong's Communists, and the Dragon Khan's Imperialists. The Communists were the early losers in the conflict, mainly because they lost the race to recruit powerful Neos to their cause. None of Chiang's Eight Immortals were powerhouses like Ultimate or Janus, but they were powerful enough to find and kill Mao and most other Communist leaders by 1947. The war then devolved into a general conflict between Chiang and the Emperor, and its resolution was the first major conflict directly involving the UN. The Freedom Legion fought on the Nationalist side during the Chinese Civil War, along with an international (mainly American) military contingent, leading to the establishment of numerous American military bases in the country. In 1948, the Dragon Emperor created an energy wall along thousands of miles of Chinese territory as well as the former Soviet Republic of Mongolia, and the exhausted combatants agreed to an armistice that divided the country in two, although Chiang's Republic of China never recognized the Empire and to this day refers to the region as "the rebellious provinces." The Pacific Alliance Treaty Organization (PATO) was configured a few years later, forming an alliance between the Republic of China, Great Britain and its Asian dominions, the US, Australia and the Philippines, among other nations (Japan, which remained demilitarized, was not allowed to join PATO until the 1980s).

By 1950, Neolympians had redrawn the maps of the world, played a decisive role in the Second World War, and made their power and influence painfully clear to humanity.

Technology and Daily Life

The 1940s saw a great deal of technological development. During the first half of the decade, military technology advanced in leaps and bounds. By the end of the conflict, jet aircraft, helicopters, radar-controlled artillery and missiles, and battlefield laser weapons were in use. The Manhattan Project led to the development of the first nuclear weapons, although they were not used in the conflict (both Japan and Germany surrendered months before the first successful atomic bomb test on June, 1945). Nuclear research switched from military applications to peaceful power production; the first nuclear power reactor prototype was developed in Oak Ridge, Tennessee, in 1949, and a huge percentage of the ensuing decade's new electrical production came from nuclear power plants.

Daily life remained much as it had during the 1930s for most of the decade, because most research and development concentrated on military applications and also because the world was still recovering from the Great Depression or suffering the ravages of the Second World War. The main change was the gradual growth of the TV industry during the second half of the decade, with a growing number of homes replacing their radios with television sets.

The Golden Age of comics went into full swing during the 1940s, with over a dozen major publishers and hundreds of titles. The most popular comics involved costumed superheroes, both reality-based and fictional. *Action Tales*, featuring Ultimate the Invincible Man, was the best-selling title of the era, with a circulation of 1.5 million copies per issue for most of the decade. Neos were also heavily featured in radio programs and movies.

The line between fact and fiction was further blurred by several movies starring real Neos. The best-known example was Colonel Wonder (nee Josiah T. Knobbs), a Type Two Neo with super-strength and the ability to fly that first appeared in Los Angeles during the late 1930s. After several well-publicized heroic deeds, and a wildly successful line of comic books by Fawcett Periodicals, Colonel Wonder agreed to star in a serial by Republic Pictures. *The Adventures of Colonel Wonder* (1940), a 15-episode episodic movie, became an instant success, as people lined up to watch an actual Neo performing incredible deeds on the screen. Josiah Knobbs was a mediocre actor at best, but he more than made up for it with his powers. After a twelve-month combat tour in Europe, he went on to star in three more serials and two feature films before his untimely death at the hands of the Doomsday Devil in 1953.

Just as the existence of real-life superhuman beings affected pop culture, said culture also influenced the behavior of Neos. People who developed special abilities were expected to dress up in outlandish costumes and behave in certain ways, and most Neolympians during that era did just that. In the US alone, over sixty Neos donned costumes and used their powers for the public good (or tried to). Another thirty or so used their powers in criminal activities. The authorities' reactions to Neo vigilantes and criminals varied from one jurisdiction to the next. In some cities, the police developed formal or informal alliances with Neo do-gooders; in others, it went after any Neos who took the law into their own hands.

The 1950s: Progress, Fear and Change

The Fifties were a time of recovery. As Europe slowly picked itself up after years of conflict, the US enjoyed an unprecedented era of affluence as the only major industrial country left intact by World War Two. The decline and fall of the Soviet Union meant there was no Cold War to worry about. Communism was viewed as a failed ideology, and after the fall of the Soviet Union in 1958, an extinct one, much like Fascism. Without the specter of Hiroshima and Nagasaki (both cities escaped being destroyed by nuclear weapons, although they were burned to the ground by conventional bombing) inspiring fear and distrust, the atomic age was welcome with open arms. The free world did not fear Communism or the Bomb; instead, its paranoia turned toward Neolympians.

A recovering Europe had to contend with the power and influence of the Dominion of the Ukraine, but for the time being the Iron Tsar seemed to be content rebuilding his domain's economy and tormenting the Russians. Without the fear of Soviet expansion, there wasn't a strong drive toward a permanent military alliance like NATO. An international force (mostly US and British troops) remained in bases across Germany and Poland for six decades, along with a detachment of Freedom Legionnaires.

Without Soviet intervention overseas, the decolonization process moved more slowly than in our timeline. India became independent in 1952; Pakistan followed suit in 1959. French Indochina became the Republic of Vietnam in 1956. Most other European colonies retained their pre-war status until the late 1960s and early 1970s, although all colonial powers agreed in principle to put their former dependencies on the path to full autonomy and took steps towards implementing it during the 1950s.

In Asia, the Republic of China experienced a great deal of economic growth, albeit it was hampered by the rampant corruption of the Chiang regime. On the other side of the Dragon Wall, the Empire of China recovered more slowly; the Dragon Emperor spent most of the decade consolidating his power over the region and trying to modernize it. Japan, on the other hand, did not recover as swiftly as in our timeline. The US occupied Japan until 1953, and restrictions on Japanese industry (to prevent any possible rearmament) delayed its economic recovery. The situation would only worsen as the Republic of China began industrializing and selling products to the US, becoming a major competitor in the ensuing decades. While Japan eventually recovered and became a major industrial player in Asia, it never reached the preeminence it did in our timeline.

The Neolympian Peril

In 1948, psychiatric facility inmate Miller Fairbanks of Santa Fe, New Mexico developed the power to reanimate the dead and to transform himself into a virtually immortal being. Monstrous Miller and his zombie army terrorized several US states, killing over a hundred thousand people before being put down by the combined efforts of the Army, the Freedom Legion and several other Neolympians. The incident was the inspiration for the 1965 film *Night of the Living Dead*. It also led to the formation of the House Parahuman Activities Committee in 1949. HPAC, led by Massachusetts representative J.F. Kennedy, compiled a lengthy list of crimes committed by Neolympians and spent the ensuing two decades investigating the possible threats parahumans posed against the country. The committee would become the focal point of government efforts to curb the actions of Neolympians.

The number of Neos continued to grow steadily, with over three hundred confirmed parahumans in the US alone by 1955. While most Neos were law-abiding citizens who tended to gravitate towards the sciences, entertainment industry, law-enforcement and military, a sizable minority became criminals, murderous vigilantes, and on several notable occasions, rampaging menaces. Neos with the ability to transform into giant creatures terrorized several cities across the world. In one of the most notorious incidents, a colossal humanoid lizard laid waste to Tokyo in 1953. Giant creatures were just one of many Neo-induced catastrophes. Other renegades triggered power blackouts, earthquakes, and hurricanes, leaving behind horrendous death tolls.

The experience of World War Two, as well as detailed analysis of several incidents in the post-war years, revealed a number of unpalatable facts about Neolympians. First, the best defense against a Neo was another Neo, ideally one of a higher power rank, or a group of Neos trained to work together. Secondly, military weapons could take down most parahumans with a PAS of 2.6 or below, but higher-ranked Neos were almost impossible to subdue through conventional means, needing either Neo intervention or the use of Neo-created super-weapons. Third, a rapid response was essential in stopping a Neo on the rampage. When a psychotic parahuman was given more than a few minutes of unrestricted action, the death toll could be catastrophic. Unfortunately, conventional forces could not respond quickly enough with enough firepower to subdue a Neo, not unless armed garrisons were stationed in every city around the country. Given that most Neos bought into the "costumed superhero" meme of the Golden Age of Comics, most US cities and states decided to allocate funds to create and maintain official super-teams, less-ambitious versions of the Freedom Legion that would be given police powers and would be at hand to stop any rogue parahuman attacks.

Texas led the way, having already deployed a Special Team of the Texas Rangers, led by the Shadow Terror, back in 1939. By 1960, twenty states and thirteen cities had followed suit. Teams like the Empire State Guardians, the Chicago Sentinels, and the California Angels ended up becoming a combination of special police force and sports team, with franchising opportunities that paid for a significant portion of their budgets (and in some cases actually made money for their sponsor localities). Neos who agreed to join super-teams were paid lavishly and got royalties off of any merchandize with their likeness on it. The Freedom Legion was somewhat grudgingly allowed to operate two bases in the US, located in New York and Los Angeles.

In addition to local teams controlled and financed by cities and states, the federal government developed three national teams. The first one was attached to the Secret Service; its primary function was to provide protection for the President and other national leaders and visiting dignitaries, but under the Eisenhower Administration it grew in size and purview to become the primary federal Neo response force to domestic threats. The Parahuman Operations Command (established in 1954, officially the United States Parahuman Operation Command, or USPOC) is a military organization that manages Neolympians in all branches of the service. The POC's best known group is Papa Force, a team of Neo combat specialists tasked with fighting threats to national security. Finally, the CIA-sponsored Project MK-Ultra, launched in 1953, led to the creation of a team of Neos specializing in psychic abilities and covert operations. The project was initially founded to study methods of mind control through drugs and psychological techniques, but Neolympian research quickly took precedence. The CIA Neo division was officially renamed MK-Ultra when the project was made public. It primarily recruited clairvoyants, mind-readers and precognitives. Because of their relatively low-pay, none of the federal branches attract the more flamboyant or ambitious Neos, and its members tend to be on the lower power spectrum, although they are equipped with an assortment of super-weapons.

The conflicting views on Neos, seen as both the source of problems and solutions, would continue to plague policies on parahumans for years to come. HPAC kept recommending restrictive laws, including the registration of all Neolympians in the US into a federal database. It also launched a series of investigations into the interference of "independent parahuman organizations" (meaning the Freedom Legion) into American domestic affairs. US-born Legionnaires like Daedalus Smith, Doc Slaughter and Janus were called to appear in front of the committee several times during the 1950s, leading to many heated exchanges. Smith retaliated by using his personal fortune to quietly bankroll political opponents of committee members; his efforts almost cost JFK his bid for the Senate in 1952, something the Kennedy family never forgot.

Outside the US, the "parahuman issue" was dealt with in several different ways, with wildly varying degrees of success.

Great Britain adopted the "super-team" model, but all such groups were given a royal charter. The MI-5 parahuman element, commonly known as the Royal Guard, kept the UK safe through many a Neo crisis, including the "Martian" invasion of 1956 (actually an attack by the mechanical creations of a deranged but powerful H.G. Wells fan).

Elsewhere in Europe, attempts to strictly regulate Neo activities backfired badly. France tried to force all native-born Neos to serve in the armed forces, resulting in the emigration of most parahumans from the country – except the criminal-minded and insane, who managed to rampage unopposed until the Freedom Legion was asked to intervene. The situation led to the fall of the French government in 1958 (and the return of Charles De Gaulle to power in the country) and less restrictive laws. In 1959, Interpol (which had been using Neolympian agents for years) created a Parahuman Branch, gathering all Neos in its employ under a central administration. Interpol Neolympians can assist member countries in making arrests and similar tasks if invited to do so by the local authorities.

In the Third World, things were less a matter of governments deciding what to do about Neos than the other way around. In Mexico, the former masked pro wrestler and Neo powerhouse known as *El Hombre Rojo* (the Red Man) won the 1952 presidential election and went on to win a referendum appointing him *Presidente Vitalicio* (President-for-life) in 1957. The political maneuvering and Neo adventures of the Mexican leader (*El Hombre Rojo* had saved the country a good dozen times before his rise to power) could fill several novels; *El Presidente* continues to rule Mexico to this day. Neo dictators seized power in such countries as Liberia, Guatemala, Uzbekistan, Bolivia and Haiti during the decade. A few were deposed by the Freedom Legion (acting under UN resolutions) when their rule became too brutal to be accepted, but for the most part were left alone if they showed enough political sense to get the US, Dominion or Empire to act as their patron.

Technology and Daily Life

Nuclear power became widespread in the US; by 1960 almost one third of the country's electrical supply was being generated by fission reactors. The issue of nuclear waste was solved by launching the waste into space, in trajectories aimed at the sun. While electricity never became "too cheap to meter," power costs went down a great deal, increasing the demand for electronic products, from washers and dryers to television sets. The Fifties were the Golden Age of television, with home sets in almost every home by the end of the decade, and four major networks offering a variety of programs. The first mass-produced electric car (the Tucker Lightning) made its debut in 1957, although low gas prices kept their demand low for the time being.

Space exploration was led by Neos. Ultimate and Janus landed on the Moon in 1952, bringing back hundreds of color pictures that captured the world's imagination. The first artificial satellite was placed in orbit around the Earth that same year, also by Ultimate. Advances in rocketry (which often combined regular technology with Neo Artifacts) and the availability of Neolympians capable of carrying large objects into orbit sparked a golden age of space exploration. A moon colony was built by a joint US-European initiative in 1959.

Popular culture changed along with the perception of Neolympians. Comic book sales suffered a steady decline for most of the decade, as the fear of Neolympians made their stories less popular and comics had to compete with other forms of entertainment like television. A growing body of non-fiction books trying to explain Neolympians also appeared, alleging alien origins and warning of past (and possibly future) Neolympian tyrannies. Immanuel Velikovsky's *Clash of Pantheons* (1951) claimed that the mythological gods of every culture were actually early Neos who had become the rulers of primitive humanity before somehow vanishing or being destroyed, a theme that would be expanded in ensuing years by such writers as Erich Von Daniken (*Thrones of the Gods*, 1968).

In music, the big band era continued throughout the decade, thanks in no small part to the survival of influential musician Glenn Miller, who continued to perform until his death in 1972. Jazz gained in popularity, led by Neo music virtuoso

Hepcat Slim. Slim worked with musical giants Duke Ellington, Dizzie Gillespie and Thelonious Monk in the 1940s and went on to become the best-known African-American performer of the decade. His influence was felt in several musical genres, from Blues to Rock and roll, and continued for the rest of the century (Hepcat Slim continues to perform in 2013 to sold-out venues). The term "hep" became widespread towards the end of the '50s to indicate someone in the know, or connected to the leading edge of art and culture.

Socially, the Civil Rights movement gained momentum in no small part due to the efforts of Cassius Jones, a.k.a. Janus, the African-American hero who had played a crucial role in winning the Second World War. Jackson was an outspoken opponent of Jim Crow laws, and starting in 1952 he helped organize a series of lawsuits, demonstrations and other forms of concerted action against them. This led to an investigation by HPAC to determine if the Legionnaire's actions constituted "outside interference in domestic affairs." Janus spent several years fighting off the allegations, and he continued backing the movement, which grew in momentum throughout the decade.

1960-1979: War, Progress, Change

At a glance the 1960s shared many similarities with the decade in our timeline: it featured a lengthy war that grew more unpopular over time, a youthful president brought down, the questioning of authority, a counterculture movement, and many changes, social and technological. There were fundamental differences, however, as the changes building up since World War Two continued to have an impact in world affairs.

The First Asian War (1964-1971)

For over decade, a tense truce had held between the two Chinas. Starting in 1959, however, the Dragon Empire started making peace overtures towards the Republic of China. Trade between the two countries increased, and ambassadors were exchanged, even though the ROC remained steadfast in not recognizing the Empire's legitimacy. The US government joined the peace talks in 1960, and became fully committed to diplomacy under the Kennedy Administration.

In 1963, the US started withdrawing troops from the Republic of China as a show of good will. J.F. Kennedy made the withdrawal from China a major talking point of his administration, citing the military budget savings that could be used for social programs or tax cuts. In June, 1964, the Dragon Empire struck. Millions of soldiers charged out of the Dragon Wall, led by hundreds of super-powered Celestial Warriors. The remaining US forces in China suffered heavy losses, and whole provinces of the Republic were overrun. Only the intervention of the Freedom Legion stemmed the tide.

The ensuing Asian War lasted the better part of a decade. JFK lost a heavily contested election to Ray "The Patriot" Stevens, the first Neolympian US president. Stevens implemented the draft, issued an amnesty to any criminal Neos willing to enlist to fight in the war, and led the country into a lengthy conflict that cost the lives of over a hundred thousand Americans. The United Nations sent contingents from several dozen nations into China, but the US and the ROC did most of the fighting and dying: the Republic lost over four million soldiers and as many civilians if not more: the final tally would never be known.

The war was fought with a bizarre combination of conventional weapons, Neo powers and bizarre pseudo-science devices. The Dragon Empire's armies were poorly armed and equipped for the most part, with little motorized transport and artillery, in many ways closer to a World War One army in terms of conventional weapons and equipment. However, it also had elite units armed with special gadgets and artifacts, including energy weapons purchased from the Dominion of the Ukraine. It also had Celestial Warriors, who allegedly were normal men granted superhuman powers by the Emperor himself. However the Celestial Warriors came to be, there were hundreds of them, the largest concentration of Neolympians in the planet. The Freedom Legion deployed a hundred and fifty Neos of varying power levels in China. The US, ROC and allied forces threw another hundred and twenty parahumans into the fray.

The Dragon Empire attacked with over five hundred Celestial Warriors.

For the first time in history, large numbers of Neolympians fought set piece battles, some of them involving more superhuman combatants than all the parahumans that fought World War Two. Villages, towns and in a few cases entire cities were erased from the map by energy exchanges equivalent to the detonation of multiple nuclear weapons. Much of the destruction of the war was never documented by the news media simply because it was too dangerous for humans to be anywhere near a large-scale Neo conflict. One vicious fight between the Dragon Emperor, Ultimate and Janus released a gigantic cloud of dust and smoke that turned 1968 into the "Year without a spring." Global temperatures plummeted for several years, leading to a "Little Ice Age" during the 1970s.

The initial phase of the war was fought in Northeast China, with a main thrust towards the ROC capital in Beijing that was barely stopped and only slowly pushed back. Other offensives in Central China followed, as the Imperials tried to split the ROC in two and failed every time. After a multi-pronged offensive was turned back in 1967, the war turned into a grinding conflict of attrition. Late inn 1969, the Empire switched tactics and launched attacks on the ROC allies' countries, infiltrating teams of Celestial Warriors into several nations to spread terror there.

Imperial terror squads wreaked havoc in the US, Great Britain and Canada. Local Neo super-teams managed to contain most of the attacks before they could do a lot of damage, but the Asian War was not something that just happened in Americans' TV sets; Imperial attacks in New York (1969), Detroit (1970) and Los Angeles (1971) killed over seven thousand American civilians and inflicted billions of dollars in property damage.

The drawn-out conflict sparked an anti-war movement early on, as people questioned the idea of fighting for the fairly corrupt and undemocratic ROC. Most of the country stuck by President Stevens' policies, however, and Stevens won a second term in 1968, narrowly defeating challenger Lyndon B. Johnson. War exhaustion was setting in by 1969, but the Imperial attacks on US soil had the effect of galvanizing public opinion in favor of the war.

The most powerful Neolympians of the planet launched a series of attacks on the Empire itself in 1971 that devastated much of the country. Stevens also threatened to use the US nuclear arsenal, which consisted mainly of small tactical devices but included several dozen hydrogen bombs. With no prospect of victory, and after losing over two-thirds of his Celestial Warriors, the Emperor agreed to a cease fire. In 1972, a peace treaty that restored the borders to their pre-war status was signed. The fact that the Emperor escaped any actual punishment sparked outrage around the world. Unfortunately, even the most powerful Neos in the world had been incapable of defeating the Emperor. The Empire also had a number of weapons of mass destruction and threatened to retaliate if any harsher demands were made on it.

The unsatisfactory peace led to the Republicans being repudiated at the polls in the next several elections, but there were few changes no matter which party was in charge. New president John Glenn continued Stevens' policies towards the two Chinas. The number of US troops in China increased dramatically, along with financial aid to the ROC to modernize its army.

Technology and Daily Life

The two decades were times of social change. Landmark legislation like the Civil Rights Act (1963) struck down many segregationist policies in the US. A sizable number of young people rebelled against traditional society and formed the core of the hepster movement, although the hepsters were never as popular or widespread as the hippies of our timeline, being restricted largely to the East and West coasts. Contraceptives helped spark the sexual revolution.

Technology kept improving. Wrist communicators (popularly known as wrist-comms), an invention of the 1940s, started becoming commonplace as national cell networks spread out throughout the country. In 1966, the wrist-comms allowed video communication as well, and by 1968 some wrist devices had the ability to take pictures and send text messages.

Computers, first introduced in the late 1940s, improved by leaps and bounds and became widespread. Innovations like magnetic and optical storage devices were developed decades ahead of our timeline by a handful of Neo geniuses (and a host of human engineers and scientists who developed those inventions into useful products). By the early sixties, "mini-computers" were commonplace at places of business, schools and universities.

The threat of rampaging Neos also spurred the development of redundant communication networks. A defense project launched in 1959 produced the first computer network (known as ARPANET) in 1962. A civilian version, the Hypernet, was developed in 1963, used primarily by universities across the world. In 1967, Project Xanadu gave birth to what would become the Xanaweb, using hyperlink documents to communicate through the Hypernet. The Xanaweb had one very important difference from our world wide web: users of the system were not anonymous. Security protocols required a biometric signature and a single personal account; identities could be faked, but with great difficulty. Privacy revolved around who had legal access to a person's account; for the most part only the authorities did, and only if they could show probably cause and get a warrant. The lack of anonymity made hacking and other cybercrimes much rarer than in our timeline, and it also prevented such plagues as spam and trolling.

The biggest new appliance of the 1970s was the Home Terminal (HT). The first models appeared during the late 1960s, used initially by the military and later spreading to business and government agencies. Hewlett-Packard launched the first personal HT model in 1969; IBM followed suit in 1971 with the HT-15, which became hugely popular. Home Terminals looked like regular color televisions with built-in cable connections, but they allowed users to connect to Hypernet hubs, giving users access to news, bulletin boards, and by 1973, movies on demand.

The devices transformed the Hypernet from a service largely limited to academia and other specialized users to something very much like Earth Prime's Internet, with a myriad services (ranging from booksellers to pornography) springing up over the ensuing decade. Home Terminals became more complex over the years, adding several peripherals like keyboards and mice and adding more computational power until they became more like personal computers, although their reliance on an external network continued.

Other inventions of the decades included sophisticated electric cars and cybernetic implants. Thanks to breakthroughs in battery technology, 35% of all new cars in the US and Europe were either electric cars or hybrids by 1980. Normal combustion-engine cars continued to dominate the market, however, thanks to greater fuel efficiency and low oil prices. The large number of war veterans with missing limbs spurred research into cybernetics. Several patents developed by Smith Industries in the early 1970s led to prosthetic limbs that could be controlled through direct neural connections and could even simulate the sense of touch to a limited degree.

Medicine continued to progress. Several forms of cancer were eradicated by Neo-invented therapies. Additionally, the growing number of Neos with healing abilities allowed major hospitals in most cities to keep at least one or two healers on staff, dedicated to handling critical cases. Demand for healers far outstripped the supply, however.

The early sixties were the Silver Age of comics, with a resurgence in demand for heroic tales. Even as superheroes went off to war, the appetite for stories about them continued, at least at first. The aftermath of the Asian War caused a backlash against Neos in pop culture during the 1970s. The Stevens presidency was highly unpopular among artistic circles, and this antipathy was eventually extended toward Neolympians in general. Many books and movies produced during the late 1960s and the 1970s portrayed Neos as dangerous and megalomaniacal beings. Mainstream novels of the period tried to ignore Neos as much as possible, treating them largely as potential natural disasters or background elements, with a focus on the lives and problems of normal human beings. Comic sales suffered a slump in the 1970s as the Silver Age of comics faltered.

In 1972, US Comics launched *Godhunter*, a fictional series about a human vigilante who used high technology and old-fashioned guile to kill Neolympians. Godhunter's victims included thinly-disguised versions of Ultimate, the Patriot and other well-known heroes, who were invariably portrayed as corrupt, decadent would-be tyrants. *Godhunter* became a hit, with sales eclipsing Buck Comics' *Freedom Legion* and *Action Tales* in 1974. The comic was adapted for the big screen in 1976; *Godhunter: The Motion Picture* was the top grossing movie of the decade and spawned no less than six sequels, although the last one, *Godhunter: Revenge* (1984) bombed at the box office, possibly a reflection of changing attitudes towards Neos (although a terrible script and lackluster direction were also to blame).

1980-1999: Closing Out the Century

After a decade without any major conflicts (by the end of the 1970s some intellectuals were predicting the end of war in human affairs), the 1980s and 1990s were largely defined by war and the threat of war. The Indian Reunification War was the first major conflict since World War Two that was started by normal humans for very human reasons, although it was ended by Neolympians. The Second Asian War was yet another surprise attack by the Dragon Emperor.

In between those conflicts, most of the world enjoyed a great deal of peace and prosperity, albeit with its share or problems and unforeseen consequences.

The Indian Reunification War (1983-1984)

Relations between Pakistan and India had been tense for decades, but Great Britain's influence had prevented outright war between the two countries. Over the years, the situation continued to deteriorate, however. Both nations built up their militaries, purchasing both conventional and "special" weapons from all over the world, including the Dominion and the Dragon Empire.

The conflict came to a head in 1981, when a failed revolt by East Pakistan's non-Muslim minorities was brutally quashed by the military dictatorship ruling the country. The United Nations condemned the atrocities but couldn't muster the votes to intervene. India, which had been providing aid to the rebellion, threatened to invade. A cease fire between the rebels and the Pakistani government was followed by year of tense talks that achieved nothing. One of the rebellion's leaders was killed by paramilitary forces and hostilities resumed. When thousands of Bengali Indians were killed by the Pakistani military, India sent troops across the borders of both East and West Pakistan.

Pakistan retaliated with multiple nuclear strikes.

The source of the nuclear weapons remains a mystery. The plutonium used in the devices was eventually traced to American and British sources, material that had been stolen decades before. The weapons were fission bombs with yields in the 25-30 kiloton range, and were small enough to be smuggled into India by several trucks. Ten trucks armed with the devices entered India while the peace talks were being held. Two of the bombs failed to detonate properly (one in Mumbai and the other in Kolkata). A third one was intercepted by the police and captured intact. The other seven exploded. One device targeted the Indian government in an attempted decapitation strike. Two were aimed at the Indian Parahuman Agency. The others were deployed against military headquarters or major economic centers, with the purpose of causing the maximum amount of disruption in both civilian and military affairs.

Over half a million people were killed immediately by the attacks, including India's Prime Minister Indira Gandhi, fifty-three Neolympians in the Indian Parahuman Agency, and several general officers and regional commanders. Another two million people were severely injured, with hundreds of thousands dying in the ensuing months of radiation poisoning, burns and other attack-related injuries. While India reeled from the attacks, the Pakistanis repelled the Indian attacks. Two more nuclear weapons were used in the ensuing week, targeted at Indian troop concentrations.

That was when India revealed its own nuclear arsenal. Over the decades, the country had built an arsenal of several dozen 100-kiloton air-dropped bombs, using plutonium produced by "breeder" nuclear power plants. Five days after the Pakistani attacks, Islamabad and seventeen other cities were struck, twelve in West Pakistan and five in East Pakistan. Three million more people died in the space of seven hours.

By the time it was over, five million more deaths later, Pakistan had ceased to exist, its cities incinerated and its territories annexed by India. A hasty intervention by the UN and the Freedom Legion prevented the use of more nuclear weapons and outright genocide of the Muslim population in the annexed areas, but the brief but brutal war was a humanitarian catastrophe whose effects continue to the present day.

The Violent Crime Control Law (1986)

In 1984, six Neo criminals escaped from Alcatraz Island's maximum security prison. All of them had been convicted of several murders but the states where they had been convicted did not have the death penalty; the escapees had all been serving life sentences. Before being apprehended or killed, the fugitives caused an additional thirteen hundred deaths, thousands of injuries and hundreds of millions in property damage. The incident served to underscore how difficult it was to keep Neos incarcerated. Between 1945 and 1975, over seventy percent of all imprisoned parahumans in the US had managed to escape at some point of their term of imprisonment.

The federal Violent Crime Control Act was devised to deal with the problem. The Act made any murders committed by parahumans a federal capital felony, and it also streamlined the appeals process to ensure a swift execution upon conviction. Opposition to the Act was almost non-existent. Most US states already had similar provisions in place, and even the ACLU only made pro forma protests about the fast-tracked appeals process.

In 1985, Neolympian serial killer Arnie "Zodiac" Allen was convicted of fifty-seven counts of murder and sentenced to death. He was executed that same year after a three-month appeals process. Since then, one hundred and sixty-three Neos have been executed by the federal government, and another hundred and thirty by state courts. An additional two hundred and eighty-two parahumans have been killed while committing a crime or resisting arrest.

The Second Asian War (1991-1992)

Twenty years of peace between the two Chinas came to a sudden end when the Dragon Empire launched a surprise attack aimed at the Republic of China's capital of Beijing. While the reasoning behind the attack remains unclear, a possible cause may have been the ROC's voluntary surrender of its nuclear arsenal following the UN-led international disarmament drive sparked by the disastrous Indian Reunification War. The last ROC nuclear weapons were decommissioned in 1990, six months before the attack. A few analysts claim the two events are unrelated, but theirs is a minority opinion.

The Empire achieved surprise by stockpiling weapons and vehicles close to the border over several years and then moving troops to their prepositioned equipment by train. The move was performed deftly enough that ROC and US intelligence agencies were caught largely unaware. Even the psychics of MK-Ultra didn't see the attack coming; the Empire somehow managed to "spoof" both precognitive and clairvoyant powers.

The drive to Beijing was only stopped by the hasty deployment of the Freedom Legion and the ROC's Immortals, who held off the invasion force long enough for conventional troops to mobilize. The Emperor himself fought the Allies' most powerful Neos before being driven away. Over three hundred Imperial Celestial Warriors were killed in the massive parahuman battle, along with some fifty Neos from the Legion and ROC contingents. Once the Celestials and the Emperor had been driven off the field, the Imperial conventional units were destroyed or captured fairly quickly.

The rest of the war consisted of an extensive air campaign against the Empire and Neolympian strikes seeking to kill of capture the Dragon Emperor. The counterattacks caused a great deal of destruction and suffering among the hapless subjects of the Empire but failed to bring the Emperor to justice. A cease fire was reluctantly agreed to when the Emperor demonstrated a "Sun-Seed Bomb" with an explosive force equivalent to a ten-megaton hydrogen bomb and threatened to launch massive strikes throughout Asia if not left alone.

The war led to some two million deaths and little else, except the ROC's quiet reacquisition of a nuclear arsenal to present a deterrent to any future Imperial attacks. The Empire's trade relations with the rest of the world suffered a great deal, leading to severe privation for the country, including a famine that killed nearly a million people.

Parahuman Brush Wars

While the Second Asian War showed there was little that could be done about the Empire (or the Dominion for that matter), attempts were made to remove various Neo-led dictatorships around the world. Brutal Neolympian Papa Doc Duvalier and his coterie of human and super-powered *tontons macoutes* (bogeymen) were deposed and arrested in 1990 by the Freedom Legion and a US-led multinational force, ending a thirty-year reign of terror in Haiti. Papa Doc was killed in the fighting.

Other parahuman dictators suffered a similar fate in Rwanda (1988), Belize (1993) and Bolivia (1997). Additionally, several attempts by Neos to take over national governments were stopped on their tracks by the Legion or regional super-teams. Neo plots to threaten or blackmail nations or entire continents also led to conflicts deadly enough to be called wars. The notorious arch villain Hiram Hades was killed in 1994 after a brutal siege of his compound in the Andes mountains that led to nearly ten thousand deaths.

By the end of the century, the most brutal dictators were gone. The ones that remained (several dozen of them) learned to be more circumspect and to play the game of international politics better. As before, the patronage of powerful countries, corporations and other movers and shakers allowed several tyrants to hold onto power.

Technology and Daily Life

Neolympian "super-science" continued to grow in influence. By the 1980s, impossible technologies were commonplace, manufactured by combining conventional technologies with Neolympian Artifacts. The term for these hybrids was "magic box systems," where one or two components in a device were hand-made by Neos and provided power or functionality that could not be scientifically explained.

A typical "magic box" device was the contra-gravity drive, which used an electromagnetic field to somehow neutralize the effects of gravity and provide thrust, even in vacuum, apparently by somehow dragging itself over the fabric of space-time or creating "dimples" in it. While the crucial components of C/G devices were Neo artifacts, they could be powered by conventional means, although the power requirements were impressive. By 1980 the US military had a force of a few hundred "flying tanks" and a handful of "flying fortresses" that could, for instance, travel around the world in a matter of hours, which turned out to play a critical role in the Second Asian War. C/G systems caused a mini-war of their own between the US Army and Air Force over who got to control the new amazing flying machines. The conflict reached a stalemate, with all branches of the service making use of them in different configurations.

The first civilian fusion power plant was built in 1979. By 1999, thousands of new plants had been built around the world. The patents, held by the Freedom Legion, were shared for very low fees (which still produced hundreds of billions of dollars for the organization); the plants themselves were cheap and easy to build and maintain, although its main components could only be produced by select Freedom Legion Neos. In the US, the new power plants would eventually deliver almost half of the country's electricity demand by the early twenty first century, almost completely displacing coal and natural gas generators and gradually replacing nuclear power plants. The development paradoxically caused a severe economic recession (1981-1987) due to a crash in the value of traditional energy industries. The world emerged from the recession stronger and more prosperous than before, however.

The first wrist-computers made their appearance in 1987; the devices allowed users to connect to the Xanaweb, use GPS navigation, and many other applications. By the late nineties, almost all new wrist-comms were computers with highly sophisticated systems, and the popular name for the devices drifted from wrist-comm to "wrist-comp" over the years. E-tablets, introduced in 1994, allowed users to watch video, read books and magazines, and surf the web on screens larger than those in wrist-comps. By the end of the decade the devices had come down in price enough to become popular.

The eighties saw a renaissance in comic books, with a new generation of writers and artists infusing new life into the medium. Fictional Neo stories became more complex and darker; the Comics Code Authority was largely abandoned by the mid-eighties, and graphic depictions of Neo violence (real and fictional) appeared in select comic series by major publishers. The Silver Age trend of portraying Neos as men and women with very human failings continued, with growingly complex storylines growing in popularity.

The new comics and graphic novels attracted an older audience and helped revive sales, making up for the slump of the 1970s. So did a number of new policies targeting comic book collectors, like variant covers and multiple new series for people chasing the presumably valuable first issues. The collector frenzy led to hundreds of thousands of people hoarding millions of utterly worthless, vacuum sealed comic books. People interested in reading (instead of collecting) comics increasingly went digital, using their e-tablets as reading devices.

Neo-centric movies and TV shows also made a big comeback as memories of the First Asian War faded. The most popular show of the decade was *Sideline* (1982), an hour-long romantic dramedy depicting the adventures of a fictional Neo heroine and her wise-cracking human sidekick and love interest; *Sideline* lasted for twelve seasons (about three seasons too long according to most critics). *Freedom Legion: Part I-III* (1985-1989), a series of movies depicting a mix or historical and fictional adventures of the group, went on to dominate the box office during that decade.

2000-2013: The New Millennium

The first decade of the century was a time of peace and prosperity, marred only by the occasional outburst of parahuman violence. There were no major wars, and billions of people in the Third World entered into the global economy. Standards of living rose worldwide. Breakthroughs in energy generation, agriculture and manufacturing made famines and abject poverty a thing of the past in all but the most (physically or politically) isolated countries. Humanity was doing fine – except when Neo-humanity stirred things up.

Third World Uplift

The effects of thirty years of (literally superhuman) efforts to help the poor and disadvantaged populations of the planet were paying off handsomely by the turn of the century. By 2001, the overwhelming majority of the world's population had access to clean water, enough food to stave off malnutrition, and basic services like electricity and sanitation systems. The Freedom Legion alone helped build over two hundred fusion power plants in Africa, Asia and South America, providing energy for hundreds of millions of people.

A decades-long effort to curb corruption continued to make an impact in the developing world. Neolympians trained by the Freedom Legion returned to their native countries and used their abilities to go after kleptocrats as well as supervillains. Unlike mere mortals who could be bribed or intimidated, Neos were able to expose and arrest even wealthy and socially or politically connected perpetrators. In the Republic of China, for example, the efforts of the *Xian* (Immortals), the national super-team, led to the downfall of the Chiang family and the arrests of thousands of prominent officials over the decades. While corruption was never completely eradicated, public officials were expected to do their jobs while lining their pockets, and to restrict their peculation to a relatively small fraction of their budgets.

Those efforts were not universally praised, of course. Many decried the "unwarranted parahuman intervention" in the internal affairs of the world's nations. Also, in many cases Neolympians were themselves guilty of corruption and harder to expose than merely human criminals. For all that, many countries benefited a great deal, as their economies were not completely despoiled by small groups of oligarchs.

Campaigns to eradicate disease also helped better the lives of billions. Environmentally-friendly pesticides and genetic methods to curb mosquito populations (the latter developed by Doc Slaughter) eradicated malaria from the planet by 2001, saving millions of lives. Several other tropical diseases were likewise eliminated. AIDS was already largely under control by the time a vaccine and an anti-viral treatment were developed in 2013.

Haiti became the best-known case study of the "uplift" movement. After the fall of Papa Doc's government, the Freedom Legion made the island nation its own pet project, with the willing cooperation of its new democratic government. The organization invested billions in infrastructure and education efforts, including the construction of one of the best teaching hospitals in the Western Hemisphere, the

Louverture Institute. By 2010, thousands of Haitians were employed by the Freedom Legion, serving as administrators, medics, peacekeepers and technicians. Experimental agriculture and managed fishing techniques led to the island becoming a net food exporter; manufacturing also became an important employer. With a 2010 GDP in the hundred-billion range, the country's success was intensely envied by its neighbor, the Dominican Republic (the Spanish half of the island), which received far less assistance during that period and benefited only tangentially from Haiti's success.

Notorious Neolympian Events

In a decade without major international conflicts, Neos were at the center of most memorable stories of the early part of the century. The influence of parahumans in everything from the prevention of natural disasters to presidential elections led Global News Network commentator Blitz Wolfen to remark that "this is the Neolympians' world; we're just living in it."

The Freedom Legion's Weather Management Program came online in 1998; it was an international project led by the worlds' most powerful weather-controlling Neos, including Tempesta, Hurricane Harry, and the Ocean Goddess. Their efforts prevented all hurricane landfalls worldwide from 1999 to 2013, and successfully contained earthquake-triggered tsunamis in the Indian Ocean (2004) and Japan (2011). The estimated benefits of the program (thousands of lives saved and billions of dollars in damage avoided) didn't prevent many analysts from denouncing the program, claiming its alteration of weather patterns was the cause of numerous floods, droughts, or basically any and all negative climatic effects of the decade.

Neo-triggered disasters, meanwhile, continued to happen with alarming frequency. Over a dozen new Type Three Neolympians appeared between 2000 and 2010, and nine of them went on rampages and had to be killed. In the US alone, there were an average of ten major (i.e. resulting in more than a hundred casualties) Neo-related incidents a year during that period, up from eight a year in the previous two decades. The number of smaller parahuman violent incidents also increased by around twenty percent, as more Neos of all power levels manifested and fell prey to "Neo Psychosis" or simple poor impulse control. Only the quick reaction of local, national and international superteams prevented the incidents from generating even bigger body counts.

Thanks to advancing technologies, human police and military organizations started enjoying more success in subduing rogue parahumans on their own. Soldiers and SWAT teams equipped with powered armor systems, energy weapons and other special devices proved able to handle Type Two Neos under some circumstances. Even those successes remained marred by higher casualties and property damage than when Neolympians dealt with their brethren, however, and the world's dependency on parahumans to protect it from other parahumans continued.

In the 2008 US elections, Neolympian candidate Johnny "Stonebender" Colletta (Reform Party) defeated the Republican and Democrat contenders in an unprecedented third-party victory, becoming the second Neo president in American history. Colletta, a First Asian War veteran, became a celebrity when he joined the Unlimited Wrestling Federation in 1975 under the nickname "Stonebender." After a decade-long career in the ring, a few movie roles, and a three-year stint with a regional super-team (the Midwest Minutemen), Colletta went into politics, joining the Reform Party, an independent movement founded by Neo billionaire Bradley Roth. The Party's ideology was loosely defined as "pragmatic small-l libertarian" in its views. In addition to favoring a reduced government presence, the Reform Party became notorious for backing Neolympian candidates (invariably former super-team members with sterling reputations) in a number of city and state elections, touting their dedication to public service and "incorruptible" stands. Founded in 1988, when Roth unsuccessfully ran for President but managed to gain enough votes to upset the election bid of Vice-President Bush, the party quickly gained momentum.

That momentum allowed Colletta to become governor of North Dakota in 1992, a position he held for almost sixteen years. The elections of 2008 provided a unique opportunity for the Reform Party, as an unpopular Republican Vice-President ran against an initially popular Democrat who was brought low by a sex scandal in the middle of the campaign and refused to step down. Colletta, who had been running neck and neck with the Republican candidate, surged ahead in the polls after the sex scandal and narrowly defeated both established parties' nominees. The Reform Party also won a sizable number of Congressional elections, with the result that no party ended up controlling either the House or the Senate. A prominent political analyst predicted the result would be "chaos and old night."

Colletta proved to be surprisingly adept at political maneuvering, however, and the Reform Party Caucus played the other two parties against each other to pass several legislative initiatives, involving everything from tax laws to the budget. He went on to defy conventional wisdom and win reelection in 2012, despite a vocal group of anti-Neo activists decrying his "parahuman dictatorship."

Technology and Daily Life

By the beginning of the millennium, the average citizen of the developed world had a wrist-comp with higher memory and processing power than a high-end home computer from our timeline, often linked to a set of "enhanced reality" goggles that allowed owners to immediately access people's social media information at a glance, or to navigate in an unfamiliar city via a virtual map overlaid onto the goggles, among many other uses. Said citizen was also largely free of cancer, allergies, diabetes and heart disease, had a life expectancy a good ten years longer than in our timeline, and enjoyed a far better quality of life throughout it. His or her car was 45% likely to be electric, and 35% likely to be self-driving (these percentages would rise to 55% and 40% respectively by 2010). On the other hand, said citizen had a yearly 10,000-to-one chance of being killed by a Neolympian in any of several bizarre and gruesome ways, ranging from spontaneous combustion to plain dismemberment.

New technologies becoming popular during the decade included neural implants allowing a direct interface between the user's brain and several devices. Costs remained high but were dropping steadily over the decade. By 2012, the Intel MindChip II retailed for $3,500 (including surgery costs). Among other things, it let users communicate with any wireless device, record sensory input (audiovisual only, although work to capture other sensory stimuli was under way) and transmit whatever they saw or heard onto the Hypernet. Such devices, as well as advances in storage capacity (the typical computer of 2010 had one petabyte of hard disk space), made it possible to record every second of a person's life and access it at will. The effects of such technologies were just beginning to be felt in the second decade of the century.

Pop culture continued to have a love-hate relationship with Neolympians. Over two thirds of all movie blockbusters of the century were costumed superhero sagas with lavish special effects, often using Neo actors and stunt doubles; in several cases famous Neos reenacted their deeds for the cameras. Tabloids dogged the steps of the more famous or notorious parahumans, documenting their every public appearance or private scandal.

World Overview

This section describes the state of the world by the beginning of 2013, when the events of *Armageddon Girl* and its sequels begin to unfold. Since an in-depth look at the world would require several books, the description touches only on a few ways in which the setting differs from our world.

In 2013, the world has a population of 7.5 billion people. The most populous country is India, with 1.4 billion inhabitants, followed by the Republic of China (950 million), the Empire of China (400 million), the United States (320 million) and Indonesia (250 million). The Gross World Product (the sum of all countries GDP) is about 125 trillion in 2012 dollars. About 15,000 people live in permanent or semi-permanent installations outside Earth, including space satellites and bases in the Moon, Mars, Titan and the asteroid belt. Finally, some 5,300 Neolympians dwell on the planet.

The United States

The US remains the wealthiest and most powerful country in the world, a position it has held since the end of World War Two. In many ways, it is very much like the US in our timeline, but there have been several notable differences. With the early decline and fall of the Soviet Union, there was no Cold War, no risk of global thermonuclear war, and a somewhat smaller military-industrial complex. There were no Korean and Vietnam Wars, but the country fought in two much deadlier conflicts in China instead. The US' biggest overseas military commitments are in Asia, due to the continuing threat of the Dragon Empire. The US has ceded many of the duties of "world's policeman" to the UN and the Freedom Legion, which while stubbornly independent is still largely controlled by American (or formerly American) citizens.

Neos in America

The US is the home of an estimated 1,400 Neolympians, the largest population in the world (second place goes to the Dragon Empire, with about 800 parahumans). Neos from all over the world come to the US in search of fame and fortune, and for the most part they find both. Neos in America are generally expected to devote some or even all of their time and energy to public service; those that do not are reviled, not least by other Neos. Criminal Neolympians are viewed with a combination of revulsion, fear and fascination.

Thirty-seven city, state or regional super-teams employ some three hundred Neos. Working in a super-team involves being on duty at the team's headquarters for eight to twelve-hour shifts, ready to respond to any emergency that may require parahuman intervention. Members are also expected to appear at a number of public functions as representatives of their locality. A costume and code name are often mandatory, even if the Neo's identity is publicly known. In return, team members get lavish salaries (six figures or more), and merchandizing rights on their costumed personas. The more successful super-team members earn tens or even hundreds of millions of dollars a year.

The entertainment industry directly employs some hundred and fifty Neos, mostly as actors, special effect specialists and stunt doubles. The term "Hollywood Neo" is applied contemptuously to parahumans who portray heroic characters without ever performing any actual heroic deeds. It's not uncommon for

"Hollywood Neos" to spend some time working for super-teams or the police to improve their image. Those publicity tours of duty often end up badly for everyone concerned.

Another two hundred or so parahumans participate in special sports leagues; Neos are not allowed to participate in regular sport competitions, for obvious reasons. The most popular Neo sports organization is the Parahuman Fighting Championship. PFC matches have very few rules and resemble nothing more than gladiatorial fights, with Neos entering large octagon-shaped rings (protected by the best force-field systems money can buy) and fighting until only one is left standing (fatalities, while rare, are not unknown). The events draw millions of viewers, with major matches happening once a month. In addition to professional fighters, the NFC often recruits "mainstream" Neo superheroes to participate in select title fights. Many NFC matches have turned into informal duels, with rival Neos working out their differences in the octagon, to the titillation of millions of viewers.

Hundreds more parahumans work in the private industry in a wide variety of jobs, with research and development being their main employer. Neo inventors and artificers typically work for large corporations or go into business for themselves. Original Neo geniuses Doc Slaughter and Daedalus Smith started a tradition of sharing their inventions with the rest of the world, and many Neo inventors follow it, releasing their patents after only a couple of years or even immediately (those that work for corporations and other institutions don't have that option, of course). About a dozen Neos with the ability to carry objects into outer space work part of full time for the aerospace industry, ferrying everything from communication satellites to passenger capsules into orbit or to and from space installations as far off as Saturn's moon Titan.

The US government employs another two hundred Neos directly. They serve in the military and federal agencies. The pay is much lower than in the private industry or even local super-teams, so many Neos only work for the government for a few years before moving on to greener pastures. The ones who make a career in government service usually do it out of patriotism (often bordering on the fanatical), or to make up for past crimes (or to avoid serving prison sentences).

The Parahuman Registration Act of 1964 requires that all Neolympians make their identity and powers known to the government, as well as provide DNA samples and other information. Using one's powers without registering them is a federal offense, with penalties of up to one year in prison and a $50,000 fine, even if the power use is not harmful. Over the years, there have been attempts to make noncompliance to the act a crime in itself, but so far none such laws have made it through Congress. Hundreds of unregistered "illegals" have flaunted the law, but only a few have been prosecuted.

A sizable number of Neo criminals and vigilantes operate in the shadows, hiding their identities and using their powers illegally. Most law-abiding Neos do not have secret identities: even those who try to hide find that it's almost impossible to do so in a world where cameras are everywhere and face recognition systems and DNA analysis make it easy to identify everyone. Most successful Neo criminals do not parade around in colorful costumes; they work for organized crime or are leaders within it, and rarely use their abilities in public. The exception are usually mentally unhinged parahumans who revel in the terror and chaos they cause. Most of those end up dead in short order, either at the hands of local super-teams or executed after their capture and trial. The ones who manage to survive are extremely resourceful and dangerous.

US Presidents, 1932 to 2016

Franklin D. Roosevelt (D) 1933-1945 (d. January, 1945, replaced by VP-elect Harry S. Truman).

Harry S. Truman (D) 1945-1953

Dwight D. Eisenhower (R) 1953-1961

John F. Kennedy (D) 1961-1965

Ray Stephens (R) 1965-1973

John Glenn (D) 1973-1981

Ronald Reagan (R) 1981-1989

Gary Hart (D) 1989-1991 (Resigns in 1991, replaced by VP Bill Clinton)

Bill Clinton (D) 1991-2001

John McCain (R) 2001-2009

John "Stonebender" Colletta (I) 2009-2017

The Freedom Legion

Formally founded in 1940 (although active in the late 1930s), the Freedom Legion started out as an informal gathering of New York-based Neolympians who decided to pool their resources to fight crime and other threats. When the US went to war in 1941, the Legion put itself at the service of the country's armed forces, although their place in the chain of command was never clearly defined, leading to a great deal of tension between the Neos and the military and government. At the end of the war, the group decided to become an independent international organization, not beholden to any country's interest, dedicated instead to "the protection and betterment of all of humankind."

By the 70th anniversary of its foundation, the Freedom Legion employed over two hundred Neos and 50,000 humans, had facilities in every continent on the planet, and had an operating budget of some ten billion dollars a year, all funded privately. In addition to protecting the world from hundreds of Neo attacks, natural disasters, and international crises, the Legion was responsible for the Second Green Revolution, which eradicated famine from most of the world, and the Fusion Revolution that brought cheap, environmentally friendly energy to the planet.

The organization is far from being universally loved, however. Its detractors accuse it (among many other things) of being a US puppet, a sinister group aimed at establishing a Neolympian aristocracy to rule the planet, a weak-willed, self-righteous group that selectively overthrows some dictatorships while allowing others to thrive, and a clear and present danger to all of humanity. There are literally hundreds of conspiracy theories about the Legion, accusing it of such secret practices as ritual infanticide, secret pansexual orgies and devil worship. Depending on which tinfoil-hat-wearing basement dweller you ask, the Legion secretly serves aliens bent on world domination, ultra-terrestrial entities from beyond time and space, or their own greed and megalomania.

Many view the organization with suspicion and fear for no other reason than the sheer amount of power it represents. The Legion's two hundred Neos include one third of the world's known Type Threes, men and women with the power to lay waste to entire countries. This makes the Legion one of the top five military powers of the world (the other four being the US, the Dragon Empire, the Dominion of the Ukraine and the Republic of China; the actual rankings vary depending on the yardsticks employed), although it lacks the personnel to actually conquer territory (the Legion can deploy only about five thousand paramilitary troops, largely trained to work as a constabulary force, rendering it incapable of holding large territories).

Organization

The Legion Council is the governing body of the organization. It consists of eight Councilors elected by the group's active Neolympian members. Councilors serve for two years. The Council has two Executive Officers picked from its members on rotating six-month tenures. The Officers act as overall leaders during times of crisis, but otherwise the Council makes most decisions.

The Legion at large is organized in Squads with four to twelve Neos. Squads are deployed in bases located in countries around the world; there are two Legion bases in the US, located in Los Angeles and New York City. Each Squad has a dedicated Auxiliary Platoon of 25-40 human personnel that includes pilots, communications specialists, medics and soldiers. Squads and their attached platoons train together extensively. Besides those groups, the Legion has about fifty Auxiliary Companies (each with three platoons) that are used when there is a need for more "boots on the ground" as well as for providing security and humanitarian assistance.

Legion members and employees are recruited from all over the world, with Haitians making the largest percentage of civilian and paramilitary personnel (ten thousand and two thousand respectively), followed by Americans (about six thousand, evenly split between civilian and military) and Chinese (four thousand), with the remainder (nearly thirty thousand) hailing from dozens of different nations. American Neolympians are still overrepresented in the Legion, comprising roughly forty-five percent of its active members.

The Legion works closely with the United Nations, including agencies like the World's Health Organization and the Department of Peacekeeping Operations. It also often works with assorted US organizations, both military and civilian, and as well as with Interpol and most countries' police and military. A lot of former Legionnaires end up working in assorted super-teams, which can lead to either a cordial working relationship or tension and acrimony, depending on the circumstances of the ex-member's departure.

Applicants to the Legion must be Neolympians with a PAS of 1.2 or higher. Candidates undergo a twelve month training, screening and testing process to verify their fitness to serve in the Legion. Upon passing, the new Legionnaire is given a spot in a Squad and remains in the Legion until he or she resigns or is expelled. Resigning members can choose to remain in the Legion Reserve, which can be called back into service in case of major emergencies. Expulsion can occur in cases of blatant rules violations and criminal conduct, and is determined by a ruling by the

Legion Council. Only about a dozen expulsions have occurred in the Legion's history.

The Dragon Empire

The largest Neolympian-ruled country in the world, the Dragon Empire is comprised of eleven Chinese provinces as well as the former Soviet Republic of Mongolia. The landlocked country is cut off from the rest of the world by the mysterious Dragon Wall, an energy construct that runs for thousands of miles along its borders. The Empire is a land of contrasts, where traditional Chinese culture (or at least its ruler's idea of traditional Chinese culture) coexists with modern cities and bizarre Neo pseudo-science. The country has a surprisingly large concentration of Neolympians (estimated at eight hundred), most of them allegedly created by the Emperor himself.

The Emperor

Very little is known about the godlike conqueror of half of China, including his birth name. Rumor has it that he was an ethnic Han who grew up in Mongolia at the beginning of the 20th century, most likely the son of a merchant or government official. The earliest reports of a mysterious man performing extraordinary deeds in the area date back to 1913, which would make him one of the oldest parahumans in history. The alleged Neo vanished without a trace sometime in 1915; no concrete proof as to whether or not that individual was the Emperor has been produced.

Some Neo scholars claim that the eventual Emperor traveled to Europe and became the Secret Master, a mysterious criminal gang leader who terrorized East London and became the shadowy ruler of the city's Chinatown during the twenties and thirties. Given that the Emperor speaks fluent if somewhat archaic English with a Received Pronunciation (high-class, cultured British) accent, it is possible he was educated in London. The Secret Master disappeared from the scene around 1935, allegedly killed by either a rival or famed London vigilante Spring-heeled Jack. The first rumors of a mysterious warlord stirring trouble in the Mongolian People's

Republic started around that time. According to the Imperial history books, the Emperor went on a pilgrimage where he acquired his superhuman powers before returning to his homeland.

The Dragon Khan, as the Neo styled himself, assembled a gang of brigands and outlaws in 1936, styling himself the protector of the country's Buddhist institutions, which were being purged at the time. The band grew, and many of its members developed Neolympian powers. By 1939, the region was in a state of open rebellion, with the Soviet government having little control outside the capital city of Ulan Bator. The Dragon Khan and a band of several dozen Neos and thousands of human followers gained followers very quickly and defeated several Soviet armies in the field.

The Stalin regime, beset by more urgent troubles in Finland and the Ukraine, largely withdrew from the area by 1940. The triumphant Khan massacred any ethnic Russians left in the country and started launching raids into China. In 1941, a ragtag horseman army captured the city of Zhangbei and killed Mongolian prince De Wang. The Dragon Khan named himself the ruler of all Mongols and also laid a claim to all of China.

Backed by a growing Neo army and wielding enough power to destroy cities by himself, the Emperor repeatedly defeated the Japanese as well as both Communists and Nationalist Chinese troops, and added Chinese recruits to his cohorts. He aimed for the interior, less populated parts of the country first. As World War Two came to an end, the Emperor's conquest of China was stalled by American and Freedom Legion intervention. At that point, the Emperor created the Dragon Wall and spent a decade and a half building up his realm before launching the disastrous First Asian War.

The Emperor's powers have grown over time. Early on he appears to have been a Type One Neolympian with a genius-level intellect. Upon his return to Mongolia he could control and produce diverse forms of energy at will, and also had the power to either awaken or develop parahuman powers in others. By 1964, the Neo could control several elemental forces and unleash explosions in the multi-kiloton range.

The motivations of the Emperor are as mysterious as his origins. He is clearly not content with ruling over his current realm, and at the very least wants to expand it to include all of China. Some of his pronouncements indicate he wants all of Asia, and possibly the world.

Rulers and Ruled

The Empire's capital is the city of Baotou in Inner Mongolia (population 3 million), where a replica of Beijing's Forbidden City has been built. The New Forbidden City is protected by an energy dome similar to the Dragon Wall, but it was still nearly razed to the ground during both Asian Wars, when several Type Three Neolympians breached its defenses and fought the Emperor and his personal guards. Both times, the palace complex has been rebuilt and restored to its decadent splendor.

The Emperor is the absolute ruler of the land. The administration of the realm is in the hands of several ministers appointed by the Emperor, often with overlapping spheres of interest, who in turn implement and enact laws through a bureaucracy loosely inspired by Confucian doctrines. Provincial governors are also picked directly by the Emperor, often as a reward for loyal services. Alongside the civilian administration, there is a parallel military system dominated by ethnic Mongols, Uighurs, Manchurians and other minorities. The third pillar of power in the Empire is comprised by its Neolympians. The Celestial Warriors and their even more powerful leaders, the *Noyan* (Commanders) all appear to have Type Two or higher power levels. There are also a group of Celestial Artificers who produce a variety of Artifacts, including copies of several Dominion weapon systems.

Most of the population of the Empire live under primitive conditions, working mostly in agriculture, with mining and oil and gas extraction being the next largest employers. A small minority in cities work in the manufacturing sector, but the Empire's economy depends largely on the sale of raw materials (coal, oil, assorted metals and rare earths), mostly to its hated rival, the Republic of China. A secondary market of Neo artifacts and designer drugs also brings much-needed hard currencies into the Empire. Much of that trade is in the hands of assorted criminal cartels in Asia and Eurasia.

The Emperor styles himself as a protector of Buddhism, and over the decades has overseen the building of hundreds of temples and monasteries around his realm. The religious establishment is left largely alone as long as its members do not criticize the Empire or its officials.

The Dominion of the Ukraine

The other great Neolympian dictatorship of the world, the Dominion of the Ukraine has about 20% more land area than the Ukraine of our world and almost twice its population (estimated at about 80 million). The country is an agricultural and industrial giant, producing a variety of "magic box" products that combine conventional technology and Neo artifacts, as well as mass-produced artifacts greatly prized around the world. While the strange country has not expanded its territory since the end of World War Two, it has subtly or overtly dominated all of its neighbors, saving most of its abuse for Russia, which has been reduced into a pathetic, impoverished and crime-ridden hellhole due mainly to the Iron Tsar's actions.

The Iron Tsar

As with the Dragon Emperor, the real name of the conqueror of Ukraine is unknown. It seems likely he was a member of a prominent noble family in the Galicia region who became involved in the Ukrainian nationalist movement after World War One. Several possible candidates have been proposed by historians, including former officers in the Austro-Hungarian Army. In any case, the first reported sightings of a man wearing a metal helmet occurred 1929, when several Soviet commissars working on the collectivization of Ukrainian farms were murdered. The mysterious "man in the iron mask" continued to launch attacks on Communist officials and support revolts across the region. By 1931, some of the rebels were using energy weapons of unknown provenance and devastating power.

The collectivization process ground to a halt; the Soviets poured thousands of Russian soldiers into the area and engaged in brutal reprisals against the population, but their losses continued to mount. A purge of the Soviet officer corps by the frustrated Stalin only made the situation worse. By 1939, as the Nazis and Soviets formed a non-aggression pact that gave the former a free hand in Poland, much of the Ukraine was ungovernable. The diversion of resources to quash the ongoing revolt is blamed for the disastrous failure of the Soviet invasion of Finland later that year. It may have also contributed to Hitler's decision to attack the Soviet Union in 1941.

After a temporary lull in activity after the Nazi invasion, the Man in the Iron Mask struck again with a nationwide uprising in 1943. The revolt crushed both Nazi and Soviet forces in the area. The Tsar did not just slaughter wantonly, even though he is believed to have personally killed some two million people during the uprising; he also proved to be a charismatic leader able to convince hundreds of thousands of Soviet (and a smaller but still-significant number of German and German-allied) soldiers to switch sides and join the rebellion.

After the war, the Iron Tsar followed a policy of amnesty to anyone willing to swear fealty to him. By 1946 millions of Russians, Tartars, Poles, Romanians and Germans had fled to the new country. Several Nazi officials sought and found asylum in the Ukraine, so long as they hadn't perpetrated atrocities against the Ukrainian people. The kingdom put all those diverse people to work rebuilding the devastated country, and took advantage of the fluid situation to carve out choice parts of Russia, Belarus, Poland and Romania, as well as the entire country of Moldova.

The chief policy of the Tsar has been to ensure that all of its neighbors are friendly allies or puppet states, or so weakened they pose no threat. He also took his revenge on the Soviet Union, encouraging rebellions in all its member states which eventually dismembered the Communist empire and isolated Russia. Finally, the Soviet government was brought down in 1958 by a military coup led by former Russian marshal Vasily Sokolovsky, who proceeded to kill off the entire Politburo and rule Russia until his death in 1971. Sokolovsky never antagonized the Dominion during his time in power; neither have any of his successors.

The entire country has been reshaped to conform to the romantic ideals of its ruler. He favors ethnic Ukrainians over all other groups in the Dominion; Ukrainian is the official language of the land, and most high-ranking positions are held by native Ukrainians. For someone so devoted to that ethcnic group, the usage of the term Tsar is unusual, since only one Ukrainian ruler in its history ever held that title (Yaroslav I in the 11th century; that ancient ruler of Kiev, perhaps not coincidentally, has been highly revered in the Dominion since its inception). His court is patterned after an earlier era, reminiscent of Russia under Catherine the Great or the Hapsburg courts, featuring old-fashioned and colorful gowns for the ladies, gaudy uniforms for the men, and regular balls and classical concerts.

As a ruler, the Tsar tends to allow his subjects a good deal of leeway to conduct their affairs, as long as they maintain their fealty toward him. Any overt dissent, however, is not tolerated.

Life Under the Tsar

The Dominion is an autocratic government thinly disguised as a parliamentary monarchy. Dominion subjects (there are no citizens) elect the members of a General Assembly (established in 1955) that mostly ratifies whatever the Tsar puts in front of it; other elective offices include city mayors and other minor posts charged mostly with municipal matters. All other civilian and military positions are appointed directly by the Tsar or his ministers.

About fifty percent of the Dominion's people work in the agricultural sector; the Dominion is a major food producer, selling grain all over Europe. The rest are largely employed in manufacturing, producing both mundane products like cars and aircraft and exotic devices including contra-gravity drives and "energy crystals" used to provide power for everything from flashlights to electrical plants.

The government holds a largely paternalistic and hierarchical attitude towards its subjects, who are allowed to prosper and thrive as long as they pay the proper respect to their superiors. Malcontents are surprisingly rare, and most of them are allowed (and encouraged) to emigrate from the country. The ones who try to foment reforms or resistance against the Tsar are imprisoned, tortured and executed; the Dominion has one of the worst human rights records In the world, with some twelve hundred executions a year (the Dragon Empire is far worse, but human rights groups have precious little information about what happens there).

Demographically, Ukrainians make up around sixty percent of the population; ethnic Russians comprise twenty percent, and a variety of other nationalities (Belarusians, Poles, and Tatars, among others) comprise the remaining twenty percent, including a large German population (2%), mostly the descendants of WWII refugees. There is a great deal of tension between the Ukrainian majority and the other ethnic groups (Germans are particularly despised, not least because they are overrepresented in technical trades and other crafts), but it is kept repressed by the government. Many analysts believe that if the Tsar's government ever falls, those ethnic tensions will likely explode violently across the country.

Neos in the Dominion are expected to serve in the Iron Guard and are lavishly pampered and compensated. The Guard has about a hundred and fifty members, including a handful of Type Three parahumans. The country's armed forces are equipped with a variety of powerful Neo artifacts, from robotic automatons to gigantic flying fortresses armed with batteries of death ray emitters, making the Dominion one of the leading military powers of the planet.

The Rest of the World

Much of the rest of the world is largely like our own. This section will make note of the more noticeable differences.

Europe

The recovery from the ravages of World War Two proceeded somewhat like in our timeline, slower in some areas (without a Soviet threat, some programs like the Marshall Plan were given less priorities) and faster in others (most countries spared Soviet occupation did better than in our world). Germany eventually bounced back from the effects of the war and became the center of gravity of the European Union. The Balkans sank into a mire of civil war that required the intervention of the UN and the Freedom Legion, and the partition of several countries, before the bloodshed finally ceased.

The European Union has provided a great deal of peace and prosperity to its fellow members, although an economic slump towards the end of the first decade of the 21st century is still making its effects felt.

Asia

The Republic of China is the most prosperous nation in the continent, and its economic growth rate is the highest on the planet, looking like it may surpass the US and the EU in several areas over the next generation. The last four decades saw a great deal of modernization and industrialization in the country; China is the world's leading manufacturer of automobiles, consumer electronics, and metal tools and parts. It's also the leading polluter in the planet, although of late has been taking steps to fight that problem.

India has the potential of becoming another international powerhouse, but the aftermath of the Reunification War still affects the country: the conflict severely damaged several cities, disrupted its economy and brought millions of unwilling Muslim citizens into India, leading to a seething terrorist problem and outbursts of brutal reprisals from the Hindu majority and the government.

Japan's growth was slower than in our history, as most Western investment and commerce flowed into the Republic of China. Japan is still a major manufacturing power, but it never reached the prosperity levels of our history, leading to growing resentment and even some longing for the glory days of the Empire. A number of Japanese apologists are vehemently anti-Neolympian, blaming Neos for the downfall of their country.

Africa and the Middle East

With a more orderly decolonization process, Africa has fared somewhat better than in our history. South Africa is a glaring exception. The country is still dominated by its Afrikaner minority, which has evaded international censure by maintaining strong trade and diplomatic relations with the Dominion of the Ukraine and by acquiring several deadly Ukrainian weapon systems and developing nuclear weapons. Attempts to reform the country from within have been met with brutal repression. The relationship with the Ukrainians have prompted some wags to refer to the country as "the Dominion of South Africa."

The founding of Israel precipitated a crisis in the Middle East not unlike in our history. Reduced interest in the entire area, resulting from far lower demand for Middle Eastern oil, has led to far less meddling from outside powers, leaving everyone involved to work things out by themselves, with varying levels of success. In general, the Middle East is a lot poorer; petrodollars have a lot less purchasing power in a world where fusion power plants and electric cars have reduced oil consumption to a fraction of what it is in our world.

Oceania and the Americas

Australia and New Zealand have developed a close working relationship with the Republic of China, to the benefit of everyone involved. There is some local resentment at the large influx of Chinese investors and business owners, especially in Australia, but by and large the Aussies don't mind the vast sums of money that come along with the immigrants.

Mexico has done rather well under the multi-decade watch of *El Presidente*. The Neolympian leader helped cut back corruption and crime in the country, often personally arresting or executing wrongdoers. Mexican manufacturing, oil production and trade are all growing steadily, and the country's main problem involves dealing with the influx of illegal immigrants from Central and South America.

The rest of South and Central America is relatively stable, despite attempts by Neo would-be rulers to take over regions or countries. Brazil is on the verge of becoming an economic superpower, but the country has been on the verge of becoming an economic superpower for several decades already.

The Final Frontier

The existence of Neos with the power to travel (and transport cargo) beyond Earth's atmosphere led to a true Space Age. At first, Neos replaced rockets as the primary "launch vehicles" to leave the planet's gravity well, but scientific advances, including such Neo "technologies" as contra-gravity and fusion propulsion have also led to the building of several kinds of launch vehicles and even a few actual spaceships. The solar system has been thoroughly explored and human-crewed installations have been built as far away as the asteroid belt and Saturn. The Earth is ringed by thousands of artificial satellites, from small communication devices to fully-crewed space stations. An asteroid mining project made its first Earth delivery (several containers of Helium-3) in 2009.

A few Neos have traveled even further. In 1973, Janus used his teleportation abilities to visit Alpha Centauri (the closest star system), where he discovered several planets but no signs of life. In 1993, the hero went on a twenty-year long pilgrimage of outer space. He returned in late 2012, but so far has not spoken publicly about what he saw during his travels.

So far, no signs of life outside Earth have been found. A research colony in Mars has made some exciting discoveries along those lines, showing indication that life may have existed there at some point, but has found no definite proof as yet. Missions to Titan have found some possible signs of life there, but again no confirmation had been discovered as of 2013. No extraterrestrial contacts with intelligent species have been confirmed. While several Neos over the decades have claimed to be aliens, they haven't offered any proof beyond their powers and special devices, all of which have been shown to be the product of ordinary (so to speak) parahuman abilities.

Roleplaying in New Olympus

(**Author's Note:** This chapter is dedicated to the tabletop RPG enthusiasts among you. If you are not into RPGs (particularly if you don't know what an RPG is), some of the material below may need some Google searching to make sense out of it. Still, I hope some of the information below sheds more light on the world of *Armageddon Girl*.)

The world of New Olympus started as source material for a roleplaying game: it was going to be one of the game settings for the Eden Studios sourcebook *Beyond Human* (slated to come out in the near future, hopefully). The basic idea was to create a superhero setting where said superheroes had made a significant impact in world history and current affairs. The basics of the setting are described in the New Olympus chapter. Here we get to the nitty-gritty: characters, potential stories, and roleplaying hooks.

There are no system notes here, or a lot of crunchy material. When describing powers, "real life" measurements will be used as much as possible, to allow GMs and players to convert those measurements into game stats using the game system of choice. Whatever rule system you end up using, keep in mind the measurements below are meant to be guidelines: if they prove to be too unbalancing for the game, feel free to modify them as you see fit. Linear-power systems (**GURPS**, for example) may need GMs to lower some of the power benchmarks of the setting to make games playable.

I hope to start posting actual game stats of characters and gadgets in several different game systems on my website www.cjcarella.com, as time permits (I'm planning on spending most of my time writing fiction, however, so those postings will happen sporadically). I may also invite other people to send me conversions for other game systems and I will happily share them with the world as long as I can secure permission from the game systems' owners. Finally, if there is enough demand, I may write a full treatment of the game setting, either as a supplement to an existing rules system (very likely *Beyond Human*) or as a stand-alone game with its own new rules.

Meanwhile, I hope you enjoy the material below and find it useful for your games.

Characters

New Olympus features a world where superhuman beings are everywhere. Depending on the kind of game the GM wants to run, several different options are possible.

Humans in Olympus: What role have the mere mortal when godlike beings walk the earth? A game where the player characters are normal men and women would try to answer that question. Possible roles include police or military personnel trying to handle Rogue Neos without parahuman support, dedicated freedom fighters trying to fight against Neolympian tyrants (or even Neos in general), or normal people who somehow become embroiled in the affairs of one or more superhuman being. They might even belong to some secret organization dealing with the messes the caped crusaders uncaringly leave behind.

This is the ultimate underdog game. Even a Type One Neo would pose a challenge for a group of humans, let alone higher level ones. Still, humans didn't become the top predators in the planet by playing fair. Smart tactics, trickery and the liberal application of firepower can deal with a lot of challenges. Trying to take down an immortal demigod may involve a quest to find some silver bullet or Achilles' heel. One mistake too many will reduce a character into a bloody smear on the pavement, though.

Down and Dirty: The characters are all Type One Neos, slightly tougher and more agile than normal humans, and blessed with fast healing and eternal youth, all of which are great until they run into someone who can make their heads explode by snapping his fingers. On the other hand, fighting everybody at a biker's bar becomes not only doable, but possibly fun.

Type Ones often do not adopt the more colorful masked personas the average person expects of Neolympians. Their jobs tend to be more mundane – hardboiled private eyes, street-level vigilantes, or secret agents. They may not grow old, but they sure aren't immortal. Enough punks with guns will put them down, so they have to use their wits as much as their catlike reflexes to survive.

This type of characters lend themselves to "action movie" games rather than full-fledged superhero stories. The supers are out there, but they can be left largely in the background, except for occasional situations where a rampaging Type Two or Three needs to be taken down, and the PCs are the only (unlikely) heroes available for the job. Costumed superheroic tales will resemble more the adventures of a certain sulking bat dude or vision impaired crime-fighter. The characters may not wear costumes at all, and their deeds may involve shooting terrorists for God and Country in between mixing up martinis, or running around with machineguns and mowing down some banana republic's entire army.

The Amazing Whatshisname: The characters are middle-weight Neos, Type Twos able to lift cars, bounce bullets off their skins, toss fireballs or other equally impressive feats. The heroes can be part of a regional super-team, a government agency, or even the one-and-only Freedom Legion, fighting the good fight while wearing latex outfits grownups shouldn't be caught dead in. In between fighting bad guys, our heroes can wrangle merchandizing deals, show up to red carpet events and get asked who they're wearing, or start their own personal soap opera plotlines.

Alternatively, the heroes can be powerful but live at the margins of society, unable or unwilling to register and be on the limelight. They can be vigilantes who must avoid the authorities as they seek justice or revenge, or villains out to fulfill their own self-serving goals.

At this level, the PCs will be influential in whatever field they decide to pursue, one of the lucky twenty-four hundred or so Neolympian powerhouses on the planet. Their deeds may be featured in comic books or movies, and pictures of their wardrobe malfunctions will likely be all over the Xanaweb in a matter of minutes. Will the characters appreciate the whole power-responsibility formula from the start, or will they need to learn it the hard way?

Top of the World, Ma! The characters are all Type Three Neolympians, veritable demigods able to change the course of mighty rivers, or to effect regime changes in a single bound. Few things pose a threat to the heroes, but the ones that do are truly nasty. Type Threes can write their own ticket from the get-go, but a surprising number let the power go to their head and end up becoming a clear and present danger to everyone around them. With great power comes great danger. Their mortality rate is the highest among Neolympians: well over two-thirds of all reported Type Three Neos are dead.

The biggest problem with characters at that level is to come up with challenging situations every week. Not all problems need to involve planetary threats, however. Defeating a dangerous but weaker opponent without causing innocent deaths can be tricky when both sides can fling around enough power to knock a building down, for example. There are also plenty of situations that cannot be resolved with atomic punches and other Neo tricks. Political maneuvering within a super-team, smear campaigns by the press, or whodunit mysteries can keep Neos busy with nary an explosion-laden scene.

Variety Pack: For the most part, super-teams aren't comprised of Neos with the exact same PAS numbers. Most Neo groups have one or two powerhouses, three of four middle-weight supers, and maybe a couple of "near normal" guys and gals more suited to skulking around than to going *mano a mano* with tank-crushing monstrosities. Balancing this may be tricky depending on the game system you use. The weaker heroes should get something to compensate for the power differential – it could be more non-super skills, a "good luck" mechanic or some other perk to help make them as effective and vital to the story as the indestructible behemoths in the party.

Neo Psychosis: A disproportionate number of Neolympians suffer from a variety of mental problems, including personality disorders, mild autism, and even outright psychosis. Almost all of them are addicted to the thrill of danger, and few are ever content leading a sedentary life. GMs may wish to attach some form of psychological problem to the "Neolympian Package."

Rules

Although this book has no actual game rules, the setting has some elements that GMs should take into account when trying to run a game there. Whatever rules book you end up using, you might want to add some home rules to keep the game faithful to the setting, or you might pick and choose which elements to keep or toss out.

Neo Powers: How They Work

Neolympians are human beings who have been altered to gain access to a powerful energy generator of unknown origin, often referred to as the Source. The Source transforms the Neos' physiology and provides the energies that fuel all of their superhuman abilities. The amount of power a Neo can draw from the Source varies widely, but it appears to be influenced by the individual's strength of will, emotional state, and creativity and imagination. During times of stress, most Neos seem able to draw more power than normal, and exceed their limits. By the same token, prolonged use of one's powers will cause fatigue and reduced power levels. Pushing powers will also lead to fatigue; extreme cases may cause a temporary ability loss, particularly if the Neos exceeded their normal limits for an extended length of time.

Additionally, Neos seem to be able to partially bypass the defenses or other parahumans, enabling weaker Neos to hurt more powerful adversaries. Even Type Threes who can bounce tank cannon shots from their skins can get bruised or injured by Type Two or even Type One attacks, yet another reason why the best countermeasure against a Neo is another Neo.

In game terms, the GM may allow the heroes to push their limits, maybe requiring some sort of skill check, with the risk the characters may burn out their powers for some time if they push too much. Also, Neo powers are more effective than conventional attacks when striking other Neos, even if they do the same damage. To simulate this in game, all Neo attacks should get some form of armor piercing or defense-bypassing bonus when used against Neo defenses.

Mental Powers

One important story element in the setting is that mental abilities create a two-way link between the people involved. Passive observation (empathy or mind-reading, for example) works like a charm, but trying to affect a mind directly (implanting mental commands, or full mind control) has a price. The psychic will feel whatever the target feels, and the psychic backlash can produce pain or even physical injuries. Trying to control another mind is an agonizing, difficult process. Even powerful Neo mentalists are rarely able to affect more than a few people at a time. Attempts to mentally control a fellow Neolympian are even more difficult; all parahumans have an innate resistance to mental powers, which appears to be proportional to their overall power level. Type Threes are almost impossible to influence mentally, or even to be mind-read.

If GMs want to stay true to the spirit of the novels, characters with mental powers should have a hard time controlling people. Snooping and brute-force effects (knocking someone out, for example) are relatively easy. Anything involving making people do something against their will should have a hefty penalty. Furthermore, if the person being controlled suffers an injury, the psychic controlling the victim will receive similar injuries. Finally, all Neos should get resistance bonuses commensurate to their power level; the more powerful the Neo, the more highly resistant he will be to all forms of mental control.

Parahuman Ability Score Calculations

Measuring a Neolympian's PAS is a complex process involving a multitude of tests. The test results are rarely accurate, but most people accept them as gospel, even Neos, who should know better. A proper PAS test rates the Neo in a hundred and fifty categories and uses a series of complex formulas that require a computer to process. To simulate the rating in a game, a couple of far simpler methods are outlined below.

To figure out a character's PAS, check out the Benchmark List on Appendix III. Take any powers with a score of 1.2 or higher, assign the appropriate PAS score to each of them, and average them. Then, take their total number of abilities with a score of 1.2 or higher, divide them by thirty, and add the result to the total.

If you'd rather not worry about that kind of calculation, just take the character's highest power's score, and drop it by one or two decimal points. This quick and dirty method is the least accurate, of course.

Example: The Teutonic Knight Shatterhand had a Protective Aura (2.4), a special explosive attack (2.6), inhuman running speed (2.0), amazing regeneration (2.3) and superhuman strength (2.4). The average of all those abilities is 2.34. He has five abilities, which, divided by 30, add an additional 0.16, for a total of 2.5. Or, doing it the easy way, take the highest power (2.6), and drop it by one decimal point to 2.5. Since the PAS number is not accurate in the setting's "reality" it really doesn't matter that much if the PAS score is not perfectly accurate.

Some PAS Benchmarks

The list below provides examples for some common Neo powers to provide some guidance in measuring a Neo's PAS score. It's far from an exhaustive list, but you can use it to give you an idea where different powers would be scored.

Agility

1.0: Above average human (could qualify for professional sports).

1.5: Olympic level athlete.

2.0: Animal-like reflexes (tiger or leopard)

3.0: About 20% faster than the 2.0 level (reflexes appear to plateau at the 2.0 level and improve only slightly after that).

Defensive Shields

Defensive shields are energy constructs that block attacks. They can protect from only one direction like an actual shield or completely surround its wielder.

1.0-1.5: No shields.

1.6: Shields will stop pistol rounds and slow down rifle bullets.

2.0: Up to .50 caliber rounds or equivalent.

2.5: Up to 75mm armor-piercing tank rounds or equivalent.

3.0: Up to 120mm depleted uranium tank rounds or equivalent.

3.5: Up to 18-inch naval artillery armor-piercing rounds or equivalent.

Energy Attacks

Effects are given in joules of power. Energy releases ramp up very quickly.

1.0: 150 joules (enough to bruise and lightly injure a human being).

1.3: 600 joules (equivalent to a large-caliber pistol round).

1.5: 2,000 joules (equivalent to a heavy rifle round).

2.0: 15 kilojoules (equivalent to a .50 caliber machine gun bullet).

2.4: 50 megajoules (10 kilograms of TNT).

2.7: 10 gigajoules (2 tons of TNT).

3.0: 10 terajoules (2 kilotons of TNT).

Healing Factor

1.0: Recover from minor injuries (bruises, sprains, shallow cuts) in a matter of minutes. Recover from serious injuries (bone fractures, non-lethal gunshot wounds) in a matter of hours. Recover from critical injuries (near-lethal gunshot wounds, multiple fractures, internal bleeding) in a matter of days. Massive trauma (second and third degree burns, destruction of major organs, spinal cord injuries) will take weeks or months to heal.

1.5: Minor injuries heal in seconds, serious injuries in minutes, critical injuries in hours, massive trauma in days.

2.5: Minor injuries heal as quickly as they are inflicted (under one second), serious injuries in seconds, critical injuries in minutes, massive trauma in hours.

3.0: massive trauma is healed in minutes, all other injuries in seconds.

Movement Speed

1.0: Can do a 100-yard dash in 12 seconds.

2.0: can run at 50 mph or fly at 100 mph

2.5: can run at 400 mph or fly at supersonic speeds.

3.0 can run at supersonic speeds or achieve escape velocity if flying.

Protective Auras

A protective aura generally conforms to the wearer's skin (although it can project as far out as a couple of inches) and it absorbs or disperses attacks, allowing only a fraction of their energy to affect the target.

2.0: reduce incoming damage by 50%.

2.5: reduce incoming damage by 75%.

3.0: reduce incoming damage by 90%.

Strength

The weights below are what a Neo can lift without pushing his limits. At 2.5 and higher, the Neo's "strength" is a largely telekinetic ability, enabling the Neo to pick up large objects that would normally fall to pieces if lifted, by exerting force evenly along its entire volume.

1.0: 500 lbs.

2.0: 2 tons

2.5: 20 tons

3.0: 500 tons

3.5: 20,000 tons

Stories

New Olympus' storylines revolve around answering the question "What if superhuman beings as portrayed in comic books existed in our world?" GMs have almost a century's worth of material (comic books, movies, TV shows and novels) from which to draw inspiration. The most common storylines in this kind of setting deal with men and women with incredible abilities confronting assorted threats while dealing with personal issues. Characters in New Olympus can save an entire country one day, deal with an unflattering post at Perez Hilton's website the day after that, and escape an (actual or character) assassination attempt the next day. Games can involve cosmic slugfests that would cost millions in CGI special effects, or intensely personal stories of friendship, betrayal and loss.

A good way to approach this kind of game is to treat each game session as a comic book issue. As with actual comic books, each issue can have a self-contained story with a beginning, middle and end, be an episode in an ongoing storyline, or a combination of both. The simplest story is the "villain of the month" action tale: bad guy shows up, bad guy starts making a mess, bad guy is confronted and put down. By itself, that kind of story is likely to get old pretty quickly, though. Ideally, some adversaries will have a more complex plan than "stomp innocent bystanders till heroes show up, then stomp them." And conflict does not necessarily involve violence, even among superheroes.

Finally, one can spice things up by adding elements from outside the setting. While a "vanilla" New Olympus game has one source of super-powers and revolves exclusively around humans and parahumans, your game doesn't have to.

Plot Complications

Here are some possible twists and story ideas that can help enliven games and go beyond "brawls of the week."

Things Are Not What They Seem: Sometimes the supposed villain of the piece is actually a misunderstood hero, and vice versa. For example, what if an alleged "Neo Terrorist" attack on a chemical factory was an attempt to stop an evil plot by a secret organization? What if the characters discover that the supposedly heroic members of a local super-team spend their time off killing hookers and transients for fun? Start with a seemingly straightforward scenario, and then drop clues indicating there is a lot more to it. If the PCs start becoming downright paranoid, that means you're doing your job.

Healthy (and Unhealthy) Competition: A lot of Neos measure their success by how much public exposure they get. They measure glory by how many social media followers they have, or how often their picture shows up in the news. Those glory-hounds may try to steal the limelight from the player characters, or even go further and attempt to ruin their reputations, leading to all kinds of problems that can't be solved with energy blasts. Even if the characters aren't interested in glory or profit, a smear campaign can damage their reputation and even lead to their expulsion from a super-team, so it would behoove them to fight back.

Politics: Put three or more people together in a room and you get politics; Neos are no different. You have internal politics, with members of the team or group jockeying for position in the organization's hierarchy. Then there is capital-P Politics: governments can change policies from one election cycle to the next, a politician may start a crusade against the player characters for any reason or none, and a tragic incident can be used by demagogues to start all kinds of trouble. To deal with this kind of situation, the characters need to develop strategies and tactics that will depend on their brains a lot more than their kewl powerz ™.

Genre-Bending

Most comic book universes mix a variety of elements: the characters' special abilities may be the result of a mutation, or alien origins, advanced technology or supernatural sources. In New Olympus, every Neo has the same origin: their powers come from the connection with the mysterious Source. But in your game that doesn't necessarily apply. Here are some ideas on adding additional themes to a New Olympus game.

Urban Fantasy and Horror: If you'd like to add vampires, werewolves and other things that go bump in the night, you could easily bring in characters and rules from other RPGs, like Eden Studios' *WitchCraft* (written by yours truly) or the vastly more popular series of gothic-punk games set in a dark world populated by assorted supernatural critters. The various supernatural races would have existed for centuries or millennia, possibly ruling humanity in secret until the coming of Neolympians upset the status quo. Modern-day sorcerers and undead can be allies or enemies of the new gods, providing lots more flexibility to character creation as well as more sources of conflict and drama.

Zombie outbreaks are already part of the setting; many Neos, from the nefarious Totenkopf of World War Two to Monstrous Miller in the 1950s, have developed the ability to animate the dead. So far those outbreaks have been contained quickly, but a Zombie Apocalypse is always possible (an entire line of RPG supplements dealing with such an eventuality is out in stores: Google *All Flesh Must Be Eaten* for more information). The most powerful Neos in the world might be dead (or even worse, they might have been zombified).

Alien Nations: Extraterrestrial visitors or invaders are a common staple of comic book stories. You could easily bring your favorite alien species from books, movies or TV into the setting, or create your own. The discovery that humans are not alone would bring massive changes to the world, likely giving even more power to the United Nations and the Freedom Legion in an attempt to present a united front toward the outsiders.

GMs wishing to add even more cosmic elements to their games can have alien armadas show up, lasers blazing, to do battle with Type Three Neos out in space, or toss in more exotic threats like space monsters determined to implant their chest-bursting embryos on unsuspecting humans, pods producing hostile replicas of their victims, or planet-eating menaces.

Historical/Fantasy: What if Neos had appeared in a different historical period? Some Neo scholars (mostly the whacky kind) think prehistoric Neos were the inspiration for the legends of mythological gods and demigods mixing it up with mortals. You could have a Greek or Norse myth game where the characters are Neos who became the inspiration for the legends of such deities as Thor and Hermes. Or you could have the "gods" show up and change history during other times, with superhuman Spartans battling (actual) Persian Immortals, or Roman Legions being led by demigods as they battle their Carthaginian counterparts.

You could move the first appearance of Neolympians to the Victorian Era, allowing characters to conduct adventures in the style of Jules Verne and H.G. Wells (the comic book classic *League of Extraordinary Gentlemen* would be to go-to sourcebook for that kind of game). Or you can have Neos visit your favorite fantasy world.

The main challenge in some of those those settings is to prevent Neos from completely outclassing everyone else. Restricting the game's power levels to Type Ones and Type Twos would probably work best.

Non-alternate historical settings are also possible: you could set your game in the 1930s (or 1940s or 1960s or whatever) for a more pulp-fiction oriented game, or for wartime stories.

Other Books by C.J. Carella

College student Christine Dark wasn't happy. Her social life sucked, she spent too much of her time playing computer games or reading sci-fi novels (and the occasional paranormal romance) and she felt like she was missing out on everything.

Fate had something special in store for her, though.

Without warning, an unknown force drags Christine out of her world and takes her to a whole new universe, an alternate Earth where superhuman beings have existed since the end of World War One. Christine soon learns she too is more than human, and that her choices may save her new home... or bring about its destruction.

Armageddon Girl is on sale now:

http://www.amazon.com/Armageddon-Girl-New-Olympus-Saga-ebook/dp/B00GPZFWL6/

Christine Dark's adventures on Earth Alpha continue. Trapped in a world where super-beings known as Neolympians have existed for almost a century, Christine must find out why she was dragged there. She and the vigilante known as Face-Off will make new allies, face enemies, travel the world, and work out some personal issues, even as dueling conspiracies and a looming world war bring together unlikely friends and foes.

Doomsday Duet will be available on the spring of 2014.